For Love and Country

VOLUME THREE OF THE
HORSTBERG SAGA

Books by Elizabeth D. Michaels

Horstberg Saga
Behind the Mask (Volume One)
A Matter of Honor (Volume Two)
For Love and Country (Volume Three)

For Love and Country

VOLUME THREE OF THE
HORSTBERG SAGA

Bestselling author Anita Stansfield writing as

Elizabeth D. Michaels

WHITE
STAR
PRESS

This is a work of fiction, and the views expressed herein are the sole responsibility of the author. Likewise, certain characters, places, and incidents are the product of the author's imagination, and any resemblance to actual persons, living or dead, or actual events or locales, is entirely coincidental.

For Love and Country: Volume III of the Horstberg Saga

Published by White Star Press
P.O. Box 353
American Fork, Utah 84003

Rose and keys painting copyright © 2014 Anna C. Stansfield
Cover and interior design by Epub Masters

Print ISBN: 978-1-939203-49-6
Printed in the United States of America
Year of first printing: 2014

To my children. May you have the courage to trust your feelings and to follow your hearts.

Chapter One

A Change of Heart

Bavaria—1840

Han Heinrich pulled back the drapes covering his bedroom window and looked down to the castle courtyard below. He lived with his parents in the nicest apartment among the many residences of the castle, but the view from *this* window was a completely different angle than any view of the courtyard that could be seen from any room belonging to a member of the royal family. His father was the duke's highest advisor, and his mother was the highest paid and most respected of the duchess's maids. Each of his parents in their own right was enormously successful and revered by the royal family as well as the citizens of Horstberg.

Han considered himself privileged to have such parents, but his pleasure in being their only son wasn't so much to do with their positions and prestige—even though he admired those things. Georg and Elsa Heinrich were loving, kind, and generous people. Han had never wanted for anything, most specifically love and perfect support in all that he'd endeavored for more than twenty years of life. But Han still didn't like the angle of his view of the castle courtyard. He felt excluded for reasons that were painful to even think about.

He closed the drapes and grabbed his jacket before he headed down the stairs for a quick breakfast with his parents. After eating, they all walked out the front door and went different directions, each attending to their individual professions in serving the most wealthy and powerful family of Horstberg. Georg would go to the ducal office. Elsa to the duchess's personal quarters. And Han went to the stables, where he both loved and hated his work. For reasons that were too complicated to untangle, he just couldn't seem to get beyond the stables and find the life he knew was meant for him. He didn't know for certain what that life entailed, but he knew it wasn't this.

Han did a quick check on every horse to make certain all was in order, and then he began the morning feeding regime. The cavalry stables were some distance up the courtyard and employed several stablehands, which was necessary to care for the dozens of horses that were kept on the ready for officers of the Guard. Han worked mostly by himself here in the family stables, assisted occasionally by a boy who came to work part time. He preferred being alone for the most part, but he also knew that too much time on his own could be dangerous when he allowed his mind to wander into memories and hopes that all seemed fruitless and subsequently depressing.

Han was pouring feed into the trough of the final hungry animal when he knew that Maggie du Woernig had entered the stables. He hadn't heard her, and his back was turned toward the doorway, but he sensed her presence. He always could, and he nearly hated her for it. He moved with deliberate slowness to finish his task before he turned to look at her, wishing there was some potion he could take to stop the reactions that typically happened in her presence. His quickened heart and sweating palms were nothing more than annoying when she only stared at him with coldness in her blue eyes. He took in her appearance: an elegant riding habit, her red hair perfectly styled and topped with a perfect little hat. As always, she looked flawless. He warded off his own reactions and spoke with a light sarcasm that hid his emotions from her as completely as she had banished her own true feelings about everything important in her life.

"So, the little princess wants to take a ride," Han said, futilely trying to avoid eye contact.

Maggie watched Han shuffle the toe of his boot over the ground as if he had all the time in the world. She didn't know why he purposely tested her patience at every opportunity, but it never ceased to make her angry.

"What makes you think you're going to get a horse saddled at this hour?" he asked. A familiar amusement sparkled in his green eyes.

Han's attitude came as little surprise, but it infuriated her none-theless. "You say that as if you never see me here this time of day.

I am almost *always* here this time of day. The sun has been up for at least an hour."

"So have I. What's that got to do with it?"

"That's when I like to go riding. You *know* that. Just . . . saddle Pagan so I can go."

"Pagan is eating his breakfast."

"Then saddle up another horse."

"They're all eating," Han stated as if she were inane. "Don't you know a hungry brood of horses when you see one?"

"Oh, never mind!" she exclaimed. Exasperated, Maggie gave up her impulse to ride before breakfast; she simply wasn't up to the typical argument with Han today. She headed for the door until a complacent chuckle stopped her.

"Now what are you laughing about?" She turned with her hands on her hips. "You're always laughing!"

"Life is fun." Han smiled, throwing his hands in the air for emphasis.

"Except when I want to go riding," she retorted. "Do you think that once—just once—you could saddle a horse for me without making an ordeal out of it?"

He smirked. "Why should I?"

"Because that's what you're paid to do. You might find this a startling revelation, Han Heinrich, but you are a stable groom. It is your job to get a horse ready for me when I want one."

"You're always reminding me." He chuckled.

"If you did your job the way you're supposed to, I wouldn't have to remind you." Maggie turned away with a silent indication that she wasn't going to press the conversation any further.

"Oh, all right." Han laughed. "Just wait another minute, and I'll saddle Pagan . . . Your Royal Impatience."

Maggie kept her back to him and blew out a careful sigh, fighting to put her temper under control before turning back to face him. She knew he only behaved this way to get a reaction out of her, and she'd told herself countless times that she would not give him any further satisfaction. But oh, how he riled her! Simply put, if it weren't for the times he'd helped keep her out of trouble, she'd have insisted he be dismissed long ago. But somehow he always managed to come through when she was in need of a quick alibi. Beyond that, he was infuriatingly rude and sarcastic, and his manner as a groom was deplorable! But then, Han no doubt had confidence that his position was not easily threatened. Maggie had only once insinuated that she would have him dismissed, and he'd come up with a long list of reasons why he never would be. Those reasons haunted her in moments like this. She almost hated him simply for the way everybody else around here liked him.

Maggie's father foremost absolutely adored Han. This was mostly due to the fact that Han's father was Cameron du Woernig's right-hand man and lifelong friend. Although Han was *nothing* like his father. They both had the same tall, lean frame and fluffy, blond hair. But Georg Heinrich was a kind, gentle man who would never speak with any degree of disrespect to a lady. Maggie often wished that Han would pay more attention to his father's example.

"It's a beautiful morning." The subject of her thoughts interrupted her musings, and she turned to see Han throwing a saddle on Pagan's back.

"Yes," she said, "I believe it is. I'll let you know for certain when I've had a chance to see for myself."

"Patience, Princess." He smiled. "Patience."

Maggie glared at him then looked away, and he chuckled again. "Why do you take everything so seriously?" he asked.

"That is a topic I refuse to discuss with you."

"Do you know what your problem is, MagdaLena?"

"I'm certain you do," she said sarcastically. "And it's *Princess* MagdaLena to you."

"Oh, knock off the formalities. Your problem," he went on, "is that you just don't know how to have fun."

"You've mentioned that before," she said in a scolding tone, but he just laughed, and she did her best to ignore him.

Han watched Maggie as she moved closer to Pagan and pressed a hand down the horse's neck in their usual greeting. While he tightened the strap beneath the horse's belly, he hardly took his eyes off of her. He liked watching her while she wasn't aware, though he rarely had the opportunity. In spite of her older brother being his closest friend, it wasn't often these days that he encountered Maggie anywhere beyond the stables. And even then, she was quickly in and out. And rarely kind.

She always wore a fine riding habit, since she owned several in varied colors and styles, but today she wore dusty blue, which enhanced her eyes of the same color. Again he noted how her rich, curly red hair was styled immaculately and set off with a smart little hat. She played her role of the princess well, but Han recalled the little girl she'd once been, romping in the castle gardens and climbing trees with the other children. He'd watched her mature into a beautiful young woman, but there had been a time when her feelings for him had been much different. To this day, he didn't understand what had changed her. But he couldn't help hoping that something of the Maggie he'd grown up with still existed somewhere.

With the saddle secure, Han held out his hand to help her mount in a manner they were accustomed to. He bent his knee below the stirrup, and she briefly set her booted foot on his thigh in order to hurtle herself into the saddle. While she adjusted her skirts and brushed them meticulously, Han took the reins and walked Pagan toward the wide door that had not yet been opened today. Turning the reins over to Maggie, he pushed against the huge door with his shoulder to open it while Pagan pawed with anticipation at the ground beneath his hooves.

The smell of recent rain rushed into the stables. When the door stopped on its hinge, Han leaned against it and held his arms out elaborately as the sun burst into the stables and Pagan bolted forward. Han saluted casually as Maggie rode past, and he watched intently until she had galloped across the courtyard and disappeared through the high castle gate. He should have been going with her, he thought; life should have been so much different for both of them. He told himself as he did every day that he should just accept the past for what it had been and let it go. But something kept him holding on to the tiniest spark of hope, even while a part of him knew it was hopeless. He forced himself to get to work, making certain all of the horses were clean and brushed and the stables in good order. But he could only think about Maggie.

The morning air felt briskly invigorating to Maggie. She drew serenity from riding and quickly forgot the tension Han always created within her. Reaching the foot of the hill that majestically supported her home, Maggie turned by habit to admire Castle Horstberg. She had never known any other home or way of life, but being the eldest daughter of the Duke of Horstberg was an honor she didn't take lightly. She took pride in her heritage and felt certain the future she had chosen for herself would serve her country well.

Pagan grew impatient from her brief admiration. Almost by his own will, the stallion turned and broke into a gallop toward the foothills. The Bavarian countryside had a beauty Maggie could never put into words. She only knew she felt a part of it on mornings like this. The forest was sparse in this favorite spot of hers, not far from the castle hill. And the meadow was just beginning to show signs of color as winter slipped away. Maggie heeled Pagan around the circumference of the meadow, relishing the wind in her face and letting whatever anxieties might have hindered this enjoyment fall away.

Maggie was surprised to realize she was not alone. At first she thought the man she could see at the edge of the woods was Erich, since her brother often rode early as well. From a distance it briefly looked like him. But she quickly realized that Erich's red hair was unmistakable, and this man's hair was dark. Enveloped with sudden apprehension, she couldn't recall ever seeing anyone else riding this close to the castle before.

As the rider came closer, there was no conscious reason for Maggie to be afraid, but there was something indefinable in his manner that disturbed her. She was accustomed to being approached with deference, and this man's boldness caught her off guard. Remembering her father's repeated warnings—however light—about being kidnapped and carried off for the duke's ransom, Maggie turned and rode away from the approaching rider, relieved that he didn't pursue her.

When Maggie arrived back at the stables, Han was there as always to help her dismount. She wasn't aware of the vague weakness in her knees until she leaned against Han's hands at her waist.

"Is something wrong?" he asked with sincerity, holding onto her longer than necessary to offer support.

"No," she said sharply and left Han staring after her.

Maggie quickly freshened up and made it to the dining room just as breakfast was nearing an end.

"Look, Abbi," her father said to her mother as Maggie entered and sat down. "I told you there was another daughter around here someplace. They always come around when they're hungry."

Maggie gave her father an affectionate glance. She was quite comfortable with his teasing. She exchanged a quick glance with her sister, Sonia, then smiled toward her mother, who replied, "If you don't stop that, Cameron, they'll all take to eating in their rooms."

"On the contrary," Erich piped in, "mealtime can be rather entertaining. I wouldn't miss it for the world."

Cameron du Woernig nodded toward his son, obviously pleased by the comment. And the mirrored image of his youth nodded back. If not for Erich's red, curly hair that was such a stark contrast to Cameron's that was nearly black—slightly spattered with hints of gray—their appearance was practically identical except for their obvious difference in age.

"I'm glad you're here, Maggie," her mother said. "You mustn't forget that you have a fitting this afternoon at three. Don't be off roaming the countryside and leave the dressmaker waiting."

"I'll be there," Maggie assured her.

"What are we getting a new dress for this time?" Erich asked.

"Don't you remember, dear?" his mother replied. "Maggie's betrothal will soon be official."

"Ah, yes, of course." Erich's tone indicated his disapproval. "The groom's family is traveling many miles to meet the bride to be. And what a festive occasion we'll have!" His sarcasm was light but true.

"Oh, hush!" Maggie insisted.

Erich gave her a sidelong glance and stood from the table. "I'm going riding, little sister. Want to come?"

"I do," Sonia volunteered, coming to her feet as well.

"Wonderful," he said. "Maggie?"

"I've already been out once," she said, recalling the strange encounter that had cut her ride short, "but I wouldn't mind going again."

"Good." Erich smiled, taking Sonia's arm. "We'll meet you in the stables. Don't be too long."

Even though Maggie's parents had finished eating, they tarried at the table to visit with their daughter while she hurriedly ate her breakfast. Maggie wasn't surprised when her father asked, "Are you ready for the big day?"

"I will be," she said easily.

"I know I've asked this before," Cameron said carefully, his teasing tone completely absent, "but I need to be certain this is what you want to do. I will not have you feeling forced into a political marriage if it's not what you want."

"Yes, Father," Maggie smiled, "you've asked me before. And I'll tell you again: I'm not being forced into anything. This was *my* idea, remember?"

"But you haven't even met Rudolf," her father argued. "How can you be willing to marry someone you haven't even met?"

"I've met his parents," Maggie said with only a hint of impatience in her voice while her mother looked on with concern. "They're a good family. You told me yourself."

"Yes, they are," Cameron agreed. "But that's not necessarily enough to make a good marriage. Why don't you—"

"Father," Maggie said firmly, "we've discussed this already. Rudolf and I have been exchanging letters for quite some time. I feel I know him well. I'm certain it will be a satisfactory marriage."

"Satisfactory?" Cameron echoed, his voice raised a pitch.

"Cameron," Abbi said gently. Maggie knew it was her mother's way of reminding him to stay calm.

"Father," Maggie leaned over the table, "you have admitted yourself that this marriage will be advantageous for both our countries."

"Yes," he had to agree, "but that's not enough reason to—"

"It's reason enough for me," Maggie insisted, her voice picking up an edge. "It's my life and my choice."

Cameron said nothing, but the muscles in his face tightened.

"I'm certain she will like Rudolf," Abbi said to her husband, and Maggie calmed somewhat.

"Like?" he chuckled satirically and shook his head. "I don't know if this is right or not."

"Really, Father," Maggie assured him as she stood to leave, "it's fine. Don't worry. I'll be happy enough."

"She'll be happy enough," Cameron repeated after Maggie had left the room. "Abbi, my love, does she have any idea what she's getting herself into?"

"I don't know." Abbi tried to smile. "She's convinced that she'll be an old maid at the ripe age of nineteen. She just wants to get married and be settled."

"Well, I hope you understand that. I don't."

"Cameron," she said gently, "you should know by now that there is no changing Maggie's mind once she's set it to something. We can't make her choices for her. I'm as concerned as you are, but the more you try to talk her out of it, the harder she will fight to defend her ground. She's come to take her role as the duke's daughter very seriously. Perhaps it's important for her to know that her life will benefit Horstberg."

"It's not enough," Cameron said. "I swore years ago I would never force my children into political marriages and—"

"And you haven't. It was her idea. She's a woman now, Cameron. If this is what she wants, we'll just have to hope it works out. Rudolf is a good man. He'll treat her well."

"But, Abbi . . . hasn't she seen in you and me what real love is like? I thought our children would want that."

"Perhaps," Abbi sighed, "she is taking for granted that all marriages are that way."

The duke leaned back in his chair and blew out a long breath of worry. "Well, I hope it's right. I'm sending the messenger out this morning with the finalizing decree. And they'll be here on Friday."

"I'm sure everything will be fine, dear." Abbi stood and kissed her husband lightly.

"I will have to take your word for it." He grinned and pulled her onto his lap to kiss her again.

Maggie found Erich and Han in the stables, laughing like children, while Sonia listened with amusement and stroked her cherished mare.

"Good morning, Princess Maggie," Han said as she entered and forced a smile toward him. Erich continued with whatever he'd been telling Han, and Maggie listened indifferently. She had become well accustomed to waiting for them.

Han and Erich were divided in age by only a matter of months. Han's mother, Elsa, had been Abbi du Woernig's personal maid even before Abbi had become the duchess, and it had only been recently that Elsa had more or less retired, still spending most of her time with Abbi simply because she wanted to. Abbi and Elsa had remained close as friends, just as their sons were. Abbi had insisted on having her children with her as much as possible in spite of her position, and she had enjoyed having Han around as a playmate for Erich, right from infancy. Han, being an only child, had been raised alongside the du Woernig children. Having grown up together, Erich and Han were naturally close as friends. And though Maggie was occasionally amused by their boyish ways, she was more disgusted by the way men of twenty-two years could act so childish.

In her youth, Maggie had often felt envious of their friendship. There had been no servant girls at the castle near her age that she'd been close to. And being a princess had left her basically secluded from the rest of the world. Her parents had always encouraged her to spend leisure time with Sonia. But though her younger sister was nice enough to be around and they had rarely quarreled, there was much more than two years separating them. Beyond their red hair, they looked nothing alike. It was difficult for Maggie to understand why Sonia was blessed with such a well-curved figure, while Maggie was so slight. Still, their differences went far deeper than appearance. Sharing little common ground, they found it difficult to have fun together the way Erich and Han always had.

"Are you two going to stand around and gab all day," Maggie demanded, "or are we going riding?"

Han's eyes glowed with amusement as he helped her mount while Erich quickly finished his story. Han smiled complacently toward Maggie, and she hated him all the more for the way he was so perfectly respectful whenever anyone else was around. If she tried to tell anyone that Han was rude and impertinent with her, no one would ever believe her. And it made her angry.

Not long after the threesome arrived at the meadow, Maggie noticed again the man she'd seen earlier, sitting on his horse near the edge of the forest. She was grateful for Erich's presence, and she and Sonia remained behind him as the rider approached. Initially, Maggie felt the same apprehension as she had earlier, but watching him come closer, her suspicion faded into intrigue.

"Good morning," he said, halting in front of them and showing an easy smile. "It is a beautiful day."

"It is," Erich replied. "You are a stranger here," he added in a tone that indicated this man did not recognize them as members of the royal family.

"Actually, no," the man replied, and Maggie couldn't help but think him handsome. His features were strong, as was his stature, and his dark hair was styled to do him justice. "I was born in south Horstberg. I've never been to this side of the valley."

Maggie knew what that meant, but he didn't appear to be the type from that area. He had a certain dignity about him that was usually absent in the common laborers who typically lived in a part of the country known for poverty and crime that often required government assistance or military intervention.

"This land belongs to the du Woernig family," Erich stated with his natural nobility.

"Ah." The man smiled and glanced overtly toward Maggie. She turned away, feeling an indiscernible rush of excitement. "The du Woernigs. *The* family of Horstberg."

Erich remained silent and the man went on. "I am trespassing then," he said with no apology in his tone. "You must forgive my ignorance." Still no one replied. Erich was well known for his silent, imposing manner.

"Allow me to introduce myself," the man continued easily, not seeming unnerved by the lack of response he was getting in this conversation. "My name is Nikolaus Koenig." His eyes darted to Maggie. "And you are . . ." He raised his brows toward Erich.

"Erich . . . du Woernig."

"Ah," Nikolaus Koenig said easily, not seeming the least bit surprised. "So I have come upon *the* du Woernigs." He looked shamelessly toward Maggie and added, "How delightful. You must introduce these lovely ladies."

"My sisters," Erich replied. Maggie couldn't tell if he liked this Mr. Koenig or not, but he gave no further introduction.

"I am very pleased to meet you," Mr. Koenig bent gallantly, "Your Highnesses."

Maggie felt herself smile as their new acquaintance met her gaze and held it. A fluttering surged through her, and she looked quickly away.

Nikolaus Koenig seemed pleased by her reaction, but he turned his attention again to Erich. "I have heard much of your family. My mother has always shown quite an interest in royal *gossip*—if you will forgive the term. But I had no idea the famed princesses were so lovely."

"It was a pleasure meeting you, Mr. Koenig." Erich eased his mount forward, and Sonia moved close behind her brother.

"A pleasure indeed," Mr. Koenig replied and Erich rode away with Sonia. But Maggie felt momentarily compelled to stay.

"Do princesses know how to speak?" Mr. Koenig asked her, showing a pleasant smile.

"Of course," she replied. "I saw you riding this morning."

"It was you," he reassured himself. "Did I frighten you?"

"Only briefly," she replied, wondering what she was feeling.

Erich noticed his sister lagging behind and turned back. "Come along, Maggie."

"It was a pleasure meeting you, Mr. Koenig," she said, easing her horse forward.

"Wait," he seemed almost panicked, "will I never see you again?"

Maggie smiled. "I'm not certain."

"Meet me," he pleaded, "later."

"Maggie!" Erich called impatiently, and she was glad her brother couldn't hear their conversation.

"I . . . don't know," Maggie said, wanting desperately to see him again but not knowing for certain what was best. *I am betrothed*, she told herself.

"Please," he said, "only for a few minutes. I would like to talk to you."

Again, Erich called for Maggie, turning around to come and get her personally. Impulsively she replied, "All right, Mr. Koenig."

"Call me Nik." He smiled and sighed with apparent relief.

"Very well, Nik, I'll come back here . . . around five o'clock."

"I'll be here," he said and turned the opposite direction, riding quickly away.

Maggie watched him a moment then rode to catch up with Erich and Sonia.

Returning to the castle brought Maggie back to reality. While she hardly understood what she was feeling, she couldn't deny the regret gradually seeping through her as she went into town with her mother and was fitted for her betrothal gown. The regret became completely unbearable by the time she returned to the meadow at precisely five and saw Nikolaus Koenig riding toward her. Suddenly Maggie didn't want to be betrothed. There was a new desire in her to experience life. And now this marriage to Rudolf, the son of a count, seemed very sordid and dooming.

"Thank you for coming," Nik said when he came near. Maggie managed a smile in spite of her oppressive thoughts. "Come," he added, moving toward the forest. Maggie followed, stopping when he did at the edge of the trees. He dismounted and tied off his horse, then he held up his hand for her. "Shall we walk for a few moments?"

Maggie hesitated before silently slipping her gloved hand into his. She felt a tingly sensation from his touch as he helped her down. She was briefly reminded of the time when she and Han had . . .

The memory prodded at something painful, and she pushed it away. Focusing on the man at her side, she wondered momentarily if it was a good idea for her to be here, for a number of reasons. But impulsively, she threw all reasoning away and walked with him.

"Princesses do speak," he said, "but not very much."

"I'm not certain what to say, Mr. Koenig," she replied.

"My name is Nik."

"I think Mr. Koenig would be more appropriate."

"On the contrary," he said easily, "walking alone in the forest calls for given names."

"I don't even know you."

"But you want to," he said with impeccable confidence, and she couldn't argue. She noticed then how tall he was. No taller than Erich or Han. But Maggie had inherited her mother's petite stature, and standing near this man, she was very aware of his height.

"May I call you Maggie?" he asked, looking toward the ground.

"I don't know if you should."

"Why not?" he stopped and turned to face her with intense question in his eyes.

"I . . . I'm betrothed."

Nik's expression hardly changed, but he asked quickly, "Do you love him?"

"I've not . . . met him," she replied, "but I—"

"Then you must call it off," he interrupted adamantly.

"I think I should go, Mr. Koenig." Maggie started to move away, but his arm came around her waist, bringing her to an abrupt halt as he turned her to face him.

"Deny it!" he challenged.

"What are you talking about?" She barely breathed, wondering for a moment if she had put herself into some kind of danger. But she couldn't think of any logical reason why he would do her harm in any way.

"You don't even know him, yet you are willing to become his wife. You hardly know me, but can you deny what you're feeling?"

Maggie wanted to say something in her defense, but she wasn't accustomed to feeling this way any more than she was accustomed to being treated in this manner. She had no idea how to react on either count.

"You see," he said softly, bringing his fingers to her face, "you can't deny it."

Maggie was trying to tell herself that she must remember her position—and the part of the valley this man was from. It wasn't right or suitable. Her mind protested as his face moved close to hers. But as his lips met hers softly, she recalled her parents talking about falling in love as opposed to arranged marriages. The very idea was so confusing, she nearly felt dizzy.

Nik's kiss left her breathless, and then he whispered close to her face, "May I call you Maggie?"

"Yes," she heard herself say, "yes, Nik, you may call me Maggie."

"Good," he smiled, still holding her very close, "I always wanted to fall in love with a princess."

Maggie wanted to tell him that he couldn't possibly be in love; they had only just met. But he bent to kiss her again, and she thought that she couldn't lie to him.

"I should get back," she said when his lips pulled away. "I will be missed if I don't return soon."

"You must call it off, Maggie," Nik whispered adamantly, and she felt almost hypnotized by the way he affected her. She made no reply, but he looked into her eyes, seeming satisfied for some reason. Maggie wondered if he could see the unrest he had already created within her.

"Can I see you tomorrow?" Nik asked, helping her mount Pagan.

"I . . . uh . . . yes."

"When?" he asked, looking up at her, holding her hand firmly. "You tell me when you can get away, and I'll be here."

"Uh . . ." Maggie paused, certain she had never stammered so much in her life. "Same time," she said.

"I'll be looking forward to it." He smiled then kissed her hand, and she rode away.

Maggie's confusion only deepened through a sleepless night. The experiences of her youth had taught her to take her role as the duke's daughter very seriously. Her family had never been very pleased with her attitude—and Han was downright belligerent over it. Though she couldn't blame him. And she couldn't really expect any of them to understand. They often embarrassed her by their down-to-earth manner in ruling a duchy. She knew her father was a good ruler, but she couldn't believe how he managed to blend in with the commoners at times. Maggie, however, felt it was important to keep the distinction of royalty very clear. She had once sworn to never marry beneath her. Her betrothal to Rudolf was something she'd felt good about. Sonia had had the nerve to say that Maggie only wanted to get away from Horstberg and be flaunted about like a royal treasure bestowed upon Rudolf's family. They'd argued for more than an hour before Maggie had finally called her sister some awful things and stormed out of the room. She didn't like the image of herself that Sonia had implied. But now as she thought of Nik Koenig, something about her motives for marrying Rudolf began to make her uneasy.

Maggie knew that Erich also strongly disapproved of her betrothal. He'd made that clear on several occasions. Her parents had attempted to discuss it with her repeatedly. But Maggie's mind had been made up, and she'd refused to listen. And now . . . Nikolaus Koenig had sparked something in her that she'd not felt in years. Or had she ever? She hardly considered her little fling at the age of fourteen to count for much in the way of experience. Though she knew Han would disagree, she felt certain it had been nothing more than puppy love. Her memories of their relationship were vague and obscure, but then the entire thing had ended so horribly that she'd chosen not to think about it at all . . . until now. What was it about Nikolaus Koenig that suddenly made her question things she'd felt so strongly about before? How could their brief encounters force her to take a hard look at her resolve concerning matters of love and marriage? And why did her thoughts carry her—almost against her will—back to her experiences with Han? Rather than contemplating too deeply *why*, Maggie simply came to the conclusion that what Nik made her feel had changed her mind. It was as simple as that. She contemplated her parents and the love they obviously shared. Her mother had no royal blood, but she was well suited to her father, and she filled her obligations as the duchess with dignity and competence. Maggie had been hearing her parents harp for years about marrying for love. Only now did it make any sense at all.

With her mind made up, Maggie finally fell asleep before dawn and missed breakfast. An intense excitement accompanied her through the remainder of the day and right up until her meeting with Nik in the meadow as she had promised. He laughed as he helped her dismount, immediately pulling her into his arms with a hungry kiss. And she offered no resistance.

Maggie waited for him to ask the inevitable question, and her answer was well prepared. She was by no means certain whether or not Nik was the right man for her. But he had made her realize one thing. The right man was not Rudolf. She had made up her mind to call off the betrothal before it was too late. And whether or not it was Nikolaus Koenig, she would marry a man she loved.

"Well," he asked impishly, "I know you've been thinking. I can see it in your eyes. Are you still betrothed?"

"Yes," she said.

"And?"

"And what?" She prolonged her answer on purpose.

"Surely you must have reconsidered this betrothal. How can you possibly go through with it?"

"You are taking a great deal for granted, Mr. Koenig. We only just met yesterday."

"You are trying to deny it again," he stated with conviction. "You must be mine, Maggie. Now that I have found you, I will not let you marry this man you do not know."

"You make it sound so easy."

"It is easy. You must know this betrothal is not right, and you—"

"That is one thing I do know," she said with a smile. "I am not certain who I will marry, but it will not be Rudolf."

"Maggie," he whispered, and his eyes widened. "Are you telling me . . . Are you still betrothed?"

"Yes," she stated then laughed, "but not for long."

"Ah," he laughed with her and pulled her up off the ground, turning her around in circles, "I knew you would do it."

"I haven't talked to my father yet," she said as he set her down and she leaned heavily against him from the dizziness, "but I will . . . tonight."

"Do you think he will be agreeable?"

"I don't know," she said, certain her father's initial reaction would not be pleasant. "But I think I can win him over eventually."

"I must know right away," Nik said intently. "I can't wait until tomorrow to find out what happened. You must meet me tonight."

"I don't know if I . . ." Maggie hesitated, recalling the many times she had sneaked out of the castle late at night just to ride—simply for the adventure. She knew she could pull it off, but she wasn't certain whether or not she should. Han had always helped her when she'd done it before, and she felt certain she could coerce him into doing it again, but she didn't necessarily want to. Still, the temptation was too great. Nik looked into her eyes, and she felt compelled to follow the impetuous mood he inspired in her. "All right," she said, and he smiled. "Meet me here a little past midnight."

Nik laughed and kissed her again. Maggie rode home, feeling real excitement for the first time in years—if ever.

"Hello, Han," she said pleasantly as he helped her dismount.

"My, but aren't we cheerful today!" He smirked, but she ignored it. Nothing could deter her enjoyment.

"Yes," she said, "I believe we are. Han?" she added carefully.

"She wants something," he said more to himself as he pulled the saddle from Pagan's back. "She's always cheerful when she wants something."

She ignored his comment. "Will you do me a favor?"

"Not another midnight ride!" He looked at her with exaggerated shock. "Just what is it that gives you these bizarre urges? Is your life really so dull that you have to sneak out all by yourself just to ride a horse in the dark?"

"Yes," she smiled, "it really is."

"And you will insist I come out here to saddle a horse for you and lie on your behalf in case anyone finds out."

"You always have before." She smiled easily.

"Only because I felt sorry for you," he said quite seriously. "You've got to have some kind of excitement. If I didn't play along with your silly games, you'd get none at all."

"There was a time you didn't think it was silly," she said.

Han turned to look at her, forcing himself to not gape in astonishment. It was the first time in over four years that she'd even hinted at any acknowledgment of what they had once shared. Determined to not let her affect him, he simply replied, "That was before you declared your royal proclamation that I was not allowed to come with you . . . Your Highness." He added the title with a subtle sarcasm that was difficult for him to avoid.

"Well," Maggie said complacently, "if you don't want to help me, that's fine. I'll go bareback and do all of the lying myself."

"My," he smirked again, "but aren't we determined! Something's gotten into Her Royal Highness."

"Will you or won't you?" she asked. "Just tell me so I'll know."

"I take it you're going out whether I help you or not."

"You're very perceptive, Han."

"Well, I'll not have no one knowing where the princess is. I'll be here—if only to make certain you come back when you're supposed to."

"Are you trying to say that you still worry about me . . . in spite of it all?" she asked.

"Are you joking?" he countered easily. "If anything happened to you, your father would find a way to blame it on me and have me hung, no less. I'll be here," he added, walking Pagan to his stall. "I don't know why I'll be here, but I'll be here."

"Thank you, Han," she said. He only glanced toward her and cursed under his breath. But Maggie ignored him. Her mind was preoccupied with the way it felt to be kissed by Nik Koenig. She was so elated, even telling her father to call off the betrothal didn't seem terribly ominous.

Chapter Two
THE REPLACEMENT

Maggie went to her father's office soon after dinner, where she found him and Erich going over some matter of business. Since neither Georg nor the Captain of the Guard were present, she knew it wasn't likely anything very urgent. Erich appeared perturbed by the interruption, but he left after Maggie insisted that she needed to talk to their father alone.

Cameron removed his glasses and leaned forward, placing his forearms on the desk. Maggie's heart beat quickly as he waited for her to speak.

"Father," she began, "I . . ." Drawing back her shoulders, she blurted it out. "I don't want to marry Rudolf."

In the following silence, an imposing quality filtered through Cameron's eyes. At such moments, Maggie became keenly aware that her father was the Duke of Horstberg. She didn't question that he was a very powerful man.

"Where are you going?" she asked frantically when he stood to leave the room.

"I'm going to get your mother," he said with no expression. "I refuse to discuss this without your mother present. She understands you—I don't!"

Maggie paced the office, wondering what was taking so long. But when her parents entered and closed the door, she wanted to be anywhere but there.

"All right," her father said after seating himself again, "I'd like you to repeat what you said before I left."

Maggie cleared her throat. "I don't want to marry Rudolf," she said quickly, and her mother's eyes widened.

"Now, Abbi," Cameron directed his attention to his wife, "you tell me if I'm wrong. Did I not ask this young lady yesterday morning if I should go through with this? And did she not—most emphatically—say that it was fine?" He stopped, waiting for a reply.

"Yes, dear," Abbi gave the only answer she possibly could.

"And have I not, several times in the past, implored her to reconsider this decision before I made it final?"

"Yes, dear," she repeated.

"Then why," he shouted, "now that the royal family of Schmautzberg is on their way here to make it all official, does she decide she doesn't want to marry him?"

"I don't know, Cameron." Abbi remained intently calm. "You would probably have to ask her."

"All right." The duke turned his attention to his daughter, who was nervously torturing a handkerchief with her hands. "Why?"

"I . . ." Maggie wondered briefly what to tell him, but figuring he would be upset no matter what, she opted for the truth.

"Out with it, girl! I want to know why you're wanting to put us on the brink of war."

"Oh, it's not as serious as all that!" Abbi interjected.

Cameron gave her a sidelong glare but didn't argue. He gazed intently at Maggie, waiting for an answer.

"I've met someone," she said and felt a degree of hope when her mother smiled.

Abbi was absorbed with deep relief when Cameron leaned back in his chair and sighed. She knew that he couldn't be angry with his daughter for falling in love. And her own concerns about Maggie making a mistake with this betrothal were put to rest.

There was an intolerable length of silence before Cameron said softly, "Who is this . . . someone? And where did you meet him?"

"Yesterday while out riding. Erich and Sonia were with me. He's very nice . . . and handsome," she added more toward her mother. "His name is Nik Koenig."

"What do you know about him?" he asked, and Abbi laughed out loud. "What's so funny?" her father insisted, turning toward his wife.

Abbi willfully sobered her expression. "I'll tell you later. I'm sorry." She put a hand over her mouth to keep from laughing again.

Maggie noticed her father smile, but he quickly suppressed it and turned back toward Maggie. "What do you know about him?" he repeated.

Reassured by her mother's pleasant expression, Maggie gave the strongest answer possible, "I only know how I feel when I'm with him."

Again Cameron sighed, leaning his head into his hands through another unbearable silence. "Well," he said at last, "I don't know how I'm going to do it, but if you don't want to marry Rudolf, I'll figure something out. You know very well that I would never force such a thing."

"Oh, Father," Maggie squealed, overwhelming him with an exuberant hug, "thank you."

"But you listen to me, MagdaLena! Until I've taken care of this, you will not say a word to anyone. I'll not have gossip started over it. And after this is settled, we will see to a proper courtship. But," he added, pointing a finger at her, "don't be thinking you have to marry this Mr. Koenig just because you . . . well, just because. You take time . . . and be careful. This is your life we're talking about."

"I'll be careful," she promised adamantly.

Cameron took his daughter's hand and gave an affectionate squeeze. She kissed her mother and left the room, more excited than they had seen her in years.

Cameron asked his wife dubiously, "Is that the same girl who was wanting to sacrifice her life for her country just yesterday?"

Abbi smiled and took Cameron's hand. "Perhaps she's finally allowing the pendulum to swing the other way." At his questioning gaze, she added, "Perhaps she's feeling more like a woman than a princess. I'm certain that one day she will find the proper balance. Until she does, we can probably expect some swinging back and forth."

"Oh, great," Cameron said with sarcasm, but Abbi only chuckled. "What's so funny?" he demanded.

"Oh, I was just thinking. You make a fine duke, Cameron du Woernig. You have little trouble being the military general and chief judge, but being a father certainly keeps you off balance."

Cameron couldn't hold back a warm chuckle. "How well you know me," he murmured, and she bent to kiss him. "It's later," he added with a subtle scowl. At her questioning gaze, he clarified, "You certainly were amused when I asked Maggie what she knew about this Mr. Koenig."

Abbi laughed again and his scowl deepened. "I've been waiting for years to hear you say that to one of our daughters." He glared at her. "Forgive me, my love," Abbi smiled affectionately, "but do you recall how little I knew about you until long after we were married?"

Cameron smiled, warmed by the memory. "Yes, but that was different," he said impishly.

"Perhaps." She touched her nose to his. "But there was only one thing that mattered, Cameron. I loved you. And perhaps Maggie will come to love this Mr. Koenig."

"So," he said with a deep sigh, "what do I tell the count when he arrives?"

"The truth, perhaps?" she suggested.

"You know, Abbi, being a father might not be so difficult if it wasn't all tangled up into political matters."

"I'm certain you'll manage just fine," she assured him.

"I don't know." Cameron chuckled again. "Maybe I should have been a blacksmith."

"I'm certain you would make a wonderful blacksmith, Cameron. But Horstberg is in your blood. You know as well as I that you'd not be happy doing anything else."

"Yes, you're right," he admitted. "And there is one aspect about being the Duke of Horstberg that makes it all worth it."

"And what is that?" she asked.

"Being married to the Duchess of Horstberg."

Maggie went through the formalities of getting ready for bed and pretended to be especially tired while Klara, her personal maid, brushed through her hair. She pretended to go to sleep for good appearances, but her excitement to see Nik and tell him the good news made it difficult to even hold still.

Maggie managed to get out to the stables a little before midnight.

She knew Han wasn't supposed to be there yet, but still she felt impatient for him to come. Pacing back and forth, she was filled with a fresh excitement, not only in the adventure of being out like this without anyone knowing, but in the prospect of her meeting in the meadow, as well.

"Boo!" Han said close behind her, and Maggie let out a gaspy scream.

"How many times," she said in exasperation, "have I told you not to sneak up on me like that?"

"You're obviously in an adventurous mood. I thought I'd add to the excitement of it all!" he concluded dramatically, and Maggie couldn't help but smile.

Han thought it best to say nothing as he saddled Pagan, but it was difficult to keep his eyes off Maggie. There was something intriguing about her when she was in the mood for her nighttime riding escapades. And he was fascinated. He wondered if her hair had anything to do with it. Only on these occasions had he seen it down since she'd turned fifteen. He felt certain there was not a more beautiful head of hair in all of Horstberg.

The du Woernig family was known for curly hair—but Maggie had gotten the most of it. The unruly curls hung in full array halfway down her back, and he wished that he could see it like that in daylight. The vibrant red would most likely come to life in the sun. Even now, in the low lamplight of the stable, her hair almost overwhelmed her. When she turned to face him after the saddle was in place, he caught something different in her eyes. And her high cheeks and full lips seemed unusually flushed with color.

"Do you want me to go with you?" he asked impulsively as he helped her mount.

Maggie wondered over his motives and glanced down at him briefly. There had been a time when they'd done this together—quite regularly. When she had severed their relationship, she'd made it clear that she would ride alone, though he'd insisted that he should be there to make certain she came home safely. She'd eagerly accepted that offer for reasons she wouldn't admit to; though somehow she believed Han understood. He'd saved her life that one time she had ridden out alone without a saddle, but the experience was all part of an episode in her life she refused to even think about. Han had never questioned her desire to ride without him even though he was there to make sure she came and went safely. But she had to admit now that if she weren't going to meet Nik, it might have been fun to have Han come along.

"Well?" he asked, lifting his brows mischievously when she remained silent.

"No," she replied forcefully and moved Pagan forward. "You be careful," he called after her. "And don't be too long. I'm not waiting here half the night . . . Your Royal Highness!" As always, his use of her title had a subtle bite of sarcasm, but Maggie ignored his remarks and galloped toward the meadow.

Nik was there waiting for her. "Hello, my love," he said, pulling her from Pagan's back and directly into his arms.

"Hello," she replied. Had he really called her "his love?"

Nik kissed her without hesitation. Maggie saw no reason to resist. Instead, she concentrated on the pleasurable sensation. She felt suddenly so alive that she began to wonder how she had ever existed before now. Perhaps that was the problem; she'd only been existing.

"You spoke with your father?" he questioned as soon as his passionate greeting was finished.

"Yes," she said, trying to remain expressionless.

"And?" he asked expectantly.

"He said that . . . well, it will be difficult, but . . . he said he would find a way to call off the betrothal."

"Oh, Maggie," he laughed, "I am so happy."

She laughed with him, and then he insisted she tell him the details of the drama. They held hands as they talked, and she enjoyed Nik's attentiveness.

Maggie lost her sense of time until she remembered that Han was waiting for her. Reluctantly she declared that she must return. Nik seemed disappointed, but he kissed her good night and helped her mount, leaving Maggie elated. Despite her hesitance to leave Nik, she rode home quickly and found Han dozing in the straw.

"Wake up!" she said, poking him in the ribs with her boot.

"The queen of the nighttime adventures has returned," he said in mock gallantry before he yawned.

"Indeed," she sneered and left the stable. Going to her room,

Maggie was so thoroughly caught up with thoughts of Nik Koenig, she felt certain she would never recover.

Maggie bit her tongue to keep from making up some kind of excuse to avoid joining the other ladies in the castle for chatting and needlework. Maggie abhorred needlework. But it was expected that a lady know how to do such things, and she *did* know how; she simply didn't like it. Abbi had taught her daughters that while needlework itself was not something she considered terribly important, it did teach a woman a certain amount of discipline and gave them something to occupy themselves when they were forced to entertain ladies who visited Castle Horstberg with their husbands and fathers when they came to conduct business. While politics and matters of echelon were being discussed at the other end of their enormous home, the women would sit with their backs straight, chat politely, and do needlework. There were no visitors at the castle today, but it wasn't uncommon for the ladies to gather—more to visit than to actually accomplish much sewing—and Maggie was often required to be present. Sonia didn't seem to mind, nor did Dulsie Dukerk—who were the only other women present of her own generation. But Maggie hated it and had to put great effort into keeping her countenance appropriate while the needle went in and out of the fabric in her hands.

Maggie stopped sewing while she listened to the conversation taking place between her mother and the two women who were at her sides as often as any family member. These women were Abbi's dearest friends and confidants. Nadine Dukerk was married to the Captain of the Guard, who not only worked closely with the duke but was also one of Cameron du Woernig's closests friends. Of course, the other woman in the room was Elsa Heinrich, whose husband was the duke's highest advisor as well as a lifelong friend. Just as the three men were rarely apart in matters of business *and* friendship, so it was with their wives. Dulsie was Nadine's only daughter and was more than five years older than Maggie. They'd never had any discord between them as they'd grown up together with the same tutors and nannies. Dulsie was quiet and well refined, and ironically, she seemed more suited to enjoying the company of the generation before her. She had little to say to Maggie or Sonia, even though she was always very kind. Elsa had no daughters, but she had always been like a second mother to Maggie and Sonia. And Dulsie, as well. In fact, Maggie considered Elsa and Nadine to be more like aunts than friends of her mother.

The group of women passively busy at their needlework and chatting casually was comfortable and the situation commonplace. But perhaps that was the very reason Maggie felt so bored. No one had anything to say that she hadn't heard some version of many times before. It was always the same. The men ran the country, and the women talked about what the men were doing, often joking that it was actually the *women* who ran the country because their husbands trusted them and relied heavily on their insights and opinions. These women were all heavily involved in ways that no outsider would ever suspect—especially if they could see them now, appearing as if not one of them knew how to do *anything* except create little pictures in fabric out of tiny little stitches. Maggie wanted to scream!

Now that she'd stitched dutifully for nearly an hour, the probability of graciously escaping became more feasible, and she considered what she might say to her mother in order to be excused. Ironically, she knew her mother wasn't terribly fond of needlework either; it rather seemed that she wanted her daughters to be privy to these conversations, as if they might learn something. Maggie just felt bored. She considered the possibility of a headache, or perhaps some feminine issue that would necessitate her needing to retire to her room. Then the door came open, which for a split second offered Maggie some relief at the idea of an interruption. But it was Erich and Han who sauntered into the drawing room and made themselves comfortable. She bit her tongue from suggesting that *they* should be taught how to make tiny little stitches while sitting with their backs straight—as opposed to the way they slouched onto the sofas in a manner that no gentleman ever would. She might expect as much from Han, but Erich had been raised to be a duke. Of course, Han had been raised at his side, so he supposedly *did* know how to behave like a gentleman. But it seemed that Han brought out the worst in Erich.

"Hello, boys," Abbi said, lighting up at their appearance. Elsa lit up similarly since Han was her only child—her pride and joy. If she only knew how her son behaved when his mother wasn't around!

"Hello, Mother," Erich and Han replied almost simultaneously, each offering their mothers a warm smile.

"What are the two of you up to?" Elsa asked.

Maggie noted that Dulsie didn't even glance up from her sewing, as if she hadn't noticed that anyone else had come into the room. Nadine gave each of the boys a smile, which they returned fondly.

Erich looked toward Han as if he expected *him* to answer the question—perhaps because it was *his* mother who had asked it.

"Erich was just going down to his laboratory," Han said dramatically, "to try a new experiment."

"How very exciting," Abbi said with a hint of dubious sarcasm. Her son's interest in chemistry was one thing she could have lived without, and she'd never pretended that she felt otherwise. However, she also respected her children's inclinations—as long as they were reasonable—therefore, she *tolerated* Erich's hobby. Maggie shared her mother's views. She thought it was silly. But Erich took it very seriously. And their father had often said that if he wasn't going to be the duke, he would have made an excellent chemist. According to opinions of experts who had helped teach him the science of chemistry, he was actually very good at it.

"Would you like to come along?" Erich asked.

"Who, me?" Sonia replied eagerly, and Maggie knew her sister was far more bored than she'd been letting on.

"Yes, you," Erich said.

"You mean you'll let me into your dungeon?" Sonia asked with an astonishment that was only a little bit wry.

"Of course." Erich chuckled.

"I'd love to," Sonia said, obviously glad to put the needlework aside.

"How about you, Mags?" Erich asked.

"I'd rather not," she said with distaste.

"Ah, come on," Erich urged. "It'll be fun."

"Forget it, Erich," Han piped in. "She doesn't like to have fun."

Maggie saw her mother smile slightly, and she wondered why Abbi might find this amusing. She knew that bringing attention to it would only make her look foolish, so instead she tossed Han an indignant glare as she said with forced nonchalance, "Going down to the cold, dark recesses of this castle to watch bottles of liquid bubble is not my idea of fun."

"But today we're doing something very interesting," Erich said. "We're going to try a new experiment. And you can be a witness."

"Oh, go along, darling," Abbi urged. "It would be good for you to do something different."

"Come along, little sister." Erich took her hand and pulled her right off the chair. She didn't want to admit her relief at tossing her needlework aside, but this wasn't the escape she'd had in mind.

"Apparently I have no say in this," Maggie said as she was dragged toward the door.

"What about you, Dulsie?" Erich asked, pausing deliberately to wait until she lifted her eyes to look at him. "Surely this must be tedious."

Abbi gave her son a comical scowl that made him laugh before he focused again on Dulsie. "Come along," he said. More to her mother, he added, "We'll take very good care of her; I promise."

"Go with them," Nadine urged her daughter with a smile.

But Dulsie said with perfect politeness and apparent sincerity, "No, but thank you, Erich. I'll join you another time."

"If you're sure," Erich said, and Maggie wondered why Erich always went to so much trouble to coax her when she rarely if ever joined them for anything.

"Yes, thank you," Dulsie smiled at him and turned her attention back to her needlework.

Maggie was rushed from the room, her arm held firmly in her brother's grasp. "So, Dulsie can choose to stay?" she asked. "But I'm bodily forced to go along?"

"Don't be such a ninny," Erich said as if they were still young children in the nursery. "Dulsie likes sitting around sewing useless things. You were bored out of your mind, and I know it. If you weren't so stubborn . . ." He laughed and left the sentence unfinished as he hurried to catch up with Sonia and Han, still holding to Maggie's arm.

They quickly traversed a typically lengthy hallway before Erich pushed open a squeaky-hinged oak door and led the way down the stairs with Sonia behind him, then Maggie, and finally, Han, bringing up the rear.

"I hate these stairs," Maggie said in reference to the winding stone steps with a wall on one side and only a rope bannister on the other. They seemed to go on and on, and she could almost get light-headed if she wasn't careful.

"Oh, they're fun," Han remarked.

"They're scary," she retorted.

"I always count them," Sonia said. "There are seventy-eight steps."

"Really?" Han laughed. "Seems like more."

Maggie began to feel dizzy and stopped briefly until she felt Han's hand on her arm.

"Are you all right?" he whispered close behind her ear.

"I'm fine." She pulled away quickly and proceeded down.

They came at last to the bottom, and Erich pushed open another squeaky door of iron.

"This place gives me the creeps," Maggie said.

"It's a dungeon." Han smirked. "What do you expect? Just think of all the ancient tortures and all the people who died down here in the—"

"Oh hush!" Maggie cut off his dramatic speech, and he grinned at her as they followed Erich into his laboratory.

Mother had insisted that if Erich was going to do this, it had to be here so she wouldn't have to put up with the odd smells or worry about fire. Erich came here almost every day without fail. Maggie thought it was all very strange.

"Now, let's see," Erich said as he lit a few lamps from the one he'd been carrying. He began picking up different bottles and looking at the labels. "Ah yes, here we go. First some of this and—"

"Don't use that!" Han said. "We decided it would need this if it was going to work." They proceeded to work intently on their project in silence while Maggie and Sonia looked on, occasionally exchanging a glance of astonishment over their antics. Except that while Sonia seemed more amused, Maggie felt mostly disgusted.

Maggie noticed, as she often did, the unique contrast in Han and Erich. They were both slender and muscular, above average height, but they looked nothing alike. Erich had red curls and blue eyes, a stark contrast to Han's fluffy, blond hair and green eyes. Maggie recalled often hearing her mother say that the two of them looked and acted very much like their fathers used to. And though the years showed in her father's face—and Han's father as well—she could see the resemblances and had to admit it was true.

"What are you going to make?" Sonia asked with interest.

"A love potion," Han said as if it were nothing out of the ordinary.

"Really?" Sonia asked with a little laugh.

"And just what is this love potion supposed to do?" Maggie asked skeptically.

"It makes people fall in love, of course," Erich said as he busily poured a number of different liquids into a vial.

"Baggage!" Maggie said, and Han chuckled.

"All right, Han," Erich said, "you know what to do now."

"Are you sure you got everything in there?"

"Of course I'm sure."

Han picked up a small vial and poured a drop of something into the mixture. Immediately it began to bubble and smoke.

"Good heavens," Maggie said, but Han only rubbed his hands together. Erich looked positively satisfied, and Sonia was quite amused.

"That should do it," Erich said, then he poured the liquid into a drinking glass and it gradually stopped bubbling. "Maggie would you hand me that . . . that rag over there?"

"What, this?" she asked, turning to pick up a little piece of cloth, which distracted her and Sonia for just a moment.

"Yes, thank you." Erich took it from her and wrapped it around the glass. "This stuff is kind of hot."

"Well," Han said with his hands on his hips, "let's see if it works."

"Here goes," Erich said. He took a deep breath and lifted the glass to his lips.

"Wait!" Maggie cried. "You can't drink that!"

"Why not?"

"It's probably . . . *poison!*"

"Oh, let him drink it." Sonia smirked. "It would do him good."

Grinning, Erich glanced toward Han and took a deep swallow

of the drink. His face went into several exaggerated contortions. He shivered visibly from head to toe. Then he squeezed his eyes shut, opened them dramatically and coughed. When the initial effect seemed complete, Erich held his breath and the other three stared with wide eyes.

"Whew!" Erich said. "That stuff is potent."

"How do you feel?" Han asked with expectation.

"No different."

Erich gazed quite obviously toward Maggie and then Sonia, as if he expected something to happen. "Nothing!" he nearly shouted. "What could have gone wrong? We did all the right things. It should have—"

"Give me that!" Han said, abruptly taking the glass from Erich. "They're your sisters. You can't expect to fall in love with one of your sisters."

"What is he talking about?" Maggie asked her brother.

"After a man drinks that stuff, he's supposed to fall in love with the first woman he sees."

"Baggage!" Maggie uttered.

They all became silent as Han took a big swallow of the golden liquid and did an exact imitation of the reactions Erich had performed. When he opened his eyes they were set on Maggie. He seemed quite stunned and overwrought with emotion.

"What do you feel?" Erich asked with intense anticipation.

"Erich," Han whispered, "I never realized your sister was so beautiful." Erich chuckled with satisfaction as Maggie's eyes widened and she backed away. "She's like an angel. I feel all tingly . . . and oh, Maggie!"

Han deftly swept her into his arms, and despite her efforts to get away, he held her to his advantage.

"Let go of me!" Maggie shrieked, barely aware that Erich and Sonia were laughing intolerably. She didn't find it funny *at all!*

"Don't speak to me that way, my love. Oh, Maggie . . . say you'll be mine. I need you in my life."

"You are mad! This is baggage!"

"How can you say such things?" Han looked genuinely hurt. "Can't you see how much I love you?"

"Erich! Get him away from me!"

"But he's in love," Erich laughed. "You can't blame a man for being in love."

"Ooh!" Maggie hissed, but Han pressed his mouth over hers with a kiss that forced her into momentary silence.

"Let go of me!" she shouted louder when he set her lips free.

"One more kiss, my love," he whispered, then overcame her with a kiss more passionate than the first.

Maggie forced back the memories stirred by his kiss and finally managed to turn her face away. Han chuckled, but she briefly caught something severe in his eyes that left her uneasy. "You'd better give her some of that stuff, Erich," he said. "She could really use some. She'll be betrothed soon and needs a little romance before the dreaded thing takes place and it's too late."

Maggie wanted to retort that she was in love and there would be no betrothal. But she bit her tongue, remembering her father's admonition to keep it a secret.

Sonia laughed and said, "I'll try some."

Erich handed her the glass without hesitation while Han continued to hold Maggie close, ignoring her continued effort to free herself. Sonia took a careful sip and chuckled. "That's nothing more than scotch whiskey. You switched glasses!"

Erich and Han laughed boisterously while Maggie finally managed to squirm out of Han's arms.

"And how do you know?" Erich asked. "Has my little sister been thieving from the duke's liquor cabinet?"

"Just a little taste here and there," she admitted with a smile.

"Well, at least you get some adventure." Han chuckled while Maggie brushed the front of her dress with exasperation. "That kiss is the most adventure Maggie's had since—"

"Han!" she stopped him.

"Sorry," he whispered and briefly put his hand over his mouth. "I won't tell. I promise."

Erich's brows went up, and Han added, "Don't ask, Erich. I won't tell a soul—not even you."

"If he does," Maggie said, starting up the stairs, "I'm certain that Georg Heinrich would be interested to know what his son has been doing in the dungeon."

"Threats?" Han called after her, but she ignored him. "Do be careful on those stairs, my love. Oh, and if you hear any serenading outside your window, it's me. I'll never forget that kiss. I could live on it for the rest of my life. But I may get desperate and come searching for more and—"

"I don't think she can hear you anymore," Erich cut him off. "If she can, she's not listening."

"Too bad," Han said. "I had so much more to say."

"Give me some more of that," Sonia said, taking the glass again from Erich. She took another sip and did her best to imitate the required reaction. Then she opened her eyes and jumped comically into Han's arms.

"Oh, Han, my love," she said, batting her eyelashes. "Let's run away together and get married."

"I think I looked at the wrong girl." Han grinned.

"Kiss me, Han. Kiss me!"

"If you insist." Han smiled and kissed her every bit as passionately as he had Maggie. But when he pulled away and Sonia started twirling around the room, he glanced toward the stairs where Maggie had gone. There was no question about it. Maggie was a better kisser—even if they were both sorely out of practice.

Maggie arrived at the stables the following morning, angry with Han even before he spoke to her with exuberance. "Good morning, Maggie, my love."

"I am not your love!"

"What's the matter, Maggie? You're extremely petulant today."

"And what would you expect? You louse! I don't appreciate being the brunt of one of your tasteless jokes."

"It was not tasteless," he said proudly. "And it was Erich's idea; a fine one at that, I might add. He thinks you're a stick-in-the-mud and that you need to have a little fun before this dreaded betrothal business takes place. And what could I do but agree?"

"You were mocking me, and you know it."

"Me?" Han questioned, his expression showing exaggerated innocence. "Now Maggie, if you think that *I* would have reason to *mock* you, then you must have a guilty conscience."

"If you'll just saddle Pagan, I will be on my way, thank you."

Han said nothing more and did as she requested. Maggie's anger quickly dissipated as she rode to the meadow and found Nik waiting for her in the usual place.

They walked and talked together, and he kissed her with a zeal he'd not shown before, sparking a fresh excitement within her. Although she felt fresh anger when memories of Han's kiss in the laboratory pushed into her mind, marring the moment. She forced thoughts of Han away, and Nik wished her luck for the canceling of her betrothal, saying he would be anxious to hear how everything turned out. As they said good-bye, Maggie felt certain that she loved Nik—though not certain enough to admit it just yet. She simply couldn't think of any other way to explain these feelings.

The minute Maggie rode away, Han's mind began wandering into paths he'd tried to shut off years ago. At first he became angry with Erich for coming up with that ridiculous love potion escapade. He'd almost forgotten what it was like to kiss Maggie, but now the memories had been rekindled, and with them came emotions he'd been attempting to be rid of for years. His anger shifted to himself—for being stupid enough to have ever believed that someone like him could be a part of Maggie du Woernig's life. He cursed himself for not being man enough to get over it long ago. Then he cursed Maggie for being so selfish and stubborn. He'd given up on the idea of ever having the chance to win her over again—or at least he thought he had. But now as he contemplated the reality of this ridiculous betrothal that was about to take place, his anger over the entire thing got the better of him. He was caught off guard to look up and see her riding in. With no premeditation he shot to his feet and took her by the waist to help her dismount. When her feet touched the ground, he didn't let go.

"You can't do it, Maggie," he said in response to her questioning gaze.

"Let go of me," she insisted, attempting to break free. But he only held her tighter.

"Are you listening to me, Maggie? How can you possibly marry a man you've never even set eyes on? Are you really stupid enough to believe he can make you happy?"

"It's my life, Han," she said, wishing she dared tell him that the betrothal wouldn't take place. "This has nothing to do with you."

"It does, and you know it," he snapped, "even if you won't admit it."

Maggie's eyes widened. He'd not spoken to her like that in years. "Let me go," she demanded, but he only pushed his arm around her waist. She attempted to ignore the electric shock that assailed her every nerve and left her more helpless than the way he was holding her.

"Listen to me, Maggie," he whispered hoarsely. "You have no idea what you're doing. Do you think passion just magically appears once you've got a ring on your finger? What are you going to do when you wake up in his bed and realize you don't want to be there? When his kiss does nothing for you, will you be able to forget what it was like to be held and kissed by someone who loved you?"

"Stop it!" she hissed, pressing her fists against his chest. When his words pricked something in her conscience, she was grateful she'd already made the decision to call off the marriage. But his methods were appalling.

"Remember what it was like, Maggie." His voice became husky. "Remember how it felt to be kissed by someone who loved you." She groaned and squirmed, but he held her tighter and pressed his lips near her ear. She credited the quickening of her breath to anger as he went on. "We were too young then, Maggie. We're not too young anymore."

At Han's overt implication, Maggie exerted all her strength and managed to pull one hand free enough to slap him hard. "How dare you say such things to me!" she snarled.

Han took a step back and touched his face where the sting settled in. "There was a time when you enjoyed having me say such things. Have you forgotten how you begged me to—"

"I was a child!" she interrupted.

Han's eyes quickly glanced down the length of her and back to her face, flushed with color. "You don't look much different to me."

Maggie looked into his eyes and tried to comprehend what she saw there. "Don't tell me you're still in love with me, Han—not after all these years."

Han was so stunned he could hardly breathe. She actually laughed when she said it, and the hurt cut deep. "You're a cruel woman, Maggie," he retorted in his defense. "The Maggie I loved would never have been so heartless, even to someone as lowly as me. And she would never have been stupid enough to give her life away to some stodgy son of a count. Oh no, Maggie. Don't flatter yourself enough to think that I would love someone so cold, so utterly foolish."

Maggie said nothing, but the hurt in her eyes was evident. He wondered why it gave him no pleasure to hurt her the way she hurt him. Still, he felt compelled to take the opportunity to say things he'd wanted to say for months but hadn't dared. "You're right about one thing, Maggie. It's your life. And no one can force you to do something you don't want to do. But think it through. And whatever you do, Maggie, don't be stupid enough to believe that marrying this way will make you happy. You told me long ago that you would never marry beneath yourself. Marry the son of a count if you must, but for crying out loud, Maggie, marry for love."

Maggie stared at him a long moment, wondering how he might react when he discovered the turn her life was taking. While it was difficult to tell if he still cared for her to any degree, she felt certain he wouldn't be pleased. She wished she could explain somehow, to help him understand. But not knowing how to fit her concern for Han into this sudden change of heart, she just turned and walked out of the stables.

Immediately, Han cursed himself for being stupid enough to expose his feelings to her all over again. He reminded himself that he was going to have to learn to cope. Pining for her all these years had gotten him nowhere. By the time he met Erich at the pub later that morning, he'd managed to push all of his feelings down just deep enough that they couldn't torment him. And he was proud of himself for being able to talk and laugh as if nothing in the world was wrong. He'd become pretty good at it with years of practice. By the next morning, he was almost convinced that the best thing for him would be to see Maggie get married and leave Horstberg. He hoped it would happen soon. The sooner she left, the sooner he could get over it and find a life without her.

Abbi du Woernig couldn't help being keenly aware of a great deal of excitement at Castle Horstberg as the day of MagdaLena's betrothal arrived. But only Abbi realized the mental anguish the duke was going through, wondering how he was going to tell their distinguished guests that no union would be made.

Maggie became caught up with an anticipation entirely different than what she might have expected when this had initially been agreed upon. Knowing that Rudolf's family had arrived and were now resting and freshening up, she could hardly sit still to think of all that would take place this evening and its impact on her life. Very soon this would all be over, and she would be free to see Nik openly. She was nearly ready to go downstairs and greet their company when Sonia came to her room, full of questions.

"Are you sure you're ready for this?" she asked cautiously.

"Under the circumstances, yes," Maggie replied.

"Is it exciting," she prodded, "to be preparing to wed?"

"Quite," Maggie said, noncommittal.

"Sometimes I wish I were getting married," she mused. "It would be such fun."

"Actually," Maggie said, perhaps in a tone of warning as she donned a string of pearls, "I wouldn't say a betrothal is fun. Rather stifling, in truth."

"Mags!" Sonia said in near astonishment. "You sound as though you're dreading it. You're not regretting the decision, are you?"

"I'd rather not talk about it," was all she said, not wanting to lie—or do as her father had warned and let anyone know what was really happening.

"Maggie?" Sonia's tone became gentle, reminding Maggie of their mother. "I hope you're not still angry about what I said before. I mean, it's your decision, and if you—"

"It's all right, Sonia." She smiled and briefly squeezed her sister's hand. "Maybe there was some truth to what you said. I don't know. But I'm certain everything will work out for the best."

Sonia was stunned into silence. She couldn't remember the last time Maggie had even mildly suggested that she might have been wrong about something. Before she could think of a suitable response, Maggie brushed quickly out of the room, saying as she went, "Come along, or we'll be late."

In the hallway, they met their mother, who smiled with approval. "You both look lovely."

"And you as well, Mother," Sonia replied, and Maggie nodded in agreement.

"You run along, Sonia," Abbi said. "I need to speak with Maggie for just a moment. We'll be there shortly."

"What is it, Mother?" Maggie asked when they were alone.

"I just wanted to remind you to keep silent about all of this and let your father handle it. He'll know when it's the right time . . . and what to say."

"I'll remember." She kissed her mother, and they headed toward the great hall where they were to greet Rudolf and his family.

Sonia arrived alone at the bottom of the stairs to see Erich and her father just now greeting their guests. She first noticed a girl who appeared to be near her own age, though a bit homely. There was another girl near the same age, slightly more attractive. Sonia knew that one was a sister to Rudolf and the other a cousin. There could be no doubt about who the count and countess were, but her eyes stopped on the young man with dark hair and deep-set gray eyes, who was just now being greeted by her father.

"Ah, Rudolf," she heard her father say.

"I am very pleased to see you again, Your Grace." Rudolf's tone was deep and mellow, and his smile intrigued Sonia as he bowed slightly and clicked his heels together. As she laid eyes on the man to whom her sister was about to be betrothed, Sonia felt suddenly and unexpectedly envious. She had never envied anything of her sister's before. Their parents had always treated and provided for them equally. But as this man gallantly took her hand to kiss it in greeting, she felt a tingly sensation that unnerved her. Feeling this inexplicable attraction to Rudolf surely had to be something close to treason.

"And this must be the lucky bride-to-be," he said with an impeccable smirk.

"Uh," Sonia heard herself say, "I . . . uh . . ."

"Actually," the duke interjected, though Sonia was only vaguely aware of the tension in his eyes. She was mesmerized by this man. "No, this is my younger daughter, Sonia."

Sonia caught the brief look of disappointment in Rudolf's eyes, but it quickly faded into a gracious smile. Her heart went heavy, wondering if she could bear seeing Maggie married to this man. She had never felt this way before in her life.

Maggie forced herself to walk slowly as she came down the stairs with her mother. For a brief moment, she was able to observe the man she had almost sentenced herself to share her life with. He was certainly handsome enough, but immediately she was glad that the marriage would not come to pass. If she hadn't already known the betrothal would be called off, she likely would have gone into a panic and made some kind of scene.

"Ah," Rudolf turned toward Maggie, "surely this must be the lucky bride."

Maggie glanced tensely toward her father whose expression was blank as he replied, "This is MagdaLena."

The introductions were all made official while Rudolf kissed Maggie's hand, then he continued to hold it possessively as they moved in a group toward the gardens where drinks and hors d'oeuvres would be served while the families and some high-ranking officials mingled and chatted. Maggie did her best to avoid Rudolf, trying not to be rude. She couldn't decide if she was relieved or a bit deflated to realize that he hardly seemed to notice her indifference toward him.

Abbi sat close to her husband's side, discreetly watching everyone involved in the unfolding drama. Maggie was clearly trying to avoid Rudolf's attention as much as possible—even though she was being gracious about it. But Maggie was apparently so preoccupied with her efforts that Abbi felt certain she hadn't noticed what had now become clear to Abbi. Rudolf was oblivious to Maggie's cool disregard because his attention was discreetly drawn to Sonia. And remarkably enough, Sonia seemed equally aware of Rudolf. Abbi could hardly believe her eyes. It seemed too good to be true, although she couldn't jump to any conclusions based on a few odd glances. But she kept observing, praying that somehow they would find a gracious way out of this mess. She wished that Cameron might have been more up front about all of this, that he would have said something to the count earlier. But he was avoiding the topic, and Abbi's nerves were growing raw.

While the parents sat close together chatting, watching the young people mingle and talk, Abbi felt certain the count hadn't noticed the duke's distress. But Abbi had noticed, and in spite of all their best efforts to remain gracious and polite, she knew what an awkward position her husband was in. And the more that time passed, the more awkward it became. Abbi was also aware of the tension in Maggie's eyes and the way she kept glancing expectantly toward her father, hoping he would get this over with. It seemed that one way or another, this was going to be a bad situation.

Abbi watched Rudolf more closely, and her deepest instincts told her that he was a very nice man. He would most likely make a good husband. And he certainly was handsome. But as she observed even more closely, asking herself if her initial impressions might actually be correct, she felt a light of hope set in. Rudolf was indeed very obviously more taken with Sonia than he was with Maggie.

Abbi's attention then turned to Sonia, needing to reassure herself that the attraction was mutual before she jumped forward any further in her conclusions. She smiled to see the obvious twinkle in Sonia's eyes every time she looked coyly toward Rudolf. As strange as the situation had become, and as opposed as Abbi had always been about arranging her children into life-altering situations of any kind, there was something deeply warm and comforting about what she felt now. She had learned at a very early age how it felt to stumble upon destiny, and she was feeling it now.

Abbi was about to whisper her observance into her husband's ear when the count began to speak. "This betrothal business can be a rather touchy situation at times," he stated.

"Yes, indeed," Cameron replied, and Abbi caught the irony in his voice.

"We try so hard to make the right choices and see that our children will be happy, when many times it's so terribly unpredictable and perhaps . . . precarious. And well," he chuckled, "we have to wonder if we're doing the right thing."

"Yes, that's right," the duke replied in a tone that let Abbi know he was determined to now say what needed to be said. "You know, I believe that perhaps—"

The count interrupted, "Your daughters are both very beautiful. I was just noticing how different they are. The elder looks very much like her mother . . . in coloring and stature. And the younger—Sonia, is it?"

"Yes."

"Sonia looks more like you, Your Grace . . . other than that red hair, of course. And from what little I have observed them, I believe their personalities are equally different."

"They are indeed," the duke agreed with a tense chuckle. "You see it's—" Again Cameron tried to begin his necessary announcement and was interrupted.

"It would appear that Rudolf has taken more of a fancy to your Sonia." The duke's eyes widened as he glanced up from his untouched glass of wine. "Again, as parents, it can be frustrating to wonder if we have made the right choice."

"Indeed," the duke replied, exchanging a brief and discreet glance of astonishment with Abbi.

"You will forgive my boldness, Your Grace," the count continued, "but it is a pity that the elder daughter would most likely be insulted," the count proceeded with a cautious tone, "if her younger sister were to become betrothed first."

Abbi fought to suppress a chuckle as she caught the relief and humor in her husband's eyes.

"On the other hand," Cameron said, "seeing what is obvious here, I dare say Maggie would want to see her sister happy."

"Perhaps then," the count smiled, seeming relieved also, "we should take young Rudolf aside for a moment and have a . . . conference, if you will."

"That would seem a splendid idea." The duke smiled, and Abbi sighed with relief as her husband and the count stood to summon Erich and Rudolf, and they went inside. Abbi wondered briefly how Sonia might feel about this, but seeing her obvious love-struck expression as she watched Rudolf leave, Abbi once again checked her instincts and believed this was right. And she knew that nothing would be made final without Sonia's full agreement.

Maggie's heart beat quickly when she saw the men leave, and she sensed what was happening. She knew Erich accompanied her father for every business affair—no matter how trivial—domestic or political. And this was both. Her tension rose, knowing what an awkward position her father was in. She wondered how it might make her appear to these people. There was some comfort in seeing that her mother didn't look terribly distressed. But as minutes ticked away and the men didn't return, Maggie became more tense and had to force herself to remain still and appear nonchalant, as opposed to giving in to the temptation to pace and wring her hands.

Sonia was shocked to realize how completely she had become caught up in a frenzy of emotions. All at once, she was excited about this new feeling she was experiencing and afraid that someone had noticed she was keenly attracted to her sister's fiancé. If they hadn't seen it by now, she was certain someone would eventually. She felt hurt, angry, and mostly covetous. She was at least grateful that Maggie would be moving away with Rudolf, so that she wouldn't have to stand by and see them together. The very idea seemed torturous, and she wondered how it could be possible to feel so strongly about something that had not even occurred to her earlier today.

When the supper hour arrived and the men still had not emerged, the women went to the dining room and were seated. Abbi sent one of the maids to tell the men dinner was being served—with or without them. A few minutes later they all appeared, each holding a snifter of brandy, all seeming jovial and at ease.

Maggie's palms were sweating while she wondered over the outcome. She nearly fainted when Rudolf's father sat down and declared, "Well, it is good to have this settled, and to see that our families will be united, and—"

"And . . ." Cameron interrupted, "may your son and my daughter be happy together until the end of time."

"Father!" Maggie stood abruptly. Her life was on the line. She glanced around to see that only the closest members of the family were near enough to hear the conversation.

"Calm down, Maggie." He smiled easily, and she wondered if he had been drinking too much, though he didn't appear that way. And she couldn't recall that he ever had.

"Everything will be fine, MagdaLena," Rudolf said calmly and quietly. But there was a subtle sparkle of humor in his eyes, and she realized her father had been teasing. Her heart threatened to explode as he continued, "Your father has taken time to explain the delicacy of the situation, and we are quite compassionate to this . . . Well, what I am trying to say is—"

"I think I'd better handle this," Cameron said, and everyone watched him expectantly. "What he's trying to say is . . . and Sonia, I hope you will trust my judgment, and of course it's really up to you, and everyone understands that, but . . ."

Maggie wanted to know what Sonia had to do with this, until her father added, "I have given Rudolf your hand in this betrothal, not Maggie's . . . only if you agree to it, of course."

Sonia stood up, finding it difficult to breathe. She felt like laughing and crying and jumping up and down. But all she could do was look numbly back and forth between her father and Rudolf, who both seemed satisfied. It was the distinct sparkle in Rudolf's eyes that made her heart want to leap right out of her throat. She impulsively hurried toward the door to the gardens, knowing that she would likely erupt with emotion at any moment, and she preferred to do so in private. She was surprised, but not at all disappointed, to find Rudolf's hand on her arm, gently guiding her in that direction as he whispered with obvious affection, "I do believe that we need to talk." Her relief was indescribable, even though she suspected that her future husband was about to see her break down into childish tears. But once they were outside and beyond the view of everyone else, that didn't seem so bad in light of what had just happened.

After everyone present watched Rudolf follow Sonia outside, and most of the guests had not been privy to the quiet conversation that had preceded their exit, the duke announced more loudly about the change in his agreement with the count: Sonia would be marrying Rudolf. Maggie nearly fell back into her chair with relief and an involuntary laugh erupted from her lips. But a moment later, everyone else was laughing as well, and she only bothered to wonder for a moment what might be taking place between Rudolf and Sonia right now in the gardens. The conversation remained light through supper, and the outcome of the situation seemed pleasing to everyone involved. They were nearly finished eating when Rudolf and Sonia returned to the table, tightly holding to each other's hands, and smiling brightly. Rudolf helped Sonia with her chair, and the maids served them their supper. The conversation went on as if nothing extraordinary had taken place, but Maggie had been saved. And Sonia and Rudolf both looked happy. For no reason beyond that, perhaps this was meant to be.

After the social gathering had officially ended and the betrothed couple had once again gone to the gardens together, Maggie sought out her parents and thanked them for all they had done for her. She then went to bed, content with excitement and anticipation. She could hardly wait to see Nik, but she fell asleep full of expectancy, certain the best time of her life was just around the corner.

Chapter Three
LIKE FATHER, LIKE SON

Maggie got out of bed early and hurried to get dressed. Knowing Nik would be impatient to hear what had happened, she headed for the stables. In the courtyard, she came across Georg Heinrich heading the same direction.

"Good morning," he said with a typical cordial smile.

"Good morning, Georg," she replied cheerily. "Did I hear that Elsa is out of the country for a few days? The death of a relative, I heard. Not someone she was close to, I hope."

"This aunt was Elsa's only living relative long before I married her, but they were never close. Elsa is making a quick trip to attend the funeral and sign some papers, and she'll be back soon." He chuckled satirically. "Not soon enough, in my opinion."

Maggie offered a gentle laugh in return, knowing that Georg and Elsa were much like her own parents. Any need for one of them to be away from the other for more than a day always caused anxiety and foul moods.

"How did the big event go?" Georg asked, changing the subject. "There was somewhere else I needed to be, and I haven't had a chance to talk to your father yet."

"It went very well, thank you," she answered as they entered the stables together.

Han couldn't help being disappointed when Maggie arrived with his father. He had been well prepared with several sly comments about Maggie's betrothal, but she knew Han couldn't be anything but perfectly respectable in Georg's presence, and she played that fact to her full advantage. She rode out obviously smug for all the nice things she'd provoked Han into saying to her.

When Maggie had gone, Han stood feeling somewhat deflated, gazing out the door. His father's voice brought him back to the recollection that he wasn't alone. "Whatever it is you're thinking, you can forget it."

"What on earth are you talking about?" Han said while getting a saddle for his father's horse.

"I've seen that look in your eyes before, son. I know what it means."

Han did his best to look innocent, but Georg continued with his point nevertheless. "She's a princess, Han. And she's betrothed," he added adamantly.

"Yes," Han replied just scornfully enough to prove that his father's assumptions were correct—at least to some extent. "I'm well aware of who she is." Han hurried to change the subject. "Where are you off to, anyway?"

"I have an early appointment with the duke's solicitors," he said then smiled at his son as he mounted. "Thank you. You do a good job, as always."

Han saluted casually as his father rode out. Once alone, he snarled under his breath, "Yes, a good job as always. It takes a lot of brains to put a saddle on a horse."

Han couldn't deny that he enjoyed his work, and he had a great respect for the care of these fine animals. But he wished with all his soul that he could get out of these stables and do something more worthy of his intellectual abilities. His father had the most prestigious position in the duchy, working side by side with the duke himself. And Han was stuck with the horses.

Erich was already preparing to inherit his father's position, but Georg had made it repeatedly clear that such a privilege was not open to Han. Georg Heinrich's position had nothing to do with birth. He had grown up doing exactly what Han was doing now. And it was only at Cameron du Woernig's insistence that Georg had agreed to work with him. Han knew it had a lot to do with the remarkable way Georg had assisted Cameron in the bizarre revolution of 1817.

Georg was well aware of Han's ambition, and he had suggested many times that Han become a member of the Guard and work his way up. But a military career wasn't what Han wanted. He had seen how hard the officers of the Guard had to work. It took years to gain any significant rank, and all those with good positions weren't so old that they'd be giving them up for many years to come. Not to mention, the military simply wasn't his forte. He would be like a fish out of water in such a profession.

Han wanted more. But he had no idea how to get it. So he worked here day after day, doing his job impeccably well, hoping that one day someone might notice that he had qualities worth much more than this. And he grudgingly had to admit that his desire to hover in the stables was mixed in with his wanting to see Maggie every day. He wondered now if he should have found a job elsewhere a long time ago. Or he might have gone out of the country to attend a university very far away—somewhere far removed from Castle Horstberg. It would have likely spared him a great deal of misery.

Han was glad when Erich came into the stables. His friendship was one of the few things that made his remaining there worthwhile. After the usual greetings were exchanged, Erich asked casually, "Has Maggie gone out yet?"

"She left quite a while ago, why?"

"No doubt to meet her beau in the forest and tell him the good news."

Han felt something stab at him as he glared at Erich, completely baffled. Erich noticed and added quickly, "I see you've not heard the news yet."

"I'm afraid not," Han said, wondering if he wanted to.

"Well," Erich began as if the whole thing amused him terribly, "apparently Maggie insisted that Father call off the betrothal because of this Nik guy she met, and . . ." He paused and chuckled. "For a while there, I don't think Father knew how he was going to pull it off. But it turns out this Rudolf character is going to marry Sonia instead, and everyone is pleased as punch—especially Sonia. Love at first sight, apparently. Lucky for Maggie. She could have had a political uprising on her conscience." He finished with another chuckle, but Han didn't find it even slightly amusing.

"Who is this . . . Nik guy?" he asked, carefully concealing his fury.

"Just some guy from the other side of the valley. I don't know anything about him . . . except that he's a bit cocky with little reason to be, in my opinion. I only met him once."

Han turned away to get Erich's horse while the duke-to-be continued rambling on about the details of the previous day. But Han paid little attention. His efforts were concentrated on hiding this sudden internal fuming. He felt as if he'd been kicked in the stomach. And then in the heart. But he wasn't about to try and explain the reasons to Erich. Admitting it aloud—even to his best friend—would be just plain stupid.

Maggie was delighted to find Nik waiting for her in their usual spot near the edge of the forest. They sat together against a tree while she relayed in detail the events that had miraculously freed her from her obligation. And he seemed to thoroughly enjoy every bit of her story.

"Now," he said when she had finished, "I must make this proper. I will talk to your father, and then I can court you officially."

Maggie smiled. "My father has already insisted. He wants to see you this afternoon at three."

"My," he chuckled, then became briefly distant, "I didn't believe all of this would happen so quickly."

"You will meet him today, won't you?"

"Of course." He laughed. "It's perfect. I've been waiting a long time for this."

Maggie thought that less than a week was hardly very long. But with how quickly their feelings for each other had grown, it could have easily seemed like forever.

"I should get back for breakfast," she said. "If I'm not present, I'm certain Father will know I'm with you. And he'll want it seen to properly."

"Yes, of course." Nik stood and helped her to her feet. "Where do I go? The castle is so big. I'm certain I'll get lost."

She told him everything he needed to know, adding a few hints on the best way to handle her father. Then he kissed her, and she rode for home.

Maggie felt a certain amount of pleasure to think that news of the bizarre change in the betrothal had most likely filtered through the castle by now. With the servants gossiping, it would no doubt spread throughout the valley before nightfall. She entered the stables to find Han alone and sensed immediately that he was in a bad mood. There was a complete absence of his light-hearted sarcasm. In fact, he said absolutely nothing as he helped her dismount, and she saw something grim in his eyes as he paused to scrutinize her.

"Whatever's wrong?" she asked.

"What difference does it make to you, Your Royal Renegade?"

"What do you mean by that?"

"Quite the little contriver, you are!" He shook his head in disbelief. "You are really something, Maggie. Tell me, do you have any method to your madness, or do you just play with people's lives to suit your mood at the moment?"

"You have no idea what you're talking about!" she retorted.

"Don't I?" he growled. "You've seen me the fool more than once, Maggie, but I'm not stupid. *You,* who have so adamantly insisted that you would marry nobility, suddenly have changed your royal decree, I hear."

"It was you who told me to marry for love."

Han chuckled with no trace of humor. "And you expect me to believe that you're doing this because of something *I* said? Oh, no, Maggie. You will never convince me of that. I thought princesses were supposed to have integrity and honor. But not you!" he added with bitter sarcasm. "Little MagdaLena can do anything she damn well pleases."

"This has got nothing to do with you, Han Heinrich, and I will not discuss it any—"

"You don't think I haven't figured out why you coerced me into the stables in the middle of the night? Meeting lovers in the forest, are you?"

"He is not my lover!"

"If he's snaky enough to get you to cancel your betrothal, I'm certain he'll manage to have his way with you soon enough."

"You don't even know what you're talking about!" she insisted. "Nik is a nice man."

"How would you know? If he was a nice man, you wouldn't have to meet him secretly."

"It's not going to be secret anymore. He's going to see my father this afternoon."

"Terrific." Han's voice dripped with sarcasm as he led Pagan to his stall. "That's just terrific."

Maggie left not knowing what else to say. She felt angry with Han for putting a dark cloud over her happiness, and refused to admit that she actually felt some regret for the way her change of heart must have appeared to him. Instead she concentrated her thoughts on Nik. By the time she arrived at the breakfast table, only slightly late, she was full of excitement over what would transpire this afternoon.

With guests present, the topic of Nik's pending visit was not brought up during the meal. But Maggie found her father alone for a moment right after breakfast and told him that Nik would be coming at three.

"Good," he said with no expression. He pointed his finger at her. "And from now on, I'll have no more secret meetings. You do it properly."

"Yes, Father." She smiled then went to the drawing room where Sonia and her mother were discussing plans for the upcoming wedding with Rudolf's mother and sister and homely cousin. Maggie paid little attention. Her mind was on Nik. When the informal meeting adjourned, she was not surprised that her mother sought her out.

"Are you nervous?" Abbi asked as they walked upstairs together.

"Yes," she admitted. "I do hope Father likes him."

"Is there a reason he shouldn't?"

"No," she laughed softly, "not as far as I can see."

"I'm certain everything will go well," Abbi reassured her. "Now you be certain to stay out of sight while he's here. I think it's best that way."

"I will," she said, "but I'm afraid I'll go mad from the anticipation."

"Why don't we go to the conservatory at three and work on a little painting?"

"Could we?" Maggie was pleased with the idea. Not that she really enjoyed painting, but she didn't want to be alone, wondering what might be happening.

"Then you can tell me all about this man. I want to know everything," Abbi said with enthusiasm, and Maggie didn't know what she would do without her. Times like this made it evident that her mother was the only real friend she had.

Before three o'clock came, Abbi was working avidly on a painting, and Maggie was seated where she could watch, chattering about how she'd met Nik and all the things she felt. Maggie wondered if other girls could talk to their mothers this way. She didn't know for certain, but she would guess that their relationship was rare. Abbi not only looked young and vibrant, but she had retained a youthful outlook on life and seemed to understand the way Maggie felt, even when it was not verbalized. Maggie had no trouble acknowledging that her mother gracefully managed to achieve a proficient balance between being a mother and being the Duchess of Horstberg.

Maggie tried to do a little sketching, but she found herself too nervous and set it aside, opting instead for conversation. When she had told her mother all there was to tell about Nik and it was only quarter after the hour, Abbi picked up the conversation and relayed how she and Cameron had met and married. Maggie had heard it all before, but she never tired of hearing it again. And it helped pass the time while she tried not to think about what might be happening right now in her father's office.

Cameron sat in the office with Erich going over some book work, when Heidi, one of the downstairs maids, informed them that Mr. Koenig had arrived.

Cameron had hardly given him a second thought since this morning. Not only had he been very busy, but meeting with this Mr. Koenig would hardly compare to what he'd had to face the day before. Hoping the meeting would go quickly so that he could get back to work, Cameron asked that Mr. Koenig be shown in.

Erich asked if he should leave, but his father said lightly, "You might as well stay so you can learn the really important aspects of being the duke."

Erich didn't admit to his father that he was actually glad to be here. He personally hadn't been at all impressed with this Mr. Koenig and felt certain Maggie was being as blind with him as she was with most of the rest of her life. He knew his father to be a good judge of character, and he was curious over how Cameron du Woernig would perceive this Nik Koenig character. Erich exchanged a wry smile with his father as the door came open and they both stood. Nik Koenig sauntered easily into the room. There was an unreasonable length of silence while Erich waited for his father to say something. But Cameron just stared at this man, seeming dumbfounded, almost weak, as he sat back down in the chair behind his desk, hardly breathing.

"You know," Nik spoke easily, smug for some reason, "my mother told me you'd react that way when you saw me. I'm glad to see that you didn't disappoint her." Only silence answered him as Cameron remained uncharacteristically quiet. "Allow me to introduce myself," Nik went on when the duke made no response. "My name is *Nikolaus,*" he enunciated the name carefully, "and I won't bother to mention the rest just yet."

Erich felt suddenly nervous from the tension growing in the room. He had never seen his father so stunned or so agitated.

"What's the matter, Your Grace?" Nik chuckled. "You look as though you've seen a ghost."

"Appropriately put," Cameron spoke at last, his voice deep and dry—but firm and steady.

"Thank you," Nik said complacently.

"Will someone tell me what is going on here?" Erich couldn't bear his ignorance any longer.

"Ah," Nik smiled toward Erich, "obviously your son hasn't heard the finer points of the story. But then, I'm certain there are a few points you haven't heard either."

"I assume you're going to tell us," Cameron said cynically.

"I thought you'd never ask." Nik smirked, and Erich saw the muscles in his father's neck tighten.

"You see, Erich," Nik went on. "I may call you Erich," he stated rather than asked. "You see, you and I are cousins."

That was all the explanation it took for Erich to understand his father's distress.

"My father," Nik went on, "was once the duke of this fair valley. All of this," he lifted his arms elaborately for effect, "was once his. And if he were still alive, it would all be mine."

"But he's not," Cameron stated.

"No," Nik added coolly, but Erich could see something smoldering in this man's eyes that made the situation increasingly uneasy. "Thanks to you, Your Grace."

"I did not kill your father," Cameron stated.

"I know the whole story," Nik said. "There's no reason to repeat it. The only thing that matters now is . . ." he paused and grinned, "well, I'm here!"

"And," Cameron stood and leaned his fists against the desk, "that doesn't mean *anything* to me."

"But it should," Nik replied with impeccable confidence.

"My brother's *bastard* is entitled to nothing."

"Are you implying that I was born illegitimate?" Nik chuckled.

"My *younger*," he enunciated, "brother was not married before he was killed."

"Ah," Nik said, "but he was. You see Nikolaus du Woernig, in perhaps a youthful, impulsive moment, secretly married a young woman by the name of Klarice Koenig. He was going to make it public, but then certain circumstances suddenly made him the duke. I'm certain you would recall those circumstances."

"I remember them very well," Cameron replied bitterly.

"In spite of appearances, he had every intention of making the marriage public. But he was killed before he had a chance."

"It was a mock marriage," Cameron stated. "He pretended to marry a number of women in order to get what he wanted, but the marriages were not legal."

"I knew you'd say that," Nik said, "but it wasn't a mock marriage at all. And I've got the document to prove it. Let me finish my introduction. My name is Nikolaus Koenig du Woernig, Your Grace. And I want what is rightfully mine."

Cameron sat back down, apparently calm. But Erich sensed his emotions seething beneath the surface.

"Erich," he said coolly, as if nothing were wrong, "will you go and get Georg . . . right now—quickly."

Cameron watched his son leave the room, hoping that Georg wasn't too far away. He felt literally sick to his stomach and didn't want to be alone with this man for even a minute.

"Do you think it will do any good to have me thrown out?" Nik asked after Erich had gone.

"Hardly," Cameron replied. "I am going to send Georg and Erich with you, and they are going to tear Horstberg apart until they find out for certain if what you say is true or false. *If,*" he said dubiously, "your mother really was legally married to Nikolaus, then you will get the allowance he would have had if he were still alive. If they find out you're lying to me, you'll regret ever having come here."

"Threats?" Nik laughed. "But not to worry. I know what they'll find, and the money does sound intriguing. But I was thinking more in terms of, well," he glanced around the elaborate office, "this is such a big place: so much space. I was thinking of moving in. It would be so cozy to have the family reunited."

"You will get an allowance and nothing more," Cameron stated calmly while his insides roiled.

"But I *want* more, Your Grace." If for no other reason, Cameron hated him for the sarcastic way he spoke the title. "I intend to marry your daughter."

Cameron stood up quickly as the shocking reality of the situation forced his anger to take hold. "You will not go anywhere near her—*ever* again!"

"Are you trying to convince me, or her? She's in love with me," he stated easily, "and I intend to—"

The office door came open, and Georg followed Erich into the room while Cameron watched and waited for a reaction, implementing his greatest self-discipline to remain in control of his anger. Georg showed little surprise at seeing Nikolaus since Erich had clearly filled him in on the details. But he seemed momentarily intrigued by the resemblance. And Cameron knew that Georg was every bit as upset by this as he was, despite his lack of expression and the fact that he said absolutely nothing. Cameron forced himself to behave like the duke as he quickly gave instructions on what he wanted done. He watched the three men leave the room, Nik tossing him one last complacent glance as he said, "Good day, Your Grace. It was a pleasure."

"Damn!" Cameron hit his fist against the desk the moment he was alone. There were so many possible problems that could arise from this that just trying to decide which one to fear the most made his head ache. At first he thought the memories being unearthed was the worst part of it. Then he thought about Maggie and wondered what he had done to deserve this.

"I should have been a blacksmith," he muttered and rose stoically to go and find his daughter.

It wasn't so much the abrupt opening of the conservatory door that made Maggie and her mother jump, but rather the manner in which it came open—hard and loud.

Maggie stood quickly to face her father. Her apprehension turned to fear when he said, "I'm glad you're here, Abbi."

"What is it?" Abbi asked, standing and setting her brush aside. "What happened?"

Maggie didn't dare speak. For the life of her, she couldn't imagine what would have made him so upset.

"Did you speak with Mr. Koenig?" Abbi asked with a calm approach that seemed an attempt to either ignore his obvious bad mood or perhaps to soothe it.

"Yes," he said. "But let us not refer to him as that." He paused to let out a harsh sigh that seemed an attempt to appropriately control some degree of anger. When his wife gave him the expected questioning gaze, Cameron went on. "We'll call him *Nikolaus*. It's quite appropriate."

Maggie saw something come into her mother's eyes that she didn't understand. "Why . . . is it appropriate?" Abbi asked with an unusual tension in her voice.

"He's named after his *father!*" Cameron shouted, perhaps louder than Maggie had ever heard.

Abbi's eyes widened in shock, but she said nothing to try and counteract Cameron's rage; it was as if she not only expected it, she somehow shared it. "Your daughter," he went on, ignoring Maggie completely, "has fallen in love with my brother's bastard son!"

Maggie felt so tangibly ill, she feared she might lose her stomach. She wasn't certain what all of this meant, but she had no doubt that the problems facing her now were not small, by any means. While she couldn't begin to imagine why her father would be so upset, logically she had to conclude it was merely some kind of misunderstanding and it could surely be sorted out. Though she knew little of her father's dead brother, she recalled that the name Nikolaus had always been spoken with a certain contempt, however briefly it had been mentioned at all. Though she felt angry that Nik had not told her this himself, she was more concerned about dealing with her father.

Abbi found it difficult to breathe, and even more so while fighting to remain calm and steady. She took a long look at her husband, then her daughter, then her husband again. Memories too horrible to think about—let alone speak of—rushed in to consume her, making it difficult to think reasonably. She knew Cameron had to be feeling the same way, which was no doubt the source of his anger. But Maggie knew only the tiniest part of what Cameron's dead brother had been responsible for, and Abbi forced herself to step in and do what she had done countless times through her years of motherhood: mediate calmly between her child and her husband. However upset she might feel, she had to remain calm. Cameron certainly wasn't; one of them had to be.

"Cameron," Abbi said after she drew in a long, sustaining breath then blew it out slowly, "let's try to at least look at this from Maggie's perspective. Simply because this man is Nikolaus's son doesn't mean that he—"

"You will never convince me of that!" Cameron interrupted. "He just stood in my office and made it very clear what his intentions are. I will not have Maggie near that man—ever. And that is final!"

"No," Maggie protested and tears burned her eyes, "that's not fair. You can't judge him by . . . by . . . one conversation, or . . . by who his father is. He's been very good to me."

"You don't even know what you're talking about!" Cameron said directly to Maggie. "You have no idea what that man is really like."

"Cameron," Abbi retorted with forced calm, "surely you are forgetting what it was like to be in love and facing difficulties."

Her statement only drove his anger deeper. "That is something I will *never* forget. Do you know why, Mrs. du Woernig? It was my brother who caused all of the difficulties you and I were facing. Surely you are forgetting what kind of *hell* that man put us through!"

"You're angry," Abbi stated as calmly as she could manage. "I don't think we should discuss this while you're so—"

"You're damn right I'm angry. He's using her, Abbi. He knows what he wants and he will stop at nothing."

As much as Abbi understood Cameron's anger, she still had

to point out, "You're being cruel, Cameron. What happened to us doesn't have anything to do with our daughter." Maggie rushed to her mother's arms, overwrought with tears.

"It's better that she find out now," Cameron insisted. "I'll not have her seeing him again. It will only get worse—for all of us."

"Perhaps you *are* judging him by your brother," Abbi felt she had to say while Maggie continued to cry.

"I am judging him by the interview we just had," Cameron growled, growing more angry. In fact, Abbi hadn't seen him this angry in many years, and she wondered what had happened to set him off so deeply. While she was considering how to defer this conversation until she could speak with him privately, he turned to their daughter and said, "Maggie." She made no response and he said it louder, "Maggie!"

"What?" She turned reluctantly to face him, wiping at her tears with the back of her hand.

"I want you to promise me you'll not see him again."

"But . . . how can I . . . I . . ."

"That's not fair, Cameron," Abbi said as gently as she could manage. "Our daughter's heart is breaking. Surely we can give this more time and thought."

Cameron glared at Abbi before he abruptly turned to leave the room, far more angry than when he'd entered.

"Where are you going?" Abbi insisted.

"I will *not,*" he said through clenched teeth, "stand here and argue with you about this. We will discuss this in private, Your Grace."

Abbi was at least glad that they agreed on the need to talk about this without Maggie present. But he upset Maggie further when he turned to her, pointing a finger, "You remember what I said!"

Maggie winced when the door slammed, and cried her heart out against her mother's shoulder, wondering why her father couldn't see the Nik Koenig that she could see. When she had calmed down, Abbi sat beside her and spoke carefully, "Maggie, I will talk to your father about this. I think it deserves another chance; at the very least we all need more information. But you must promise me you won't see Nik without talking to me first. We'll give your father some time to cool down and just take it on the best we can."

"Thank you, Mother," Maggie said with a loud sniffle. Then she went up to her room and cried so hard that she felt sick again. She simply could not understand why her father would be so upset. She'd grown up seeing him rule a country, and when he stepped into the role of being a sovereign, there was no contending with his authority. Still, he was respected by all who knew him, and he was known throughout Bavaria as being a just man with integrity and honor. Maggie had known him to be a firm father when he needed to be, but he'd been more prone to leave the biggest matters of discipline up to Abbi. The du Woernig children had grown up with a father who was quietly involved in their lives, teasing them, playing with them, and always there with a predictable fatherly strength. What she had seen today was something she had *never* seen in him before. Her father had become the duke over matters of the heart. To her knowledge, it had never happened before, and it didn't make sense. She tried long and hard to figure it out, but in the end, all she could do was cry. Her heart was breaking as she felt torn and utterly confused. And how would Nik ever understand what was going on when she certainly didn't?

Abbi didn't comment at the dinner table on her husband's foul mood. Since Maggie had asked for supper in her room and the other children were present, she didn't even want to bring it up. Cameron had been occupied with meetings in the office since she'd last seen him, and there had been no opportunity to speak to him privately. She noticed that he ate very little then excused himself and left the room briskly. Knowing him as well as she did, she thought it best not to follow him. They would be able to talk later.

It was late evening when Abbi walked across the courtyard to one of the fine apartments in the fortified group of buildings that comprised Castle Horstberg. She knocked lightly on the door and smiled at the young man who answered.

"Your Grace," Han said easily, "please come in."

"Thank you, Han," she said, moving into the neatly arranged parlor. "Is your father here?"

"I think so," he said. "Please have a seat, and I'll see if I can find him."

"Thank you, Han," she said, making herself comfortable.

Han returned a moment later and said, "He'll be right down. Can I get you anything? A drink or—"

"No, thank you, Han." Abbi smiled at him again, amazed as always at how just seeing him brought on such strong memories of Georg when he was that age. He even dressed like his father, wearing high black boots, narrow dark breeches, and a blousy white shirt, topped by leather braces.

"When will your mother be back?" she asked him.

"The day after tomorrow, I believe."

"So, her aunt finally passed away. She's been ill almost as long as I can remember."

Han hovered in the room but remained standing. He didn't want to be impolite, and the duchess was practically like family to him, so he didn't feel uncomfortable, but he felt anxious to be elsewhere. Still, he said with easy nonchalance, "Which would be longer than *I* can remember." He was glad when his father came in and he was able to make a gracious exit, knowing that Erich was waiting for him at the pub.

"Abbi," Georg said pleasantly after Han had excused himself. He took the duchess's hand and placed an affectionate kiss to her cheek.

"Georg," she replied, relieved already just to be in his comfortable presence, "it's good to see you. I don't very often, you know."

"That husband of yours keeps me busy." He smiled as they sat down together. "If he doesn't keep me locked in that office, he sends me off to represent him elsewhere in one capacity or another."

Abbi smiled, knowing how much Cameron trusted him; he always had. And Abbi trusted him too, which was her very reason for coming to see him.

"We must have you in for dinner when Elsa returns," she said, preferring to remain engaged in small talk while she gathered her thoughts. "How are you getting along without her?"

"Not so bad," he smiled remarkably. "Han isn't such a bad cook." She knew he was mostly joking since there had always been hired help that came in to clean and do at least some of the cooking. She also knew that Georg and Elsa had made a point of teaching Han to be self-sufficient, and he likely *was* able to cook. Abbi laughed softly then remembered her purpose for this visit.

Georg's brow furrowed as he took in her countenance. "What's the matter, Abbi?" he asked gently, and she appreciated his perception.

"I need some advice, my friend."

"Now that's something I've been giving you since you were old enough to talk."

"That's why I'm here," she said softly.

"So, what's the problem?" He relaxed and crossed his ankle over his knee.

"It's Maggie," she said, "and Cameron. Well, that's the problem actually. I know that I should stand behind Cameron in his decisions, but I'm not certain that what he's doing is right."

"Could you be more specific?" he asked.

"I'm sorry," she said. "It's about Nik Koenig."

Georg blew out a long breath, and she knew he'd already known the answer to the question, but he'd wanted *her* to clarify. "What about him?"

"Do you know what's happening?"

"I do," Georg stated. "Cameron asked me to find out some things about him earlier today."

"What did you find out? Please tell me all you know. Cameron said very little. He was shouting too much." Georg looked surprised and tightened his gaze on Abbi with silent questions which provoked the sting of tears in her eyes. "I haven't seen him like that in many years, Georg, and never with one of the children. Please help me understand."

"Well," Georg began with compassion, "to begin with, Nik Koenig is not illegitimate. Nikolaus really did marry this Miss Koenig. She kept her maiden name because the marriage was never made public."

"That's incredible!" Abbi said. Since they'd both been keenly aware of the ridiculous number of mock marriages Nikolaus had set up in order to make women believe they were the only one, it was astonishing to realize that he had actually married this Miss Koenig. The implications were enormous, but one fact stood out strongly in Abbi's memory, and she felt sure Georg was remembering the same. "Nikolaus was betrothed to a princess from Kohenswald. What could he have possibly been thinking?"

"I don't know for certain what Nikolaus had intended to do

about it." Georg shook his head. "The more time that passes, the more Nikolaus's actions prove how absurd and ridiculous his thinking must have been. But that doesn't matter now. What matters is that this Nik is entitled to certain things."

"Which are?" Abbi's heart began to tighten as the reality started to settle in. There had clearly been valid reasons for Cameron's anger, but she had a feeling she hadn't begun to know the least of them.

"Mostly money. Cameron already offered him the allowance that would have been his father's—if we proved his legitimacy, which we have."

Something didn't make sense to Abbi. "As upsetting as all of this could be for . . . well . . . for all of us who . . . saw the damage Nikolaus caused, I still can't imagine Cameron being so upset over . . . an allowance."

"You know your husband well," was all Georg said when she was hoping for more information. But the implication was clear: Cameron would *not* be that upset over paying Nik Koenig an allowance simply by right of being legitimately attached to the du Woernig family. She was wondering how to ask when Georg said, "What is the problem, exactly?"

"Cameron has forbidden Maggie to see Nik again, but Maggie is heartbroken. She feels he is being unfair and judging Nik by his father's deeds. I have never taken sides in family matters, and Cameron and the children know that; they know that I will only side with what I believe is true and right. I don't have to tell you how bringing Nikolaus up at all is . . . disconcerting for me."

"To say the least," he said with an intensity in his eyes that made it clear he knew exactly what she meant.

"So . . . I can see why this would stir up some difficult feelings for Cameron, but . . . he was *so* angry. And Maggie, she's young and in love. I was younger than her when I met Cameron. How can I use that as an argument without being a hypocrite? I can see both points of view, and I feel compassion for each of them. I haven't had a chance to talk with Cameron yet, which is probably best. Hopefully he will cool down. But . . . I don't know what to do. You've always been there for me Georg; help me know what to do."

"Have you met Nik?" he asked.

"No," she said.

"You are a very perceptive woman, Abbi. I dare say Maggie lacks that perception at this point in her life. In my own opinion, age and wisdom rarely go hand in hand. You were especially wise and insightful when you met Cameron. I don't believe Maggie has those same qualities. I say that as if she were my own daughter; I'm not being critical."

"I understand. You're right, I know. You're just stating what's true. I can see that."

"Perhaps you should meet Nik Koenig and see for yourself. If you feel good about him then you can perhaps convince Cameron to give him a chance. And if you don't, then you'll know that backing him in this is the right thing."

"That makes sense. Although you know that when it comes right down to it, I would always stand by Cameron first . . . even if I disagreed with him."

"I know." He nodded and smiled just slightly. "You've always been a good wife to him. And through many years of disagreements, you've always managed to come to some kind of agreeable compromise. I think you need more information, and Cameron *does* need to cool off."

"I knew you would help me see the situation reasonably. You always do." She paused and looked directly at Georg. "You've met him."

"I have," he said with no expression.

"And what was your impression?"

Georg smiled again, but there was caution in his eyes. "I think it's best that I keep my opinions to myself. You should judge him for yourself, not by my impression."

"But you already know, don't you," she stated.

"Know what?"

"What my decision will be."

"I do," he said with confidence. "I know you well, Abbi. I have no doubt what the outcome will be." He chuckled then squeezed her hand. "And I'm glad I'm not in your shoes."

"Georg." She narrowed her eyes. Knowing he wouldn't say anything more, she stood and he did the same.

"I take it that was all you needed."

"Yes, Georg. Thank you."

"I'm glad I could help." He smiled and walked her to the door. "And you don't need a crisis to stop by. It's good to see you."

"And you," she said, pressing her hand to the side of his face. "You've hardly changed in twenty years, Georg."

"And you, Abbi." He smiled with affection and gave her a quick kiss. "You're as beautiful as ever."

"Thank you again," she said.

"No problem," he replied and stood in the doorway, watching her walk away. Abbi glanced over her shoulder once to reassure herself that he was indeed still watching. If he didn't know there were officers of the Guard situated in several places around the castle courtyard, he probably would have insisted on walking her back. It wasn't that he had any reason to be concerned over any imminent danger; he'd simply always looked out for her, and she knew he always would. His advice had helped her through many challenges and dilemmas, but she was especially grateful for it now. She only feared that doing what needed to be done would not necessarily go well.

Maggie finally felt drained of tears and knew she had no choice but to face the challenge before her—even if she had no idea what to do. She loved Nik Koenig. But could she ever make her father see him the way she did? She loved and respected her father, which made the dilemma storming through her mind all the more difficult.

Despite her desire to ride out and meet Nik, Maggie knew she must do as her mother had requested and not see him until she had talked with her father. After brooding in her room all evening and far into the next day, she felt overcome with boredom and ventured on a walk through the castle. She'd tried to remember all she'd heard about her Uncle Nikolaus. Though she knew very little, she did remember that somewhere in this castle was his portrait.

Going to the long hallway where the family gallery was located, Maggie slowly examined each painting. She had a certain fascination with an artist's interpretation of a face and scrutinized them closely. It was one of the few interests she had retained from the art training she'd received in concordance with her mother's hobby of painting. She wasn't much interested in the really old portraits, since they seemed to hold little bearing on the present. The first one she looked at carefully was her grandfather—a stern-looking man with dark hair and a goatee who had reigned as duke until his death in her father's youth. Then there was her grandmother Sonia, a Norwegian princess with pale hair and blue eyes, who seemed quite a contrast to her husband.

Maggie liked the portraits of her father's sisters—the ones she had been named after: Magda and Lena. She found them both fascinating women, and the portraits had captured their uniqueness. She wondered how they were doing; it had been years since she'd seen them.

And then there was her father's portrait. She thought it looked very much like him, but there was something about his youth that intrigued her. She could almost believe it was a painting of Erich, except for Erich's red hair.

On one side of Cameron du Woernig's portrait was her mother's, and Maggie wondered if she truly looked as much like her as everyone said. Abbi was a beautiful woman, with dark red hair and vivid green eyes. Maggie believed the artist had captured her well, and she had changed very little in the years since it had been painted.

On the other side of her father was a subtly harsh-looking woman. The inscription read Gwendolyn du Woernig. She was pretty as well, but Maggie caught something the artist had captured in the eyes which made her think she would not like this woman. She knew little about the death of her father's first wife, except that it must have been very traumatic by the way everyone seemed to avoid talking about it.

"Hello, Maggie." Her mother's voice startled her.

"Hello, Mother," she replied and couldn't help the sad tone.

"The portraits are intriguing, aren't they?" her mother said in a wistful tone. "When I first came to the castle I would look at them for hours. Especially the one of your father. It was painted before I met him, and I used to look at it and try to comprehend what he'd been like before we'd fallen in love."

Maggie turned her attention to the portrait of Gwendolyn and asked, "What happened to her?"

Abbi hesitated and wondered if finding her daughter here right now had been an answer to her prayers. She knew that Maggie needed some insight on the other side of the story, but she suspected her daughter wouldn't necessarily understand. She could only hope that in the end everything turned out all right as she took a deep breath and just said it, "Your Uncle Nikolaus killed her."

Maggie gasped and met her mother's eyes, which were starkly absent of any hint of humor. A part of Maggie wanted to know more, but at the moment, the topic came too close to the dread she'd been trying to avoid, so she quickly changed the subject. "I love the wedding portrait," she said, turning to the other wall to look up at the life-sized, full-length depiction of her parents. "Why are there no wedding portraits for anyone else here?"

"It was something different your father wanted to have done," Abbi explained. "Because our wedding was tied into his return to Horstberg after being in exile, and also into his reclamation of the country, he wanted it to be commemorated with something special." Abbi looked up at the portrait and sighed. "It was a very challenging time for both of us. The day of our cathedral wedding was one of the happiest of my life, and yet the most difficult." Abbi paused and looked at her daughter. "Nikolaus was killed that same day."

Maggie realized they weren't going to be able to avoid the subject of her father's wicked brother. But perhaps addressing the situation would help her mother understand that Nik was nothing like his father. "Where is Nikolaus's portrait?"

"Oh," Abbi laughed softly, but still there was no evidence of humor, "it's in some odd room that we never use. He was rather a vain man, and the painting was huge in comparison to these. It looked quite out of place here."

"I'd like to see it," Maggie said.

She saw her mother's barely concealed hesitance and felt sure she would avoid Maggie's request, but she pulled back her shoulders and said, "I think we could find it."

Maggie followed her mother through long stone hallways, feeling as she often did that she could almost become lost in her own home. They came at last to a room where Abbi pulled back the drapes so they could see, and dust flew from the fabric. When the sunlight filtered in, Maggie was taken off guard—not only by the size of the portrait, as her mother had said, but by the uncanny likeness to the man she loved. It was almost unnerving to see the full-length painting and know that it had hung here for many years, yet it was an almost perfect reflection of Nik Koenig.

"What are you thinking?" her mother asked.

"It looks just like him," she whispered.

"Nikolaus was a handsome man. I met him before I met your father, and I must say that I was intrigued. In fact," she laughed again with no humor, "I was quite caught up with him for a time."

"What happened?" Maggie asked curiously.

"I realized quickly that he was not an honorable man. And once I'd fallen in love with your father, I was grateful that I had realized it in time. What I felt for your father made my experience with Nikolaus seem trite and sordid."

Maggie didn't like the implication of her mother's words. She continued to gaze at the portrait, feeling somehow closer to Nik by being there. "Is that why Father hated him so badly," she asked, "because he killed Gwendolyn?" Maggie couldn't help wondering about her. Such a thing as another woman in her father's life was difficult to comprehend.

"There's more to it than that," Abbi replied cautiously. "Your father's marriage to his first wife was not necessarily good. It was a marriage of convenience. But Nikolaus not only killed Gwendolyn, he framed your father for the crime and forced him into exile for years. During that time, Nikolaus ruled Horstberg very badly, and there were many problems as a result."

Maggie took in this new information and realized that the story she and her siblings had been told all their lives about how their parents had come together had been entirely focused on the positive aspects of the situation. It had become practically a legend, almost like a fairy tale, but obviously those who had experienced it had chosen to omit the unsavory details over the years.

"So, how was Nikolaus killed?" she asked.

Maggie could see that her mother was struggling with the conversation, but like a duchess, she drew a deep breath and stated, "Your father and Georg found proof of his guilt, and . . . a difficult encounter occurred. It was the Captain of the Guard who killed him."

"Captain Dukerk?" Maggie asked. She knew him so well; he was almost like a member of the family. It seemed surprising that he could have done such a thing.

"Yes," Abbi stated then seemed eager to change the subject. "Maggie, my dear. I have felt torn since yesterday on what to do about this, but I have come to a decision that I hope you will accept. I've talked with your father, and he agrees."

Maggie's heartbeat quickened as if her life might either begin or end in that moment.

"I would like to meet Nik," she said, and Maggie smiled, so relieved she could have fainted.

"Oh, yes, Mother. If you meet him, I know you'll like him."

"I've always trusted my instincts, Maggie. I know you know that because I have taught you to do the same, but it can take . . . practice . . . to know if what you're feeling is correct, or if it's being blinded by some other emotion." Maggie felt certain her mother was admitting that her parents' bias toward Nik's father had likely tainted their initial response, and she was eager to hear what else her mother had to say. "If I can be with him and feel good about the situation, then I think I could talk your father into letting him court you. But Maggie," she added adamantly, "if I decide that I agree with your father, I must implore you to honor his wishes. It is your well-being we are concerned about. You must trust me!"

Maggie looked down quickly, not wanting to make such a promise. But she thought of how kind and charming she knew Nik to be, and it was easy to say, "I will."

"Very good, then." Abbi kissed her daughter on the cheek. "We will send a message and ask him to dine with us this evening."

"Oh, Mother, you are so good to me!" Maggie laughed, her dread and fear completely vanishing behind the hope of seeing Nik—here in her home. "What should I wear?"

"I don't know, dear." Abbi smiled and closed the dusty drapes before she ushered Maggie out of the room and closed the door. "Let's go upstairs and see what you've got."

Maggie went quietly with her mother, grateful for her kindness and understanding, and excited beyond measure at the prospect of seeing Nik again.

Chapter Four

THE DUKE'S RANSOM

One of the downstairs maids came to Maggie's room and announced that Mr. Koenig was waiting in the drawing room.

"Thank you, Heidi," Maggie replied, trying to conceal her excitement. Checking her appearance once more in the long mirror, she went quickly downstairs, glad to find him alone.

"Maggie," he laughed her name and pulled her into his arms. "Oh, you look beautiful." He bent to kiss her.

"I've missed you," she said.

"Yes," he replied sadly, "I feared after what happened that you wouldn't be able to get away."

"Exactly what *did* happen?" she asked pointedly, recalling how his withholding information had put her into a terrible situation. "And why didn't you tell me who you are?"

"I'm sorry," he said sheepishly. "I wanted you to love me for me, not because of who I am. But I didn't realize your father hated my father quite so much. When I told him who I was, he got rather upset."

"I should be angry with you for keeping secrets from me."

"Yes, you should," he agreed adamantly. "But you're not going to be, are you?" he added with a confident smile.

"How could I," she said, "when I have missed you so desperately?"

"I'm curious," he said. "After having been rudely dismissed from your home, why have I now been invited to dinner?"

"Mother wants to meet you. And if she likes you, she will convince Father to let you court me."

"Ah," he said, "so I must be my most charming self."

"You must indeed. Come along," she said, "or we will be late."

Maggie noted how Nik slowed his pace as he walked beside her, observing his surroundings with great interest. She allowed him the opportunity to do so; it was far from the first time she'd seen newcomers to Castle Horstberg overcome with its enormity and fineness. They entered the dining room a few minutes late, and Maggie could immediately see that her father was tense. But she knew he had excellent diplomacy skills, and she could see in his eyes that he was willing to remain civil. Erich and Sonia seemed intrigued by the unfolding drama, and it occurred to Maggie only then that Erich had probably been near their father through much of this, and he had no doubt told Sonia all he knew. She could only be grateful that Rudolf and his family had returned to their home country, which kept them from being privy to their family challenges. Maggie and her siblings had never been prone to keeping secrets from each other, but she felt annoyed to think of them gossiping about her. They each tossed her a brief smile that was closer to a smirk, but she ignored them and kept her attention mostly on her mother. It was Abbi du Woernig's opinion of Nik that would determine the outcome of all this.

Maggie made formal introductions, noting that her mother's eyes were almost mesmerized by Nik. She could imagine that for Abbi, seeing Nik might have been very much how Maggie had felt seeing the portrait of Nik's father. As they were seated and began to eat, Abbi paid very close attention to Nik. Maggie felt sweat rising in her palms, wondering what the outcome would be. But she smiled often at Nik, and he returned her smile with kind affection, silently reassuring her of his love.

The conversation remained light even though there were long stretches of uncomfortable silence in between. Maggie questioned whether or not she should have informed Nik of the duchess's reasons for wanting to meet him, when she realized that Nik would occasionally look right at Maggie's mother, boldly meeting her eyes as if he were silently challenging her to accept him. Knowing her mother as she did, Maggie wondered if that was the best approach. Even if Nik was as decent as she believed him to be, it might be possible that a display of arrogance could set off the duchess. Maggie knew well enough that her mother was not impressed by arrogance. Maggie felt decidedly nervous but did her best to conceal it.

After Abbi and Nik shared a long mutual gaze, Maggie saw something come into her mother's eyes—decisive rather than puzzled. But her father kept glancing back and forth between them, looking as though he'd like to tear Nik apart with his bare hands.

"You must excuse me," the duchess said, standing abruptly and throwing her napkin onto the table. "I'm not feeling well."

Nik shot a worried glance toward Maggie just as the duke stood and followed close behind his wife.

"Perhaps I should go for now," Nik said toward Maggie. Erich and Sonia just watched, apparently amused by the drama. And Maggie wished they weren't there.

"I'll walk you to the door," Maggie said, and they left the dining room together.

"I'm afraid, Maggie," he said as he stood to face her in the grand entry hall. "I'm afraid she sees my father in me and will not accept me."

"I will talk with her," she said. "Meet me at midnight."

"I will," he said, then kissed her softly and left.

Maggie went stoically to her parents' bedroom and knocked on the door, wanting to forever avoid this but knowing it had to be faced. Her father answered and silently moved aside for her to enter. She saw her mother sitting on the bed crying, and a tangible fear crept down her spine. Maggie wished her father would leave, but he sat down with a clear indication that he was staying, and she knew the worst was yet to come.

"Maggie," her mother began, indicating she come sit by her on the bed, "it is time I told you some things about the past that . . . perhaps you should know." She glanced timidly toward her husband, and Maggie caught a glimpse of compassion in his eyes.

"I told you earlier today," Abbi went on, still crying quietly, "the circumstances that your Uncle Nikolaus forced your father into. But what I didn't want to tell you before—yet I feel you should know—is exactly what happened the night he was killed. It was the day of our cathedral wedding." She glanced toward Cameron again then back to her daughter. "Your father went to free the witness who could prove his innocence, and while he was gone, Nikolaus came into the castle by a secret passageway and . . ." Abbi paused as her emotions got the better of her, and Cameron finished.

"Your mother and I had been married privately some time earlier," he said. "Your mother was pregnant, and Nikolaus . . ." Maggie saw her parents exchange a meaningful gaze, as if they had some silent form of communication, and she knew beyond any doubt that they had made a mutual decision to omit certain details. A part of her wanted to know those details, but a bigger part of her was relieved when her father seemed resolved to move past them. He turned firmly to Maggie and continued. "He took your mother rather brutally out of the castle to find me. He made some horrible threats, Maggie, including implications that he would kill the baby when it was born . . . if it was a boy—which it was," he added, referring to Erich.

"When Captain Dukerk killed Nikolaus," Abbi inserted, "he was . . ." She stopped when her tears overwhelmed her again.

"I don't think the rest makes any difference, Abbi," Cameron said strongly. "Maggie could never comprehend what Nikolaus put us through. It has no bearing on this. Nik Koenig is not to be held responsible for his father's actions."

"Then you . . ." Maggie began, feeling a light of hope.

"I'll take him on his own merits," Cameron interrupted. "And he's a greedy, underhanded son of a—"

"Cameron!" Abbi stopped him, and Maggie started to cry.

"I'll let you handle this," Cameron said and turned to leave.

"Wait," Abbi said, and he turned back to look at her with eyes that were nothing but tender and compassionate. His voice was the same as he said to his wife, "She will never understand what he did to us . . . what he put us through. And she will never see this man the way we see him, because he's deceiving her, Abbi. You know what that's like. Maybe you can talk some sense into her." He glanced at Maggie then back to Abbi. "If you don't, it could be the undoing of us all."

He left the room and didn't slam the door as hard as Maggie knew he was capable of doing. Still, she winced and then turned to her mother and pleaded, "You must understand, Mother, how I feel about him. Please . . . please don't tell me that you've—"

"Maggie, my darling," she said, "there is something in his eyes. There is a lack of goodness there. I can't explain. I only know it's true. I would not trust that man to make you happy, Maggie—no matter who his father was. I must agree emphatically with your father. You will not see him again."

"No!" Maggie shouted as she stood. "I love him. You can't expect me to—"

"Maggie! It is for the best. You must trust us. When I was young . . . when I was so infatuated with Nikolaus . . . there was no one to guide me . . . or perhaps I wouldn't have gotten myself into so much trouble. You are blessed to have parents who care about you. Believe it or not, we do have some wisdom and insight in such matters." Abbi leaned forward, and her countenance intensified. "Love is not enough, Maggie. There are millions of women in this world who *love* men who do deplorable things, and they excuse all of the bad behavior in the name of love. You deserve better than that. You deserve respect and trust, as well as love. You must trust me, Maggie; you must!"

Maggie knew she likely wasn't being entirely rational, but there was something hurt and angry inside of her that seemed to block out most of what her mother had said. She could only think of how Nik Koenig was being banished from her life, and she just couldn't live with it!

"You're judging him by his father," Maggie growled. "Do you see yourself? Look how emotional you've gotten . . . because of his father—not him. You can't see him the way I do."

"You're only seeing what you want to see." Abbi remained calm in spite of the way Maggie was speaking to her. Normally, talking to her mother in such a tone would have been reason enough to be severely reprimanded. But there was a tender pleading in Abbi's eyes. "Infatuation can be very blind, Maggie. You must believe me. You've got to search your feelings carefully and listen to what your instincts are telling you. Have you spent any time at all with him in the midst of real life? Do you know anything about his character? Does he have integrity? Is he kind when things are difficult? You don't know, Maggie. You don't know him."

Again Maggie could only feel her own heartache. She broke into fresh sobs and ran from the room, crying into her pillow long after the household had retired and it was time to meet Nik and tell him the horrible news. She was more careful than usual in getting out of the castle, certain that her father would be especially alert. Having spent her entire life in this fortress, she knew exactly how to avoid the officers of the Guard who were always posted in certain positions, and she slipped by them all unnoticed. She wished she'd had a chance to arrange for Han to help her, but it occurred to her that he likely would have refused, given all that had happened. She mounted her horse bareback, as much as she hated it, and rode to the meadow.

"Oh, no," was the first thing Nik said when she dismounted and fell into his arms. Even in the darkness of a partial moon, she knew there was no hiding her tear-swollen eyes or the heaviness of her countenance.

"What will we do?" she asked. "They have forbidden me to see you . . . ever again."

"You must marry me," he stated.

Maggie could hardly breathe. She'd certainly not expected *this!* "Nik . . ." she muttered, "I . . . I don't know. It's been so short a time and—"

"Don't you love me?" he asked.

"I . . . yes, I . . ." Her mother's cautions haunted her, but she felt so strongly drawn to Nik. And he was so convincing.

"Then you must marry me. We'll run away and get married."

"But Nik . . . my parents. I don't want to leave here, and I—"

"We'll just leave long enough to get married. When we come back, there is nothing they can do. They'll just have to accept it. And they will, I promise."

"I don't know," she said. "I must . . . I must think about it."

"Meet me here tomorrow," he said, "at the same time . . . and we'll make plans."

She made no reply, and he kissed her fervently. Maggie felt torn as he helped her mount, and she rode home feeling the confusion deepen over her dilemma. Her thoughts were full of turmoil when she rode slowly into the stables. She wasn't the least bit prepared to have Han come out of the darkness with a very loud, "Boo!"

"Ooh," she said scornfully, dismounting on her own, "you will be the death of me!"

"Not I," he smiled slyly. "If anyone is to be the death of you, it will be this Nik bastard."

"He is not a—"

"That's strictly a matter of opinion."

"Thanks for cheering me up, Han," she said with sarcasm. "Before I left I was feeling as though the world was against me. Now I'm certain it's true. You've confirmed it."

"No, Maggie," he said, "the world isn't against you. You're just the only one stupid enough to believe that Nik Koenig is a nice guy."

"Ooh," she repeated for lack of anything better to say, but he only chuckled.

"You'd better be nice to me." He smirked as he led Pagan to his stall.

"And why is that?"

"I wonder what your father would say if I happened to mention that I saw his daughter coming into the stables long past midnight."

"You wouldn't!"

"Of course I wouldn't." He smiled easily. "But I just thought I'd remind you what a nice guy I am, so you don't forget."

"You're deplorable!"

Han laughed as she turned to leave. "Yes," he said, "but I know your secrets, so you have to put up with me anyway."

Maggie tossed and turned through the night, wondering in vain what she should do. On one hand, the thought of running away and marrying Nik was so exciting that it took her breath away. She loved being with him and knew it would be wonderful. But on the other hand, it would devastate her family. And that was a difficult thing to balance out. She *loved* her family. For all that they had their differences, she had been raised well, loved and cared for, and she felt safe and secure here with them. How could she leave that behind? How could she not accept Nik's offer and simply do the most exciting thing that had ever come her way? Surely her family would forgive her. Wouldn't they?

She slept at last from exhaustion, waking long after breakfast was over, and decided to go riding to ease these frustrations. Perhaps the fresh air would clear her mind and help her come to a decision before tonight when she was to meet Nik again.

"Good morning," Han said cheerfully when she entered the stables, "Your Royal Midnight-Rider."

"Oh, hush!" she insisted. Caught up in her dilemma, his teasing was more irritating than usual.

Maggie stood with her back to the door, watching Han as he picked up the saddle. He was about to throw it over Pagan's back when he dropped it to the ground and, with fearful eyes, ran toward her.

Hearing something from behind, Maggie turned just in time to see Erich fall off his horse, almost right on top of Han, who tried to catch him.

"Good heavens!" she shrieked. "What happened?"

Erich's reply was a guttural moan, and Maggie panicked when she saw the blood.

"I've been shot!" Erich managed to say, and he groaned again.

Han shouted at Maggie, "Get someone to send for a doctor—now! I'll get him inside."

Maggie did as she was told and became quickly caught up in a whirlwind of panic until she found herself sitting outside of Erich's room with Han while the doctor attended to her brother. Her parents had gone into town with Georg and, as of yet, had no idea what had happened.

Maggie's thoughts rushed frantically back and forth between wondering how she would survive if Erich didn't and what she should do about Nik Koenig. She longed to be in Nik's arms, wanting to feel them around her, giving her comfort. She wished desperately that he was here now.

"Are you all right?" Han asked quietly. She'd almost forgotten he was there.

"I'm fine," she whispered and no sooner broke into tears.

"He'll be all right, Maggie," he said gently, pulling her head onto his shoulder, where she wept.

Han reminded himself to keep his thoughts in check while Maggie cried in his arms. He steered his mind toward his prominent concern for Erich and felt some assurance to know that at least he and Maggie had *that* in common.

The doctor came into the hallway, and Maggie quickly wiped at her tears as they both stood to hear the verdict.

"The bullet went straight through his shoulder," he stated. "He's lost a great deal of blood, but he's going to be fine."

"Oh, thank heaven," Maggie said and felt Han's arm come soothingly around her as they both laughed in relief.

A moment later, Cameron came running up the stairs with Abbi and Georg close behind. "What happened?" the duke demanded.

Han spoke quickly. "Erich was shot, but he's going to be fine."

"*Shot?*" Cameron shouted. "How did it happen?"

"I don't know," Han said. "You'd have to ask Erich."

"Please, Han," Abbi said fearfully, "tell us all you know."

"He rode into the stables, said he'd been shot, and collapsed."

Cameron moved into Erich's room with Abbi close behind. Again, Maggie sat with Han in the hallway, not certain what they were waiting for. Georg sat silently with them, and it was some time later before Cameron came back out, directing his attention to his friend and highest advisor as he stated the facts. "He was riding the lower meadow when somebody shot him. He's certain it was deliberate, but all he saw was a shape in the trees."

"Well, that doesn't give us much to go on," Georg replied soberly.

"Damn!" Cameron said and threw a scornful glance toward Maggie.

"What?" she asked.

"I knew as soon as he walked into my office that something like this was going to happen."

"Don't be absurd!" Maggie snapped. "This has nothing to do with him!"

"No? Who would inherit the duchy at this point if Erich were dead?" Cameron demanded.

Maggie remained silent, but Han boldly volunteered the answer with a mere touch of drama in his tone, "Nikolaus Koenig, of course."

Maggie thought his comment was rude and out of line, but of course, her father tossed Han a quick glance that suggested some kind of approval.

"You've all gone mad!" Maggie stormed away, making up her mind in that moment. She was going to marry Nik.

Maggie's ride that night was like a fantastic whirlwind. She told

Nik of what had happened to Erich, and he seemed distressed. But knowing that Erich would be all right, his concern was quickly replaced with an intense excitement when she willfully accepted his proposal of marriage. She could hardly believe he wanted to leave the following night. But his insistence that he had to have her—and his declarations on how wonderful and exciting their life together would be—made it impossible to not consent.

Nik gave her instructions to meet him at a point far enough from the castle to be discreet where he would have a carriage waiting. Then he kissed her good night and rode away. It wasn't until after he'd left that Maggie wondered how she would possibly get to their rendezvous point without a horse. And she couldn't just leave the horse there. It was stupid to have forgotten such a detail. But she wouldn't have another chance to talk to Nik, and she made up her mind that she would surely be able to coerce Han into helping her—even if she had to bribe him.

Maggie was disappointed that Han wasn't in the stables when she returned—even though that would mean he'd know what she'd been up to. But knowing she would have ample opportunity to talk with him tomorrow, Maggie went up to bed feeling excited and complacent over the glorious adventure she was about to embark upon that would change her life forever.

Abbi spent most of the night in Erich's room, just to be certain he was all right. She knew there were plenty of people available who could watch over him for the asking, but he was her son and he'd been hurt, and she and Cameron agreed that his parents should be the most frequent faces that he saw as he drifted in and out of sleep, aided by a pain tonic the doctor was having him take at regular intervals. Even though she and Cameron had taken turns getting some rest, Abbi didn't feel at all rested—or calm. She just couldn't get the scene out of her head that Erich had described. Shot? Her son had been *shot!* Memories of a time when Cameron's life had been in danger mingled into her present concerns, and she found it difficult to keep up the proper facade that she was calm and in control. Was this the plague of being royalty? She could hardly think about it.

Alone with Cameron, she could be herself and cry all she wanted to. With the exception of a few close friends—who were either presently away or very busy—Cameron was her only ally. And how grateful she was for him! But they both knew that this horrible thing that had happened to Erich was not their only concern. Maggie's state of mind was perhaps even more disconcerting—especially since Cameron had declared that his gut instinct told him the two situations absolutely had to be connected. He didn't believe in coincidence, and neither did Abbi. Her instincts were completely in alignment with her husband's.

Despite a solemn mood at the breakfast table, due mostly to concern over Erich, Abbi couldn't help but notice the change of attitude in her daughter. Cameron seemed preoccupied with his thoughts, and she felt sure his mind was heavy with worry over his son—even though they were certain Erich would come through this just fine. It was future attempts that concerned Cameron now. Nik Koenig was surely on Cameron's mind as well. But since Maggie had been given the edict of never seeing him again, Cameron and Abbi had both agreed that there was nothing more to be done about him for the time being.

However, observing her daughter at breakfast, Abbi's concerns shifted abruptly. She knew her daughter well, and something wasn't right. She thought it through carefully before she sought out Cameron as soon as breakfast was finished.

"Come here," she said, dragging him into a little-used room.

"What on earth are we doing in here?"

"I need to talk to you . . . privately."

"Fine. Talk."

"Cameron," she whispered, "I fear that Maggie's going to run away."

"What?" he shouted.

"Shhh."

"What gave you that idea?" he whispered.

"I just know. I can see it in her eyes. She's accepted the circumstances too easily. You know as well as I do that when she doesn't get her way, she pouts . . . for days sometimes. She's too content, almost smug. I know her, Cameron. And I know she's going to run away with him."

"Damn!" Cameron muttered.

"You've been saying that a lot lately," she scolded.

"I've had good reason to."

"What are we going to do?" she whispered with panic.

"I don't know," Cameron drawled with quiet adamance, "but I'll think of something. Georg is waiting for me. I must go. Maybe *he* can think of something."

"Think fast, Cameron," she implored. "She may do it as soon as tonight."

"Tonight?"

"There's no way of knowing. But can we take any chances?"

"Oh, Abbi." He put aside his need to hurry for a moment and took her into his arms. They shared a tight, lengthy embrace that was common between them. Even though they were both very busy, they needed each other, and such moments gave them strength. "You know," he said, pushing a stray strand of red hair back from her face, "everything would have been much easier if I had been a blacksmith."

"So you keep telling me." She smiled and kissed him. "You're far too brilliant a man to do anything but run a country."

He let out a weighted sigh. "So you keep telling me."

Han looked up from oiling a saddle to see his father walk into the stables, but there was something unusual in Georg's eyes—a firm determination that let Han know his reason for coming here had nothing to do with horses.

"Hello, Father," Han said, pretending not to have noticed.

"I'll take over here for a bit," he said. "The duke wants to see you."

"He what?" Han's heart began to pound.

"You heard me. He wants to see you—and it's official. You'd best treat it as such." He glanced toward Han's hands and said, "Wash up first."

"Of course," Han said and ran to the apartment where they lived to wash his hands and face, change his shirt, and comb his hair. He looked at himself in the mirror, blew out a long breath, and walked slowly across the courtyard, trying to gather his wits and remain calm. He was surprised by the memory that appeared in his mind, as clearly as if it had been yesterday.

Han kissed Maggie once again, feeling as if he'd die without her. She moaned pleasurably and threaded her fingers through his hair. He marveled that a young lady of fourteen could be so passionate in response to a perfectly chaste kiss. He had to continually remind himself that they were too young to be involved beyond the innocent kisses they exchanged on occasion, and they had to be extremely careful. Somewhere in the midst of their kiss, he realized they weren't alone. Erich cleared his throat elaborately, and Han met Maggie's eyes with a self-recriminating grimace. He moved away from her and lay back casually in the straw, as if nothing in the world was out of the ordinary.

"What on earth are you doing?" Erich asked in a voice fitting of the next Duke of Horstberg.

Maggie eased close to Han, as if she would defend him—or perhaps she was hoping he would defend her.

"What does it look like?" Han asked, determined to not apologize. When Erich only folded his arms in apparent disgust, Han added, "Good heavens, man, we've got our clothes on. It was only a little necking."

"That's my baby sister you're necking with, Han. I thought I knew you better than that."

Han stood up and held out a hand for Maggie, helping her to her feet. "You do know me, Erich. So think about it and you won't have to wonder what I might be doing here. There's only one possibility. And she's not a baby; or hadn't you noticed?"

"I can assure you that Han has been a perfect gentleman," Maggie said in his defense.

"A perfect gentleman does not—" Erich began, but Maggie interrupted.

"If you're angry, be angry with me. I'm the one who—"

"It's all right, Maggie," Han said, watching Erich closely. They'd been as close as brothers since the nursery, but he'd never felt any discord between them—until now. He wasn't certain how to handle it. The obvious question slipped onto his tongue. "Do you think I'm not good enough for her, Erich?"

"It's not that, and you know it."

"If I knew it, I wouldn't have to ask. The fact is, she's the duke's daughter, and whether I was raised at your side or not, I am the son of servants. Would finding me in the straw with your sister be more tolerable if I were the son of a baron, or a count?" Erich said nothing. The insinuation of his silence was

something Han didn't even want to think about. "I love Maggie," he said firmly, and she eased a little closer to him. "I can assure you that her best interest is my highest concern."

"Then why all the sneaking around?" Erich demanded. "Is there a reason you don't want my father to know you're involved with Maggie?"

Han could have told Erich that Maggie seemed to prefer it this way. But instinctively, he knew it would be better to have it out in the open, for many reasons—and now seemed just as good a time as any. Without a word, Han took Maggie's hand and rushed past Erich.

"Where are you going?" Erich called, following after them.

"I'm going to talk to the duke. You're welcome to come along."

"Han," Maggie protested, "my father will—"

"I don't care what he does. Erich's right. It's time our families knew what's going on between us. We have nothing to hide."

Han hurried across the courtyard and into the main entrance of Castle Horstberg, walking briskly down the hall toward the duke's office. He knocked at the door, and Maggie's father called for them to come in.

Han strode into the office, holding tightly to Maggie's hand. Cameron du Woernig looked up from the paperwork on his desk. Georg Heinrich sat up a little straighter in his chair to the left of the duke's. Cameron removed his glasses. His eyes were drawn overtly to Han and Maggie's clasped hands, then briefly over the expressions of his three visitors.

"May I help you?" Cameron asked.

"There's something I need to tell you, Your Grace," Han said with no hint of apology in his voice. He exchanged a quick glance with his father, hoping there wouldn't be hell to pay for this later. But he reminded himself of his feelings for Maggie and knew he would gladly take any consequences to have her a part of his life.

"I'm listening," the duke said with no expression. Georg sighed and folded his arms over his chest as if he sensed what was coming.

"I must confess—I've been necking with your daughter."

For a long moment nothing happened; no one moved. Maggie sucked in her breath loudly. Erich looked astonished at Han's boldness. Georg looked as if he were restraining himself from slapping Han here and now. And the duke was completely unreadable.

"I see," Cameron finally said. "And may I ask why?"

"Why?" Han echoed. "Well . . . because I care for her, very much . . . Your Grace. I know we're young yet, but one day . . . when we're older . . ." Han *stopped himself from getting too specific with his feelings. He didn't want to have them discredited due to his youth.*

"Well, then," Cameron said, almost smiling, "I suppose it would be appropriate for you to have dinner with us this evening." He put his glasses back on as an obvious indication he'd said all he wanted to.

"That's it?" Erich demanded. Cameron looked up at him, apparently baffled. "Well, aren't you concerned about Maggie's . . ."

He didn't finish, and Cameron asked, "Maggie's what?"

"Well," Erich glanced at Maggie, and she blushed visibly, "you know."

Cameron turned to Han and asked, "Is there a reason I should be concerned about Maggie's welfare?"

"No," Han said, lifting his chin firmly, "I would never do anything to hurt Maggie."

"Good," the duke said, "we'll see you at dinner." He looked at Han over the top of his glasses. "Unless there's something else?"

"No, Your Grace. I'll be there. Thank you."

Han glanced toward his father as he turned to leave and felt certain he'd hear about this later.

"Oh, Maggie," Cameron said, and she turned around, her eyes wide with fear. "There's straw in your hair, sweetheart."

Maggie nodded and left the room with Han. Erich brushed past them and hurried away. Once they were alone, Maggie spoke in an angry whisper, "I swear sometimes, Han, if I didn't love you, you would drive me completely crazy. I can't believe you just did that."

"Well," he smirked proudly, "now that it's not a secret anymore, we won't be so likely to get into trouble." He glanced both directions down the hall to be certain they were alone before he kissed her quickly and whispered, "You're far too passionate to keep me in line forever."

Maggie gave him one of those smiles that seemed to force its way through her attempt to be angry with him. They walked down the hall holding hands, and Maggie said, "What do you suppose has gotten into Erich?"

"He'll get over it, whatever it is." Han pulled a few pieces of straw from Maggie's hair. "If he doesn't, it's his problem."

"He's your best friend, Han. Would you let me come between the two of you?"

"Once Erich realizes I'm not just toying with you, he'll come around. He loves you. He just wants what is best for you."

"Then you have something in common," she said warmly, and Han felt certain life could be no better than this.

Later, Georg didn't express the anger that Han had expected. He brought it up by simply saying, "I trust you're being a gentleman with Maggie."

"Of course," Han insisted.

"Good," Georg stated and said nothing more.

"That's it?" Han asked.

Georg smiled subtly. "Well, I could tell you what His Grace said to me after you left earlier, if you're interested."

"Let's have it," Han said, wondering if he wanted to hear this.

"He said he would far prefer that his daughter be necking with you rather than some idiot he didn't know and couldn't trust. He expressed good faith in you to not compromise Maggie in any way. I'm certain you won't disappoint him."

"No, I won't," Han assured his father, and he meant it.

Han drew courage and pushed the memories away as he knocked at the door to the duke's office. He took a deep breath when he was asked to come in. Closing the door behind him, Han found himself alone, face-to-face, with Cameron du Woernig. He couldn't recall ever being in this room since the day he'd confessed his involvement with Maggie. He'd been seventeen at the time, but at the moment, he nearly felt like a child all over again.

"You wished to see me, Your Grace."

"Please sit down." Cameron motioned toward a chair.

"I think I would prefer to stand, Your Grace . . . if you don't mind."

"Fine," Cameron said and sat behind his desk. "We have a little problem going on here," he began, "that is, you might say, like father like son. I'm certain you know what I'm talking about, but I want to repeat some of the finer points nevertheless.

"Nikolaus Koenig, my brother's son, seems to be far from satisfied with the allowance I have allotted him for the dubious honor of being born a du Woernig. Somehow he's convinced my daughter that she should be in love with him, and well . . ." He paused cautiously. "You know Maggie well, Han." It was not a question.

"Well enough," he admitted.

"There was a time when I know you quite liked her, but I know circumstances have changed." The duke met Han's eyes intently. Han didn't like the course of this conversation at all.

"How do you feel about her now, Han?" he asked. While Han

was contemplating an appropriate answer, the duke added, "Do you like her?"

"She's not an easy girl to like, sir . . . if you'll excuse my saying."

"I'll excuse it," he chuckled and went on. "Let me get to the point. The direct problem at the moment is that my wife is convinced—because she knows Maggie so well—that she may very well attempt to run away with this Nik."

Han looked surprised but only asked, "Excuse me, sir, but what has this got to do with me?"

"I did say the problem was like father like son. I believe the answer is the same. And in fact, so does your father."

"I don't follow you, sir."

"I trust your father completely, Han. He is the best man I have ever known, and I believe you have some of the same qualities."

Han's heart beat wildly. He'd always hoped someone would notice he was worth more than a stablehand. But the duke himself? It was incredible!

"So, I'm giving you a new job," Cameron du Woernig said. "That is, if you want it. It won't be easy, but it could be beneficial for you."

Han waited expectantly. In his wildest imaginings, he couldn't begin to think what the duke wanted of him that would have to do with Maggie.

"I want you to kidnap my daughter."

Han held his breath until it erupted into a brief but loud burst of laughter. He felt certain it was disrespectful to react that way toward the duke, but he just couldn't hold it back.

Cameron smiled. "You find it amusing, but do you think you can do it?"

"Oh, I could do it," Han said, "but I'm not certain I understand why you want me to."

"I have never believed in arranged marriages, Han. I've seen their destruction, and I swore I would never push it with my own children. But in Maggie's case, despite my relief that Sonia is happy, well . . . what I'm trying to get at is that . . . Maggie is the most stubborn, willful woman the world has ever seen, and she's blind as a bat! She can't see her nose in front of her face, and if she marries Nik Koenig, he will undermine this duchy just like Mordred did in Camelot."

"Camelot?"

"Come now, Han. Surely you've heard the legend of Camelot."

"Briefly, sir."

"Well, the kingdom certainly had its problems, but when Mordred, the long-lost relative, moved into the castle, he stirred everybody up and made mountains out of molehills and destroyed the entire kingdom. And I am not going to let that happen here. If Maggie was away from him for a good, long time, I think she would eventually figure out that she can live without him. That's why I want you to kidnap her. She's too bull-headed to listen to reason. Frankly, I've got no choice. And you're the only man I would trust to do it. So what do you say, Han? Are you willing?"

"Kidnapping is pretty general, sir," Han said with a straight face that belied the bubbling excitement inside of him. "I'm willing, but before I agree to this, I'd like to know exactly what you expect me to do."

"All right," Cameron said. "Are you sure you don't want to sit down?"

"I'll sit down," Han said breathlessly and took a seat across the desk from the duke.

"The main thing is that I want her gone for at least six months. I need that much time to make certain the problem is under control."

Han couldn't hold back a smile. This was sounding better by the minute. "What do I do with your daughter for six months?"

"Just keep her entertained." He laughed. "I'll send lots of money with you. Call it the duke's ransom." Han chuckled, and the duke joined in. "Buy her presents. Take her all the places she's never been. Just show her a good time."

"Your daughter isn't known for having fun, sir. It could be difficult to convince her that she's having a good time."

"I know," he said apologetically. "What she needs is a good dose of humility. But I think you can handle her. There is one other thing," he said cautiously.

"What?" Han asked with dread in his voice.

"I am the duke. If my daughter disappears, I can't stand up and declare that I hired one of my stablehands to kidnap her. I realize this requires a fair amount of deception, which I'm generally against—and I know you are, as well. But I can't see any other way out, and the situation is very delicate. She's my daughter, Han. She is dear and precious to me. And I must order my military force to do their best to try and find her."

"What are you trying to say, sir?"

"You will most likely be pursued."

"Oh, boy!" Han shook his head. "So, let me see if I've got this straight. I'm supposed to kidnap your daughter and—"

"Tonight," Cameron interjected, and Han's eyes widened.

"Tonight," he went on. "I need to keep her away from here for at least six months and make certain that no one can find us. I'll probably be running from the Duke's Guard, not to mention I'm certain Nik Koenig isn't going to let her go for nothing."

"You've got it straight, Han."

"Well, I—"

"Before you accept my proposal, there is more."

"How could there possibly be more . . . sir?"

"If . . ." the duke smirked, "you can get her to fall in love with you, I'll—"

"Wait a minute," Han laughed satirically, hoping to hide the painful knot that erupted inside of him at the mere mention of *that*. Already he could see a dark side to this proposition. He held up his hands in defense. "Your daughter doesn't like me very much. That sounds impossible to me."

"There was a time when she was rather fond of you."

"As you said, sir, circumstances change."

"Forego love. Get her to marry you and—"

"Marry me?"

"Do whatever you have to."

Han couldn't believe the duke was saying this. It was unbelievable. "Now I understand," Han said strongly, "why you were talking about arranged marriages. But you want me? Really? *Me* . . . to marry your daughter?"

"I do."

Han was stunned.

"Don't you want to marry her?" Cameron asked with concern. "I mean, there isn't anyone else, is there? You're not in love with—"

"No, sir. There is no one else. I *do* care for Maggie. I always have.

I could accept marrying her, but I can't quite believe you'd want a stablehand for a son-in-law."

"That's irrelevant to me, Han. But if you can get Maggie to marry you—by whatever means necessary—and succeed with all of this, I will guarantee you your father's position, working along with Erich as he takes over the duchy. Being Georg's son does not guarantee that position. It's an important one, and I expect it to be earned. But from what I've seen so far—and if you can pull this off—I think you'll deserve it."

Han was stunned beyond words. It was like having the world fall into his lap. Not only would he have Maggie right where he'd always wanted her, but he would have the position he'd always dreamed of—and had sensed was right for him. He knew, as the duke had said, it would not be easy. Maggie wasn't fond of him, and she was a fighter. He felt some hope in believing that something of the Maggie he'd fallen in love with still existed somewhere. But not only would he have to be extremely clever and crafty, he would have to be on his toes continually. It would not be an easy six months. But if he could survive it and do all the duke was asking of him, he'd have it all. Already he was creating strategic plans in his mind, and he thought, if nothing else, it could sure be a lot of fun. And it would certainly be better than working in the stables day in and day out—whatever the results might be.

"Well?" Cameron asked expectantly after giving Han a reasonable amount of time to think about it.

"I'll do it," he said, standing in a courageous gesture.

The duke threw back his head and laughed. "I knew I could count on you," he said. "Now," he added soberly, "do you have any questions?"

"I don't know," he said, "I haven't had time to think."

"You'll manage, I believe," Cameron said with confidence as he pulled a key from a drawer and turned to open a safe behind the desk. He groaned, pushing the stubborn handle to the correct position, and then pulled out a pouch of money and handed it to Han.

Opening it, Han caught his breath. "Good heavens, sir. This is a lot of money!"

"The duke's ransom." He grinned. "But it's a small price to pay to save my duchy. It won't be cheap keeping that girl happy for six months. I fear growing up as a princess somehow stifled the spirit I believe she has in there somewhere. You teach her how to have some fun, will you, Han?"

"I will certainly do my best."

Cameron shook Han's hand, and the latter said, "I'll see you in six months . . . Father."

Again Cameron laughed with boisterous confidence. He clearly believed he was doing the right thing. Han just hoped that with time, Maggie might come to agree.

Han walked back to the stables with the pouch of money buttoned inside his shirt. He wondered exactly how, within a matter of hours, he was going to kidnap the Princess MagdaLena du Woernig. Arriving at the stables, he found a boy there who usually worked doing odd jobs in the cavalry stables.

"Hello, Mr. Heinrich," the boy said. "Your father told me to take over your job. He said you had some things you needed to do and to tell you I'd take care of everything while you was busy."

Han chuckled and thanked the boy. On his way out of the stables, he almost ran right into the purpose of his quest.

"Good afternoon," he said, barely able to behave normally, "Your Royal On-the-Brink-of-Adventure."

"What are you talking about?" Maggie asked scornfully, wondering if he somehow suspected what she wanted.

"Well, aren't you?" he asked, playing innocent.

"Han," she whispered, "I need you to help me."

"I was right!" he boomed.

"Shhh," she said and ushered him outside where the boy couldn't hear. "I need you to meet me tonight and—"

"Can't you saddle your own horse this time?" he asked with well-acted dismay. "I could use some sleep." He stifled a yawn. "I haven't been getting nearly enough."

"This is important!" she demanded. Maggie knew she had to confide in Han. If he was going to help her, he'd find out soon enough anyway. With courage she just blurted it out. "I'm going to run away with Nik . . . tonight. And I need you to help me."

Maggie had expected him to argue, or at least retort with some sarcastic comment. But all he did was smile.

"Just what is it that you want me to do?" he asked.

"I need you to take me to where I'm meeting him so that you can bring the horse back. It's too far to walk."

"And what's in it for me?" he asked and couldn't help smiling still. It couldn't have been easier if she'd held out her wrists and asked him to tie her up. He laughed from his thoughts, and she glared at him.

"I'll . . . well, I don't know. What do you want?"

"Oh," he said, "I don't need anything. If you want me to help you, I will. But are you sure you're doing the right thing?" he asked with unusual seriousness.

Han saw a flicker of doubt in her eyes, but she covered it quickly. "Of course I'm sure," she said firmly.

"Well, all right. When and where, Princess MagdaLena?"

"My, but aren't we agreeable!"

"I confess," he said, "I've surrendered—temporarily, at least." If only she knew just how temporary his agreeability would be.

"Meet me here at midnight," she whispered then walked away, and Han fought to keep from letting out a boisterous whoop.

Realizing he had much to do, Han began organizing in his mind and spent the following hours paying his debts at the pubs and talking with Erich. He said nothing about his plans, certain this was supposed to be confidential. And there were certain things that he and Erich had never quite agreed on and avoided talking about.

It was past ten when he arrived home to pack. With a combination of nerves and excitement, Han nearly went mad trying to think of what he needed.

"Han," his mother said, standing in the doorway of his bedroom while he threw a few clothes into a saddlebag, "what are you doing? I've only been home a day, and you're—"

"I'm going away for a little while, Mother," he said, grateful that she *had* come home from her aunt's funeral before he'd left. He would hate to think of leaving for so long without seeing her.

"Are you in trouble?"

"No," he laughed, "don't worry. I'm not in trouble. I'm just going away."

"How long? And where?" she asked in a panic.

"Oh, I don't know. A few months, maybe more. I just thought I'd wander a little. Have some fun."

"But what about your job?"

"I'll get a new one when I get back," he said easily.

Deciding he'd packed all he needed from the bedroom, he went downstairs, and Elsa followed close behind.

"Have we got any food I can take?"

"I suppose," she said while he rummaged through the kitchen, stuffing a few things into the saddlebag. "I know you're a man now, Han, and I know you've been discontent, but . . . still . . . isn't this all very sudden? I've always tried to be reasonable and let you find your way, but . . . help me understand."

"Mother," he said and took both her shoulders into his hands, "I can assure you that I'm not being impulsive, and I will always do my best to behave the way you've taught me to behave. But . . . I really do need to get away. Please . . . try to understand."

"I've already discussed it with him." Georg's voice startled them both. "I think it's fine."

Han smiled at his father. The only discussion they'd had was conveyed through the duke. Elsa remained silent, but her expression still wore the concern of a mother, and Han wondered if she would figure it out when both he and Maggie ended up missing.

"Hey," Han said, picking up one of the towels commonly used in the kitchen. "Can I have some of these?"

"What on earth do you want with those?" Elsa asked, wrinkling her nose as he pulled one tightly between both hands to test its strength.

Georg chuckled, and Han wondered if his father knew what he was thinking. "Let him take them," Georg said. "I'll get you some more if you need them." Han saw his mother look anxiously toward his father, who gave her a reassuring nod that seemed to silently put the matter to rest.

With everything Han needed packed neatly into his saddlebags, his mother having rearranged it all for him, Han kissed Elsa and hugged her tightly. His father walked with him toward the stables.

"Here," Georg said, handing him a folded sheet of paper, "I thought you could use this."

"What is it?" Han asked, taking it from him.

"A map." Georg lifted his brows subtly.

"Thank you," Han replied with a knowing smile.

"Han," Georg said in a familiar quiet voice, "I'm not unaware of your feelings for Maggie."

Han stopped walking and met his father's eyes in the moonlight. He was tempted to try and deny it, but his father's expression clearly expressed that it was pointless. Georg Heinrich was a perceptive man. There was no point in trying to pretend with him.

"That's the biggest reason I proposed this plan to His Grace the way I did. I know you'll want what's best for Maggie. While the stability of the country appears to be in jeopardy, it is equally important that you and Maggie are happy. I trust you will have the good judgment to know what's best on all counts. I hope you'll agree that it was the best possible option under the circumstances."

Han didn't know what to say. Impulsively he embraced his father, muttering simply, "Thank you. I won't let you down."

"I know," Georg said. They briefly gripped forearms, and then Han hurried on toward the stables. He almost saddled Pagan but opted for a horse that was not only more sturdy, as it would need to carry both of them for a good distance, but also wasn't so valuable that it couldn't be traded for other modes of transportation along the way if it became necessary.

With everything ready and the time drawing near, Han sat down in the stables to study the map. He was surprised to find a suggested route outlined by his father, as well as a note and a key tucked inside. Han chuckled to himself as he read it. With his mother's towels in his back pocket for handy retrieval, he waited for the princess to appear.

Chapter Five

A PRINCESS SCORNED

After dinner, Maggie felt the urge to give each of her parents a firm embrace, but knowing it could look suspicious, she refrained. She talked with Erich for a while but left when Han came in. He whispered to her as she passed by, "I'm looking forward to our midnight rendezvous, Your Royal On-the-Brink-of the-Best-Time-of-Your-Life."

Maggie gave him a scolding glare and went to her room. When Klara came in to help her dress for bed, Maggie asked, "Could you lay out something conservative for me to wear tomorrow, please?"

"I could do it in the morning, Miss," Klara replied.

"I'm certain I'll be going out before you get up," Maggie said. Klara nodded and went to the wardrobe. "While you're at it, put out two changes." Klara gave her a dubious glance. "So I can choose." Maggie smiled innocently.

With the clothes laid out, Klara took down Maggie's hair and brushed it through. After going through the necessary motions of preparing for bed, Klara left, and Maggie packed the simple clothing and a few personal items into a valise before dressing again and donning a cloak. She left a note on her bureau that simply said: *I'll be back. Love, Maggie.* Then she went with haste to the stables, knowing it was nearly midnight.

Han was waiting with a horse saddled and gave her the usual annoying greetings. Maggie was so caught up with excitement that she didn't bother to question the weighty saddlebags on the horse when he secured her valise there.

"Why aren't we taking Pagan?" she asked.

Han was proud of himself for his own nonchalance as he answered her. "This horse will hold both of us better." He smirked at her carelessly. "Are we ready, then?"

"Yes," she said, and he caught a fresh flush of color in her cheeks.

Maggie was distracted by a quivering sensation in her stomach as Han helped her mount and got behind her in the saddle. As he put his arms around her to hold the reins, a memory caught her off guard.

"Just like old times," he said, but she ignored him, not wanting to admit she'd had the same thought.

Han didn't want to count how many years had passed since he'd been this close to Maggie, but he liked it. Knowing they would be together for months, he couldn't hold back a chuckle.

"What are you sniggering for now?" she asked scornfully as they descended the hill from the castle.

"This is kind of fun, don't you think?"

"I suppose," she said. Keenly aware of being sandwiched between the pommel and Han's body, she felt certain it would be more fun if he were Nik. "Do you know where we're going?" she asked.

"Of course I know."

"Then why are we going this way?"

"I know a shortcut."

"But we don't need a shortcut. It's not that far."

"I know, but this way will be much more adventurous—I can assure you."

They rode in silence for several minutes, and Maggie began to feel uneasy. "Han, we should have been there before now. Are you certain you know what you're doing?"

"I know exactly what I'm doing," he said with a complacency that increased her uneasiness.

"Han! Nik is waiting for me. This is no time for games!"

"I'm not playing games," he said right behind her ear. "I'm quite serious."

"Serious about what?" she asked skeptically.

"About what I'm doing."

"What *are* you doing?" Maggie asked, her uneasiness turning to panic.

"I'm taking you for a ride."

"Han! Take me to Nik—now!"

"No," he replied calmly.

"Han!" Maggie retorted, trying to squirm away. But his arms tightened around her, and she could hardly move. "Have you gone mad? Let go of me!"

"You're the one who's gone mad. Did you really think I would safely deliver you into that bastard's hands?"

"He's not a—"

"That's strictly a matter of opinion."

Maggie tried to remain calm. Han had the horse at a full gallop, and he was holding her to his complete advantage. "So," she said haughtily, "if you had no intention of taking me to Nik, why didn't you just refuse to help me?"

"Because you would have found another way, and I'm not going to let him have you."

"Han! You have no right to—"

"I'm stronger than you are," he said, and Maggie could almost hear him smirk. She felt like tearing his eyes out. "And that is all the right I need at the moment."

"Take me home!" she demanded. If he wasn't going to help her elope, she wanted to go home.

"What? Now? After I've gotten you so conveniently away? Oh no, my love, we're not going home."

"I am not your love!" She tried squirming away again, but he'd caught her wrists into one of his hands, and she was completely helpless.

"Besides," he added as if discussing the weather, "your father would hang me if he discovered I had intentionally assisted in your eloping."

"Ooh!" she seethed, her anger kindling.

"If you'd hold still it would be a lot easier on both of us," he said calmly. "We've got a long ride yet, my love."

Like a splash of cold water on her face, Maggie fully realized what he was doing. Consumed with scorn and anger, she threw her weight back against his chest and twisted her hands from his grip. She managed to get the reins from him in the struggle and pulled the horse to an abrupt halt, jumping down and falling on her backside. But before she could get to her feet, he was on her like a lion, pinning her to the ground. She kicked and screamed and beat against him with her fists. She went for his face with her fingernails, but he caught her wrists again and laughed like he was having the time of his life.

Han had predicted such a reaction from her and was readily prepared. With extreme efficiency considering the ongoing struggle, Han pulled a towel from his back pocket and tied her wrists firmly together. Her anticipated protests ended abruptly when he used another towel for a gag, tying it at the back of her head. Her ranting continued, but he was satisfied with having it muffled enough that he could survive.

Maggie couldn't believe this was really happening. In all her wildest nightmares, she would have never conceived anything like this. *She hated Han Heinrich!* She didn't care what his motives were; she only knew she had to get away from him.

Maggie was completely appalled when he put a towel in her mouth. But when he put one over her eyes, she nearly went mad with fury. She fought with everything she had, but it didn't take long to figure out that it was a futile waste of energy.

Han was glad for all of his years working in the stables and the physical strength it had given him. Maggie's slight frame made it easy for him to pick her up much like a sack of grain and put her back on the horse, tying her bound wrists to the pommel. She squirmed and moaned for a few minutes, but when he mounted behind her and began to ride again, she became still. Han chuckled. He had the princess right where he wanted her.

Maggie's mind went wild with fear while it seemed that they rode forever. Her back ached up into her neck. Were she not so uncomfortable, she could have drifted to sleep from sheer exhaustion. Han said nothing as they rode, but she sensed a smug attitude about him nevertheless.

Hours passing forced Maggie to unwillingly relax, letting her back rest against Han's sturdy form until she realized what she'd done and sat up straight, chiding herself for allowing such close contact. She wondered where Nik was right now and what he might be thinking. The possibilities made her so angry that she kicked her heels into Han's shins. He only laughed, and she realized her kicking would have little effect through his bootlegs. But oh, how she hated him!

When they stopped at last, Maggie would have sighed audibly with relief had it not been for the towel in her mouth. She felt Han dismount and lead the horse for a moment. He untied her from the pommel but left her wrists bound as he lifted her off the horse and set her rather firmly on the ground.

"We're here, Your Royal Saddle-Soreness." He laughed as he pulled the towel from her eyes, and she did her best to express all of her fire and scorn in the glare she gave him.

"We're going to sleep now," he stated. Maggie glanced around to realize they were in a barn, which brought on muffled protests. "Yes, right here," he smiled, "in this very lowly place, my love." She moaned some more. "Obviously you've got a lot you'd like to say," he said sternly, "so I'll make you a deal. I'll take that thing out of your mouth if you'll promise to keep your voice down. If you don't," he smirked, but his voice held a threat that actually frightened her, "you'll be mute for a week. Do I make myself clear?"

Maggie nodded willfully, but she didn't cease to glare at him with all the hatred she felt. Han cautiously untied the towel from around her head.

"My father is going to kill you!" she said through clenched teeth, even though she heeded his threat to keep her voice quiet. Han just smirked, then he chuckled.

"It's not funny!" she insisted. "None of this is funny, Han Heinrich! How could you do this to me? You must take me home at once! I don't know why you're doing this, and I don't care. I just insist that you return me home at once. The longer you keep me away, the worse trouble you're going to be in, and I—"

Han placed his hand firmly over her mouth and held her face very close to his. "Shut up, Your Royal Run-Off-at-the-Mouth. I am not going to tolerate that kind of attitude, my love. I am not going to take you home. And I am most certainly going to think this is all very funny if I wish to. You can make the most of this and resign yourself to your fate, or you can make things difficult for me and spend the forthcoming span of your life in bondage."

"Just what is my fate?" she asked scornfully when he removed his hand.

"That's a secret for now." He grinned.

"I hate you, Han," she spat like venom.

"I suspected you might." He chuckled. "But that makes little difference to me at this point. Now, why don't you get some sleep? We've got a lot of riding left to do."

"Where are you taking me?" she gasped, still disbelieving of all this.

"That's a secret, too." He smiled carelessly. "That's why you're going to be blindfolded until we get there."

"So," she said, "you're just going to carry me off, and I'm supposed to go along cooperatively despite not having any idea what's going on."

"Very good, Your Royal Perceptiveness. Now let's stop talking and get some sleep."

"But I have to . . ." She hesitated with embarrassment.

Han pointed behind her. "There're some great bushes right out that door. But if I can't see you, I want to hear you."

Maggie scowled at him and hurried to relieve herself, telling him all the while how much she hated him. She was barely decent when he took her arm and escorted her back into the barn. Her mind frantically considered possible methods of escape until Han proved exactly how perceptive he was—or perhaps how well he knew her. "Getting away from me may seem like a nice thought." He grinned while tying her bound wrists to his belt with a short length of rope. "But it won't work."

She cast him one more glare of hatred then made herself as comfortable as possible in the soft straw and fell quickly asleep from complete exhaustion.

Cameron sat with Georg in his office, more staring out the window than accomplishing anything. It wasn't unusual for them to meet here and get some work done before breakfast, but no one else knew what he and Georg knew. He wanted to talk about the situation, but there was little to say that hadn't already been said. Just a little while earlier, Maggie's maid had frantically come to Cameron and Abbi's room in tears, holding the note that Maggie had left. Abbi had become as emotional as if she'd been informed of the death of a family member, and Cameron had felt helpless in any attempt to comfort her. He mostly felt grateful for Abbi's hunch the previous day and that he and Georg had acted on it quickly. Otherwise, his own grief would have undone him. This, combined with Erich's present condition—and the reasons for it—felt momentarily beyond his ability to bear.

Georg had suggested that they wait even a short while to tell their wives the truth—just long enough for the servants to observe their legitimate grief and worry. So Cameron had left his wife crying with the reassurance that he was going to do everything he could to make certain Maggie was all right. Thankfully, Georg had been waiting for him, and they were able to commiserate in silence. They had each already said that they hoped their children were all right and that their plan hadn't been foiled. Now they just had to carefully go through the motions of this plan that they had painstakingly discussed the previous evening.

The door coming open startled them both, but neither man was surprised to see Captain Dukerk. Very few people would dare enter the office without knocking or being announced. But it would have been about five minutes ago that the captain had arrived at his office, where he would have been immediately informed that the princess had run away from home in the night.

"This is a disaster!" Lance Dukerk bellowed with no preamble as he slammed the door closed behind him. "Forgive me, Cameron," he said in a voice that was only slightly more calm. With the personal relationship shared by these men, Lance often called Cameron by his given name when they were alone, but his doing so now seemed to indicate that he was gravely aware of how serious a matter they were dealing with. Even more softly he went on, "I can't even imagine how upset you must be to have Maggie do something like this, and your concern as a father must be . . . well, I cannot imagine. But it was not two days ago that I sat here and listened to *you* recount all the possible political repercussions of what might happen if Nik Koenig had *any* access to this family. And it's only logical that he is the reason Maggie is gone. We also have to consider the possible implications in regard to what's happened to Erich. I have to take every possible precaution. Please don't take my concerns as indifference toward your position as a father, but *my* position makes it mandatory for me to pursue them with all the manpower available—although they must be hours away from here by now."

Cameron turned to Georg once the captain had finished his declaration. He felt suddenly choked up as the father in him tried to imagine the possibilities of his little girl being subjected to Nik Koenig's evil ways. Even believing that she was safely in Han's care, he had to face the reality that she was gone, she was likely frightened, and he wouldn't see her for months. The possibilities of how things might turn out if Han failed made him sick to his stomach. He was grateful beyond words that Georg could read him so well, and he seemed to understand it was presently impossible to speak, but the captain needed his orders.

Georg turned to Lance and said with quiet gravity, "Yes, Captain, do everything you can. See to it and then come back here. We need to . . . discuss the possibilities."

Lance nodded then looked again at Cameron. "Are you all right?"

Cameron waved his arm through the air and fought back his temptation to cry the way Abbi had cried at the news. "Just . . . see to your orders, and . . . we'll talk."

"Very good," Lance said and left the room abruptly, again slamming the door on his way out. Captain Dukerk was known for his commanding presence and a keen ability to do his job well. He was also known for remaining controlled and calm, even in the most difficult situations. He obviously wasn't calm right now.

Once Cameron and Georg were again alone, Cameron said to his friend, "We have to tell him." They'd already decided their wives needed to know; neither of them were in marriages where secrets could be kept. But they had debated over whether or not the captain should be told the truth. They knew Lance could be trusted, and he needed to handle the situation accordingly.

"You know," Georg said, "I recall a time when he proved himself to be a very good actor. He certainly had *you* fooled. And Abbi. Nikolaus too, for that matter."

"Yes, you're right," Cameron admitted, even though he hated the memories. "And there is no man more trustworthy. He needs to know."

"But first I think we need to tell our wives. The longer we wait, the more furious they will become."

"Agreed," Cameron said and sighed loudly. "Ready whenever you are," he added, but neither of them moved. Cameron just turned again to look out the window, hoping and praying that his little girl was safe.

Elsa walked briskly up the stairs toward the duchess's rooms. She was far from chipper and felt certain this day would be no better than the previous night. An uneasiness had hung over her since Han had left. And she'd wrestled with her concerns through the night, wondering what he could be up to. It just didn't seem like him to be so frivolous, running off and leaving his job like that. Having worked as Abbi du Woernig's lady's maid for the better part of her life, they were more friends than anything. Even now that Elsa had retired and her work had been turned over to someone else, she spent a great deal of time with Abbi, and she knew she could talk to her friend about this. Knowing the duke was long to work by now, Elsa entered the duchess's bedroom without knocking and found her sitting on the bed crying.

"What is it, Abbi?" Elsa eased beside her and took her hand, setting her own concerns aside at the evidence that something was terribly wrong. She wondered if Erich had taken a turn for the worse.

"Oh, Elsa," Abbi said, "I hardly slept a wink. I was afraid she would do something like this, and I told Cameron to be prepared, but she . . . oh, Elsa!"

The duchess broke into fresh tears, handing Elsa a piece of paper as if it would explain. Elsa opened it and read: *I'll be back. Love, Maggie.*

"I don't understand," Elsa said quietly.

"Klara found it in her room this morning," Abbi cried. "She's run away . . . with Nik Koenig and . . . oh, if she only knew what she'd done! It's so awful, I . . ."

Again the duchess became lost in her tears, but Elsa felt something connecting in her mind that made Han's bizarre behavior of the previous evening seem a little too coincidental. Could he possibly be linked to such a thing?

"Abbi," Elsa said firmly, "I really don't know . . . if it's just a coincidence, but . . . Han left home last night and . . ."

Abbi's eyes shot up, and her tears ceased.

"The curious thing is," Elsa said carefully, "well . . . Georg seemed to know what was going on, but he wouldn't tell me. You did say you told His Grace that you suspected Maggie might . . ." She trailed off into silence, but their eyes met and they seemed to grasp at the same moment what the other was thinking.

"Come along, Elsa." Abbi moved toward the door with purpose. "We're going to have a little talk with our husbands. Something's going on, and I want to know what it is." Elsa followed the duchess down the stairs where she entered the duke's office without knocking. The women moved past the officers standing guard as if they weren't there, and Abbi slammed the door behind her, clearly not caring if the officers suspected any discord between the duke and duchess.

Cameron and Georg came to their feet, both silently astonished at the stern expressions of their wives. But something in both their eyes betrayed that they weren't at all surprised by their wives' appearance, nor their foul moods. Silence hung heavily in the room until Cameron turned to Georg, saying soberly, "I think we're in the doghouse, Georg."

"All right, Your Grace," Abbi said to her husband, "I want to know what is going on and I want to know now! I want an honest answer when you tell me why Han disappeared last night, as well."

"Um . . ." Cameron said but couldn't seem to get anything more out of his mouth. He turned helplessly toward Georg.

"Georg!" Elsa demanded, looking her husband in the eye. "You knew what Han was up to. If it's got something to do with this, you'd better speak up now."

Only silence answered.

"Georg Heinrich!" Elsa demanded. "Our children are gone, and we want to know why!"

"And we have every intention of telling you all we know," Georg said. "Just . . . sit down and try to be calm, and we'll . . ."

A knock at the door interrupted him, and a maid entered while an officer held the door for her.

"Message for you, Your Grace." She gave a slight curtsy.

"Thank you, Berta," Cameron replied and took the piece of paper she held out. The maid hurried to leave and the door was closed again. They all remained on their feet while Cameron read the note then handed it to Georg, who also read it, and the two men exchanged a slight smile, which provoked a harsh glare from each of the women.

"We're waiting," Abbi insisted.

"Well," Cameron cleared his throat, "you mentioned, of course, that you thought Maggie might run away and . . . well . . ." He looked expectantly toward Georg.

"Well," Georg continued, "we figured that not only was it a matter of Maggie's future, but of political security as well, and . . ."

"And we had to figure out something that we believed could not fail," Cameron stated. "Looking at the long-term perspective, we felt that—"

"Get to the point, Your Grace," Abbi insisted. Cameron continued to marvel at how she could so naturally put the ruler of Horstberg in his place. But he couldn't help smiling at her; it was one of many things he loved about her.

Cameron looked at Georg, then at his wife. "I hired Han to kidnap Maggie."

"You *what?*" Abbi's astonishment made her gasp and move unsteadily to a chair. Elsa followed her example and did the same.

"You see," Georg said gently, his eyes moving back and forth between Abbi and his own wife, "if Han can keep Maggie away from here for a—"

"But, Cameron," Abbi interrupted, "what about her reputation? Han is a wonderful boy, but—"

"Abbi," Cameron replied, taking a chair close to Abbi so that he could hold her hand, "I told him to marry her."

Abbi was so stunned she couldn't speak. She took in her husband's announcement, at first shocked and then remarkably relieved. She exchanged a long gaze with Elsa, who was equally stunned, then they both glared at their husbands, perhaps to make certain this wasn't some kind of joke. With the severity of Cameron and Georg's expressions, Abbi turned again to look at Elsa. While they needed to share a long conversation about all of this and its enormous implications, Abbi felt relatively certain that Elsa would feel as pleased about this as she did. With all that they had shared, having their children marry seemed appropriate. They both knew that Han and Maggie had once cared for each other deeply and had speculated over marriage at some later date. And then something had changed in Maggie that had left them all confused—and disappointed. Abbi couldn't begin to imagine what Cameron might have said to Han, or how all of this had come together, but she felt deeply comforted to think of Maggie in Han's care. In fact, she couldn't think of anyone more capable of handling her very stubborn and difficult daughter.

Without a word spoken, Abbi sensed Cameron's relief at seeing acceptance over his decision in her eyes. If she was feeling anything else, he would have known just by looking at her. She felt good about what Cameron and Georg had done. It was easy to see their reasoning, and it made perfect sense. She could also see that Elsa felt the same, and with mutual relief, they both started to laugh.

"I think we're out of the doghouse now," Georg said to the duke.

Cameron explained the details of all he'd instructed Han to do, and he implored the ladies that they must continue to appear upset and concerned over their children's disappearance, as if they knew nothing of what had really taken place.

"I would assume," Cameron said, "with Maggie leaving the note that she must have been attempting to run away with Koenig last night. But at best, I would like it to appear that Han and Maggie eloped."

"What if Han didn't succeed?" Abbi asked, feeling a surge of panic at the thought.

Cameron handed her the message he'd just received. She read it and looked up at him in question.

"That just came from Nik Koenig," Cameron stated. "If he's requesting to see Maggie, then she must not be with him."

Complacent smiles bounced around the room before Abbi and Elsa left their husbands to their work. Abbi squeezed Elsa's hand the moment they were in the hall, and they both wore appropriate masks of worry and concern until they were beyond the view of the officers stationed in the hall.

"I cannot imagine," Abbi said to Elsa as they walked up the stairs, "what Maggie must be thinking. She's probably furious."

"No doubt," Elsa said with a quiet laugh of relief. "Do you think Han can handle her?"

"If anyone can handle her," Abbi laughed and heaved her own sigh of relief, "it's Han."

Cameron and Georg walked across the courtyard toward the keep where the captain's office was located. They entered to find him leaning over a map and quietly talking to two lieutenants.

"Your Grace," one of the lieutenants said, and they all came to some form of attention.

"At ease, gentlemen," Cameron said, and the men relaxed a little. "Could you give us some privacy with the captain, please," he added. As always, his word was heeded without hesitation, and the two lieutenants hurried from the room, one of them closing the door. "Sit down," Cameron said to Captain Dukerk. "We need to talk."

"Has something happened?" Lance asked, alarmed.

Cameron and Georg also sat down before Georg slid a piece of paper across the desk. Lance picked up the message from Nik Koenig and read it, his brow furrowing. "I don't understand."

"If Koenig is looking for Maggie," Cameron said, "then he is not *with* Maggie."

Lance's brow furrowed more tightly as if he were trying to figure out the implications. While he was still thinking, Georg said, "I know you're a good actor, Captain. You once helped save this country by pretending that something was completely different than you knew it to be. We need you to use those same skills now."

Lance's face relaxed slightly, but he still looked puzzled. "I'm listening," he said.

Georg continued, "Han left the country last night, as well."

Lance's eyes widened. "That cannot *possibly* be a coincidence! Do you think she's safe? Can we assume that he knew Maggie's plans or—"

"Lance," Cameron leaned forward, grateful for the decades of perfect trust they shared, "what I am about to tell you cannot be repeated to anyone beyond the three of us. Our wives know, but only for their peace of mind as mothers, and they are sworn to secrecy."

"I'm listening," Lance repeated, his voice more deep.

"I hired Han to kidnap Maggie and keep her away from here for at least six months."

Lance took in a sharp breath and leaned back in his chair. "Well, I'll be damned." Lance chuckled. "I have never heard of anything so ludicrous—or brilliant—in my life."

"It can't be any more ludicrous than your pretending to be betrothed to Abbi so that I could steal back my country."

"I don't know." Lance chuckled and shook his head. "It's pretty close." He shook his head again, as if he were trying to fit the pieces together in his mind. "So . . . you knew she was going to run away?"

"Abbi had a hunch," Cameron said. "And you know we do *not* ignore Abbi's hunches."

"No, we do not!" Lance said, mocking absolute terror. Given that he was as close a friend to Abbi as Georg, the gesture made the other men laugh.

"So," Georg said with a tone of declaration, "we have to assume that Han has succeeded in getting her far enough away that Nik couldn't find her, and Han knew that officers would pursue him once they were informed. You obviously have to do your job and have your men continue searching, but I believe that after twenty-four hours, it's a fair decision for the captain to declare that any further searching would be a waste of manpower, and she has likely run away with Han. We are going to treat this as if we assume that Maggie ran away with Han to elope."

"Elope?" Lance echoed.

"I . . . encouraged it," Cameron said. "Better for their reputations that way, and . . . he's a fine young man. Not so long ago, she was willing to have me arrange a marriage for her. Now I've arranged this one. With any luck, she'll forgive me some day."

Lance sighed and seemed to still be taking in this new information. A minute later, he said, "In the meantime, I intend to discreetly have officers keeping an eye on Mr. Koenig. I don't trust him."

"None of us do," Georg said. "But I think we'd all rather have him *here* as opposed to out looking for Maggie."

"Yes," Cameron said with a worried sigh. "We can hope for that."

Nik Koenig waited at the rendezvous point until almost dawn, then he went home to get some sleep, completely infuriated with the way his plan had been foiled. He was certain that for whatever reason Maggie hadn't shown up, it was not of her own doing, and he nearly went mad with fury.

Early afternoon, he finally sent a message to the castle, and it came back with a reply from the duke saying: *The princess is not available.* He sent another the following morning, which was left unanswered completely. At last, he made up his mind to go to the castle. If nothing else, he might be able to bribe some gossip out of the servants and at least get a clue as to what might have happened.

After getting past the officers in the courtyard, he was met at the main entrance by a young maid, and he could tell immediately this was going to be easier than he'd hoped.

"Could you tell me," he asked, discreetly slipping a fair amount of money into her hand, "how I might see the Princess Maggie?"

The maid looked at first skeptical, but Nik gave her a winsome smile, leaning casually against the doorframe, and she seemed taken with his charm. Few women weren't, and he'd learned to spot those kinds very quickly.

"Oh, sir," she said, "I'd love to help you, but she's not available right now."

"Why not?" he asked easily, showing a spark of interest in his eyes that he hoped she would interpret as something beyond his curiosity about the princess, something more personal.

"Well, sir, everybody knows. Surely you must have heard. She's run away from home."

"Run away?" He lifted his brows and actually felt afraid, wondering what might have happened to her between leaving the castle and making it to their meeting place. "Do you know anything else?"

"Where have you been, sir? Surely the whole valley knows by now." He didn't bother explaining why he and his mother had hardly left their home since his failed attempt to leave the country with Maggie. Instead, he just listened, and she went on. "Young Han from the stables is gone too. The duke fears that they've eloped. He's sent out an alert, and officers have been searchin' for them, but my belief is that they're long gone by now. That Han's a clever one."

"Do you have any idea where they might have gone?" Nik asked, trying to conceal his fuming anger. He wouldn't be surprised if the duke was somehow behind this.

"Why, sir, if I knew that I'd be sittin' pretty. With the reward His Grace is offerin' for her safe return, I'd not be standin' here talkin' to you."

Nik left without further comment. Consumed with more

rage than he'd ever possessed, he made up his mind—one way or another—that he was going to find her. At all costs, Maggie would be his.

Erich squinted toward the light shining through his window and wondered how long he'd been lying in this bed. He'd never hurt so badly in his life, never been so weak. He felt a hand slip into his and turned his head, focusing on his mother. She was rarely not here, but as she frantically wiped tears from her face, he knew she hadn't expected him to be awake.

"What is it, Mother?" he asked, squeezing her hand gently.

"Oh," she laughed softly, "we've just been terribly worried about you. You've had a fever. But the worst is past. Doctor Furhelm says you'll be fine."

"That's a relief." He managed a smile. "How long have I been here?"

"Three days."

"Whoa. Has Han been here? I need to have him take care of—" He stopped at his mother's obvious distress. "What?" he insisted.

"Han is gone, Erich. He left here the night after you were shot."

"Gone?"

Abbi wondered how much to say. While she couldn't leave Erich to worry and wonder, she knew she had to be careful. "You're his best friend. We were hoping he'd told you something of his plans."

"He didn't say a word. Are you trying to tell me he just . . . *left?* Did he say anything to anybody?"

"Very little."

Erich shook his head, not wanting to admit how uneasy he felt at thinking of his best friend just leaving here without a word. He looked to his mother, seeing something more in her eyes. "What else?" he asked.

"I would swear you can read my mind," she said.

"My father tells me I inherited that from you."

Abbi smiled timidly and looked away.

"What is it, Mother? What's wrong?"

"It's Maggie. She's . . ."

"What?" he demanded when she faltered. He tried to sit up and groaned from the pain. "What's happened? Where is she?"

"Calm down, Erich." She urged him back to the pillow. "I'm not going to tell you if you don't promise to stay calm."

"Where is she?" he asked more quietly.

"We don't know, Erich. She left a note that said she would be back. Nothing more. We suspected that she was planning to run away with Nik Koenig and marry him, but—"

"What?" Erich shouted and leaned forward. "How could she be so *stupid*? Someone's got to go find her. You can't just—"

"Calm down, Erich," Abbi insisted. "She's not with Nik. He's been here looking for her."

"Then where is she?" he shouted again. His ordeal had not damaged his vocal cords.

"As I said, we don't know exactly where she is, Erich." Fresh tears trickled down her face. "But our hope is that she's with Han."

Erich's heart quickened as he attempted to put the pieces together in his mind. It seemed so out of character for both Han *and* Maggie that he could hardly comprehend what might be going on.

Abbi leaned closer and lowered her voice to a whisper. "Erich, we have reason to believe that Han's intention was to keep Maggie away from Nik Koenig. If that's the case, his motives are surely honorable. He's a good man; we all know that. But . . . if that's the case . . . they may be gone a while. However, we must not say anything to anyone. You understand."

Erich nodded. Lying here with a bullet hole in his shoulder, he understood all too well the precariousness of having personal matters tied into politics. While his mother's explanation made some degree of sense, he still found it difficult to comprehend Han and Maggie together at all—for any reason. Their involvement as teens had ended with bitter feelings, and the years since had made it evident they could hardly tolerate each other. There were facets of this that concerned him deeply, but there was one thought that made him chuckle.

"Is something funny?" Abbi asked, grateful that he had calmed down.

"If your assumptions are correct, do you think Han will come back in one piece?"

Abbi smiled. "Now, Erich, is that any way to talk about your sister?"

"I love my sister dearly, Mother, but admit it, Maggie is a shrew. That girl is hellfire and brimstone personified."

"Oh, it's not as bad as all that," she argued.

"No, not usually. But if Han's trying to keep her away from Nik Koenig against her will, I'd wager money it's almost as bad as that."

Abbi tried to smile, but tears came again. Erich touched her face and said gently, "You're worried."

She nodded. "And I miss her."

"If she *is* with Han, he'll take good care of her."

"I know."

Erich managed to appease his mother's concerns, but after she'd left him alone to rest, he had trouble appeasing his own. He would trust Han with his life any day of the week, but thinking through the possibilities, he wondered if he trusted Han with his sister. He felt certain Han would never do anything to hurt any woman, but Han's relationship with Maggie was something he'd never been comfortable with. Under the present circumstances, he wondered why Han would go to so much trouble to keep her away from Nik. Were his loyalties to Horstberg so deep? Or was there more?

When the unanswered questions began to make his head ache, Erich tried to force himself not to think about it. But it didn't take long to realize the obvious. He missed them. It was difficult to comprehend even getting through the week without either one of them. And he wondered how long before they would return.

Abbi was dabbing oil onto a nearly blank canvas, trying not to worry about Maggie, when Sonia came into the room. Just as with Erich, Sonia had been told that they hoped Maggie was with Han, since they had both disappeared the same night. But neither of them had been told that their father had actually asked Han to take Maggie and keep her away from Horstberg.

"Are you all right?" Abbi asked, noting her obvious distress.

"I've been thinking about Maggie," Sonia said quietly, sitting down nearby. "You know, Mother, she and I were always so different, and I never could quite understand her, but . . . well, like for instance, I could never understand why she spurned Han the way she did and treated him so badly. He was always good to her. And why—now—would Han be involved in this? Surely he can't still care for her after the way she's belittled him all these years!"

Abbi sighed, wishing she could tell Sonia the full truth, but just as with many things pertaining to Horstberg, her children's ignorance was for their protection. At times the line between political matters and family loyalties became too fine.

"You know, Sonia, it's difficult to know why people behave the way they do. I believe we are all born with our personalities, and then the circumstances we grow up in help shape those character traits. And many times the combination isn't good. For some reason, being a princess did not suit Maggie's personality well at all."

"Or perhaps a little too well," Sonia suggested. "It got so she could be nothing *but* a princess."

Abbi nodded in agreement and became lost in thought, wondering what had happened to the free-spirited little girl Maggie had once been.

"Mother," Sonia said with a severe tone, and Abbi looked up abruptly, "I've been thinking a lot about this since Maggie left . . . about the way she behaves, and how she seems . . . so *unhappy,* and . . . well, I remembered something that was rather disturbing. The more I thought about it, the more I wondered if it's affected the way Maggie feels about herself."

"What?" Abbi asked, her heart quickening.

"Do you remember that nanny you fired . . . when you discovered she was rather prone to excessive drinking on the sly?"

"Yes," Abbi said. Already she didn't like this. "What was her name? I don't remember . . ."

"Helga."

"Ah, yes," Abbi nodded. "Helga. I remember how sick I felt when I found out, wondering if she'd mistreated you, or—"

"Maggie and I were almost always together with her. I'm quite certain that nothing horrible ever happened. It's just that . . . she always treated Maggie . . . *differently.*"

"How so?" Abbi asked pointedly.

"I remember seeing her whisper things in Maggie's ear, and the way Maggie would glare at her when she did, as if it made her angry . . . whatever it was. She was usually quite kind with me, but often when she'd speak to Maggie, she would be brash and snippy. I know Maggie was more prone to speak her mind and talk back to her. But it was as if the nanny didn't like Maggie for that reason, and she treated her very badly."

Abbi became lost in thought again as a smoldering sickness rose inside her. She'd avoided leaving her children with nannies and governesses as much as possible, but there were times when her obligations had made it necessary. And Helga had always been proper and perfectly respectable in Abbi's presence. The very idea that someone would mistreat her children made her so angry, she could almost scream. She had to wonder now as she looked at the difficulties Maggie had in trusting her feelings and having confidence in herself, if some of it didn't stem from Helga's mistreatment.

"Once Helga was dismissed," Sonia continued, "I never really thought much about it. But one time I mentioned it to Maggie. I asked her if she remembered Helga. Maggie refused to talk about it, and she got so angry I was shocked. I never brought it up again. And that was years ago. But while I was thinking about what Maggie's done now, trying to understand it, I couldn't get that out of my mind. Do you think the way Helga treated Maggie has something to do with the way Maggie treats herself and those around her?"

Tears brimmed in Abbi's eyes. "It very well might, sweetheart." She was astounded by Sonia's insight and deeply concerned for whatever Maggie might have buried inside herself. "We may never know. I only hope that she can find a way to be happy—whatever happens."

Chapter Six

MADNESS

Days dragged incessantly for Maggie with the same routine repeated with such exactness that she had come to predict their schedule. She had no idea where they were going since she had mostly been kept blindfolded. And when she wasn't, she saw no recognizable landmarks. Han stuck to back roads and stayed completely away from civilization. But of course he would; he was a fugitive now. He'd kidnapped a princess. She chose not to speculate over his reason for doing this. She only knew she hated every minute of it. And when she thought of Nik Koenig, she felt downright ill.

Han was continually smug and sarcastic and left her tied to him constantly, except for brief moments of necessity, and even then he wasn't far enough away to give her any opportunity for escape. Not that she hadn't tried. Maggie had fought with everything she had to get away from him. But he always managed to predict her ploys, and his advantage of height and strength left her helpless.

As her weariness from the journey increased, Maggie gradually gave up on her futile attempts to get away. Han always used her defeats to his advantage, treating her all the more smugly for having outdone her. She wasn't about to let him live in peace however, and she continually threatened him with what her father was going to do when he caught up with them. And she never let him forget how much she hated him.

During rare moments when she wasn't obsessed with her hatred for Han, Maggie wondered what Nik was doing now. She missed him dreadfully and hoped with all her heart that he would somehow find them and rescue her from this nightmare.

They slept mostly in barns at first and ate little more than bread and cheese and jerked meat. But one night, Han opted to stay in a secluded spot in the forest and sleep beneath the stars. As usual, Maggie was full of protests, but Han ignored them with good humor.

Another change came in their routine when Han left her tied to a tree for what seemed hours. She fell asleep while he was gone and woke up in response to the smell of something cooking. She opened her eyes and sat up abruptly. The forest was dark except for a small fire next to which Han was kneeling, turning a makeshift spit over the flames with some kind of meat on it.

"You lucky princess, you." He smiled when he saw that she was awake. "You get gourmet tonight."

Maggie said nothing as he cut away some meat and gave it to her. She was extremely hungry, but only stared blankly at it while he went ahead and ate. Finally he said, "Well, go on, eat it."

"What is it?" she asked skeptically.

Han smiled, thoroughly loving this moment. "It's edible," was all he said, opting to not tell her. He knew she had eaten the same hundreds of times in her life, but it was more fun this way.

"What is it?" she repeated.

"It's good! Taste some."

"Not until you tell me what it is."

"Listen to me, Maggie, my love," he said with no hint of anger, "that is what you get for supper. You can eat it or you can starve. And I will not feel sorry for you tomorrow if you tell me you're hungry or too weak to ride."

Maggie gave him her usual scornful glare, then hesitantly began to eat. Han had to chuckle when she managed to eat more than he did. At least she had a healthy appetite.

When their semblance of a meal was done, he sat down with a well-worn map, just as he had many times, and studied it carefully.

"Won't you ever tell me where we're going?" she asked.

"When we get there," he said without looking at her, "I'll let you know that we've arrived."

Maggie wanted to tell him how much she hated him, but she had learned from experience that doing so would never accomplish anything in her favor. She attempted to get comfortable enough to go to sleep, thinking how grateful she would be for a bed—any bed.

The monotonous routine continued on the same, except one morning when Han woke her very early and tied the towel around her mouth before she could make a sound. She saw a pistol tucked into the front of his breeches and wondered where he'd been hiding *that* before now. She realized someone was coming into the barn where they'd been hiding. Han muttered a few curses under his breath while throwing her onto the horse, then he rode carefully and quickly out the other side of the barn, and nothing else transpired. But the incident got Maggie's mind churning. One of these days, they would have to come in contact with people for one reason or another. And it would take little effort to let someone see that she was in trouble, and she would be able to get some help. She became obsessed with plots of escape—something really good that would work despite Han's craftiness. If it took her the rest of her life, Maggie was determined to find a way to be free of Han Heinrich.

"Welcome home, Maggie, my love," Han said, and her head shot up. She felt him dismount the horse and realized she must have drifted to sleep.

"I'm not your love!"

"Not yet," he grinned, and the words haunted her in ways she refused to even think about.

"Where are we?" she asked while he untied her wrists and helped her down, and she noticed they were in a small stable.

"I told you, we're home."

"Hardly."

"Temporarily anyway. No more riding for a while."

"That's a relief," she said with some sarcasm. A change in the routine sounded nice, but having no idea what to expect left her unnerved. Once the horse was cared for, he flung his saddlebags over his shoulder.

"Come on." He took her arm in one hand and her valise in the other, leading her firmly outside. Despite it being dark, Maggie could see a small cottage situated among the trees. Otherwise, all she could see was trees. They were in the forest. That didn't tell her anything; they'd mostly been in the forest since they'd left Horstberg.

"Whose place is this?" she asked when he turned a key in the lock and pushed the door open.

"It's mine," he said, dropping the bags to the floor. "No more trespassing."

She didn't believe him but didn't want to pursue it, so she changed the subject while he searched for a lamp without letting go of her arm. "How long have we been gone?"

"A week," he said, "give or take a little."

Maggie groaned, and he chuckled as he always did at her indications of misery. When the lamp shed light over the room, they both turned to survey their surroundings. They were standing in a small common room with kitchen facilities at one end and a parlor area with a large fireplace at the other. In the center was a narrow, enclosed staircase that ascended to the second floor. As if he had read her mind, Han started up the stairs to investigate. There was only one bedroom with a large four-poster bed, a nice bureau, and a big bathtub. Other than the furniture looking a little dusty, she doubted it had been too terribly long since this place had been lived in. But her thoughts were centered on that tub.

"Oh," she said, "a bath. The first thing I'm going to do is take a bath."

"Tomorrow," he said. "It's late and we should get some sleep. We came a long way today."

"Don't I know it!" she groaned, and he smiled.

Han untied her wrists, which he did very rarely. "Is the warden going to give me some freedom?" she demanded with a snideness that he paid no attention to.

"You'll get freedom when you've proven you deserve it," he said soberly, but she ignored the comment and sat on the edge of the bed to test it.

"Not bad," she said. "Where are *you* going to sleep?"

"I'm going to sleep in that bed," he said with no expression.

"No, Han," she said adamantly, "*I* am going to sleep in this bed."

"I didn't say you couldn't sleep in that bed."

"But it's the only bed we've got!" She was appalled at his implication.

"There's plenty of room," he said, motioning elaborately toward the bed with his hand.

"Han!"

"You've been sleeping tied to me for a week now. Barns or beds—I don't see much difference."

With no further comment, Han left her alone in the bedroom with her bag. For the first time since this escapade had begun, Maggie changed into a nightgown to sleep, longing for that much-needed bath. When she heard him coming up the stairs, Maggie got quickly into the bed. Relishing in the comfort, she pulled the covers up to her chin.

Han grinned at her when he entered the room and sat down to remove his boots and stockings. Maggie looked fearful when he began unbuttoning his shirt, but he assured her he'd not embarrass her and left his breeches on.

"Aren't you going to tie me up?" she asked with sarcasm, but he only grinned and pulled a key out of his pocket. He locked the bedroom door from the inside and elaborately tucked the key into a pocket in the front of his breeches. Han laughed as if he'd thought of a joke, but Maggie didn't see any humor in the situation at all. Actually being alone with him in a locked bedroom, she became fearful over what his intentions might really be. She hadn't allowed herself to give the idea much thought before now. She had been too obsessed with trying to think of ways to escape and counting the ways she hated him. As he extinguished the lamp, Maggie's mind went wild, imagining what her fate would be now. She heard him fumbling with something in the dark and kept waiting for him to do as he'd threatened and get into the bed beside her. Then he became silent, and she realized that he'd made a makeshift bed on the floor with some extra blankets and a pillow. She couldn't deny her relief, but this gesture of apparent respect seemed to contradict his previous attitude, and she felt confused.

Long after Han began snoring softly, Maggie lay gazing at the ceiling, wondering what kind of perverse plans he had in mind for her. Now that they had apparently arrived at their destination, she felt certain the circumstances would change. She knew he hated her. Ever since she'd brought an end to the ridiculous puppy love they'd shared as children, Han Heinrich had treated her terribly. Had she hurt him far worse than she'd ever comprehended? Did he have some deep-rooted resentment against her that he was seeking revenge for?

Whatever the reasons, she felt certain that she would not leave this place unscathed.

Maggie woke up alone with daylight filling the room. Noting that the door was unlocked, she hurried to get dressed and went downstairs to find Han eating breakfast.

"You'd better eat and take your bath," he said, pointing to a plate of food left for her. "I've got to go into town and get some supplies."

"Can I go with you?" she asked.

"No."

"Then you will no doubt leave me tied up."

"Very perceptive," he grinned, "Your Royal Intelligence."

Maggie made a snarling noise toward him that made him chuckle. But the hunger growling in her stomach drew her full attention to the food which actually tasted impressively good. The moment she had the last bite into her mouth, Han handed her a bucket.

"What's this for?"

"If you're going to take a bath, you're going to need some water."

"But, Han I . . ." She had never prepared a bath in her entire life. She didn't even know what to do. What she wouldn't give to have Klara here now!

"If you would prefer," he said, "there's a nice pond not far from here. I tried it out early this morning."

"But wasn't it cold?"

"Of course it was cold." He grinned. "That's what made it so invigorating," he added with overstated exhilaration.

The decision wasn't easy, but Maggie opted for the choice that would leave Han with the least opportunity to criticize her. Since she was wearing the clothes she'd had on last night—for days, in fact—she took a change of clothes and some soap and shampoo with her and set out toward the pond.

When Han followed her, she said, "Where do you think you're going?"

"I'm not letting you out of my sight."

"How on earth am I supposed to bathe while you're watching me?"

"I won't look when I could get embarrassed." He smirked.

She didn't retort, but she seriously doubted anything would embarrass him.

Han leaned against a tree, and she insisted he cover his eyes with both hands while she undressed and got in the water.

"All right," he said, "but I want you to keep talking so I know you're still there."

"Fine! Let me tell you what I think of you," she said while removing her clothes that were so soiled, if she had brought more than two other changes with her, she'd have thrown them away. "You," she said emphatically, "are a scoundrel! You're the worst kind of rogue! You're a louse!" She fought to keep her voice steady so that he wouldn't know how the coldness of the water was affecting her; still, it felt refreshing, and she was grateful. "You're a wretched man who steals innocent women away from their homes and drags them around the country in bonds. But one of these days you are going to pay for all of this. My father is going to kill you, if I don't first."

"Threats. Threats." He shook his head with his eyes still covered. When Maggie was in the water and it was unlikely he could see anything as long as she remained submerged, she stopped talking. As expected, Han removed his hands to be certain she was there.

"See," she said, "I didn't run away."

Maggie was silent as she bathed, doing her best to ignore Han, who watched her far more closely than he'd have needed to. She noticed the pistol tucked into his breeches and realized she'd not seen it for a couple of days. While it was difficult to imagine him using it on her, she couldn't help feeling unnerved by its presence.

Han found himself more fascinated with Maggie than ever before. As the sweat and dust of traveling gradually washed away from her skin and hair, he thought she looked more beautiful than he'd ever seen her. He felt a certain amount of satisfaction recalling his final quest in all of this. It was only a matter of time before Maggie was his, completely and irrevocably.

"I'm finished, Han," she called to him. "Close your eyes."

He covered them while she repeated word for word the speech she'd given before. He opened them to see her dressed in a simple dark skirt and white blouse, wringing the water out of her hair.

"Why don't you point that gun at me?" she asked while he watched her obtrusively.

"Do you think I should?" he asked.

"You're not only a kidnapper, you're an *armed* kidnapper."

"Does that frighten you?"

"Do you think it should?" she retorted.

Han smiled. "Not to worry, my love. The gun is only to protect you."

"Protect me?" She laughed. "The only thing I need protection from is *you.*"

She started back toward the cottage, and Han silently followed. Maggie noticed that in daylight the place looked rather quaint with its thatched roof and brightly painted shutters. Despite its small size, it was much better than a barn.

After Maggie had a reasonable amount of time to brush through her hair, Han came into the bedroom and said rather arrogantly, "Now that you are your old beautiful self, you need to make up the bed and wash the dishes. And the place could use a little dusting."

"Han! I will not do—"

"It's just you and me," he interrupted firmly, "Your Royal Spoiled-Rottenness. And you are going to do your share around here. I've got to get supplies, but I'm not leaving until this place is cleaned up. And if I don't have time to get them today, you're not going to have anything to eat tonight."

Han left the room and closed the door. Maggie threw her hairbrush at it, which did little to ease her anger. After pouting a few minutes, she reminded herself that Han had proven he did not make idle threats. Begrudgingly, she made the bed up the best she could and went downstairs. While Han cleaned the floor and stacked freshly chopped wood by the fireplace and cooking stove, she cleaned the dishes and washed her dirty clothes and hung them outside to dry.

Han was careful to never let Maggie out of his sight long enough for her to try something foolish, but he did his best to be silently pleasant while she went about her chores. He smiled to himself more than once as he observed her efforts. He knew he could have done a better job at the housework, but she'd never had to do it before. He felt certain that by the time they left here, she'd be plenty efficient at menial tasks.

Maggie wondered again about the cottage and who owned it. But knowing that Han likely wouldn't tell her even if she asked, she just remained quiet until all the work was done and he announced that he was leaving. When he asked her to go upstairs, she refused, certain he was going to tie her up. Without a word, he picked her up and threw her over his shoulder, carrying her to the bedroom while she beat her fists against his back and screamed at him. Setting her firmly on the bed, Han tied her wrists to the bedpost with soft towels, gagged her, and left, locking the bedroom door from the outside. She couldn't believe he would be so odious! But given his behavior since this nightmare had begun, she concluded that perhaps she should simply accept just how odious he could be.

Maggie managed to lie down comfortably on the bed, but it seemed that Han was gone forever. At first Maggie thought about Nik, longing as always for him to rescue her from this. She wanted to be in his arms and feel him kiss her. Oh, how she missed that! Then she thought of her home and family, and for the first time since this ordeal had begun, Maggie cried. She had wanted to cry many times, but she'd never been out of Han's sight long enough to do so privately, and she refused to let him see her in tears.

Maggie cried long and hard in an effort to release all of her pent-up emotion and stress, wondering what was to become of her now. When she heard Han return, she hurriedly pulled her face down to the towels that bound her hands and wiped the tears away. She could only imagine how he would mock her to know that she'd been crying like a baby.

Han came upstairs and silently untied her. She gave him a scornful glare, but he ignored it and said, "Come on. You can help me unload this stuff."

Maggie followed him downstairs and was surprised to see several boxes of food in the kitchen. She recalled seeing a wagon next to the little stable, which was the only way he could have possibly transported so much.

"How long are we staying?" she gasped.

"Long enough," he smiled carelessly, but she became filled with dread.

"When are you going to let me in on your big secrets?" she said as they worked, trying not to sound concerned.

"Do you think you're ready to hear them?" he smiled at her as if they were exchanging small talk back in the stables at Castle Horstberg.

"Of course I am!" she insisted, aching for any information that might help her understand why he had chosen to do something so ludicrous.

"Well," he said, "if you're a good girl, I'll tell you after supper. Do you have even the vaguest idea how to cook?"

"No," she said.

"You're about to learn. We're not eating bread and cheese and poached game anymore."

"You mean *you* know how to cook?"

"I didn't hear any complaints about your breakfast." He smirked. "I can cook."

"Then why don't you just do it and forego the lessons?"

"It's the principle of the thing," he said. "I'm not going to have people say Han Heinrich can cook, but his wife doesn't."

Maggie dropped the can she was holding, and it landed on her foot. "You *what?*" she shrieked, the pain in her toes emphasizing her words.

"Oops," he said with a broad, conspiratorial grin, "I let it slip out, and we haven't even had supper yet."

"You must be mad!" she said, so shocked that she couldn't comprehend her own anger.

"Yes," he said, "I believe I am. A man could be no less than mad to take on someone like you. But I've made up my mind to it, and I'm not about to let you go now."

Maggie was stunned beyond belief. She couldn't believe it. "Well, let me tell you something, Han Heinrich," she shouted. "You've got a surprise in store. I will not ever—ever—*ever* be your wife. You can just pack away your perverse ideas and take me home! If that's what this is all about, you can forget it!"

"Why?" he asked simply, as if it were a completely reasonable question and he couldn't understand why there would be a problem.

"*Why?*" she echoed. "It's totally preposterous. It's ridiculous. You and I?" She chuckled satirically, but he remained severe. "Really, Han."

"I want to know why it's so preposterous." He put his hands on his hips, unaffected by her anger.

"You don't know?" She was appalled. "Han, I'm the duke's daughter, and you're just . . ." She stopped when she saw the way he pressed his lips together firmly and a blatant intensity came into his green eyes.

"I'm a what, Maggie? Tell me what I am."

She remained silent, mostly due to her fear of his reaction. He'd never actually hurt her, but she didn't like that look in his eyes at all.

"There was a time when you were obsessed with wanting to marry me, Maggie," he said, sounding more calm than he looked. "You talked of little else."

"That was a long time ago, Han. Things change."

"Yes, they certainly do," he said with cynicism. "You neatly justified it all away by slapping me in the face with the declaration that you would never marry beneath you. But you were willing to marry Nik Koenig."

"He's my cousin," she replied emphatically, and Han's cool exterior faded.

"You didn't know that when you called off the betrothal! He's a bastard! That's what he is!"

"He is not!"

"That's strictly a—"

"Matter of opinion," she finished for him with intense sarcasm.

"You're better off without him, Maggie," Han said, visibly trying to remain calm. "And one day I'm going to make you realize that."

"Are you trying to tell me," she said, "that all of this has been for the single purpose of trying to get me to marry you?"

"That's the only reason I'll admit to," he said.

"Have you ever thought of proposing like a normal person?"

He let out a scoffing laugh. "I have no doubt what the results of *that* would have been. Besides, you were ready to run away with Nik Koenig. I had to take drastic measures."

"It will never happen." She turned away abruptly and returned to her work, if only to keep herself from trying to strangle him.

"We'll see."

"Doesn't it make any difference to you that I'm in love with another man?"

"No."

"Why not?"

"Because I believe you don't know Nik Koenig well enough to know the true nature of his character, and how can you love someone under such circumstances? As I see it, you're choosing to ignore what love really is. My belief is you've not yet discovered the full depth of it—and I know you won't find it with somebody like Nik Koenig."

"And I suppose you're certain I'll discover it here . . . with you?"

"You might. But I don't care if you do. I'm going to marry you, nevertheless."

"Not if I can help it. You can't *force* me to marry you. And," she turned to him and pointed her finger as a new idea struck her, "just what do you think my parents would think of this? Do you really think my father would approve of your marrying me? Not to mention kidnapping?"

"I don't care about that, either."

"You're taking a great deal for granted, Han. It won't work."

"No, Maggie," he said more intently than she'd ever seen him, which made her realize just how serious he was, "you are the one taking things for granted. You really believe that Nik Koenig loves you, but you're the only one who can't see what he really is and what he's really after. Your family can see it. And so can I. He's using you, Maggie. And you deserve better."

"And I suppose you think that *you* are better."

"I'm a lot better than that . . . Forget it, Maggie. Now you know why you're here, and now you know what your fate will be. You can like it, or you can tolerate it. But you're going to have to live with it."

He stood silently facing her—so confident, so calm. And she hated him. She hated him so much she wanted to tear him apart with her bare hands. After the shock subsided, her natural responses took hold, and she lunged toward him, like a tigress, claws extended.

Maggie cursed his strength and agility as he caught her arms before they could reach him. Then with an efficiency resulting from much practice, he threw her over his shoulder and carried her up the stairs. Han tossed her onto the bed and once again caught hold of her forearms. She screamed and squirmed when he put his face close to hers. He managed to briefly press his lips to hers before she turned away. His kiss was demanding but controlled, and she knew he was trying to prove what he was capable of doing. But she wondered how far he would go.

"I hate you!" she spat when he let her go. But he only kissed her again before he spoke breathlessly against her face. *"That,"* he enunciated strongly, "is your fate, my love."

"You bastard!" she shrieked.

"That is strictly a matter of opinion."

With his threats conveyed, Han stood and left the room, locking the door behind him. And he didn't bother to bring her any supper.

Han didn't come up to bed that night, and Maggie didn't see him until he unlocked the bedroom the next morning and told her it was time for breakfast. They ate in silence and did the usual housework, and he never let her out of his sight for more than a minute. Inwardly, she was seething with hatred for this man. But he had her cornered for the time being, so she kept mostly silent and did everything he told her to do, wishing with all her might that someone would find her before it was too late.

Captain Lance Dukerk hurried out of his office, across the castle courtyard, and into the main entrance of the castle where he quickly traversed the long hall toward the duke's office. It was a walk he'd taken thousands of times through more than two decades of working closely with the Duke of Horstberg. He couldn't count the times he'd needed to inform the duke of some unsavory news. Together they'd dealt with many challenges and had come up against a number of evil or delusional people who had been determined in one way or another to undermine the peace and safety of the good people of this country. Some issues had been more personal to the du Woernig family; some had been personal to himself. And some issues had been personal to them both. But rarely had a threat felt more ominous than this, even if it was difficult to explain the reasons. He knew he didn't have to explain his gut feelings to Cameron, because he felt them too. There were no words needed between him and Cameron—and Georg as well. They'd been through enough together to know when they unanimously felt a scourge of wicked intent in the wind.

At the office, one of the men in uniform guarding the door quickly opened it for him with no words exchanged. Lance heard the door close behind him and watched Cameron and Georg look up from the desk. He was glad to note that Erich was absent and also glad that no meetings were taking place that would draw more attention to his need to speak with the duke immediately. Their ability to practically read each other's minds was made evident when Cameron removed his glasses and demanded, "What's wrong?"

Lance just said it. "Koenig has left the country." Neither Cameron nor Georg commented, but he saw their faces tighten almost identically. He knew they wanted details, and he was prepared to give them. "We've had him watched carefully, as you know. You also know there have been times when he's slipped away and we've not known of his whereabouts for a day or two. We couldn't have him followed too closely or he would become aware of our observation and that would be worse. From the information we've now gathered, we know that he left the country sometime in the last few days, and at least three other men—comrades of his who have extremely atrocious reputations—have also disappeared and are likely with him."

Cameron cursed and hit his fist on the desk as he stood up. He turned to look out the window and sighed loudly. "And what do you think the chances are that these men might catch up to them?"

"It's impossible to know," Lance said. "The reality is that we know nothing at all, and our lack of knowledge is as much a disadvantage as it is a protection—for Han and Maggie as well as for ourselves."

Cameron sighed again. "Of course."

"We have no valid reason to pursue Koenig, and he's been gone too long to do so anyway. We can only hope and pray that Han is as clever as we want him to be."

"Yes, we can hope for that," Georg said with wry severity. Han had always been known for his cleverness, but the fate of the country had never been involved.

"Thank you, Captain," Cameron said with a tone of sincere friendship that contradicted the use of his title.

"If there is anything you would like me to do . . . Your Grace," he replied. "Anything at all . . ."

"As you said, there's nothing to be done." Cameron turned to look at him. "But thank you. As always, I am grateful beyond words to have *you* in this position."

"As am I," Georg said.

Lance nodded at his friends and took a seat, needing to set aside the formality of their positions now that all the vital information had been conveyed. Cameron sat back down, but nothing was said for several minutes. The heaviness of an undefinable threat hovered in the air like the smoke of stale cigars. But none of them, with all their power, could do anything about it.

Maggie lay awake far into the night, counting the reasons she hated Han. When she ran out of things, she started over and went through the list again until she became frustrated to realize it was already the middle of the night. She'd not gotten any sleep because her mind was so caught up in turmoil over this ludicrous situation. She still found it difficult to believe that Han thought he could succeed with his ridiculous quest. But she couldn't help wondering what her fate would be. Whether she wanted to marry him or not, she was a prisoner here, and so far, there was little to be done about that.

At the realization that Han had been sleeping soundly while she had stewed about this for hours—and he would no doubt have her up early cooking breakfast or some other odd chore—she became even more angry with him.

"Han." She reached a leg out of the bed and kicked him, but he only moaned, so she pushed and kicked at the same time. "Han, wake up."

"What do you want?" he said, his voice slurred with sleep.

"I'm hungry. Go get me something to eat."

"Forget it. If you want something, get it yourself."

"Give me the key, and I will," she said lightly.

"Go back to sleep," he said, rolling his face into the pillow. "You can eat in the morning."

"I'm hungry. I want to eat something now."

"It's the middle of the night," he protested.

"I like eating in the middle of the night. I used to sneak down to the kitchens and get food all the time."

"That sounds like you," he muttered. "Sneaking to the kitchen sounds typical of your royal adventures—truly exciting and unforgettable."

"Oh hush! Just give me the key."

"Go back to sleep."

"No. I'm hungry."

Han sighed and rolled over. "You're not going to let me sleep until you get something to eat, are you."

"You're very perceptive."

"Fine," he conceded. "Let's go."

"What are you doing?"

"Did you really believe I would let you out of here alone?"

"No," she sneered, "but it was worth a try."

Han sneered back then retrieved the key from its hiding place to unlock the door. He followed her to the kitchen and watched while she collected an odd assortment of things, then they went back upstairs where he relocked the door and got back into his bed on the floor.

"Now hurry up and eat so I can get some sleep," he said.

Maggie nodded and ate very slowly. When she was finished at last, she brushed the crumbs off the sheets, extinguished the lamp, and crawled back into bed.

"Han," she said lightly.

"What?" came the muffled reply.

"What day is it?"

"It's not day. It's night."

"But what is the date?"

"I don't know. Ask me tomorrow. My brain only works in daylight."

"I'm not certain it works then. Well, I know you come up with ways to torture me. But I'm certain it all stems from a degree of madness."

"No doubt," he complied. "Now will you please be quiet and let me sleep?"

"Whatever for? I've been awake all night. Why should you have the pleasure of sleeping?"

"It's not my fault you haven't slept."

"It most certainly is. How is a woman supposed to sleep without peace of mind? And how is a woman supposed to have peace of mind when she's being held prisoner . . . in the middle of nowhere . . . by a madman who takes advantage of her . . . and threatens her . . . and—"

"Maggie!" He stood up and covered her mouth with his hand. "If you say one more word I will make certain you are so tired by tomorrow night you won't have the energy to think about how miserable you are."

"And you're a tyrant," she added boldly when he moved his hand.

"That does it," he said, moving toward the door. "I'm going downstairs to sleep, and I'll be thinking of cruel things to make you do."

"What a brilliant idea," she said exuberantly. "Do have a nice night."

"And you," he said, "get some sleep while you can. You're going to need it."

"Threats, threats," she mimicked.

Han glared at her before he left the room and locked the door, and Maggie felt great satisfaction in defeating him—if only a little. She snuggled down into the bed, relishing the freedom of being all alone in the room.

The following day, Han did as he'd promised and had Maggie busy before daylight had fully appeared. By late afternoon, she was so tired and so angry that she felt on the verge of insanity. She was cleaning the bedroom floor when she noticed Han's pistol under the edge of the bed. It only took a moment for her to gather the courage to pick it up. Her father had taught her how to use guns properly, and she felt a surge of confidence as she hurried down the stairs, holding the pistol in the folds of her skirt. She found Han stirring something by the stove, humming casually as if he didn't have a care in the world.

"Take me home," she said, trying to imitate the way her father would order the officers of the Guard to do his bidding.

Han glanced toward her and smiled. "I will take you home only when you have my name, Princess MagdaLena." He turned his attention back to the stove, as if her marrying him might be the most natural thing in the world and she would be a fool to not agree with him.

"Take me home, Han. I'm quite serious."

He glanced up again and his expression changed immediately. Maggie cocked the pistol and corrected her aim.

Han considered how this might have been avoided, but then he put his focus completely on how to deal with the problem and avoid having anyone get hurt. He took a deep breath and stepped back from the stove.

"What do you think will happen if you kill me?" he asked, hoping she couldn't sense his nervousness.

"I would be free again," she said firmly.

"Do you think you can survive here on your own?" he asked, pleased to hear the calmness in his own voice. "Do you think you can find your way back?"

"I can if I have to," she insisted, and he felt certain she was right. "I want you to take me home. I want to leave now. Either you help me, or I'll kill you."

Han put his hands up and took a step toward her. "Do you think you can kill me, Maggie?" he asked.

"Don't come any closer," she insisted, and he was unnerved most of all by her anger. He knew she wasn't thinking clearly, but then, he couldn't be certain she'd been thinking clearly for years. "I swear I'll do it," she shouted, and a part of him couldn't deny the possibility that she might.

"Then do it," he said, anger tinging his voice. "Because quite frankly, Maggie, I'm getting tired of fighting you. Believe it or not, I have my reasons for bringing you here. And my motives are—more than anything—for *your* benefit. But if you can't trust me enough to get us through this, then I'm not sure I want to live. So, go ahead and shoot me, Maggie. Put me out of my misery."

Maggie could only hear how utterly delusional Han's thinking had become, but she was taken off guard to realize how many steps toward her he'd taken while she'd been so preoccupied with his little speech.

"Go ahead and do it, Maggie," he challenged, standing directly in front of her. He narrowed his eyes intently and leaned his chest against the barrel of the gun. For a long moment she seriously considered his challenge and couldn't decide if she was relieved or disgusted to realize that he'd been right. She could never kill him. As much as she hated him, she could never do it. He leaned forward even further, and she gasped, taking a step back, suddenly fearing the gun might go off accidentally. And she could never live with that. In one agile movement, Han grabbed the gun and wrenched it from her hands.

"Damn you!" she hissed. In spite of knowing she could have never killed him, she would have still preferred to keep the gun in her possession and maintain some degree of control over the situation.

"That's highly possible," Han retorted with a breathlessness that made her realize he'd been far more nervous than he'd let on.

Maggie winced as he aimed the gun toward the floor and fired. But there was nothing but six empty clicks. She looked at him in astonishment as he said, "It works better with bullets."

"You knew it wasn't loaded," she snarled.

"Actually," he admitted, feeling almost shaky from the reality, "I had no idea if you had found the bullets or not."

Han took her chin and looked into her eyes. "Do you really hate me enough to kill me, Maggie?" he asked sadly. "Or do I just remind you of something you're afraid to face?"

Maggie stared at him a full minute, feeling as if he could read her mind. Then she turned and hurried up the stairs, so confused and upset she wanted only to be alone in her anguish. But it wasn't long before she realized that she had work to do, and Han would never let her have any supper or get any sleep until it was done. So she pulled herself together and returned to her chores.

Han was grateful for some time alone in the kitchen while Maggie was upstairs. The image of her pointing a gun at him wouldn't leave his mind; the implications of her feelings toward him made him feel literally ill, as if facing the possibility of death hadn't already made him feel ill enough. He wondered what might happen now, and if he had it in him to keep this up long enough for Maggie to have a change of heart—if such a thing was even possible.

Maggie said nothing to him the remainder of the evening; she wouldn't even look at him. She hurried off to bed as soon as the dishes from supper were cleaned and put away, and he found her sound asleep when he went upstairs and crawled into his makeshift bed on the floor. He'd expected to feel complacent in thinking she'd sleep well tonight, and she'd not be likely to disturb his own sleep. But how could he sleep, so utterly unnerved by his encounter with Maggie pointing a pistol at him? He began to wonder if he knew Maggie as well as he thought he did. Whether or not he knew her at all had now become irrelevant. There could be no backing out now, and he prayed that he would be able to succeed with this quest before it undid both of them. He considered the possibility of returning Maggie to her father's care—unwed and full of fury—and that ill feeling returned. Believing that his endeavors were for a greater good, and recalling how right it had felt to do what the duke had asked of him, He prayed for God's guidance and aid, knowing he would never get through this without divine intervention. In the midst of his ongoing prayer, he finally relaxed enough to be able to sleep.

Maggie gasped and came awake, breathing sharply while she mentally accumulated the evidence that she was safe and she'd only been dreaming. Sleep had come as such a pleasant reprieve after such a dreadful day; having it intruded upon by such a horrible dream left her uneasy and disconcerted. She knew from experience that thinking about her present situation would only make her more agitated. And she couldn't think at all about those moments when she'd had a pistol pointed at Han, making herself believe somewhere deep inside that she could actually pull the trigger. What kind of madness was overtaking her?

Forcing away all thoughts of Han and the current circumstances, Maggie could only think of the dream that had frightened her out of sleep as if coming awake had been much like jumping off a cliff in order to save herself from the fear she'd been experiencing. Muddled images swirled around in her mind with no particular order or continuity; memories from her youth, thoughts of her home and family, Erich being shot, Nik kissing her and begging her to run away with him. And the helplessness she'd felt since she'd first realized that Han Heinrich had actually stolen her away from her home and was holding her captive. But this bizarre collaboration of memories in her dream had not felt frightening. It was only when they had all disappeared in a vapor, like a wisp of fog being blown away by a rush of wind. Then she'd been standing in the forest, surrounded by nothing but trees and darkness. Every direction she turned looked the same; she had no sense of direction, no idea of where she might be. Then she heard something behind her—or rather some*one*. She caught a glimpse of the dark figure of a man at the same moment her every nerve sensed danger, and she turned and ran. It seemed as if she ran forever, as if hours of her sleep had been consumed with running and falling and getting up again to run some more, always aware of a man close behind her, threatening her life if he caught up to her. Coming awake had saved her from the dark villain in the forest, but it hadn't spared her from the vivid memories of what she had seen and felt in her dream.

When thinking about the dream became as maddening as thinking about the fact that she was locked in a cottage in the middle of a forest against her will, she tried to distract herself with thoughts of *anything* else. A moment later, she became aware of sounds she'd never heard before—or at least she'd never paid any attention to them. She couldn't hear anything terribly loud, no indication that there were any great beasts lurking outside, but as her mind became carried away with these noises, mixing them into the images of her nightmare, she couldn't help feeling afraid. Realizing she had always slept within the walls of a great fortress, and now she was in a very small cottage in the middle of a forest, she became certain she would not make it through the night alive—even if she had already made it through many nights during their journey without the protection of shelter.

Sitting up in the bed, Maggie pulled the covers to her chin as if they alone could protect her. In her mind the insects and owls became horrid beasts that were going to break down the walls and devour her. For what felt like at least an hour, she adamantly refused to even consider waking Han. At best he would probably make fun of her. He was more likely to punish her with extra chores for interrupting his sleep. But as the drama in her head worsened, Maggie's fear overcame every other concern, and she sat on the floor beside Han, whispering his name fearfully.

"What now?" he asked, perturbed the moment he realized he was awake. "Are we going to make this a nightly ritual?" He wondered what kind of game she might be playing with him in some attempt to manipulate him, or simply to pester him to a point where he might give in and let her go home.

"Han," she said, "I'm scared."

"Go back to sleep." He didn't believe her and wasn't impressed.

"I'm really scared. Don't make fun."

"Why should I believe you?" he asked, resisting the temptation to start listing all the times she had been dishonest with him.

"Han! What are those noises?"

"What noises?"

"Listen."

"I don't hear anything," he said after a worthy effort that he hoped would appease her so that he could go back to sleep.

"How could you not hear anything?" she asked, her voice genuinely frantic. "It's so loud. There it is again. What is it?"

"You really are scared," Han said, turning toward her. She wouldn't be this close to him if she weren't. Either way, it put her threat of killing him into perspective.

"Of course I am. If you weren't so stupid, you'd have figured that out before now."

"Well, there is no reason to be," he assured her gently and couldn't help chuckling. He drew courage enough to put his arm around her. And surprisingly enough, she let him.

"But what is it?" she asked again.

"Well," he said, "if my calculations are correct, there is a big bad wolf coming from the east, and probably half a dozen bears coming from the south, and—"

"Han!" she scolded but made no attempt to move away.

"Maggie," he said more seriously, "it's probably some crickets and squirrels, maybe an owl. There," he added in response to a noise outside, "that is definitely an owl."

"Are you certain?"

"Yes, my love, I'm certain."

"I am not your love," Maggie said, feeling better. Though it was more from the distraction of bantering with him than deriving any comfort from his reassurance—at least none that she would admit to aloud.

"Not yet," he stated coolly.

"Are you certain it's just an owl?"

"Yes," he chuckled, "I'm certain. Go back to sleep."

"I'll try," she said in a voice that reminded him of the Maggie who had once been a completely different person than the woman she was now. She said nothing more, but he could feel how tense and alert she was, and he wondered what had happened to set her off. Rather than questioning the reasons, he just kept his arm around her, enjoying the moment while it lasted. Keenly aware of everything about her, he could feel her relaxing and getting sleepy. He was hoping she would fall asleep there beside him, but she crawled back into bed without saying anything, and he knew she had gone back to sleep within minutes. Han lay awake for quite some time, wondering if a day would ever come when she'd even slightly comprehend how he really felt about her.

Chapter Seven

TALES FROM THE BLACK FOREST

Maggie knew she had no choice but to accept her captivity, in spite of how thoroughly she hated it. She had completely lost track of how long they had been living in the cottage, but it seemed like forever. She often felt like crying, but she was never alone long enough to do so in privacy. And she would not give Han the pleasure of seeing any evidence of how miserable he had made her. With all the silence between them, Maggie pondered extensively over Han's motives. It momentarily crossed her mind that he might actually still love her in some bizarre way. But it only took a second thought to realize it was more likely that he'd become slightly deranged in the mind, and he was drawing some great perverse pleasure from all of this.

Maggie was nearly finished cleaning the breakfast dishes when she heard Han call her name. She went outside to find him sitting on the ground near the door. It was a beautiful day with blue skies, but the trees surrounding them left the area heavily shaded.

"What?" she asked in her usual cynical tone.

"Shhh," he whispered, "sit down and be quiet."

She did as he said, certain he was mad. Then she watched as he threw a small piece of bread on the ground. A few moments later, a tiny animal appeared from behind a fallen log to retrieve it.

Maggie was only vaguely interested until another one came out, and then a few more. Gradually Han urged them closer with more tidbits of food, and after a short while he had them eating out of his hand. She watched the little animals with curiosity, thinking they were awfully cute. Then her attention turned to Han. He was smiling.

It was obvious that he derived pleasure from the simple experience. To watch him now, he hardly seemed like the type of man to kidnap a princess and tie her up. But then, she hardly understood him. She didn't want to.

Maggie was surprised when he turned to her and spoke softly so he wouldn't frighten the little creatures, "Do you want to try it?"

"No," she said, "I'll just watch. What are they?" she added.

"I think," he said with no expression, "they are wolves and bears in disguise."

Maggie stood with disgust and went back inside. She purposely slammed the door, knowing the noise would scatter the little animals back into the woods.

The following day, a misty rain settled over the forest, bringing with it enough of a chill to implore Maggie to hover near the fire whenever she wasn't working. She wished she had something to occupy her time. Housework and contemplating her misery were becoming more and more tedious. Han spent a great deal of time reading, since there were several books in the cottage, but Maggie didn't like to read, and she found herself mostly just bored and miserable.

On the third afternoon of straight rain, she was surprised to turn from where she sat by the fire to see that Han had fallen asleep on the sofa. It didn't take a second thought to sneak quietly upstairs, pack her bag, add a little food from the kitchen, and escape outside. She wished she could have found the gun and taken that as well. But she'd not seen any sign of it since the night Han had confiscated it from her. She sighed with relief to realize she'd gotten out without waking him. Heart pounding, she began to walk quickly through the forest, trying to ignore the rain. And she wished the memory of that night-mare of being pursued in the forest hadn't just leaped into her mind.

Han was barely aware of sounds in the cottage as he hovered close to sleep, but the door closing brought him completely awake. "Blast!" he muttered when he realized she was gone. He pulled on his boots and set out running on the only trail available except for the one that led to the pond. It started raining harder, but he knew she was getting just as wet as he was. He sighed with relief when he caught a glimpse of her through the trees ahead of him.

"Maggie!" he shouted, and she began to run.

Maggie ran with everything she had, lifting her skirts high so they wouldn't impede her. Memories of her nightmare consumed her and her heart pounded painfully. It only took a minute for Han's long legs to gain an advantage and she felt his arms come around her, pulling her to an abrupt halt.

"Let go of me!" she shrieked, turning to hit him.

"And just where would you go if I did?" he demanded, trying to get hold of her wrists to keep her from hitting him.

"I don't know. I don't care."

"You'd better care," he said and caught hold of her forearms, which made her more angry. "You would do nothing but find yourself very lost in this forest, and then the wolves and bears *would* get you. Now come along. We're going home."

"No!" she screamed and wormed out of his arms, right into a mud puddle.

Han couldn't keep from laughing. "You make quite a picture, my love. Rain becomes you." His words sparked a memory, and by the intensity in Maggie's eyes, he felt certain she was remembering too. Her pain was briefly evident, but he had yet to understand its source. She glanced away, seeming ashamed as he lifted her up and carried her back to the cottage. There had been a time when she would have laughed *with* him over such a thing, and he wondered for the millionth time what had changed her. Perhaps hoping to understand, he decided to stop avoiding the topic and just take it head on. She couldn't possibly hate him any more than she already did. "I seem to recall doing this once before. But I'm not certain you were completely conscious the last time."

"That was the worst day of my life," she growled. "Must you remind me of such things?"

"Well, the worst day of my life was three weeks later, and I'm reminded of it every time I look at you. Fair is fair."

Maggie's eyes narrowed on him, sensing an honesty in him that she rarely saw these days, and she wished that she understood what he meant. He set her down inside the cottage and said firmly, "Get some dry clothes on before you get another of those fevers. I haven't recovered from the brain damage you got last time."

"I do not have brain damage," she retorted, wishing she had heard some evidence of sarcasm or teasing in his tone. But he still seemed completely honest and sincere—so much so that his words left her decidedly uncomfortable.

Maggie's discomfort only deepened when he added with the same severity, "You were never the same. It sure seemed like brain damage to me." She stared at him long and hard, wanting to ask what he meant but terrified of the answers. In fact, she was terrified to think about it at all. So she pushed all thoughts of it away and huffed up the stairs to change. If anybody had brain damage, surely it was Han.

When they had both changed into dry clothes and had hung the wet ones near the fire, Maggie scornfully went to work preparing supper. She was surprised when Han began helping her. They usually took turns doing the meals, and he had never helped when it was her turn except occasionally checking in on her to give instructions or offer criticism over her lack of knowledge.

"Han," she asked, trying to sound sincere, "why don't you just take me home and forget all of this madness?"

"I can't do that," he said firmly.

"Just what is it that compelled you to do such a ridiculous thing as kidnap a princess?"

"Isn't it obvious?" he smirked, all seriousness suddenly absent. "It was that love potion. It only took one swallow to never be free of you again."

"Baggage!" she said. But if Sonia hadn't clarified that it was only whiskey, she would have almost believed it. Han chuckled, and her mind went back to her failed attempt to escape. She wondered if he'd been right, that she would only find herself lost in the forest. Recalling her nightmare, she shivered.

"Where are we, anyway?" she asked.

"You don't know?" he said in mock surprise.

"How could I?" she retorted. They were both well aware she had no idea. The only thing she knew for certain was that they were a long way from the small Bavarian country of Horstberg.

"We," he said in his typical melodramatic way, "are in the Black Forest. The land of fairy tales and enchantments, where legends never die and dreams come true."

Maggie said nothing. To her it was all a lot of baggage. This was nothing more than a very bad nightmare—perhaps literally.

The nightmare intensified the following morning when Maggie awoke feeling not quite right. She did her best to ignore it and went about her usual routine. But when she was cleaning the breakfast dishes, a distinct lightheadedness overtook her and she bent over and leaned her head against the counter and moaned. Suddenly cold, she decided she was going to bed, whether the dishes were finished or not. She straightened slowly but felt dizzy, and would have collapsed if she'd not leaned back against the counter.

"Han!" she called.

"What?" he asked blandly from where he sat reading.

"Help," she said weakly.

Han looked up from his book to see Maggie bent over the counter with her face almost flat against it. He would have chuckled except that he realized something was really wrong.

"What's the matter?" He was at her side immediately. When his hands came to her shoulders, she weakly turned and fell against him.

"Good heavens, Maggie!" he said, pressing his hand to her face while the other arm went around her waist to support her. "You're burning up."

"That's impossible," she whispered. "I'm freezing."

Panicked, Han lifted her into his arms and carried her upstairs. Setting her on the edge of the bed, he pulled off her shoes and stockings while she seemed completely dazed, then he put her into bed and tucked the blankets tightly around her.

"Han," she said, "I don't feel very well."

"I know," he whispered softly, pressing his hand over her face, "but I'll take care of you. Just rest."

Maggie closed her eyes, hardly able to keep them open. It seemed only minutes before an intense ache succumbed her entire body. She drifted in and out of consciousness while bizarre dreams mingled with memories, all revolving around Han. In her mind, she kept hearing him say it over and over. *Rain becomes you. Rain becomes you.* Associated memories thrust forward from the darkest recesses of her mind, and she was far too weak to force them back.

Maggie held her new gown in front of her and admired it in the mirror. She laid it carefully over the bed, anticipating the envy she knew the baron's daughters would feel when they saw her wearing it. She was actually looking forward to their visit, wanting to explore the dress shops with the only girls she knew—beyond

Sonia—who shared this side of her life. She was contemplating which necklace to wear with the gown when Sonia stuck her head into the room and tossed something on the floor.

"Note for you. Got to go. Mother's waiting."

The door closed, and Maggie bent to pick up the folded paper. She smiled as she opened it and read: Meet me in the garden. It's raining.

Maggie glanced at the clock. She had plenty of time before the Baron Von Bindorf arrived with his family, and there was little as enticing as walking with Han in the rain.

Wearing her most comfortable skirt and blouse, Maggie hurried downstairs where a door from the main hallway exited into the gardens. A drizzling rain met her as she moved deftly across the lawn and into the maze of shrubbery. She was just wondering where Han might be hiding when his hand clapped over her mouth and he chuckled behind her ear. She wanted to scold him for the way he enjoyed startling her, but he pressed his mouth to hers as soon as he removed his hand. Maggie savored his kiss, loving the combined sensation of being in his arms with rain falling over her face.

"Oh, Han," she whispered, "sometimes I wish you weren't so noble."

"What do you mean by that?" He chuckled and kissed her again.

"Sometimes I can't help wondering . . . what it would be like." She pressed her hands over the wet fabric covering his shoulders. "Meet me at midnight, Han," she whispered and urged him to kiss her still again.

"Did you want to go riding in the rain?" he asked with a little smirk.

"No," she said severely.

"Maggie," he drawled with a scolding tone, and she smiled coyly at him. He gave her a loving sidelong glance and put some distance between them. They walked hand in hand for a few minutes, then she sat on the wet grass and he sat beside her. She urged him to kiss her and began to feel lost in it, wanting more than anything for it to go on and on.

"Please, Han," she murmured against his face. She felt sure he knew what she meant. He'd often accused her of being careless and impetuous, and perhaps she was. But a part of her believed that experiencing the full extent of Han's love would somehow ease her deepest doubts, feelings that had hovered uncomfortably inside of her since her childhood.

"I just can't do it, Maggie." Han groaned and eased away from her, pushing a frustrated hand through his wet hair. Maggie sighed loudly in exasperation.

"Why not?" she asked after a grueling silence. "I thought you loved me, Han."

"I do *love you, Maggie. That's just it.*" He looked directly at her. "*I can't do this. Not here; not like this. Not until we're properly married. You know as well as I do that under any other circumstances, it's just not right.*"

Maggie eased close to him and pressed a hand over his face. "*Then let's run away and get married,*" she whispered. She knew of many women who had married at her age, but her parents had made it clear that they expected their daughters to first reach a certain age and level of maturity.

"*No, Maggie. You don't understand. We're just too young. We can't . . . not yet. When we're older, we can get married, then—*"

"*That could be years, Han. My parents would never approve of my marrying so young. They would—*"

"*That's the point, Mags. If you're too young to marry without your parents' permission, then you're too young to get married. And you're certainly too young to be giving yourself to* anyone. *It's as simple as that. I won't let you do it.*"

Maggie moved away abruptly and sighed. While a part of her couldn't help but respect Han for his concern, she was more consumed with the intensity of what his kisses did to her. She'd always been taught to follow her instincts, to trust her feelings. In the months that she and Han had been seeing each other, her emotions had become tangled with a consuming desire that she could neither explain nor deny. It was difficult to accept that being fourteen years of age made it inappropriate for her to follow these feelings. And though Han's reasons made sense, a desire that she longed to understand burned inside her. But even more prominently, she felt rejected—something she was quite unaccustomed to. She turned to look at him over her shoulder, needing to know the full depth of his motives.

"*Don't you want me, Han?*" she asked, hating the vulnerability that seeped into her voice. A familiar uneasiness rose inside to haunt her. And she felt certain that the validation of Han's love would somehow ease it.

"*Want you?*" he chuckled as if it were absurd to think otherwise. "*Maggie, I have wanted you since I was old enough to know what it meant. You are all I have* ever *wanted. But I'm seventeen, Maggie. I'm not in a position to take responsibility for you—not yet. I'm beginning to think it would have been better if I'd just kept my feelings to myself until we were older. Anything beyond a kiss isn't right, and you know it. You're the duke's daughter, for heaven's sake.*"

"*Does that make it different?*" she asked tersely.

"*No,*" he insisted, sitting close beside her. "*It's just that I have a great respect for your father, Maggie—and he's trusting me to not take advantage of you. The decisions you make may eventually have an affect on the country.*"

But most importantly, royal blood or not, I care for you too much to put passion before your well-being."

"Don't you think I can make those decisions for myself?" she demanded.

"Maggie," he whispered, kissing her quickly, "I love you. Time will go quickly—you'll see. It won't be so long before we can be married—properly and with respect. And everything will be perfect." She gave a begrudging smile, and he kissed her again.

Maggie giggled in the midst of it, and then her voice became severe. "But how can I regret something that I know in my heart is right?"

Han lifted his head to look at her. "What do you mean?" he asked.

"It's just that . . . when you kiss me, everything feels right, Han. I just want it to last forever."

Han smiled. "Well, I'm not going to stop kissing you. We just have to be very careful." He tightened his embrace. "And one day . . ." He kissed her as if to seal his unspoken promise.

When they were both very wet, Han insisted that Maggie go inside before she caught cold. They walked hand in hand toward the door while Maggie tried to distract herself from the feelings for Han that consumed her. She wondered how she could possibly cope with feeling that way for the years left before they could marry. Turning her mind to the Von Bindorf family arriving later that day, she knew she would spend the following two days being strictly a princess. As if she could store up this feeling of freedom to get her through, she urged Han to walk the circumference of the garden with her once more. She liked the way he toyed with her hair that hung in a wet mass down her back. When they finally came inside, she was soaked to the skin and her skirt was splattered with mud. Maggie didn't give a second thought to her appearance until she came into the hall, face to face with the baron's daughters, who had just arrived—hours early.

Maggie turned hot with embarrassment at their obvious astonishment. She looked down at herself, and the shame deepened. Han's hand tightened in hers, as if to tell her it was all right. But as the girls eyed him with some kind of shocked amazement, Maggie knew that he couldn't possibly understand. Without a word, she hurried upstairs to make herself presentable, hoping the visitors would be gracious enough to not draw attention to it later. She convinced herself that even the Princesses Von Bindorf must get wet and dirty occasionally.

Maggie came downstairs at the appointed time, feeling beautiful and elegant. Her gown was the latest fashion, and her hair was styled into one of Klara's newest accomplishments, custom-designed for her thick mass of red curls. But the afternoon wore on with subtle gibes about their earlier encounter. When the girls separated from their families, the comments toward Maggie became more overt. They told her it was difficult to distinguish the servants from the royalty in Horstberg, and they wondered if there was any distinction at all. Then they laughed and didn't seem the least bit concerned when Maggie didn't laugh with them. They teased her about cavorting with the stablehands and asked if her parents knew anything at all about teaching their children what was proper for a princess. Childhood taunting stormed through her mind, pressing the wounds deeper. When Maggie could bear it no longer, she hurried away, fearing she would erupt into tears and give them one more thing to torment her about. Once beyond their sight, she ran. Heedless to the continuing rain, she ran across the courtyard and into the stables. She managed to bridle her horse in spite of the way her hands were trembling. Knowing she'd never manage a saddle, she hurled herself onto the horse bareback, lifting her silk skirts—already ruined from the rain—high above her knees. She was barely on the horse when Han emerged from the storage room with two buckets of oats.

"Maggie!" he said, dropping them. "What are you doing?"

Their eyes met, and she knew there was no point trying to hide her tears. She urged the stallion toward the door, and he dashed in front of her, attempting to stop her.

"What are you doing?" he repeated. "What's wrong?"

"Get out of my way!" she demanded.

"You can't go out dressed like that. You'll catch your death."

"Get out of my way!" she shouted, and he had no choice but to jump aside when she nearly ran him over, thundering across the courtyard and through the castle gate. She blindly galloped the horse toward the meadow, wishing the speed and the driving rain could push away her shame and humiliation. How could she ever face them again? For the rest of her life, she would be forced to endure social events with these people almost monthly, and she felt certain they would never let her live down the embarrassment. And far worse, she had to wonder if some of the things she'd been told as a child were true, things she'd tried futilely to ignore all these years.

Maggie's hurt and anger merged into fear when the rain suddenly turned to sheets, and thunder cracked overhead. She found it impossible to get her bearings, and the horse resisted her control. Thunder cracked again, and the stallion reared back.

Maggie remembered nothing after she hit the ground. Her next awareness was of being lifted and carried. Her coherency came back to her partially as she was taken into a thick patch of trees where the rain was deflected enough to be tolerable.

"Are you with me, Maggie?" she heard Han say as he set her down.

"What are you doing here?" she snarled with chattering teeth.

"Well, at least you're conscious," he chuckled and removed his cloak. He threw it over her shoulders and pulled it tightly around her. "I'm here to make certain you don't kill yourself," he replied. "Or would you rather be unconscious in a downpour with no horse?"

"I don't care," she insisted, shivering uncontrollably. Her head was pounding horribly, and she felt a little dizzy.

While Han studied her for a minute, she briefly drifted off again. When he spoke it startled her. "You do look lovely today, Your Highness. Rain becomes you."

Maggie felt the hot tears returning as he unwittingly jabbed where it hurt most. "Oh, leave me alone," she snapped, turning away from him in an effort to hide her tears.

"I would," he said, urging her to her feet, "but if I don't get you home, you're going to freeze to death. That cloak's too wet to do much good."

Maggie was shaking so hard, she couldn't find the will to protest as he lifted her onto a horse and mounted behind her.

"Keep your head down," he said, "and I'll try to hurry."

Maggie was barely aware of the pelting rain and Han's arm firmly around her waist. It was difficult to tell if she was shivering or sobbing as they seemed to go on forever. She realized she'd lost consciousness again when she felt him pull her down from the horse, and she knew they were in the castle courtyard. She was barely aware of him carrying her inside and up the stairs. He shouted something at one of the servants, but she couldn't discern what. She felt the sensation of being on a bed, while a mixture of voices surrounded her in frenzied tones. Her mother's stood out strongly, and she knew everything would be all right.

"Mother?" she said and felt Abbi's hand slip into hers. And then it was gone.

"Mother?" Maggie whimpered over and over in delirium, while Han wondered if he had ever been so afraid in his life. He'd seen Maggie go through this before, but the duchess had been at her side, and a doctor had been on hand. When he had agreed to do this, he'd certainly not anticipated something so dreadful.

Han stayed beside her, keeping cool cloths against her skin, trying with what little knowledge he had to keep the fever down, all the while praying that Maggie would be all right. He drifted in and out of sleep, lying close to her, while the situation spurred memories he'd rather be free of.

Time trickled slowly for Han as he sat in the hallway outside Maggie's room, waiting for the verdict. His clothes were still wet from carrying her in out of the storm, but he hardly noticed. It seemed as if the doctor had been in there half the night. Erich and the duke sat across the hall, looking as concerned as he felt. No one had anything to say, so they each avoided the other's gaze and waited. Han wondered by Erich's demeanor if he was blaming him for this.

When the door finally opened, the three of them stood all at once. Doctor Furhelm emerged, looking weary and glum.

"What?" the duke demanded.

"I believe she'll be fine," he reported. "She appears to have a mild concussion, which would explain her confusion and dizziness. There should be improvement on that count within a day or two. But she's running a fever, and we'll just have to keep a close eye on her. I'll check back first thing in the morning."

Han didn't see Maggie until the next day. He took a handful of wildflowers to her room, but when he timidly entered, it was immediately evident that she was very ill.

"Hello, Han," Abbi said with her usual kind voice, barely glancing his direction while she gently pressed a wet towel to Maggie's peaked face.

"How is she?" he asked, absently setting the flowers on the bedside table.

"It's difficult to tell," Abbi said with a voice so weary, Han wondered if she had been there all night. He sat down on the opposite side of the bed and took Maggie's limp hand into his. He and the duchess shared no conversation, only a silent concern.

Han took a fresh bouquet of flowers every morning, but for five days, Maggie only slept or hovered in delirium from a fever that the doctor admitted was severe enough to possibly cause permanent damage—if she survived it. Han spent every moment he wasn't working sitting at her side as much as they would allow him. At times he felt as if his heart would break. In solitude he prayed and cried, sleeping only when exhaustion took hold, wishing he understood what had urged her to go out in the storm like that to begin with.

On the sixth morning, he entered Maggie's room to see her propped up in bed with pillows. She looked so peaked and frail, it was difficult to imagine the vibrant Maggie he loved. Their eyes met briefly, then she glanced away, seeming somehow uncomfortable.

"She's doing much better," Abbi reported with a smile, "as you can see." She added to Maggie, *"Han's brought you flowers every day."*

Maggie made no response.

"I'll let you look after her for a while," Abbi said to Han, making a gracious exit.

Han appreciated the opportunity to be alone with Maggie, but he couldn't think what to say. "I thought I was going to lose you," he finally admitted, setting the flowers on the bedside table. Maggie made no response, wouldn't even look at him. He sat on the edge of the bed and took her hand, but it felt limp and cold. Uneasiness crept down the back of Han's neck. Something had changed—something beyond enduring a serious illness. Her attitude toward him was different—a difference that frightened him for reasons he didn't want to explore too deeply.

"I'm alive, as you can see," she said, mildly terse. Still, she didn't look at him.

"What's wrong, Maggie?" he asked.

"That's a stupid question," she retorted, taking her hand from his. "After what I have been through, you ask what is wrong?"

"That's not what I mean. I get the impression you don't want me here. Is there a reason why you—"

"I don't want you here," she interrupted, finally turning to look at him. The scorn in her eyes was unfamiliar, and it chilled him. He could almost wonder if her brain had suffered from that fever. This was not the Maggie he knew.

"Why not?" he asked.

"That's another stupid question."

"Not if I don't know the answer," he retorted. "I know what you've been through is difficult, but—"

"You have no idea what I've been through," she insisted. Her voice softened slightly. "Please go, Han. I want to be alone."

Han reluctantly stood, frantically searching for words that might allow him to stay with her and somehow break past this wall. Coming up empty, he simply said, "We'll talk when you're feeling better, then."

"Fine," she said, "just go."

Han stepped into the hallway and had to lean momentarily against the wall to force back the emotion hovering in his throat. Hurrying out to the stables, he tried to convince himself that she would be her old self in no time, and they would be able to resume their comfortable relationship. But something deep inside nagged him to doubt it. She'd changed. He didn't understand it. And he hated it.

For several days, Han worked hard and tried not to think about Maggie's sudden absence in his life. He spoke with her mother every day and knew from the duchess's reports that Maggie was improving steadily. But Abbi repeatedly apologized for Maggie's unwillingness to see him, assuring him that everything would be fine once she got feeling better.

Three weeks beyond Maggie's destructive ride into the storm, Han looked up from currying a mare to see her walk into the stables, dressed and styled to perfection in a deep blue riding habit and matching hat.

"Well, hello," he said, wishing his heart hadn't reacted at just the sight of her. "It's good to see you up. Feeling better, I assume?"

"Yes, thank you," she said with cool deference. While Han tried to find words to approach her, she added, "Would you please saddle Pagan for me? I'm in need of some fresh air."

Han swallowed hard. He'd never felt so keenly the impact of being her servant as he did in that moment. "Are you sure you're up to it?" he asked easily, hoping to remind her of the relationship they shared.

"The doctor said it would be fine, which is no concern of yours."

"It certainly is *my concern, MagdaLena. I am extremely concerned for you, whether you want me to be or not."*

"Well, I don't *want you to be."*

"Maggie," he asked breathlessly, "what are you saying? This isn't like you to—"

"Perhaps you don't know me as well as you thought you did." She turned her back to him abruptly.

Han moved cautiously toward her. "We grew up together, Maggie," he said, as if to convince her. "We're practically lovers." He took hold of her shoulders, and she stiffened visibly at his touch.

"Not even close," she snapped. "Or have you forgotten how you rejected me?"

"Rejected you?" he echoed. "Is that what this is about?"

"No, it's not."

"What's happened, Maggie?" he whispered behind her ear, pressing his lips into her hair in a manner that felt familiar and right. But she recoiled and moved away as if they were strangers. When she said nothing more, he added firmly, "Don't play games with me, Maggie. Our relationship is no small thing. But something has changed between us, and I have a right to know what's going on."

Maggie looked Han straight in the eye. "I've done a lot of thinking these past few weeks, Han, and . . . well, I can't go on this way."

While Han tried to figure what exactly she meant, she fidgeted nervously with her hands and seemed to have trouble standing still. Thinking all of this through briefly, he felt he had to say, "I know that whatever sent you raging out into that storm had something to do with me, but I don't understand what. Maybe we should talk about it. That is where all of this started, isn't it?"

"You have no idea what you're talking about," she snapped, but her eyes told him he'd hit somewhere close to the truth—a truth she apparently didn't want tampered with.

"Let's talk, Maggie. We can work this through."

"No," she insisted, turning her back again, "we can't. It's over, Han. It's as simple as that."

Once Han convinced himself to take a breath, a chuckle of disbelief erupted from his chest. "Surely you can't mean that you—"

"I mean that it's over!" she shouted.

Han pressed a hand over his heart, as if he could literally feel the pain settling in. "After what we have shared," he said breathlessly, "you would just turn your back on me . . . just like that?"

Maggie looked directly at him, saying coldly, "It was nothing—puppy love. That's all. Face it. You said yourself that it would have been better if we'd kept our feelings to ourselves."

"That's not what I meant."

"Well, it's obvious now that we would both be better off to pretend that nothing ever transpired between us."

"Like hell we would!" he retorted and stepped toward her, taking her upper arms into his hands before she could retract. "How dare you stand there and try to tell me what I'm feeling and what would be better for me! I love you, Maggie."

"Surely we are too young to understand anything at all of love, Han. Don't be such a fool."

Han shook her slightly, as if he could shake some sense into her. "Being too young to carry on an adult relationship is entirely different from being old enough to know love when you feel it. You're the one who told me that it felt right in your heart. You begged me to marry you, Maggie." She closed her eyes briefly as if she didn't want to hear it, and he shook her again. "This isn't you, Maggie. Something's happened. Where is the part of you that loved me? Where is the Maggie I love more than life?"

"You loved a child, Han. She's not there anymore."

"I don't believe that."

"I've grown up a great deal in the last few weeks—enough to know that we're just not right for each other."

"I don't believe that, either," he insisted, wondering how he could ever

convince her that she was making a mistake. He looked into her eyes and saw something that contradicted what she was trying to convince him of. It gave him the hope that they could eventually get beyond this. If he could only understand what had upset her so badly and catapulted her into this madness! He reminded himself that he would still be seeing her often. He would have the chance to win her back . . . to convince her. Just when he began to believe he could find a way to live with this—at least for the time being—she stepped back and shattered his dreams like a hammer to glass.

"You see, Han, I've come to realize that I will never marry beneath me. It's a simple as that. And it can't be changed. I hope that eventually you will be able to forgive me. But whether you do or not is up to you. I am a princess, and this is the way it has to be."

Han was so stunned, he could neither move nor speak. She stared at him long and hard with a coldness in her eyes he couldn't fathom. Then she turned and walked away, saying haughtily, "Forget the saddle, Han. Perhaps I'm not up to riding today, after all."

Han had no idea how long he stood there, feeling as if he'd turned to stone. He realized he'd been holding his breath when his chest began to burn for want of air. Instinctively, he pressed both hands there as if they could help him draw a breath. He gasped and sank to his knees as the stone crumbled into a million unfixable pieces.

After Han sat in the corner of a stall and cried for over an hour, a numb despair settled over him. He couldn't believe it. Everything he'd ever hoped for was gone. And he didn't even understand. Perhaps if he knew why, he could learn to cope.

Han finally forced himself to his feet and his senses. Maggie may have robbed him of his dreams—temporarily at least—but he would not allow her to take his dignity. He managed to push himself through his responsibilities, forcing smiles toward his parents and the du Woernig family and anyone else he had to face as he methodically saddled their horses and saw to his work. Gratefully, Maggie didn't show herself for three days. By the time he saw her again, he'd almost become accustomed to the pain enough to mask it. He was prepared to tell her that he would not let an arrogant little princess destroy him, but she came into the stables with Erich, and he had no opportunity to say anything at all. While Erich rambled about something he'd heard at the pub the day before, Han saddled Maggie's horse and helped her mount, as if just touching her didn't put his every nerve on fire. He stood and watched her ride out, feeling his heart break all over again. Then he remembered that he wasn't alone and adjusted his demeanor.

"What's up between you and Mags?" Erich asked pointedly.

"Apparently nothing," Han retorted coldly, turning away to saddle Erich's horse.

Han knew Erich was watching him closely even before he asked, "Are you still—"

"No!" Han snapped.

"Well, what—"

"Apparently, it was nothing," Han said, if only to get it over with. "Apparently, it was puppy love."

Erich paused to absorb this before he said, "Apparently, you don't really believe that."

"Apparently, what I believe is irrelevant."

Han was relieved when Erich didn't press the matter any further. A few minutes later, he was alone. A few stray tears fell unleashed over his face. Then he forced his emotion back and resigned himself to keep going through the motions of living.

Weeks passing made it easier to pretend. His gift of wit and humor served him well as he adjusted to the future Maggie had sentenced him to. Their brief encounters were cold, and it soon became evident that her walls were impenetrable. But Han managed to tease her as he'd done since their childhood, and he learned to laugh off the hurt she inflicted as if it were nothing. And he never stopped dreaming, even if a part of him eventually stopped believing that such dreams would ever come true.

Han snapped his head up when Maggie moaned. He watched her in the dim glow of the lamp, forcing his mind to return to the present. When she was still no better by the next morning, he went into town to get a doctor, not the least bit worried that she would try to run away. She could hardly move.

The doctor was kind, and Maggie remained silent while he checked her. He said to Han, "It doesn't appear to be anything serious. The fever should break within a day or two and then she'll be fine. If it doesn't, come back and get me, and we'll see that your wife is properly cared for."

Han knew that Maggie overheard, and he could see that she wanted to set the doctor straight, but her weakness worked in his favor when she said nothing. She did, however, manage to give Han a stony glare. But Han knew that if this doctor believed Maggie was anything but his wife, a great deal of suspicion could be aroused.

He took the doctor back to town and got some supplies, as well as a few extra things he thought they could use. He returned promptly and stayed by Maggie's bedside, doing everything he could to make her comfortable and keep the fever down. On the third night of her illness, the fever finally broke, and Maggie slept peacefully. Han did as well, knowing from what the doctor had said that she would likely feel weak and far from normal for a few days yet. But the worst was over, and he felt greatly relieved.

Maggie came awake and assessed that her body was no longer aching. She felt terribly weak but could tell the illness had passed. When she opened her eyes, she knew by the shadows in the room that it was late morning. She turned to see Han sprawled in a chair near the bed, looking exhausted and unkempt. The moment he realized she was awake, he leaned forward abruptly, looking pleased and relieved.

"How are you feeling?" he asked.

"Awful," she said. "I want to go home. I need my mother."

"You'll have to settle for me," he said, actually sounding regretful. "I bought you something," he added quickly. "Perhaps when you're feeling better it will help occupy your time."

"What?" she asked, not even trying to be the least bit gracious.

Han retrieved a package from the bureau and tossed it on the bed. Idly, she opened it, surprised to find a large sketchbook and several sketching pencils. She felt too stunned to comment and said feebly, "Thank you," before she wrapped them back up and set the package on the bedside table.

Han brought her breakfast when she expressed some appetite. But then she declared she felt too weak to eat and told him she didn't want it. He propped her up in bed, sat down beside her, and held out the spoon for her.

"You're not going to feed me!"

"I am if it will help you get your strength back."

She opened her mouth to take a spoonful then said, "It tastes better than it looks."

Han chuckled, relieved beyond measure to know that she was going to be all right—even if that meant her returning to her usual scornful self. He gladly fed her until she was full, then afterward she soon fell back to sleep, and he left her alone. After he had all of the household chores completed, he went back up to the bedroom to find her awake and declaring that she was bored but far too weak to do anything about it.

"Would you like me to tell you a story?" he asked dramatically. He expected her to refuse the offer, but she simply said it was better than watching dust accumulate on the furniture.

"Well," he began, "we are—as I told you before—in the Black Forest. And as I also said, it is the land of fairy tales." She didn't look the least bit interested, but he continued nevertheless. "My mother used to tell me all of the fairy tales and legends of this place. I know them well."

Her look of disinterest gradually faded into one slightly attentive as he began a legendary tale with a certain amount of histrionics. When he'd completed the story, she asked him to tell her another. He managed to come up with enough stories to last that day and the next, but Maggie still didn't feel well, so he started them over.

She asked for her hairbrush and pulled all of her hair over the front of one shoulder, attempting to smooth the tangles out. But she quickly gave up when her arms felt too weak.

"Do you want me to help you?" Han asked in the middle of one of his stories.

"Don't be ridiculous," she insisted. But she made no protest when he sat beside her and took the brush. He continued his story while he methodically pulled the brush through her hair in long, even strokes. He marveled at its thickness and beauty, and relished the opportunity to touch it as he'd not been able to for years.

Maggie watched Han closely as he elaborated on the finer points of a story about some poor girl being taunted by a wicked queen. He glanced back and forth from her face to his meticulous attention of her hair. She was surprised at how comfortable he seemed with the chore, until she realized he was treating her much the same way he would one of the horses in his care. The thought was actually touching. She knew he was good at what he did, and he treated her family's horses with the utmost respect.

"It's not a horse's tail, you know," she said lightly when his story was finished.

"It works the same," he replied. "Do you want me to braid it?"

Maggie shrugged, conveying indifference. But she enjoyed watching him deftly weave her hair into a snug, even braid.

"You're good at that," she said as he tied a ribbon around the bottom to hold it. "Perhaps you could find work as a lady's maid."

Han looked at her with no trace of humor.

"I'm sorry," she said. "That wasn't very nice of me, was it."

"No," he answered. "But then, I've become quite accustomed to your not being very nice to me."

Maggie thought about that for a minute. "So why do you put up with it?" she asked.

"I work for you. I have to put up with it."

"You're not working for me right now."

"I'm not putting up with it right now. I'm just not being very nice in return. Or hadn't you noticed?"

"You're being nice to me today."

"You're not feeling well. But then, I think I could tolerate being a lady's maid—as long as you were the lady."

"Why would you want to do that," she asked, "when I'm not very nice to you?"

"Because I know it's only because you're unhappy."

Maggie took a sharp breath. "What makes you think I'm not happy?"

"I don't think we should talk about that right now, Maggie." He set the brush on the bedside table. "If you start trying to hit me, you'd probably pass out."

She was silent a long moment, pondering how much she agreed with him: she didn't want to talk about that right now—or perhaps ever. Instead she said, "Tell me another story."

Han smiled and complied. Between the stories and his bringing a bouquet of fresh wild-flowers to her each morning, Maggie didn't feel nearly as displeased with his company as she usually did. Gradually, she regained her strength and began doing a little around the house, just in time for Han to come in from chopping wood one afternoon, insisting that he was going to die. She was surprised when he declared that he was going to lie down, but she went upstairs to find him curled up in bed, burning with fever.

"Han," she said, touching his face, "now you've got it."

"Very perceptive," he managed to say.

Han's first fear was that Maggie would most likely leave. He certainly didn't have the strength to keep her here. But he hurt so badly that he figured there was little to be done about it, and he had no choice but to resign himself to this illness. He only prayed she wouldn't get herself lost—or worse. If nothing else, he hoped her fear of getting lost might keep her here. How could he keep her safe when he couldn't even stand up?

Maggie couldn't help feeling sorry for Han, and she stayed close by his bedside, keeping cool, wet cloths against his face. He'd taken good care of her while she'd endured this illness; surely she at least owed him the same. It took her off guard to realize that she actually *wanted* to be there, to help him through this. She felt a formless emotion more than once while she ran her fingers over his feverish face. She remembered her mother telling her that women have an instinctive sense to care for others in need, and she felt certain that's all she was feeling. Whatever the reasons, she remained close to Han, trying to keep his fever down and hoping he would come through all right.

Han drifted into consciousness, overcome with an unnatural heaviness. He forced his eyes open, having no sense of time passing; he had no idea how long he'd been in this condition. He was surprised not only to see Maggie, but to feel her hand gently pushing his hair off his face.

"Have I died?" he whispered.

"Hardly," she replied with scorn.

"I was certain," he said feebly, "that I was beholding an angel."

"Well, I'm not."

"I won't argue." He closed his eyes since it was difficult to keep them open. "Why are you still here?"

"I'm not going to be a fool and let myself get lost in this forest. I'll just have to figure something else out."

Han smiled and opened his eyes again. "That's a pretty poor excuse, but I'm glad you're here anyway."

"I'm not going to bring you flowers or tell you stories, so don't get too cocky."

Han managed a feeble chuckle and closed his eyes again. Within hours his fever broke, and he slept deeply. When he awoke, feeling rested but still weak as he'd expected, he was surprised to see Maggie sitting on a chair not far from the bed with her sketchbook, the pencil very busy. She made no remark when she saw that he was awake. As she kept glancing between him and the sketchbook, he realized she was drawing a picture of him. He made no comment about it until she began spending every spare moment, between the housework and seeing to his needs, with that sketchbook in her hands, watching him.

"I'm certain," he said, "there are a lot of things around here more worthy of your talent than me."

"I like drawing faces," she said, "and yours is the only face around. So, hush up and hold still."

When Han finally managed to get out of bed and Maggie was busy downstairs, he found the sketchbook in a bureau drawer and chuckled when he opened it. The picture was no doubt him. He'd seen that face in the mirror before, and he was impressed by her ability to capture facial features. It was a rare gift that even some of the best artists didn't possess, and the ones who did were usually in demand for painting portraits.

The amusing thing was the way she had depicted him. He looked downright ruthless. In the drawing, his head was lowered, the hollow cheek line intensified, the eyes narrowed and dark, and the expression nothing short of cruel. He looked at it a long moment then turned the page to find another picture of himself. But this one was worse. Again, despite the simple black and white structure of the sketch, the likeness was uncanny. But the pose was a bit different and the lips were spread slightly to show clenched teeth.

Turning the page there was another, and he laughed to see himself like a wild beast, growling and foaming at the mouth. The following page was himself with horns like the devil. And on the last sketch she'd done, which was only partially completed, he looked dead. But then, he figured he'd looked mostly that way for the past several days.

Maggie got angry when she found him looking at it, and she pulled it away abruptly.

"You do very nice work," he said as a genuine compliment. She looked perhaps disappointed that he'd made no comment on the artist's interpretation of the subject.

Maggie continued drawing pictures but refused to let him see them. As his health gradually returned, she was careful not to leave the book unguarded.

Han took Maggie by surprise one day when he said out of nowhere, "Now that I'm quite recovered, I think it's about time we get down to business and get married."

"Forget it!" she replied with an indignant glare.

"Ah, come on, Maggie. It would be fun. I'm not really such a bad guy."

"You're worse than bad. I will not marry you."

"Why not?"

"I hate you."

"No you don't," he chuckled. "In actuality, you like me."

"Now I'm certain you're insane," she muttered. "Where on earth do you get such delusions?"

"You took care of me while I was sick. That's a good start."

"I had little choice."

"Sure you did. You could have run away and left me to wallow in my misery."

"I would have gotten lost." She gave him his own argument. "Besides, you took care of me while I was sick."

"Because I like you," he smiled.

"Well, I don't like you!"

"Sure you do," he said with impeccable confidence. "You're just so preoccupied with that Nik bastard to be able to see it. If you'd figure out that he's just a good-for-nothing low-life, then I bet you'd like me."

"You are mad, Han Heinrich!" she insisted and left the room.

Once alone, Han huffed a labored sigh and hung his head. At this point, he had no idea how he was going to get himself out of this mess now that he'd gotten himself into it. And he'd not predicted how his own emotions would become so tangled into her stubbornness and anger. It took everything he had to keep his cool exterior with her, but he was determined to not let her see how deeply his heart was breaking.

That night Han found himself restless and unable to sleep. He stared blankly toward the ceiling, keenly aware of Maggie lying in the bed, breathing in gentle rhythm. He thought over all that had happened since he'd kidnapped her. And though he had never known for certain how he was going to manage to get her to marry him, he couldn't help feeling discouraged to see that the situation was looking hopeless—at least from a civil point of view. He thought about the duke's insistence that he get her to marry him by whatever means necessary, and he wondered exactly what means the duke had in mind. He'd like to have the opportunity to ask him that question right now, certain it would be answered with a lot of empty stammering.

Han almost wondered at times if he should go through with all of this . . . or if he even wanted to. But there was a vision he brought to mind in moments of doubt that made it all seem worth it. Not only for the sake of Horstberg—but for himself as well—he knew that he had to see this through. His vision could perhaps turn out to be nothing more than a disappointing delusion. But the duke himself had asked Han to do this, and he would not let it all fall apart now, simply because Maggie was obstinate and narrow-minded. One way or another, he would have Maggie for his wife, no matter what he had to do. For now, he simply had to keep his emotions out of it; he couldn't possibly manage to keep forging ahead if he didn't. And yet he couldn't resist, if only for a moment, allowing himself to consider how he really felt about her.

Kneeling beside the bed, Han watched her sleeping. Even in the faint moonlight, he sighed at her beauty. "If you only knew, my love," he whispered, running his fingers repeatedly through her fiery hair. "Perhaps one day you will." He couldn't resist pressing a kiss to her brow. She moaned and shifted but continued to sleep. He watched her a few more minutes then impulsively sat beside her, pulling her into his arms. She came awake and immediately tried to pull away.

"Please don't," he whispered. "Just let me hold you."

"Why should I?" she said, continuing to struggle.

"Why not?" he asked, holding her tightly enough in his arms that she had to know struggling was futile. He had proven it far too many times.

Maggie made no reply, so he asked quietly, "Don't you ever want to be held, just because it's nice, because it feels good, and it's . . . comforting?"

"Yes," she said, "but I would prefer to be held by someone who cares for me."

"Nik," Han stated.

"Yes, Nik."

"And you don't think I care for you?"

"If you did, you would not have kidnapped me and forced me to live here . . . this way . . . with you."

"Would you believe me if I told you my motives were admirable?"

"Oh, really, Han," she said as if it were preposterous.

"If Nik cared for you, would he have asked you to run away and defy your parents' wishes?"

"You are hardly in a position to say such a thing. You, who have kidnapped me. I'm certain my parents are thrilled about that," she added with sarcasm.

"I'll make it up to them," he said. A moment of silence passed. "Maggie, why do you hate me so badly?"

"Where do you want me to start?" she asked, and he chuckled, trying to keep the mood light even though he hoped for some serious conversation.

"What do you hate most about me, Maggie? Name it."

"I hate the things you say about Nik. You have no idea what kind of man he is."

"Do you?"

"I know how he made me feel when I was with him."

"I'm certain he would say or do just about anything to get what he wanted."

"I don't want to talk about Nik."

"All right, why else do you hate me, Maggie?"

"You kidnapped me," she said like a pouting child.

"Don't think of me as a kidnapper, Maggie. Think of me as the hero. I'm the one who saved you from the evil villain, and maybe I saved Horstberg, too."

"Baggage!" she muttered.

"If I were the hero, would you like me then?" he asked.

"I didn't like you even before you kidnapped me," she said through a yawn.

"No, you didn't like the way I teased you. Actually, you liked me a lot. You just didn't want to admit it because I'm a scoundrel and a louse . . . and I'm just a stablehand."

Maggie decided not to make any further comment, knowing she didn't want to have this conversation. She was tired and wanted him to leave her alone, but it was obvious he had no intention of letting her go. Once she made the decision to just relax and remain quiet, she fell back to sleep within minutes. When she woke up to daylight, he was still sitting against the headboard, his arm around her. She found him watching her intently, and she snarled, "You can let go of me now. It's morning."

"So?" Han asked, not wanting to let go of the serenity he'd felt while she'd slept in his arms.

"It's time to get up."

"I don't want to. I'm rather enjoying myself."

"I'm not."

"Maggie," he whispered adamantly, "look at me." He held her chin with his hand and forced her to meet his eyes directly. "You are beautiful," he said softly.

Maggie turned her face away, and he insisted, "Look at me." She did so immediately, and he realized she was afraid of him.

"Do I frighten you?" he asked soberly.

"You disgust me," she replied with arrogance.

"Why can't you see that I would take good care of you?"

"I told you last night, if you cared for me you would—"

Han cut off her words with a kiss. Maggie struggled as he'd expected, but he held her tightly and kissed her again. Gradually, she stopped fighting his kiss, but rather became dormant, like a cold stone, and he wondered which was worse.

"Maggie," he whispered, holding her closer. "Don't you remember," his lips moved close to her ear, "what it was like to be in love with me?"

"That's irrelevant now."

Han felt her tension increase, but he chose to ignore it and pressed kisses to the side of her throat. "Remember, Maggie, how you wanted me to marry you? How you begged me not to stop when—"

"I was a fool," Maggie muttered. Her heart pounded while she wondered why it felt as if she were lying. Since this escapade had begun, she had often wondered if Han would take advantage of her. But with the time that they'd been alone together, she had come to assume that was not his motive for abducting her. He had proven his apparent disinterest in that regard with the many nights he'd spent close by. She had almost forgotten that worry, assuming that even Han would not stoop so low. But now, being held this way, she wondered if he *did* have dishonorable intentions. And she felt suddenly afraid for her virtue. She strained to break free, but he only held her tighter.

"What's the matter?" he asked, seeming genuinely innocent.

"That is a stupid question. You have no right to hold me this way and—"

"Why not?"

Maggie turned her face away, and he added sternly, "Look at me, Maggie, and tell me why not."

She looked directly at him, finding his face very close to hers. Trying to think of an appropriate answer, she found herself briefly distracted by his eyes, wondering what made them seem to glow with their unusual green color.

"Answer me," he whispered, and memories flooded into her mind against her will.

"Han," she said softly, finding herself weak for some reason, "you are . . . just a . . . groom, and I . . ."

"I'm a man, Maggie," he said, holding her closer. "If you would take the shades from your eyes for more than a moment, you might see that I am a man." Gently, yet with force, he took her hand into his and pressed it against his face, over his lips, down his throat, and finally against his chest, holding it there. "I'm a man," he whispered. "If I were a prince, or a count, or a baron, I would still feel the same."

Han waited intently for some kind of cruel retort, some harsh reaction. But she only stared into his eyes, seeming momentarily lost in them. He felt her breath become subtly labored, and he kissed her again, tentatively teasing her lips with his. Something almost indiscernible seeped through her response. He pressed his lips to her throat and felt her soften in his arms. His heart began to pound, and he realized how desperate he'd become for any indication that she might actually learn to trust him and care for him again. He kissed her once more, and her response was acute, even torrid.

"Maggie," he whispered, then immediately regretted even speaking. The spell was broken when she stiffened, and he pulled back to look at her, reading nothing but hatred and scorn in her eyes.

"Get dressed, Maggie," he said in a light tone that he hoped would hide his frustration and discouragement as he abruptly let her go. "It's your turn to fix breakfast." He resisted cursing aloud as he silently reproached himself for allowing his emotions to get caught up in all of this.

Maggie knew she should have felt relieved when Han let her go and moved away, but she didn't. She sat silently in the bed, watching him put on his boots while she searched for any possible reason that might explain how she had just behaved. Several minutes after he left the room, she was still trying figure it out. She could only conclude that pondering the question too deeply jabbed at something inside of her that refused to be examined too closely. More minutes passed while she almost felt like two different people: one of them desperately trying to convince the other that her declarations concerning the way she lived her life—and how they had impacted Han—were right and she would not back down. And yet another part of herself squirmed with discomfort and even some degree of fear at the very idea that perhaps she'd done something wrong somewhere along the way. But she was who she was, and it couldn't be changed. Could it? She had to stand her ground or she would never survive this. Still, she found it difficult to pull herself away from a myriad of indiscernible emotions and get out of bed.

Chapter Eight

MAGGIE'S DEFEAT

$\mathcal{M}$aggie became keenly aware of an awkward silence that settled between her and Han. But she didn't know what to do about it. Days passed with hardly a word passing between them unless speaking was absolutely necessary.

Fearing she would go mad from the silence, Maggie asked late one morning as lunchtime was approaching, "How long have we been here?"

Han replied that it had been over six weeks, and Maggie felt despair. His next comment took her completely by surprise—especially given his recent reluctance to say anything at all. "And to celebrate, we're going out to pick wild berries. I just happen to know where we can find some, and they should be perfectly ripe about now."

"I don't feel like it," she insisted, still stuck on the reality of how long she'd been away from home. She didn't feel like doing *anything*.

"Well it's either that or tied to the bed, Your Royal Pain-in-the . . ." He didn't finish, and she glared at him, knowing what he was thinking.

"But we haven't eaten yet," she protested.

"We're eating out," he said, and she watched him load a hamper with food. He picked up a blanket and opened the door, motioning elaborately for her to exit.

Maggie glared at him as she passed by, but he only smiled in return and followed. She wondered what diabolical plot he had formed in the guise of a picnic. They sat together on the blanket and ate in silence, which seemed innocent enough. And she couldn't deny that it felt good to be out of the cottage. After they'd eaten, he led her to the wild berries he'd spoken of, and they proceeded to load the empty hamper with them.

"How did you know this was here?" she asked, and he lifted his brows as if to question her motives. Or perhaps he was considering how much information he should give her. Probably both, she concluded.

"I came here more than once when I was a child," he said, and she was genuinely surprised. He smiled and went on, "The cottage belonged to my mother's aunt. She died recently, and my mother—being the last remaining relative—inherited the property."

"Then you weren't lying to me," she said while they continued to pick berries, side by side.

"I've never lied to you, Maggie." She gave him a dubious glare. "I've perhaps been a *little* deceptive," he smiled comfortably, "but I've never lied."

Han wished his declaration would provoke her into an argument, or better yet, an honest and sincere conversation—although an argument was more likely. But he would have preferred to have her say anything at all. These silent days were driving him insane.

Deciding to fill in the silence himself, he spoke wistfully, "I remember coming to this very spot and having a picnic with my parents. We had cold chicken and black bread and cheese, and we ate these berries. My father had a bottle of wine, and it was the first time I tasted it."

"And did you like it?" she asked, sounding bored.

"I thought it was ghastly." He chuckled, but she made no response. "I've since acquired a taste."

"Some wine would be nice right now," she commented more to herself. "It might be nice to get drunk and forget about all of this for a while."

Han couldn't hold back his surprise. "I dare say you have never been drunk once in your life, so how would you know?"

"I *don't* know, but it sounds nice right now."

Han ignored the insult of the implication and said, "I doubt you'd like the hangover."

"Couldn't be any worse than this." She turned accusing eyes toward Han, but he chose to ignore her still.

Silence set in again, and Han began eating berries as he picked them, watching Maggie as she worked. She looked so beautiful. He liked the simplicity she had gained since he'd torn her away from her upper-class world. The few clothes she'd brought were simple and practical, and she rarely wore her hair up since it was difficult for her to do so on her own. But he liked her this way. It reminded him of the way she'd been as a young woman—except for her constantly downcast eyes. That he hated.

"Is it really so bad?" he asked in a tone of simple curiosity.

"What?" she asked.

"Being here . . . with me."

"It's not where I want to be," she stated flatly. Then she added when he made no remark, "I don't want to marry you, Han."

"Why not?" He saw anger flash into her eyes and immediately added, "There's no need to get riled. Just stay calm and tell me why you don't want to marry me."

She took a deep breath. "I love Nik."

"Don't you think you could live without him?"

"I don't want to live without him," she said abruptly and turned and left.

Han followed her back to their picnic spot and found her sitting on the blanket with her knees against her chest.

"Maggie," he said intently as he sat beside her. He knew she expected him to say something deep or pleading, but he only held a berry up near her mouth and whispered, "Taste this."

She hesitated but bit into it and licked away the drop of juice it left on her lip. "It's good," she said. Han left his hand near her mouth. When she had swallowed, she spread her lips slightly and he put the rest of the berry there for her to take. He felt her tongue unintentionally flick against his finger, then he watched with gratification at the pleasure she found in the sweet taste of the fruit.

"Can I eat some more," she asked with the innocence of a child, "or were you going to make preserves or something out of them?"

Han laughed. "You can eat all you want," he said. "I can cook to survive, like when my mother was too busy taking care of your mother, and our housekeeper wasn't available. Making preserves is not among my talents."

"What are your talents?" she asked with only a trace of cynicism as she began eating the juicy berries.

"I know everything there is to know about horses," he said, then chuckled.

"What's funny?" she asked.

"I don't know if I have any other talents."

"You tie a wicked knot," she said as if she truly meant it as a compliment.

"So I do." He lifted his brows, pretending to be proud of himself.

"And you are quite a storyteller."

Again he smiled, glad to know his stories had left even a little bit of an impression on her. "And what are your talents?" he asked. "Other than drawing cruel pictures of me."

"I don't have any," she said.

"Doesn't it take talent to be a princess?"

"No," she stated. "I just have to be in certain places at certain times and say certain things to certain people."

Han chuckled. "Now that takes talent." She remained silently melancholy, and he added, "You play the piano."

"My father says that I am gifted. I don't enjoy it much."

"You don't enjoy anything much, do you, Maggie." It was not a question.

"Of course I do," she said in defense.

"Tell me," he challenged, "the last time you had fun."

Her first thought was of Nik, and she said, "I would be having fun now if I were with Nik."

Maggie had hoped to rile him, but he only said, "What do you suppose you would be doing?"

"I don't know. But I always had fun before when I was with him."

"What did you do that was so fun?"

"We . . . would ride, and walk, and . . . talk."

"Did he kiss you? He'd have been a fool not to."

"Of course he kissed me."

"Was it fun?"

She got a nostalgic look in her eye, but still she didn't smile. "Fun would not describe it. But I enjoyed it nevertheless."

"Did you do anything else?" He lifted his brows mischievously.

"Like what?"

"Like . . . what happens beyond a kiss."

Maggie blushed and turned away, leaving him satisfied that she was innocent. His relief was more immense than he wanted to admit.

"You see," Han said, "you didn't really have fun with Nik. You just enjoyed being with him because he was no doubt pleasant and charming, the same way his father was."

"Nik is not like his father!"

"How do you know?"

"How do *you* know?" she came back quickly.

"My father told me everything about Nikolaus du Woernig."

"But you don't know Nik."

"Neither do you, Maggie. You could not have possibly spent enough time with him to know anything at all about what he's really like."

Maggie shot an angry glare at him, and he smiled. Arguing with her was far better than awkward silence, and that was something he'd wanted to say for a long time. "I'm sorry," he said, but he didn't mean it. "We shouldn't talk about that. Let me go back to my original question. When was the last time you had fun—before you met Nik?"

Maggie remained silent, but he could tell she was thinking very hard. He let her think a good long time before he said, "You don't remember, do you."

"I went to a party last year that was fun."

"Yes," he said lightly, "you probably danced a little, drank some champagne, chatted a bit, showed off your new gown. I bet you had a glorious time," he finished wryly.

Again she remained silent, but he caught something in her eyes, something genuine he'd rarely seen in the past few years. "Did I hurt your feelings?" he asked with sincerity.

"No," she said adamantly.

"Then what's the matter?"

"Perhaps princesses aren't supposed to have fun."

"Who told you that?" As shocked as he was by her statement, perhaps it gave him a clue to the way she had changed so dramatically.

"No one told me," she said, her voice rising defensively. "They didn't have to. It's just the way it is."

"Sonia has fun."

"How do you know?"

"She goes with me and Erich sometimes. She laughs a lot, you know. She knows how to have fun."

"Sonia and I never had much in common."

"That's fine. You don't have to be like your sister. But you could still have fun. We used to have fun, Maggie. Remember?"

"We were children."

"We didn't kiss like children," he said, and she turned away. "You know, Maggie," he moved a little closer, "you haven't even smiled— not even a little bit—since we left Horstberg."

"I've had little to be cheerful over," she said with an accusing stare.

"Well, let's think of something."

"Take me home."

"Besides that."

"There is nothing besides that."

"Maggie," he whispered, "how long has it been since you've walked in a mud puddle in bare feet and squished the mud between your toes?"

"I don't remember."

"How long since you lay down in the snow to make angels?"

She didn't answer.

"Remember when we climbed trees to see what the world looks like from up there?"

"No."

"Have you ever jumped into a pond with all your clothes on?"

"No."

"Well," he said authoritatively, "not only have you forgotten how to have fun, you don't know how to use your senses."

"What are you talking about?" she asked, genuinely baffled.

"Look at the sky, Maggie. What do you see?"

She looked up contemplatively. "Sky. A few clouds."

"I see an endless sea of blue and floating images."

"You're seeing things," she said dubiously.

"Take a deep breath," he said, and she did. "What do you smell?"

"Nothing."

"Can't you smell the earth?"

"No."

"The trees, the flowers, the berries?"

"No."

"The berries," he said, holding one near her lips. "Close your eyes. Take a bite—slowly—and tell me what it feels like."

Maggie did as he said, but her boredom was still apparent.

"Well?" he asked expectantly when she swallowed it then opened her eyes.

"It tasted the same as the last one."

Han sighed in exasperation. "Here. Take the rest—slowly." She pulled it from his fingers with her lips, and he said, "What do you think?"

"You've got berry juice all over your fingers."

He chuckled then said with challenge, "Get it off."

"What?"

"You got it there. Get it off." She reached for a napkin, but he stopped her hand with his. "The same way you took the berry," he whispered.

"You are very strange, Han Heinrich."

"Do it anyway. Humor me."

Maggie shrugged and sighed, then she stuck out her tongue and licked the drops of juice from his fingers. Han couldn't resist putting his other hand to her face, longing for even a tiny piece of evidence that the real Maggie still existed. The way she'd returned his kiss not so many days ago gave him hope, and he looked directly into her eyes as he whispered, "You look pretty today, Maggie." He became as mesmerized by her gaze as she seemed to be with his, and he moved his face slowly toward hers. At the very moment his lips were about to meet hers, she pushed him away with an angry groan and stood abruptly.

"And you can go to . . ." Maggie withheld the last word on purpose, figuring if he could speak with unfinished sentences, so could she. She felt so angry and confused and . . . *furious* . . . that she wanted to break something. All she could do was walk away.

"I'll meet you there, Your Royal Pain-in-the . . ." Han called and hurried to follow her toward the cottage, cursing the Duke of Horstberg for offering him this job. After six weeks of this, he'd be more than happy to be a stablehand for the rest of his life.

With the passing of more days, Han came to believe that Maggie had set her mind to making him so miserable that he would be glad to free himself of her and just take her home. And he was tempted. But his vision of the future kept him going. He had to stick it out—for himself as well as for Horstberg. In his deepest self, he knew there was another side to Maggie still hiding in there somewhere.

He loved to think about the little girl who had followed him and Erich around, insisting she be a part of their play. As a child, Maggie had climbed trees and played in the mud. She hadn't been afraid to get dirty, or laugh, or have fun. Even at a young age, she had been able to play the part of the princess well when it was necessary, but she'd had no trouble setting it aside just to be Maggie. Her parents were both very much that way in their roles as duke and duchess; therefore, it was only natural that their children should follow that example. Han had considered many times the oddness of Maggie's behavior in contrast to the other members of her family. They each had the dignity and discipline to fill their positions, but they had no trouble putting the business aside and behaving like ordinary people. Han nearly felt like a part of the du Woernig family; he always had, given the way his parents were so close to the duke and duchess. And he'd enjoyed many good times and much laughter with them. But a day had come when Maggie stopped laughing. And she'd never been the same.

Analyzing the situation for what seemed like the millionth time, Han wondered how this woman could even *be* a du Woernig. If she didn't look so much like her parents, he'd have been certain they'd found her under a rock somewhere. Maggie's mother was a patient, kind woman with a sense of humor and a great deal of compassion. And her father was a good man who knew how to laugh and have a good time; he was deeply committed to his responsibilities, but he could set them aside and enjoy life. Han might have wondered if perhaps they'd done something wrong in raising their children, except that Erich and Sonia were both very much the same. And there *had* been a time when Maggie had fit in comfortably with her family. He just didn't understand, but if all of his analyzing had taught him anything, it was that he would likely *never* understand unless Maggie could grow to trust him again. And the last several weeks had taught him that such a possibility seemed as out of reach as the moon.

He'd come to the Black Forest believing that what Maggie needed most was some humility, to help remind her of what was truly important, to help her remember who she had once been. He'd done his best to put the two of them on equal ground, and she had certainly learned some competence at household chores. But humility was nowhere to be seen, and Han didn't know what to do about it. She held to an attitude toward him that made him cringe. If he wasn't certain that somewhere beneath all of that was something of her parents in her, he'd have given up long ago. This was not the woman he wanted to spend the rest of his life with. But he had to believe there was something better hiding somewhere. Surely the Maggie he loved was simply lost in the midst of something hurting and unhappy that she didn't want to face. If only he could reach her!

To top it all off, Han had the uncanny feeling that time was running out. Though he'd been careful, he couldn't help thinking that sooner or later Nik Koenig was going to find them. Han had been into town enough that people knew they were here. It was a small town where everyone knew everything. Given what Han knew about Nik's motives, he felt certain he'd have the nose of a bloodhound. Sometimes Han could convince himself that he was just paranoid, but at other times his instincts told him they couldn't stay here indefinitely, that they would both be in very real danger if Nik Koenig caught up with them. Not to mention the fate of the country of Horstberg!

But Han didn't dare go dragging Maggie around the world, never knowing what to expect from her. He couldn't show her a good time—as her father had requested—if she didn't want to have one. He had to admit that it was unreasonable to expect Maggie to love him against her will. He simply had no control over another person's feelings. But marrying her was another matter. From the moment the duke had proposed his idea to Han—given his own history with Maggie and the strong connection between their families—Han had believed it was right, and he considered the situation critical. If this was an arranged marriage, he could live with that. It just had to be done. But how?

He pondered the matter and prayed a great deal, knowing he was never going to get out of this on his own. From stories his parents had told him of how Cameron du Woernig had taken back his country from the hands of his tyrannical brother, there was no denying that God's hand had been involved. Georg and Elsa both believed firmly that God would always intercede on behalf of the good of Horstberg because for the most part it was a good country with good people residing there. But they also believed that God's hand had been in each of their individual lives—that He truly cared about each person and wished to bless, assist, and guide them. Han had grown up believing in such a God, and he had to believe now that God's hand would guide him to help spare Horstberg from the hands of Nik Koenig, and that God would also want both him and Maggie to be safe and happy. He was counting on it. But each passing day made him wonder if God was involved at all; or perhaps Han just didn't know how to properly interpret any message that God might send him.

Baffled and frustrated as he was, Han fought to keep up his light-hearted attitude around Maggie. He didn't want her to see how she was getting to him, so he always had a good sarcastic comment to match each of hers. And he put serious effort into thinking of funny things to say that might make her laugh. But he was running out of comical versions of addressing a princess, and she'd not once cracked a smile in all these weeks. If something didn't change soon, he surely *would* go mad.

On an especially dark night when Han found it particularly difficult to sleep, he itemized all of the facts of the situation as he knew them. He prayed and then went through the list again. And prayed again. He finally went to sleep but woke up to find it still dark. He was barely conscious when the idea came into his mind the he needed to focus on using Maggie's sense of honor, the fact that she *would* marry a man if her virtue had been compromised. The thought felt inspired, but as Han considered the only possibilities he could think of, he felt certain God would not be condoning *that*. He could not marry Maggie against her will, and he certainly *wouldn't* compromise her virtue outside of marriage. They were only a few minutes from civilization; a marriage could be arranged easily enough—if the bride were the least bit cooperative.

He stared into the darkness for what felt like hours, wondering if this was the first true sign of insanity. If he couldn't use her sense of honor against her without compromising his *own* sense of honor, then it just wasn't possible. He couldn't do it. It was as simple as that. His *answer* seemed contradictory and made him even more confused. What he needed was a miracle.

Han tried all through the day to figure out some way to play upon Maggie's sense of honor without doing something that God would surely disapprove of. Long after Maggie had gone upstairs to go to bed, he was still trying to figure it out, and he knew he couldn't sleep. He sat outside the cottage far into the night, trying to make sense of this situation. With an imaginary scale, he attempted to balance his feelings with the facts. He wondered where to draw the line between honor to his country and honor as a man who had been raised with good moral judgment. He analyzed all he knew of Maggie's feelings and tried to mesh them with his own, added upon by his assignment from the duke. It was all such a mess. His head ached just thinking about it.

He finally went to bed, but he just ended up uttering the same prayer over and over, hoping that God would hear it. Deep into the night, Han finally had an idea. He could see no other choice but to put Maggie in a position where she felt she *had* to marry him to maintain her honor. But he also knew that he had enough ingenuity and sensitivity to handle the situation in a delicate manner. Maggie would still hate him, but at least he could live with himself. Having a woman marry him because she believed she had to wasn't very flattering, but he was learning more and more to keep his own emotions out of the equation. There were far more important facets of the situation to be considered.

Throughout the day, Han figured the plan out carefully in his mind, praying that all would go well and that God would be with him in spite of the absurdity of this whole thing. If nothing else, he hoped that God would consider the security of Horstberg a higher priority than all of Han's scheming.

Late in the evening while Maggie busily dusted the bookshelves in the parlor, Han plopped down on the sofa and noisily opened a bottle of wine. Chuckling loudly, he poured himself a healthy glassful, took a long swallow and sighed with some forced drama. He knew he could be a very good actor when he needed to be; he just hoped Maggie would fall for it.

"What are you doing?" Maggie asked, much to his pleasure.

"I'm having a glass of wine," he said, not even glancing toward her.

"Where on earth did you get wine?"

"I bought it, of course," he answered, "the last time I went into town. I thought it might come in handy one of these days."

"In handy for what?" she asked skeptically.

"Oh, I don't know," he shrugged and discreetly observed her. "Perhaps we could celebrate."

Maggie glanced warily at the second glass sitting empty near the wine bottle, then she turned back to her dusting and gave a huffy little grunt. "Celebrate what?"

"Anything you want," he said. "Is it anybody's birthday?"

"I don't think so," she huffed again, "but then I don't have a clue what day it is, so how should I know?"

"Ah, no matter," he sighed, "we don't need a reason to celebrate."

She only glared at him skeptically and continued dusting.

"Maggie," he said after a reasonable silence, "what are you doing?" She didn't answer and he added, "You've dusted those books five times this week."

Maggie stopped dusting but said nothing. A minute later she stopped and asked liked a child wanting candy, "Could I have some?"

Han tried to keep his smile from showing how perfectly pleased he felt. "This other glass isn't for the big bad wolf." She sat down, and he poured her a glass of wine and gave it to her.

"What are you up to?" she asked.

Han smiled again. "I can assure you," he said, touching her glass with his, "that my intentions are purely dishonorable."

Maggie watched Han and wondered if she should trust him. As usual, she couldn't tell if he was teasing or serious. More likely teasing, she concluded. For all that he had kidnapped her and kept her captive, she still couldn't fathom Han doing anything *dishonorable*.

Not certain what to think—or do—she simply sat there, holding her glass, until Han bent close to her and whispered, "You told me yourself it would be nice to just get drunk and forget about all of this for a while."

She looked at him closely, as if that might help her discern his possible motives. Perhaps he too was growing weary of this tedious pattern they were in, hardly uttering a word to each other. With that thought most prominent in her mind, she took a careful sip and declared, "It's good."

"Of course it's good. It ought to be for what I paid for it." He sighed and stretched out his legs, leaning his head back as if he really didn't care what she did or didn't do. She almost believed he might actually get drunk and give her a perfect opportunity to escape. But as he'd pointed out on many occasions, where would she go without getting lost?

Maggie glared at Han dubiously, which made him chuckle. But when he took a long swallow of his drink and closed his eyes, paying no heed to what she was doing, she couldn't resist slowly emptying her glass, enjoying the sweet, smooth flavor of the wine. She thought of how they'd always had wine with dinner at Castle Horstberg, and she missed her home and family.

Han poured himself a second glass of wine, sipped a little and relaxed again, so Maggie decided to do the same.

"What are you doing?" Han asked abruptly.

"Are you blind?" she retorted. "I'm having another glass of wine."

"Are you sure that's a good idea?" he asked, and she gave him an icy glare. "Erich's told me you don't hold liquor well. Perhaps one glass is enough."

"Oh, mind your business and go to sleep. It tastes good, and I want more." She took a long swallow then stared at her glass as if it were a priceless treasure. "This is one of the few nice things you've done for me since we've come here, so let me enjoy it."

"But, Maggie," he protested, taking the glass from her and setting it down, "what if you lose control of your senses? Do you think that's wise, considering . . . well, what if it made you forget how much you hate me? If you did that, you might like me, and who knows what might happen?"

"Don't count on it," she said scornfully.

"Oh, I'm not counting on it," he replied, smiling at his own honesty, "but I thought it might be worth a try."

"Mind your business," she repeated and emptied her glass again. Han just sat back and smiled.

Maggie savored the full essence of the wine and closed her eyes, trying to imagine other times and places where good memories were rooted. Since she'd never even tasted hard liquor, it didn't take much wine to make her feel relaxed. In fact, she'd likely never had more than one glass with dinner—ever. By the time she'd finished her second glass, she basked in a strange tingling sensation in her limbs and a pleasant heaviness in her head. Oblivious to Han, she embarked on her third glass, more relaxed than she'd been since this ordeal had begun and dearly enjoying a brief escape from the present circumstances.

Han watched Maggie and felt utterly pleased with himself over how well this was going. He'd had a small glass of wine to begin with, and then had only poured out a small amount from which he'd only taken a sip. He needed to remain in complete control of his senses, whereas Maggie was losing complete control of her own, much more quickly and completely than he'd anticipated. He chuckled to realize she had consumed all of the bottle except for what little Han had drank. He chuckled again when she asked in slurred voice, "I've never been drunk. Is it fun?"

"You tell me." Han smirked, and she giggled. He'd not heard such a delightful sound come through her lips in years. All he could do was watch her, mesmerized and drawn back to the time when she had loved him as much as he loved her. He turned more toward her and asked in a soft voice, "Have I ever told you that you're beautiful?"

"Yes, you have," she admitted, "but I never believed you."

"Don't you think you're beautiful?" he added.

"I suppose I'm not bad to look at," she replied distantly. "I mean, everyone says that I look like my mother, and she is beautiful. Let's just say I never believed that *you* really thought I was beautiful."

"Oh, but I've always thought you were beautiful," he insisted.

"Is that why you've always been so cruel to me?" she asked carelessly.

"Am I cruel to you?" he asked.

"Oh, yes," she said matter-of-factly. "I don't know why. I'm really not such a bad person. I can't help it that I'm a princess," she added almost sadly, and Han momentarily felt sorry for her.

"I can't help it that I'm a stable groom," Han replied in a light tone.

"But you do make a good groom, Han."

"I do?"

"Oh, yes. It's always more fun to come to the stables when you're there. I mean, you can be annoying at times with all your silly jokes, and you are cruel to me sometimes, but you are fun . . . sometimes."

Han chuckled, surprised by her confessions. This was already going so much better than he'd hoped.

"You know," she continued, "I had such fun riding in the middle of the night. I missed you when you didn't ride with me anymore."

"That was your idea," he said gently.

"I know, but I don't think I'm very smart. I just didn't know any other way to fix the problem."

Han's brow furrowed. "What problem?" he asked, his heart quickening. He hadn't anticipated that this might be the means to figure out much of what had troubled him. Any little tidbit of information he might get out of her could be helpful.

Maggie looked disoriented. "You never asked me again if you could ride with me. You should have, you know, Han. I wanted you to. But you never offered until one night when I was going to meet Nik. Of course, you couldn't come along then. You should have offered sooner. We could have had fun. I mean, it was fun anyway, but I must admit, you are fun, Han—most of the time."

Han smiled even though he felt saddened. It wasn't much, but knowing what she'd just shared made the present situation not seem quite so hopeless.

"I don't understand you, though," she rambled on. "I mean, most of the time you're so witty . . . and . . . joking . . . and laughing." She said the words so loudly that Han couldn't help laughing. Then she became thoughtful, and he listened. "But other times you look at me in that way of yours and I feel certain you don't like me."

"Why wouldn't I like you?" Han asked carefully, wondering if his efforts to hide his feelings all these years had been misinterpreted.

"I can't blame you for not liking me. It was cruel of me, the way I treated you after . . . after . . . well, you know." She met his eyes and smiled.

He forced a smile in return, but he was still trying to understand what had changed inside of her that had made her so cruel. Having her admit it held a degree of vindication, but he wanted even more to be able to understand it.

"You know, Han, sometimes your eyes glow when you look at me. You have the most unique eyes, and when they look at me, they . . ." She moved a little closer as if to assure herself and added firmly, "See," she pointed at him, "see there—like that! They glow!"

"Are you sure?" he chuckled, leaning closer still. Perhaps she wouldn't give him any more answers, but he enjoyed having her so near to him without having to force her.

"Oh, yes," she proclaimed, so close he could smell the wine on her breath.

Han wanted to touch her but didn't dare. She was dazed from the wine and apparently mesmerized by his eyes. It was as if she were under a spell, and he didn't want to break it. He wished she could always be this way, talking freely to him, relaxed and cheerful. And he wanted her to know the reasoning behind the way he'd behaved with her. Taking a deep breath, he decided it couldn't hurt to at least try and say some of the things he'd always wanted to say—even if she might not remember them tomorrow. "I never stopped caring for you, Maggie."

"Really?" she asked dubiously, still looking into his eyes.

"Do you want to know what I really wanted to do all those times when you came into the stables, wearing one of those cute little riding habits you own?"

"What?" she asked as if she couldn't begin to imagine.

Han lifted his hand slowly to her face and felt relief when she didn't retract from his touch. Rather than speaking, he carefully threaded his fingers into her fiery hair and she leaned her head back into his hand with a long sigh.

Han took a deep breath. This was going much better than he'd expected, but still he was afraid to break the spell. Gingerly he leaned toward her and whispered in her ear, "I always wanted to kiss you, Maggie. Even when you hated me, I wanted so badly to just take you in my arms and kiss you."

She pulled back to look at him in surprise, and Han was afraid he'd lost her. "Whatever for?" she asked with wide eyes.

"I thought it might be nice," he said, certain that an evasive answer would be safer than admitting to the full truth.

"Well, you've kissed me not so long ago," she retorted, "And it wasn't very nice. You were cruel to me."

"I'm sorry," he said with sincerity, then decided it was now or never. "If you let me kiss you now, I'll be nice. I promise."

Again she looked searchingly into his eyes. She didn't give any consent, but she didn't protest either. Carefully, Han leaned forward and touched his lips to hers.

"Hmm," she muttered in contemplation when he pulled back slightly, "that was nice enough, but I think I liked it better when Nik kissed me."

"And how was that?" Han asked, more amused than anything. Or perhaps he just preferred to avoid thinking too much about Nik Koenig kissing Maggie *at all.* Focusing on the humor of the situation was simply easier.

"Like this," she said, and Han found his shoulders in her hands and her lips pressed firmly over his.

"That's it?" Han laughed when she pulled away, concealing his surprise at her boldness.

"It was nice," she said, her voice dreamy.

"Nice enough, I suppose," he said nonchalantly, attempting to conceal what her kiss had done to the pace of his heart. "But I can do better."

Maggie eyed him with challenge in her expression, and it was all the permission Han needed. With purpose, he pushed one arm around her waist and put the other behind her head. His lips claimed hers elusively at first, then gradually, he let the fervency of his feelings seep into his kiss. Just as he'd hoped, Maggie melted within his grasp and responded willingly.

"You like that, I see," he smirked, but she only looked at him in dazed silence. With no hesitation, he kissed her again, easing her completely into his arms. Her response urged him on, and he kissed her undauntedly, savoring every moment, trying to comprehend the years he had longed for just this. Her mouth became warm, and it tasted of wine. The effect was doubly intoxicating, and he kissed her on and on.

"Oh, Han," she said breathlessly while he kissed her throat. "I'd forgotten how good you were at this."

"Am I?" he chuckled close to her ear, then he nibbled on it, and she trembled in his arms.

"Oh, yes," she murmured.

"Better than Nik Koenig?" he asked, easing her closer still.

She nodded and urged his lips to hers briefly before she said, "It must have been that love potion."

"Oh, no, Maggie. I loved you long before that," he said and kissed her again. "Don't you remember?" She made a dreamy noise, and the moment became almost timeless as Han absorbed this unexpected evidence that Maggie *did* feel something for him beyond her outward malice. For the first time in years, he blessed these feelings he had for Maggie, rather than cursing them. As he observed her in that moment, free of all inhibition, he could almost believe his feelings for her were leading him to his destiny. And the evidence that a part of her cared for him—even trusted him—gave him the hope that eventually her feelings would come back to her and bring them together.

"Maggie," he whispered and pressed his mouth over hers again. She whimpered and pressed a hand into his hair. Abruptly, she drew back, looking startled.

"Oh, my," she said, seeming embarrassed and distraught.

Han stood up and hurried to the kitchen. He returned with another bottle of wine and quickly uncorked it while she sat looking stunned and bewildered. He poured some into her glass and handed it to her.

"I thought it was all gone."

"I found more," he replied impishly.

Maggie lifted the glass to her lips and drained it with little effort. "Oh, I do believe this bottle tastes even better than the last one." She held up her glass, and he filled it again. She drank this one a little slower, but when she wanted more, he began to fear she'd surpass loosening up and pass out. He filled her glass again, then impulsively pretended to trip as he tried to sit down. Or perhaps it wasn't *entirely* impulsive. He *had* considered this earlier as a possible course of action, depending on how the rest of his plan played out.

"Oh, I am so sorry," he said when she gasped and looked down at the wine she'd spilled down the front of her blouse and skirt. "Not to worry," he added, setting her glass aside. "We can soak the blouse in the morning and get the stain out." Since the skirt was black, staining was not a concern; a simple laundering would do.

He touched her chin and smiled to see her immediately become lost again in his eyes. "You *do* like me," he said and kissed her again. She warmed to him with little urging and wrapped her arms around his shoulders. She gave a pleasant moan, and before Han set her lips free, he came to his feet, lifting her into his arms.

"Where are we going?" she asked.

"I'm taking you to bed, Maggie," he replied, already halfway up the stairs.

"But I'm not tired."

"Neither am I," he replied, kicking the bedroom door closed and setting her on her feet.

"What are you doing?" she asked calmly when he began unbuttoning her blouse.

"You can't go to bed with wine all over your clothes, Maggie," he said. "You'll make a mess of the sheets."

She took over undoing the buttons and glanced down, sighing to see that the wine had soaked through to her underclothing. Han appealed to his sense of decency and extinguished the lamp to darken the room.

"What are you doing?" she asked with another giggle, and he turned his back, well aware that she was getting completely undressed.

"You don't want me to see you without your clothes, do you?" he asked innocently. "At least not until we're married."

"I can't marry you, Han," she said, crawling into the bed. "Nik wouldn't like that."

Han thought about the way that came out and wondered how much of Maggie's desire to be with Nik stemmed from Nik's ability to play on her stubbornness and naivete. What kind of man was Nik Koenig, to take advantage of Maggie's weaknesses for the sake of his own gain? Then he heard Maggie giggle and wondered if he was doing the same thing. He sat down to pull off his boots and quickly evaluated his motives. His plan couldn't have gone more perfectly, but it did take great willpower to not move beyond the line upon which he now stood.

"Kiss me again, before we go to sleep, Han," she pleaded like a child. He hesitated only a moment before he complied, keeping the bedding between them. He thought how easy it would be to just take her in his arms and take advantage of her. But perhaps if he was lucky, enough had already transpired to accomplish what he needed.

He simply had to brace himself to endure her inevitable hangover. Focusing on the moment, Han just kissed her, relishing the hope it gave him.

"Oh, Han," Maggie muttered while he pressed kisses over her face, "where did you ever learn to kiss like that?"

"You taught me," he stated. "Don't you remember? Or at least we learned together."

"Oh, yes," she said and giggled.

Somewhere in the midst of his next kiss, Maggie slipped into oblivion. Han chuckled and urged her head to his shoulder. He longed for a time when they could share these feelings mutually, and prayed that she might remember even a little bit of the tenderness she had revealed to him. But at least he had hope.

Now that Maggie was sleeping contentedly, Han felt momentarily guilty for purposely getting her drunk with the intention of manipulating her into believing something that wasn't true. But he had to admit he was desperate. And hopefully he had now gained some leverage that would work in his favor.

"Han," Maggie murmured, barely discernible as she stirred slightly.

"Yes, my love."

"Will you cook breakfast? I don't think I feel well."

"I would be happy to," he said, and she eased closer to him.

"Maggie," he whispered a few minutes later, and she grunted softly, "say you'll marry me. I want to be with you. I want it to be this way forever."

"Oh, I couldn't do that," she said, at the same time moving closer to him.

"Why not?" he asked.

"I told Nik I would marry him." Han wanted to tell her just how he felt about that. But he knew it wouldn't make any difference, and he didn't want to break the mood of the moment. "Besides," she added, "we must go home. Mother will be worried." She yawned and eased her arms around him. "What will we ever tell Mother?"

With that, Maggie drifted off again, and Han eased away to try and get comfortable in his makeshift bed on the floor. But it was hours before he let himself sleep. He knew Maggie's wrath was just beyond her waking, and he wanted to cherish these precious few moments with her sleeping peacefully. He concentrated on his vision of sharing a life with her. And he prayed a day would come when she could trust and respect him, if nothing else. With that vision foremost in his mind, Han finally drifted to sleep.

Heady from the effect of the wine, Maggie drifted into an unusually deep sleep, where pieces of the past merged into her experiences of the evening, and her memories became her dreams. She moaned contentedly at the thought of Han kissing her, and that first time she'd found herself in his arms became so vivid, she could almost smell the damp ground of the castle gardens.

It was Erich who regularly organized mature versions of their childhood games to play at night. Han gathered all of the servants' children together who were the right ages, and it became a common occurrence during the summer months.

During the third round of hide-and-seek in the dark, Maggie was sneaking stealthily near a length of shrubbery when she felt a hand clap over her mouth and she found herself sitting on the ground beneath the bushes. A strong arm came around her waist, holding her powerless. Her heart pounded fearfully until she heard Han chuckle close to her ear.

"Be quiet," he whispered, "and they'll never find us."

Maggie nodded slightly to indicate she understood, and he moved his hand from over her mouth. She caught her breath when he made no effort to let her go, and she realized how close he was sitting beside her.

"You shouldn't hold me this way, Han," she whispered.

"Why not?" he asked, tightening his arm around her waist.

"It's not . . . proper," she said, while inside she could find no will to protest. He said nothing for several moments, but she could feel his breathing against her face. She became intrigued with sensations she'd never experienced before and wondered what his motives might be.

"Your hair smells nice, Maggie," he whispered. "It smells like . . ." he buried his nose in it and inhaled deeply, "roses."

"My shampoo has rose oil in it," she reported, trying to ignore the quickening of her heart.

"Oh, of course." He moved his fingers methodically through the tangled curls and added, "I love your hair best when it's . . . free."

"Han," she said quietly, "they'll be looking for us."

"That's why they call it hide-and-seek, Maggie. We're hiding, and it's a fine spot if you ask me."

Maggie attempted to move, but he only eased his arm around her shoulders and chuckled. "Ooh," he said, "this is nice. We should do this more often." She felt his breath against her eyelids as his voice lowered. "When you're old enough, you should marry me Maggie, and then we can do this all the time."

She wanted to tell him the very idea was absurd, although she couldn't be certain whether or not he was only teasing her. But an unexplainable tingling erupted deep inside at the very idea. She didn't understand why, but she felt no desire to resist Han's attention. She wondered if it was her imagination that his lips were brushing elusively over her face, then she felt them just to the side of her mouth in a manner that could not be misconstrued as anything but a kiss. Maggie heard pulse-beats in her ears as she turned her face just slightly, almost against her will. She felt more than heard Han take a sharp breath. Then his lips met hers. The kiss was so soft and quick that Maggie hardly had a chance to absorb it. She was contemplating a way to ask him why he was behaving this way when it became evident they had been found. Han moved away abruptly and shot to his feet before anyone could see that she was sitting on the ground, huddled between the hedges. Once it had been declared by the others that Han had been found, the group moved on, and they were alone again.

"Come along, Maggie," Han said, holding out a hand. She took it, and he helped her to her feet. For a long moment he just stood facing her, the darkness shadowing his expression. Her heart quickened again as he bent toward her, and she hoped that he would kiss her again. His lips met her brow, and she was only mildly disappointed.

Saying nothing, they walked hand in hand back to where the others were going inside for hot cocoa. Han let go of her and stuffed his hands into his pockets before they came into view. He kept his distance the remainder of the evening, but Maggie often felt his eyes on her. She wondered what made them nearly glow when she looked discreetly at him. She thought of feeling his lips on hers, and a swarm of butterflies rushed through her.

The following day, Maggie didn't see Han at all. She avoided the stables in spite of her desire to go riding, and stayed away from the places in the castle where she knew that he and Erich might be in their spare time. She felt certain that staying away from him would put these feelings in perspective. But her mind was unwillingly drawn to him—almost constantly. And she didn't understand. Han Heinrich had been a part of her life for as long as she could remember. He *was almost like family—just as his parents were. How could her feelings for him suddenly change this way? She'd always thought he was silly and a bit obnoxious. Now she could only think of how it felt to be close to him. She reminded herself that she was only fourteen. But having been taught that she was too young to be involved romantically did not make the feelings go away.*

Two days after their little escapade in the gardens, Maggie rose early and put on her best riding habit. She had Klara brush through her hair, then she tied it back with a ribbon and headed for the stables. She entered to see Han bent over, examining the shoe of a horse. While he was unaware of her presence, she just watched him. She absently wrapped an arm around her middle in an effort to squelch the eruption of butterflies inside her at just the sight of him. She noticed the way his high boots fit over his lower legs, and the leather braces he wore over a loose-fitting white shirt. Her heart quickened when he glanced over his shoulder, as if he'd sensed her presence. His face broke into a pleasant grin as he gently set the horse's hoof down and straightened himself. He looked so tall, and she wondered when he had sprouted up to somewhere near the height of his father. But Maggie had surpassed her mother's height more than a year ago, and people were often telling her that she had every appearance of being a mature adult. Why would she not think the same of Han when he was three years older?

"Good morning, MagdaLena," he said. "I take it you're going riding." He glanced comically past her shoulder, as if he was looking for someone else. "Not alone, I hope."

"I . . . don't know if Erich or Sonia are even up yet. Perhaps if—"

"Good morning," Erich boomed, coming in behind her. Maggie tried not to show her disappointment. Now that her brother was here, she had no good reason to request that Han escort her. She enjoyed her ride with Erich, but when they returned, he hovered in the stables, talking with Han as he often did. Maggie went in for breakfast and tried to keep her mind on something else through the day. Late afternoon, she went to the east winter parlor where there was a piano, and she played through several of her favorite pieces. When she finished a particular sonata, she gasped to realize she wasn't alone. She turned to see Han, leaning back in a big chair, clapping with enthusiasm.

"Very nice, Your Highness," he said.

"Thank you." She nodded slightly. "What are you doing here?"

"I was listening to you play."

"And that's all? Is Erich—"

"Erich is busy with your father. I came to see you."

"Whatever for?" she asked, hurriedly glancing through the pile of sheet

music on the piano, if only to appear busy. She hoped he couldn't sense the way her heart had quickened in his presence.

"Well, it's just that I was thinking . . ." He rose and sauntered slowly toward her, his hands in his pockets. "I must be one of the luckiest guys in the world."

"Why is that?" she asked.

Han sat on the piano bench beside her, his back to the piano. She caught a subtle aroma about him that was familiar from being close to him in the garden. Shaving lotion, she guessed. She glanced up at him, then darted her eyes quickly away, unnerved by the intensity in his expression.

"You see," he said in a whisper, "I've been wondering how someone as common as I could be so lucky as to kiss a princess."

Maggie couldn't keep herself from looking at him then. He held her gaze as if he had some power over her, and she was helpless to turn away.

"And not only did I kiss a princess," his voice lowered further, "but I suspect it was the first time anyone *had ever kissed her." He touched her face as if she were made of porcelain, and she closed her eyes to more fully absorb his touch, or perhaps to avoid his gaze. "Did you give me your first kiss, Maggie?"*

She nodded slightly and felt his thumb press over her lips. A moment later, he put his mouth there to replace it. His kiss was brief with the innocence of youth, but Maggie couldn't deny what it awakened inside her. She didn't understand these feelings, but she longed to explore them. She held her breath as he put his lips close to her ear and said, "Have you ever gone riding under a full moon, Maggie?"

She pulled back, surprised by the question. "I can't say that I have."

"There will be a full moon tonight. There's nothing like midnight on a full moon. It's incredible." His voice lowered as if he feared the walls might overhear. "Meet me in the stables. Share it with me, Maggie."

Maggie's heart quickened at the thought. She didn't think about how she might sneak out without being noticed, nor did she consider whether or not it was proper. She just nodded, instinctively knowing the experience would be worth any risk.

Han smiled and touched her face again quickly. "Midnight," he whispered and came to his feet. She watched him walk to the door. He turned back and smiled briefly before he left the room. Maggie wondered why she had never noticed what a remarkable smile Han Heinrich had.

Maggie could barely contain her excitement as she counted the hours to midnight. She went through the ritual of going to bed as usual, then she lay staring at the ceiling until it was nearly time to go. Dressed in a conservative skirt and blouse, with her hair pulled back in a ribbon, she went carefully out to the courtyard and scurried into the stables. A lamp was burning low, but she saw no sign of Han. A moment later, he chuckled behind her ear.

"Don't sneak up on me like that," she gasped.

"It's fun," he said. She watched as he urged a stallion out of its stall, already saddled. "Your mount, my lady," he said, bending his knee just beneath the stirrup. She took his hand and briefly set her booted foot on his thigh in a manner they were accustomed to from his years of working in the stables. She hurled herself onto the horse, her skirts lifted high enough to straddle it comfortably. Han glanced at her booted lower legs and smiled, then she realized she was not sitting on her own saddle. Her feet wouldn't even reach the stirrups. Before she could question Han, he mounted behind her, sandwiching her between the pommel and his body. Maggie's heart quickened as he took the reins in one hand and pressed the other around her waist. They were at a full gallop before they exited the castle gate, and she heard him laugh behind her ear.

It didn't take long for Maggie to understand what he'd meant when he'd given this experience the humble description of incredible. The full moon illuminated the meadow, surrounded by trees on every side. Han took the reins into both hands and pressed the horse to its full potential. Maggie unintentionally grabbed onto his legs at her sides as the speed took her breath away. He galloped the circumference of the meadow a few times, then he urged the reins into Maggie's hands and pushed both arms around her waist. She heeled the horse to a full gallop and leaned forward, laughing at the exhilaration of being in control of such an experience.

Suddenly out of breath, Maggie pulled the horse to a halt and paused to survey her surroundings. Han slid from the horse and tethered it, then he reached up to help her dismount, his hands at her waist. He swung her to the ground as if she were weightless, and she felt briefly in awe of his strength.

"Come," he said, taking her hand, "walk with me."

They walked together in silence until he stopped and turned her to face him. "Oh, Maggie," he murmured, "tell me I'm not dreaming."

"You're not dreaming," she whispered, and he pressed his lips over hers. The newness of the experience felt mildly awkward to Maggie. She hardly knew what to do and sensed that he felt the same way. But as he kissed her again, the awkwardness gradually dissipated. She took hold of his shoulders, certain they'd spent their brief lifetimes waiting only for this moment. And Maggie wanted it to never end.

"We should go back," Han said, and she reluctantly eased away.

Maggie said nothing. She was too in awe of the feelings surging through her to have the will to speak. She concentrated on the feel of his hand in hers as they walked back to where the horse was tethered. When he settled into the saddle behind her, she felt somehow comforted by the arm that came around her waist, holding her tightly as they rode back toward Castle Horstberg.

Maggie dreaded being separated from Han the moment they rode into the stables. She said nothing as she watched him unsaddle the horse and care for it with tender expertise. He walked her partially across the courtyard and kissed her quickly in the shadows.

"Good night, Maggie," he whispered. "We'll do it again soon."

She nodded, still unable to speak. He kissed her again and walked away toward the servants' apartments where he lived with his parents. Maggie sailed up to bed, but sleep eluded her for hours. Her mind was absorbed with Han Heinrich, and she could hardly wait to see him again.

Contemplating why she might feel this way, Maggie realized that beyond finding Han terribly attractive, their long history together as friends made it evident that he knew her well, he understood her, and he cared for her—just as she did him. Perfectly content with this new turn her life had taken, she finally drifted to sleep.

Maggie slept later than usual and woke with only one thought in mind. She dressed hurriedly and brushed through her hair before she hurried out to the stables. She didn't see Han right off, but it only took a moment to realize he was in the corner of one of the stalls, brushing down her mother's stallion.

"Good morning," she said, peeking over the side of the stall.

Han flashed her one of his remarkable smiles, and she erupted with a fresh swarm of butterflies.

"Did you sleep well?" he asked.

"Hardly at all, actually," she replied.

Han chuckled. "We must be suffering from the same ailment. I didn't sleep much myself."

"What do you suppose it could be?" she asked, glancing coyly away.

Maggie felt his gaze intensify before she looked back up to meet it. He tossed the brush down and moved toward her with purpose. Her heart quickened as he deftly took her shoulders into his hands and kissed her.

"What if someone finds us?" she asked breathlessly.

"Erich and Sonia went out just a few minutes ago," he said and kissed her briefly. "And our parents never ride before breakfast."

Stealing clandestine moments with Han became a quickly established habit that carried them into fall. Once their relationship was discovered, he became even more a part of the family, often sharing meals and activities with them when it was appropriate. But nothing was so wonderful as the minutes they would steal here and there when he'd kiss her and hold her as if the world began and ended with their love.

"Oh, Han," she murmured and heard the words come back to her ears, somewhere on the edge of her coherency.

"I'm here," he whispered, and she instinctively squeezed the hand that slipped into hers.

"Kiss me, Han," she said and immediately felt his mouth over hers. Somewhere in the midst of his kiss she drifted back to sleep, content with the evidence that he loved her.

Chapter Nine

DELUSIONS

Han awoke before Maggie and felt a fresh rush of emotion in recalling what had transpired. He watched her for a long moment, marveling at her beauty, and he wished that she could always be this way. But he knew this serenity wouldn't last long. She was bound to wake up with a bad hangover—and the fury of a woman scorned.

Han sat on the bed and leaned against the headboard, soaking in the beauty of her full lips and tangled hair. He wanted to kiss her and knew that if she were awake he'd never accomplish it, so he bent down and pressed his lips softly over hers. She moaned and stretched, which made him smile, and he kissed her again.

Maggie felt deeply comforted and eased close to the warmth next to her, barely recalling hazy images of her dreams. Coming slowly awake, she felt different somehow. Her head ached horribly, and she groaned when she tried to open her eyes. But beyond that, something wasn't right.

"Good morning, Maggie," she heard Han say cheerfully. Just the sound of his voice intensified her headache.

"It's not a good morning," she muttered, pressing her hands over her head with another groan. "I think I'm getting sick again, Han. I don't feel at all well."

"Nonsense," he said lightly, and she made no more effort to move or speak. "Did you have sweet dreams?" he asked with mischief in his voice.

Maggie vaguely recalled hazy images that had something to do with Han. The memory was almost disturbing, and yet it seemed to have been somehow pleasant. Not wanting to admit that she might have had such dreams about Han, she replied tersely, "I don't remember."

"You don't remember *anything?*" he asked carefully.

"No," she said sharply, then she groaned again and squeezed her eyes shut more tightly against the light in the room. "Really, Han," her tone changed to misery, "I think I'm getting sick."

"I think you drank too much wine," he stated. A moment later, Maggie's eyes shot open in alarm as she recalled her last vivid memory, which was Han telling her that his intentions were dishonorable.

"The wine!" she exclaimed, ignoring the pain as she sat up abruptly in the bed, fearing the reason Han looked so smug. She felt Han's eyes move quickly over her before she looked down to realize she was wearing absolutely nothing beneath the sheet that barely concealed her.

"Oh, good heavens!" she cried, pulling the sheet up to her chin and trying to ease away from Han, who was sitting on top of the bedding.

Han steeled himself for the fury that was about to be unleashed against him, but still he couldn't keep from enjoying the look on her face.

"What have you done to me?" she demanded, and Han saw the color of her cheeks go from pale to dark pink in an instant.

"Nothing that you objected to," he said calmly.

Maggie could only stare at him in disbelief. Was it possible that the situation was truly as it appeared?

"How could you?" she spat. "I would have never believed that even you would stoop so low as to get a woman drunk and force yourself upon her."

"I thought you said you didn't remember," he replied calmly.

"I don't!"

"Then how do you know I forced myself upon you?"

"Because I . . ." she faltered.

"Maggie," he said softly, looking her straight in the eye, "I told you not to drink too much wine. I told you my intentions were not honorable. I warned you about losing control of your senses, because you might forget that you hate me—and you did. Last night you actually liked me—a lot," he added with a chuckle.

"I don't believe you."

"Believe what you want," he stated, "but you enjoyed what happened every bit as much as I did. But do you know what I liked best?"

"What?" she asked skeptically.

"You admitted," he touched her chin playfully with his finger, "that I am a much better kisser than Nik Koenig."

"That's absurd!"

"That's what I thought when you were showing me how he'd kissed you." Maggie's eyes widened. "But I gave you one after that which was . . . well, one thing led to another, and . . ." Han leaned against the headboard and interlaced his fingers behind his head.

Maggie wanted to yell and scream and tear his eyes out, but she felt scared and didn't know how to react. How could she have done something like that and not even remember? Her uneasiness and fear swirled together and threatened to overtake her. She had to concentrate all of her efforts into not falling apart with helpless sobbing.

"Would you like a hot bath, my love?" he asked.

"I am not your love!" she retorted.

"Oh, but you are." He smiled carelessly, and she looked away in shame. "A hot bath really might help, my love," he offered. "I'll fix one for you if you—"

"I don't want a bath, thank you," she interrupted, barely holding back the heat in her throat and the sting in her eyes.

"Perhaps some breakfast, then," he added, swinging his feet to the floor.

He turned to look at her over his shoulder. Their eyes met, and she felt humiliated, wondering if he was telling her the truth. How could she have been such a fool to set herself up for this?

"Get out of here!" she shouted at Han, then groaned from the pain in her head. "Leave me alone," she added more softly, not wanting him to see how he had undone her.

Han glanced toward her with a sly sparkle in his eyes, then he pulled on his boots and left the room. As soon as she was certain he'd gone down the stairs, Maggie curled up in the bed and cried. Her shame exploded into the horror of what this meant to so many different facets of her life that she had to force herself to not think too deeply about such things, or she would never be able to even get through the day.

After a long bout of tears, Maggie got dressed, convincing herself that whether she had been drunk or not, what Han had done was unforgivable. Hurt and angry, she pulled the sheets from the bed to wash them, as if it could wash away what she was imagining had happened there. She found her clothes on the floor, a huge wine stain on her blouse and chemise. Her skirt also had wine spilled on it; even though it was too dark to see, the fabric had a large patch that felt stiff and sticky. She was all the more disturbed at having no memory of spilling wine on herself, or removing her clothes. Or had Han removed them? She groaned at the thought and hurriedly washed the sheets, leaving the stained clothing to soak in the tub. Then she hung them outside to dry before breakfast.

They ate together in typical silence while Maggie tried to avoid his constant gaze that was not typical at all. Something had changed in his eyes, and it haunted her with uncertainty. Disjointed memories probed into her mind. Had she really let him kiss her that way? Or was her imagination playing tricks on her? She'd nearly convinced herself it was the latter, but as she ate, Maggie became aware that her lips were just slightly tender. How much kissing did a woman have to do to feel physical reminders of it the next morning?

Trying to push such thoughts away, tangible warmth rushed to her face at the very idea. Han chuckled, and she covered her face with her hands, wondering if he could read her mind.

Han watched Maggie closely, wishing he knew how she really felt. There was a sad, distant look in her eyes, and a complete absence of the raging anger he'd expected. Perhaps hoping for a scolding, he provoked her a bit. "What's the matter, Maggie, my love?"

"You ask what is the matter," she snarled, "after you . . . purposely . . . seduced me! You have taken something from me that can never be replaced. You have confiscated my virtue, and I hate you!"

"What makes you so certain that any such thing happened?" he asked.

"I woke up . . ." She couldn't bring herself to say it.

"Naked?" he finished, and she scowled at him. "Surely there are all kinds of reasons for that," he said. "Actually, you spilled wine all over your clothes. And you were apparently too tired to put anything else on once you got them off."

Although his explanation rang true with the evidence of her stained clothing, she said with sarcasm, "Oh, that's a likely story."

"On the other hand, maybe I cleverly lured you into taking your clothes off, just so I could hold you in my arms and try to imagine what it might be like if you were in love with me."

Maggie blushed again and pressed her aching head into her hands as he continued. "Or maybe," Han reached across the table and lifted her chin with his finger, looking directly into her eyes, "you freely gave me something very precious that no one else can ever have; something I would treasure, Maggie—always. And if you gave it to me freely, Maggie, then perhaps your feelings for me aren't what you think they are."

Maggie looked away petulantly, her face darkened with shame. Han quickly pushed away any hope of appealing to what he believed were her most genuine emotions. Instead he forced the correct attitude to face her. "Well," he smirked, determined to make the most of this, "wouldn't it be nice if you were carrying my baby? Then you'd have to marry me."

"Ooh!" she said and tried to slap him, but he caught her hand and laughed. "I hope Nik Koenig hunts you down and kills you."

"He just may do that," Han said casually, "but if he did, where would that leave you? Do you think he'd want a woman who got drunk and can't even remember why she woke up with some other man . . . *naked?*" he added in a loud whisper.

"You've really done it, haven't you. You've accomplished your quest."

"Not quite," he said, "but we're getting there."

"Well," she said in defense, "Nik will still want me. He loves me."

"Is that why he tried to kill your brother?"

"He did not!"

"Oh, come on, Maggie! It's as plain as the nose on your face. If it wasn't him, he hired someone to do it. There is only one thing Nik Koenig wants, which makes me realize he would probably still have you . . . no matter what. He wants the duchy, and he will stop at nothing to get it."

"I'm not going to argue with you anymore," she said sadly. "It doesn't do any good."

"It really was an enjoyable evening," Han said, hoping to provoke her again. He could handle her yelling at him better than her sadness. "Don't you want to hear more about it?"

"I don't care," she said. "I don't care about anything anymore."

Han tried to ignore the despair in her statement as he idly finished his breakfast and watched her do the same. He attempted to provoke her with lewd glances, but she said nothing.

When Han was finished, he stood from the table, announcing, "I'm going into town later on. Would you like to come along? I think you could use some new clothes," he finished with a smirk.

Maggie couldn't believe he was actually inviting her to go with him. He never had before. If he had, she would have jumped at the chance—not only to get away from the cottage for a while, but with the hope of alerting someone's attention to the fact that she was being held captive. But it didn't matter anymore. Han was right. No one would want her if she was carrying his child. She would be stuck with him for the rest of her life.

"I don't care," she said and meant it.

Han stood watching her a long moment, baffled over how to react. He wondered if he liked her better the way she'd been before. Without even looking at him, she proceeded to clean the dishes, dust the entire cottage, mop the floor, and mend Han's breeches. She finally managed to get the stains out of her blouse. By then the sheets were dry, and she made the bed up freshly. She was just smoothing the spread into place when Han came into the room. He couldn't help feeling a certain amount of satisfaction to see how neatly everything was done up. She had gained a real finesse with menial tasks in the weeks they'd been here, and he felt proud of her.

"Should we go?" he asked.

"I'm ready," she complied and followed him outside.

Maggie made no effort to hide her sour mood, and she was glumly quiet as they rode together into a small town. She saw no reason to be anything but cooperative. She didn't even bother trying to find out where they were or make any public scene whatsoever. She'd imagined doing so a thousand times; now the opportunity had come, and she simply didn't care. Han bought her some new things which she made no comment over, then they returned to the cottage, had dinner, and went to bed.

Maggie felt certain that Han would force himself upon her again, and she had prepared a plan in her mind of how to defend herself. She was surprised when he climbed into his bed on the floor and didn't even attempt to touch her. But still she waited, believing it would happen. It wasn't long, however, before Han began snoring softly. Maggie was relieved but baffled. She fell asleep with thoughts of Nik, hoping beyond hope that he would somehow find her. And if she was not carrying Han's child, perhaps he would still want her.

When days passed and Han made no further physical advances, Maggie became hopeful that she was not already with child. She wondered if Nik would be willing to raise another man's child as his own. Did he love her that much? The idea only encouraged her discomfort over the whole situation, so she pushed it away. She wondered how likely it might be for a pregnancy to happen after one encounter. Truthfully, she had no idea. But it didn't seem very likely. As long as she was not pregnant with Han's baby, she felt certain she could still find happiness with Nik when he rescued her.

Maggie tried to ignore Han as much as possible and became increasingly annoyed by his light-hearted attitude. He just couldn't seem to resist making jokes or wry remarks, even though Maggie rarely said anything in response, and she never gave him the satisfaction of seeing anything in her expression that might give him a clue to how she truly felt. She didn't understand Han, but she didn't want to. He surely had to be mad; of that she was certain.

"What should we name it?" he said one morning at breakfast. His comment only deepened her theory about his lack of sanity.

"Name what?"

"The baby."

"What makes you think there is going to be a baby?"

"Maggie, didn't your mother tell you where babies come from?"

"She most certainly did, and I am quite certain it would take more than once."

"Ah," he smiled, "but you never know."

"Well, I pray I am not."

"Just in case," he smirked, leaning on one elbow, "what should we name it?"

"You're mad!"

"Now, let's see," he ignored her comment. "If it's a girl, we could name her after your sister, Sonia. Or your mother, Abbi. But then it's not just Abbi. What is it?" She made no response, so he answered his own question, "Abilee Amelia. An English name. Her mother was English; her name was LeeAnna. And your grandfather's name is Gerhard. And his father's name was Josef."

"How do you know so much about my family?" she said as if she resented it.

"My father told me," he stated. "He used to work for the Albrechts before your mother met your father. You know," he smiled, "your mother and my father have been friends since they were children. I wonder what would have happened if—"

"Don't be absurd!"

"Well, I'm glad it didn't happen," he smiled, "because I don't want to be your brother."

"And I most certainly do not want to be your sister!"

"That's a relief," he chuckled. She only glared at him, and he went on, "You didn't realize just how connected our families are, did you."

"Why? Because your father and my mother were friends? That is hardly connected."

"It's a lot more than that, my love. Did you know that Erich is named after my father?"

"He's got so many names I can't keep track."

"He's a prince. Erich Cameron Georg Gerhard du Woernig. A regal sounding name, don't you think?"

"I suppose."

"And yours," he said, "After your aunts, Madeleine and Helena, and your mother and grandmother as well. MagdaLena Amelia LeeAnna du Woernig . . . Heinrich."

"Forget it!"

"And," he said, "as long as we're talking about family connections—"

"We weren't. *You* were."

"I was named after your great-grandfather."

"You were?" She was genuinely surprised.

"My second name is Josef," he said. "My father loved Josef Albrecht a great deal, and he's told me much about him."

"Your father tells you everything."

"He's one of my best friends."

"So where do you suppose they came up with the name Han?"

"I have no idea. But now that we've done all this analyzing," he said easily, "what do you think we should name the baby?"

"There isn't going to be any baby," she stood huffily and went upstairs.

From the sofa in the common room, Maggie looked up from her sketchbook to see Han carrying two buckets of water up the stairs. A few minutes later, he went up again with more.

"What are you doing?" she asked.

"I'm preparing a bath, my lady," he said with mock gallantry.

"But it's the middle of the afternoon. You never bathe in the middle of the afternoon."

"I didn't say it was *my* bath," he said.

Maggie looked at him sideways. "What are you up to?"

"You know, Maggie, it's not polite to always assume the worst of someone. I can assure you that my intentions are purely for the intent of making you feel pampered like a princess."

"Why?" she asked, longing for a hot bath even as they spoke, but at the same time skeptical of his motives.

"Because you've worked very hard the last several weeks, and I figure you've earned it. You really should learn to be more trusting," he said and hurried up the stairs.

A short while later, Han stood before her and held out his hand. "Your bath is ready, my lady."

Maggie refused his hand but stood and walked past him up the stairs. As soon as she entered the bedroom, she could smell the aroma of fragrant bath salts in the steaming water.

"Oh, Han!" She couldn't restrain her enthusiasm.

He chuckled and said, "Enjoy!" Then he closed the door and left her alone.

Maggie wondered briefly over his reasons for doing something so nice for her, but she couldn't remember the last time she'd had a real bath. Han had bathed in the tub several times since they'd arrived here, but he'd insisted that if she wanted to bathe she'd have to get the water and heat it herself. And she simply hadn't been up to all the work it would entail. So she had settled for bathing in the cold pond, always with Han remaining nearby to make certain she didn't run away.

Fearing he might return, she hurried to get out of her clothes, deciding to leave on her long chemise for the sake of maintaining a degree of modesty—on the chance that he *did* have some hidden motive. Carefully, she slipped into the water, loving the barely tolerable heat. It was just the way she liked it. With the water clouded by bath salts, she felt some comfort knowing that Han couldn't see anything beneath it even if he did return. Choosing not to concern herself with the possibility, she lay back in the tub, letting her hair absorb the fragrant water. Inhaling the sweet aroma, she wondered what it might be. Seeing the bottle on the floor, she reached for it to read the label. *Rose oil and vanilla.* Well, he had good taste. She could give him credit for that.

Maggie closed her eyes and could almost imagine herself at home with Klara in the next room laying out fresh clothes, and dinner waiting downstairs to be shared with her family. Overcome with a sudden bout of homesickness, she let the tears roll down her face while she relaxed so completely, she nearly drifted to sleep. She gasped when Han touched her face; she hadn't even heard him enter the room.

"What is this?" he asked gently, indicating the moisture of tears.

"I'm sitting in a bathtub, Han. Would you not expect my face to be wet?"

"Oh, of course," he said, only slightly sarcastic.

"Which is the same reason that you should not be in here."

"And why not?" he retorted, sitting down and crossing his legs with every indication that he intended to stay. She noticed that his feet were bare and his shirt untucked.

"It's not proper for you to see me without my . . ." Maggie stopped and felt her face turn warm when he smiled.

Han loved to see her blush, simply for the way the color in her face enhanced her natural beauty. He wanted to tell her, but their relationship certainly didn't allow for genuine compliments. If he told her right now that she was beautiful, she would throw it back at him, attached to something cruel. So he kept the thought to himself and continued matter-of-factly with the conversation.

"Actually," he said, "it was dark that night. I turned out the lamp so I wouldn't get embarrassed."

"You're deplorable."

"I just hauled in four thousand buckets of water and heated it so you could enjoy a bath, and you're calling me deplorable? Not to mention, I bought you that smelly stuff you're soaking in."

As Maggie shifted slightly in the water, Han noticed the wet chemise over her shoulders. "You're bathing in your underclothing?"

"A woman does what she has to. I feared you'd come parading back in here, so I took precautions."

"You're too clever for me," he said with a shake of his head, keeping his sarcasm too subtle to be noticeable.

"Are you just going to sit there all day?" she demanded.

"Well," he said, "it just so happens I have this expensive little bottle of shampoo that is the same fragrance as what you're soaking in."

"Well, where is it?" she demanded.

"What will you give me if I get it?" He raised an eyebrow with purposeful mischief.

"And you have the gall to try and convince me that your preparing my bath was for purely selfless reasons? You *are* deplorable."

"Maybe I am," he admitted, "but you're not exactly an angel, my love."

Maggie said in a voice of forced kindness, "That was very sweet of you to prepare a bath for me, Han. Thank you. May I please use the shampoo?"

"Very good," he drawled with exaggeration and rose to open a bureau drawer. He stood next to her and held out the bottle, but as she went to grab it he pulled it back. "What's it worth to you?"

"I've already given you everything I have," she said a little too seriously.

Han almost felt guilty for misleading her, but he figured she would find out the truth soon enough. And he'd have to deal with that when it happened. He was mostly just making this up moment by moment as he went along. In the meantime he just smiled and said, "But you don't remember. I kissed you better than Nik Koenig ever did, and you don't remember that either. You can't imagine how that hurts my feelings."

"I don't believe you," she said.

"That you kissed me, or that you hurt my feelings?"

"That it was better than Nik."

Han smiled. This particular moment was going much better than he'd expected. "All right. You give me a fair chance to prove it, and I'll let you have the shampoo."

Maggie resisted the urge to gape at him in astonishment. She couldn't believe how crass and brazen he could be, but perhaps worse than that was how she always managed to allow him to provoke her into such things. Knowing she would have no peace until she agreed, she rationalized that he'd kissed her many times before anyway—even if she couldn't remember the more recent kisses which he'd declared to be so wonderful.

"Oh, very well," she said haughtily.

Han grinned and knelt by the tub. She retracted slightly, and he said, "Now you can't expect it to be fair if you don't participate, Maggie. A good kiss works two ways, you know. You have to give it a fair chance."

"All right." She forced herself to relax. "Just get it over with."

Maggie willed her heart to stop pounding as he leaned toward her. Butterflies rushed through her insides, catching her completely off guard. She knew she should have felt disgusted, perhaps even afraid, over such a ridiculous gesture. But she felt neither, not even close. And she gasped unwillingly as he touched her chin with his finger. Just before he touched her lips to his, he pulled back and said, "Now, you have to be honest, Maggie." His voice took on a huskiness she'd never heard before. "If I kiss better than Nik Koenig, will you be honest enough to admit it, even if you aren't drunk? If you're not going to be honest, let's just forget it."

Maggie's breath quickened while something inside her felt as if she would die from wanting his lips to touch hers. "Very well," she agreed, trying to sound disgusted so he wouldn't realize how disarmed she'd become over the unbearable anticipation of his kiss. "I'll be honest. Just get on with it and kiss me."

Han nearly touched her lips again, then pulled back a little. "Now be careful, Maggie. You might forget you hate me, like you did when you were drunk. Then what?"

"Just get on with it," she ordered breathlessly.

"Yes, Your Highness," he smiled and pressed his lips over hers.

Maggie wondered what was happening to her as she found it impossible to not enjoy this. He kissed her meekly at first, then she felt something mildly torrid seep into it as his hand pressed into her hair, his fingers kneading the back of her head. Almost by their own will, her arms came up out of the water and around his shoulders.

Han drew back slightly and smiled at her dreamy expression. He nearly tingled from the hope it gave him that they might yet be able to move beyond her aversion to their relationship.

"You like that, I see," he said.

For a moment, Maggie tried to come up with a protest. She didn't want to admit it, but she'd told him she would be honest. And how could she deny what he'd already figured out without making a fool of herself?

"You can't blame me for being human," she said.

Han chuckled. "Nor can you blame me," he replied and kissed her again. And again.

"Oh, Han," she said when he finally set her lips free, "where did you learn to kiss like that?"

"You've asked me that before," he said.

"Did I? What did you tell me?"

"You taught me, Maggie. There's never been anyone else who could kiss the way you do."

"Is that true?" she asked skeptically.

"I've never lied to you, Maggie. I've just been—"

"Slightly deceptive. Yes, I know."

He smiled. "So, you admit it."

"Admit what?"

Han sat on the floor next to the tub and idly twirled his fingers in the water. "That I kiss better than Nik Koenig."

Maggie begrudgingly had to say, "Yes, I admit it."

Han smiled triumphantly. "That's because I care for you more than he does."

Maggie could not accept *that* as being true and was ready to tell him so when he quickly handed her the shampoo. "You've earned it," he said.

"Thank you," Maggie said, her anger disintegrating as the little bottle changed hands and their fingers touched briefly. She felt a deepening confusion as something sparked inside her that had nothing to do with Nik Koenig.

"Smile, Maggie. We're having fun."

"Are we?" she asked dubiously, wondering what his intentions were now. While a part of her wanted him to leave, if only so she could put her feelings into perspective, she couldn't find the will to ask him to go.

"Of course," he said. "Let me help you wash your hair, and I'll prove it."

Maggie said nothing. She felt too numb to know how to respond. While she was trying to convince herself that she should protest, Han stepped into the bathtub, fully clothed, and sat in the opposite end. Water splashed out onto the floor, and he laughed when she retracted as far as possible.

"What are you doing?" she insisted.

"I'm having fun!" he said as if it should be perfectly obvious.

"What kind of a man sits in a bathtub in his clothes?"

"Would you prefer that I remove them?" he asked, lifting his brows quickly.

"No!"

"Forgive me, Your Highness, but it seems I'm not the only one sitting in a bathtub wearing clothing."

Maggie looked down at her wet chemise, submerged nearly to her shoulders, and couldn't hold back a chuckle. "You got me there, Han."

"Here, turn around," he said, taking her arm to help maneuver her. He urged her head back and lifted water into her hair where it didn't hang into the tub. She handed him the shampoo and he poured out a ridiculous amount.

"You have the most beautiful hair," he said softly, working it into a healthy lather.

Maggie said nothing. With her back to Han, she leaned forward and wrapped her arms around her legs, allowing him to have his way with her hair. The aroma of the shampoo filled her senses, and she closed her eyes, allowing herself to absorb the luxury. She unconsciously moaned with pleasure as his fingertips gently massaged her scalp then worked down through the length of her hair. She could feel the lather falling over her shoulders and dripping into the water.

Just when she thought he would play with her hair forever, she felt his hands on her shoulders, pressing the excess lather up and down her arms. She set her arms on the sides of the tub, and watched his hands move toward hers, pushing lather between her fingers as he threaded them into his. She felt his chest against her back and relaxed as his hands moved back up her arms, caressing her shoulders then moving into her hair again. Maggie shifted slightly and felt no will or reason to protest when his arms came around her and her head fell naturally to his shoulder.

"Are you having fun yet, Maggie?" he asked, pressing his hand over her shoulder.

"I wouldn't call it fun, but it is nice . . . I have to admit."

"Yes," he agreed, "it is nice."

Again Maggie tried to understand what she was feeling, but it was all so confusing that she pushed her speculations away and just allowed herself to enjoy the moment. For the first time since he'd taken her from her home, she didn't feel lonely. In truth, she felt safe and secure, though she wasn't about to admit it aloud. She lifted her head slightly to look up at him. Their eyes met, and she wondered what made his nearly glow when he looked at her that way. Not certain if she really wanted to know, she impulsively pulled a handful of lather from her hair and pushed it into his face. Han laughed and spit soap out of his mouth.

"Now," she laughed, "I'm having fun."

"You little vixen!" he snarled with a chuckle, wiping the lather off his face. Maggie laughed and tried to move away, but he caught her around the waist, tickling her ribs until she writhed with laughter. With her head back in the water, she squirmed and wiggled until nearly all the shampoo had rinsed away.

"Oh, Maggie," he said, giving up at last, "it is so good to finally hear you laugh." He leaned back in one end of the tub and hung his long legs over the sides.

Maggie relaxed at the other end and chuckled. "You're deplorable, Han Heinrich."

"Yes," he agreed, "but I'm a great kisser."

"So you are," she had to admit.

Han watched her and just allowed himself to absorb the sweetness of this moment. If only he could make it last! "You know,

MagdaLena," he said, gently earnest, "for the first time in years you almost seem like the little girl I used to play with in the castle gardens. Remember how we climbed trees and made mud pies with the other children?"

"I remember," she said distantly.

He chuckled. "Remember how we'd hide in the shrubbery and kiss while the others were frantically searching for us?"

"I remember," she repeated, but all evidence of happiness fled from her expression.

Han attempted to read between the words and felt compelled to ask, "What happened, Maggie? One day you just . . . stopped laughing. It was the same day you rode out into that storm and nearly got yourself killed."

Maggie looked at him in astonishment. She attempted to feign ignorance, convincing herself that he had no business knowing her well enough to read her thoughts and feelings. But the memories rushed in so hard and so fast that she could only turn away and hope he wouldn't press her.

"Maggie?" he asked so gently that she could almost believe he really *did* care for her. The very idea only added to her confusion when she tried to fit it in with her reasons for not wanting to be here. With no warning, her turmoil rushed in to meet the unwanted memories, colliding in a torrent of emotions.

Han felt momentarily helpless as Maggie pressed a hand over her mouth and squeezed her eyes shut. She whimpered, then moaned, and tears trickled down her face. She tried to turn away, but there was nowhere to go.

"Maggie," he repeated as a stifled sob erupted from her throat. Without her permission, he reached over and pulled her into his arms. She briefly attempted to squirm away, then she took hold of his shoulders and pressed her face to his throat and wept. Han just held her and let her cry. If nothing else, he appreciated the evidence that she had made some progress in trusting him.

Long after she stopped crying, Maggie lay with her head against his shoulder, playing idly with his wet shirtsleeve. Then with no warning, she stood up in the tub and wrung the water out of the hem of her long chemise. Han exercised great self-control to keep his eyes turned downward. He only stole one quick glance at her as she turned away from him and stepped out of the tub, her hair hanging down her back like a length of rust-colored satin. She walked behind him but said nothing. He could hear her removing the chemise and putting on dry clothes, then she left the room.

By the time Han was dressed and had the bedroom floor mopped up, he found Maggie putting dinner on the table.

"It's very good," he told her while they were eating, but she didn't comment. They worked together to clean the dishes afterward. But still she said nothing. They slept in the same room as they had nearly every night since this escapade had begun, but Han felt as if she were a thousand miles away. He'd never felt so lonely and discontent in all his life.

Maggie woke the following morning not feeling well. She quickly realized the reason and took care of the problem. With the evidence that she was not pregnant, she tried to concentrate on her habitual thoughts of getting away from Han and finding a future with Nik. But it was difficult to find the zeal she'd found previously. And she wondered why.

Through the next few days, Maggie tried to figure it out. The more she thought about it, the more memories of her past relationship with Han crowded into her mind. When she came to no conclusions that would rest well with her conscience, she forced such thoughts away, certain that everything would be fine once she was able to get away from here and marry Nik.

Early in the evening, Han came in from chopping wood and sat uneasily at the table.

"What's the matter?" she insisted, noting he looked a little pale.

"I've got a sliver," he said.

"A *sliver?*" she echoed with a little laugh that made him glare at her.

"Yes, Maggie, a sliver. Would you help me, please?"

Maggie gathered a needle, tweezers, and some disinfectant and sat down beside him. She took his hand to examine the problem in the fleshy part of his hand, just below his thumb. "Good heavens," she gasped, "that's not a sliver. That's a tree!"

"Somewhere in between, I think," he said. "All I know is it hurts like hell, and you've got to get it out."

"I'm not sure I can," she protested.

"You have to." He pulled out his pocketknife and unfolded the blade with his teeth. "Here," he said, handing it to her. "Sterilize that. You're going to have to cut the skin to get it out. The knife is sharp enough. Just do it."

"Han? I can't."

"You've got to!" he insisted. "Just do it and get it over with! If you don't, it will get infected, and . . ."

Maggie wanted to suggest they go into town and have the doctor do it, but it was almost dark, and she knew the distance they'd have to travel would not be feasible.

"All right," she said. "I'll do my best. But don't watch."

Han sighed with exasperation and laid his head on the table, fearing he might actually pass out otherwise. The procedure didn't take as long as he'd expected, but he couldn't hold back the evidence of how badly it hurt, and he let out a long breath when she said with triumph, "I've got it. I think it came out pretty clean."

Han lifted his head to see that his hand was bleeding profusely, then he put his head back down and clenched his teeth while Maggie poured disinfectant into the wound and bandaged it carefully. When she announced that she was finished, he sat up straight and examined the results with approval. He felt certain it would heal just fine once it stopped hurting.

"Very good," he said, "especially for a spoiled little princess."

"I've learned a thing or two about being resourceful," she said. "Mother insisted."

"Your mother is a very wise woman."

"Yes," Maggie agreed, and Han knew by the look in her eyes that she was missing home.

"Han, I want to go back to Horstberg."

Han looked into her eyes and wished with everything he had that he could just tell her the truth and make her understand. But the progress he'd made with her was minimal, and he knew her loyalties were still with the enemy.

"We can't," he said gently. "Not yet. You must trust me."

"Why?" she asked.

"Why should you trust me?" he asked, trying to keep the conversation light.

"Why can't we go back?" she asked in frustration.

"That's a secret," he said.

"Enough secrets!" she shouted, and hot tears burned into her eyes. "I have a right to know why!"

"All right," he leaned toward her, fixing a partial story in his mind, "I'll tell you why." He took a deep breath. "We can't go back to Horstberg yet, Maggie, because someone is trying to take over the country, and he's trying to use you to do it. As long as I keep you away from him, Horstberg will remain secure. That's why, Maggie. Your being here with me is a matter of political security."

Maggie stared at him a long moment, then she shook her head as if his story was the most pathetic thing she'd ever heard. She stood up abruptly and left the room, saying over her shoulder, "I don't know where you get your delusions."

The following day, Maggie went to the pond to wash her hair, and Han followed.

"You really should marry me, Maggie," Han said while he watched her pull lather through her hair. "It's the only honorable thing to do, since I've kidnapped you and got you drunk and—"

"Don't you dare say it!"

He smiled. "Since I've compromised your honor, Maggie, I must make it right and marry you. How can you go back to Horstberg without being married? What would it do to your royal reputation?"

"Last night it was a matter of political security, now it's my honor and reputation. Which is it, Han?"

"Both, actually."

"You're running out of ideas, Han. You might as well give up. I'm never going to marry you—for honor *or* politics."

"I'm never going to give up," he retorted. She glared at him, and he added, "Looks like we've got an adventurous life ahead of us, doesn't it . . . my love."

"I am not your love!"

"That is strictly a matter of opinion."

Maggie was glad to be finished, and as always, it felt good to be clean, but it took great willpower not to scream at Han. Or worse.

It was nearly dusk when she started up the trail toward the cottage, with Han following closely. A bristle of fear rushed through her the same moment she heard a hard thud just behind her. She turned abruptly, expecting to find Han trying to frighten her, then he would laugh to see that it had worked. Her fear became very real when Han fell against her, forcing her to the ground with the weight of his body. He landed face down in her lap, and any thought of this being a practical joke vanished when she saw the blood gleaming in his hair. For a long moment she couldn't move, couldn't even breathe. She looked around frantically, wondering what had happened and what she should do. Her heart pounded with fear when she heard a noise, and she felt certain they'd been assaulted by thieves or vagabonds and her fate was sealed. But every moment of the last several weeks became hazy and dreamlike when she looked up to see Nik Koenig standing above her.

"Maggie," he said, pulling her abruptly to her feet, which left Han to fall face down on the ground. "Are you all right?"

"Yes," she said breathlessly, "I'm fine. I . . . can't believe it. How did you find me?"

"It wasn't easy," he laughed and kissed her. "Oh, Maggie. I have never been so happy to see anyone in my entire life!"

He grimaced toward the body on the ground. "I could kill him." He took a pistol from his belt and aimed it toward Han's back.

Frantically Maggie put a hand on his arm to stop him. "No," she said, "don't. He didn't hurt me. Please."

Nik met her eyes in question, and Maggie felt decidedly uneasy as it seemed he would ignore her plea. *Was he really the kind of man who would shoot an unconscious man in the back?* She pushed the thought away, certain he wasn't; he'd surely only been concerned about her safety and had overreacted. She sighed when he retracted the gun with a begrudging groan. "Come on," he said, "let's get out of here. I have a carriage waiting nearby."

"Shouldn't I get my things?" she asked.

"No," he said, "I'll get you whatever you need. We're going home."

Maggie ran behind him holding his hand, torn between the excitement of being with him again and wondering if Han would be all right. Knowing she could do nothing about the latter, she recalled the countless hours she'd spent longing for this moment, and she convinced herself that she was happier than she'd been since the night Han had waylaid her meeting with Nik.

"I knew you would rescue me," she said as he helped her mount a horse and got into the saddle behind her.

"Of course," he laughed. "I need you. I could not possibly be happy without you."

Maggie laughed with him. She felt confident, despite everything that had happened, that Nik would still want her. She was certain that he loved her. He had rescued her. And she felt sure that Han would be all right, and he could certainly take care of himself once he regained consciousness. Everything would be fine now. Everything. She just knew it.

Han opened his eyes to see the ground about to swallow him up. He groaned when the pounding in the back of his head hit with full force. Gradually, he managed to get to a sitting position and spit the dirt out of his mouth. The reality of what had happened struck him, and he stood up quickly, only to bend over from dizziness, fighting for equilibrium.

Finally able to get his bearings, Han got the horse from the stables and prayed that he could do what he needed to do in spite of the injury that was making his head pound. And he prayed that Maggie would be all right. And that she wouldn't do anything stupid! He had no idea where to start looking, but he had to find her. If he didn't, he was certain the duke would have him hung at the very least. And if Nik Koenig so much as laid a hand on her . . .

Han couldn't even think about that. He just had to find her!

Maggie vacillated between relief and fear during the brief ride to where a carriage had been left. It was dark by the time they arrived, and she wondered if Han was all right. Nik shouted something to a driver, and someone else took his horse. She wondered how many people had come with him as he opened the carriage door and ushered her inside. Once seated next to her amidst the plush interior, he smothered her with kisses, laughing intermittently to express his happiness. Maggie laughed with him and enjoyed his affection fully, refusing to think at all about anything else that might mar this experience. She'd been waiting for this moment for more weeks than she could count. She'd never been so happy in her life. While they traveled, she told him all that had happened, leaving out some details that were best forgotten, and he absorbed her tale with compassion and intermittent kisses.

"Now that I have you back," he said, "we are going to ride straight through for a day or two to avoid any trouble, then we will stop and get married and honeymoon our way back to Horstberg." She laughed, and he added, "And whether your father likes me or not, he'll have to give me the reward he's offered for your safe return." They laughed together and talked until Maggie started yawning. She laid her head against his shoulder and fell into a contented sleep, grateful to have been rescued at last.

Maggie's next awareness was coming awake on the carriage seat alone. It was evident they had stopped, probably to feed the horses. Though it was still dark, she sensed morning was nearing and felt a certain peace when she heard Nik's voice just outside the carriage, talking softly.

"Well, I got her, didn't I?" he said proudly, and Maggie smiled.

"Is the girl asleep?" a man's voice asked. Maggie almost announced herself, but curious to hear what they would say about her, she remained down on the seat with her eyes closed. She heard subtle noises to indicate that Nik was peering through the curtain covering the carriage window to check.

"Yes," he chuckled with certainty, "she's sleeping like a baby. She is pretty, I have to admit."

"Pretty or not," a woman with a harsh voice spoke, "the important thing is to get the two of you married."

"It won't be long now, Mother," Nik said, "and we'll have it all. I can't wait to see the look on the duke's face when I show up as his son-in-law. And once I'm underfoot all the time, it will be easy to get what I want."

"If I'd have known years ago," the other man chuckled, "that you were going to be the Duke of Horstberg, I'd have been a lot nicer to you."

"You can make up for it now," Nik laughed. "It won't be long, and it will all be mine. All for the price of an innocent, young beauty."

"We'd best be on our way," his mother said. She called more loudly, "Are those horses about finished?"

"A few more minutes," a voice called from the distance.

Maggie couldn't breathe. *This was a nightmare!* Any minute she would wake up and find the Nik she loved holding her. But the pounding of her heart convinced her that this was no dream. She felt angry and hurt and scared. But the only thing that mattered now was getting away from Nik. If she allowed him to marry her, the fate of Horstberg was sealed—not to mention her own. *Everything Han had said was true!* She felt so humiliated and sick to think how blind she'd been. But this was no time to sort out her feelings and react to them. She had to get out of here! Easing her way down to the floor of the carriage, she carefully pushed open the door opposite of where Nik had been standing. She peered both directions to make certain no one was there before she stepped out, bending low to avoid being seen. She paused at the back corner of the carriage and looked around it, glad to see no one. A frantic assessment of her surroundings gave her some relief. They were on a road going through thick forest. It only took a dozen careful steps away from the carriage before she was able to lose herself in the trees.

Once certain she was far enough away that she wouldn't be seen or heard, she ran like mad, not knowing where she was going or what she would do. She just ran, praying with everything inside her that she would not regret this. Out of breath, she stopped and leaned against a tree. With the initial escape behind her, she figured it would be easy enough to avoid staying hidden in the forest. But then what? Could she find her way back to the cottage? Not likely. She'd been blindfolded when they'd arrived, and she'd paid little attention to landmarks on the one occasion she'd left it. And what about Han? She'd assumed he would wake up eventually, but it occurred to her now that he could actually be dead from such a blow to his head. The thought sickened her. He had been right. All along he'd been right. Despite his cruel methods and his touch of madness, he had been right about Nik Koenig. And she hated herself for being so stupid, so foolish, so utterly naive.

Maggie wanted to cry but couldn't even force tears. Unable to think, she just started walking through the trees, trying to stay in one direction—away from Nik Koenig. She felt a prickly sensation run down her spine that reminded her of how she'd felt just before Han had been hit over the head. When she heard movement not far behind, she froze and perked her ears. Her heart went mad and her knees weak. She'd never been so afraid in her life as she wondered if she would be safer hiding against a tree in the darkness or running as far and as fast as she could manage.

Maggie had just made up her mind to run when a hand clapped firmly over her mouth. Her heart nearly stopped from fear, until she felt the gauze bandage—the one she had tied there just last night. The familiarity took hold and left her breathless. She nearly slumped with relief as the old reliable towel went over her mouth, then she heard an endearing chuckle as Han threw her over his shoulder and said, "Why do you make it so blasted easy to kidnap you, my love?"

Maggie would have laughed had she not been gagged—and so full of despair.

Han added, "I've been following this carriage wondering how I was going to get you out, and here you are."

Now that Maggie knew she was not lost in the forest and she would actually survive this, the reality of her delusions set in. Her mind was in turmoil when he tied her to the pommel of the saddle then mounted behind her and rode quickly through the night. As sad and ashamed as she felt, as broken as her heart had become, at least she felt safe. At least she knew Han would take care of her.

Just past dawn, they came to the cottage, and Han went in, leaving her tied to the horse. He came back a few minutes later with their bags, some blankets and food, and the cottage shut up tightly and locked. She met his eyes with question as he tied the supplies onto the saddle. He smiled at her and said, "We're not staying here anymore. They'll find you here, and I'm not about to let them get you away from me again."

Han expected to see scorn and fire in her eyes, but he saw nothing but anguish. *Poor girl*, he thought, *she really does love the bastard*. But he quickly reminded himself that it was for the sake of his country, and he got into the saddle behind her.

They rode all day, staying deep in the forest and far from any roads, stopping only twice for necessities that didn't include the luxury of eating. He knew both their lives were in danger, and a keen desperation drove him to put distance between them and Nik Koenig.

As the sun was going down in the west, Han trotted the horse directly into what appeared to be the ruins of an old abbey. He tied off the horse where it could graze and helped Maggie down. She sat numbly on the ground while he took their things off the saddle.

"Hungry?" he asked, knowing she had to be.

Maggie shook her head and cast her eyes downward sadly. It was obvious to Han that she wanted to be with Nik, and if he didn't have the Duke of Horstberg to back him up in this, he'd have probably taken her back to him. He knelt beside her and removed the towel from around her mouth, saying softly, "You should eat, my love."

"I don't want to." She then added much to his surprise, "I'm glad you're alive, Han."

"So am I," he chuckled.

"Are you hurt badly? There's still blood in your hair."

"I still have a headache, but I'm fine."

"He almost shot you," she said without meeting his eyes, "but I stopped him. I'm glad I did."

"Why is that?" he asked gently, wondering over the source of her mood. This was not at all what he'd expected.

Maggie shook her head to indicate she didn't want to talk, and he silently handed her some bread and cheese, which she ate idly.

"You can untie me," she said. "I won't run away."

Han didn't bother to ask why. Whatever the reason, he knew she was sincere. He gently untied her wrists, rubbing them for her.

"Thank you," she said and meant it.

They finished eating in silence before he spread a blanket out in one of the corners of the ruined structure and told her to lie down. She did as he said, and he lay next to her, throwing another blanket over both of them as dusk filtered into darkness.

Han lay silently staring upward, noting the stars beginning to show in the sky above them. There wasn't any roof left in this place at all. He knew something was terribly wrong with Maggie. But for the life of him, he couldn't figure what. He'd have assumed she'd be overjoyed to have Nik rescue her, and she would have fought like mad at being recaptured by her evil kidnapper. Knowing she had been running when he found her in the forest gave him a clue. Perhaps she had figured something out about Nik. That had to be it, he thought with a certain amount of confidence. He was just wondering what might have happened when he heard her sob. She was lying with her back to him, but even in the darkness he could see her shoulders tremble as her crying increased.

"Maggie," he whispered, leaning up on one elbow. "What is it?"

"Oh, Han," she said, turning toward him and burying her face into the folds of his shirt. He had been cruel, and she hated him for all of the things he'd done. But he was all she had now, and she cried all of her pain out against his shoulder.

"What is it?" he whispered again when her emotion had settled somewhat.

"It's all true," she cried. "I heard them talking, and it's all true. He was using me just like you said he was. Oh, I'm so humiliated. How I must have hurt my family! Oh, Han, it's so awful. I'm so glad I didn't marry him, but I . . ." She broke into fresh sobs, and he pulled her close to him, stroking the back of her head gently in an effort to comfort her.

Han sighed with indescribable relief. It was a miracle! The worst was behind him. As long as Maggie knew the truth, they could make it through this together. "Maggie," he whispered. "Maggie, my love. It's all right. It doesn't matter anymore. I will take care of you—always."

In spite of her confusion, Maggie absorbed the much-needed comfort he was offering and instinctively nuzzled closer to him, hanging desperately on his words. He was all she had.

Han took in her willingness to be close to him with amazement and gratitude. Silently, he lifted her chin with his finger, smiling as he wiped away her tears. "You look lovely tonight, Your Royal Beauty."

Maggie looked into his eyes, as if she were searching for something, and she made no resistance when he bent to kiss her. His lips met hers soft and quick, and then he pulled away briefly to watch her eyes. He read there a yearning for comfort, and with the desire to give it, he kissed her again. He was surprised to feel her lips part subtly beneath his. But he took advantage of the opportunity, and she moaned softly as he eased her closer.

Maggie pushed away her horrible thoughts of Nik and focused

on the comfort and security she found in Han's kiss. Before his lips set her free, she found herself completely in his arms. Memories of being with him like this in the past trickled into her mind. Fighting to push the bitterness of her delusions away, she moved effortlessly into his embrace. She felt his heartbeat quicken in time with hers as she set her hands against his chest. Falling completely under his power, she caught fire with an excitement she'd never experienced before. Or had she?

Han began to lose himself in Maggie's affection—knowing she was sober. He was surprised to find her unbuttoning her blouse.

"Maggie," he drew back, "what are you doing?"

"I don't remember, Han," she whispered in a raspy voice, "but I want you to—"

"No, no, Maggie." He sat up, taking her hands into his. "We mustn't."

"Why not?" She sounded deflated as she sat beside him. Han had to tell himself he wasn't dreaming. Maggie du Woernig was asking him to make love to her, and he was trying to stop it. He wondered what kind of horrible insecurity smoldered in her that would make her so willing to do something that he knew went against everything she'd been taught.

"There's something you need to know, Maggie," he said carefully.

"I'm listening," she said, and her voice alone made him want her.

"Maggie," he took a deep breath, "you know how I said that I'd never lied to you?"

"Yes," she agreed. Then she asked skeptically, "*Did* you lie to me, Han?"

"No, not exactly. I mean . . . I was only—"

"Slightly deceptive."

"That's right."

"About what?"

"Well, the only thing that matters now is . . . well . . . I just—"

"You're stammering, Han."

"Yes, I am. You see, Maggie. Nothing happened that night. I mean, what I said about us kissing, and you taking off your clothes . . . all of that was true. But then you just . . . went to sleep."

Even through the darkness, Han felt her gaze harden on him. "But you said that—"

"No, Maggie, I never said that it happened. I was simply specu-
lating over the possibilities of what *could* have happened."

Han heard a huffy little noise, then silence. While he waited for
her reaction, he imagined being catapulted back into dealing with
her fury. Feeling the need to make a point, he added, "Your honor
and virtue are still intact, Maggie. And I'm certainly not going to
compromise them *now*. In spite of what I might have implied in the
past, I would never dishonor you."

A minute passed before she said, "You are a scoundrel, Han
Heinrich. You're a deplorable louse! And a horrible tease. And . . ."
Something close to a laugh broke the tension. "And you're a fabulous
kisser."

Han chuckled with relief, but silence fell between them again,
and he held his breath. When she finally spoke, her voice was soft
with emotion. "I'm scared, Han. So much has happened that I don't
know what to think . . . or what to feel. But I need you. Will you
hold me, Han . . . like you did before . . . without compromising my
honor and virtue?"

He chuckled warmly. "I think I could probably manage."

Maggie touched his face and added, "Will you kiss me, Han?"

"Your wish is my command, Your Highness."

He said it as if he truly meant it, and Maggie allowed all her fears
and worries to flee as she relaxed in Han's embrace and allowed him
to kiss her freely. She pushed a hand into his hair and marveled at
its softness, being careful not to touch his head where it was surely
very tender from the injury he'd received. He lay close beside her
and kissed her again. She felt safe and secure. Nik Koenig was the
furthest thing from her mind.

"Maggie," Han whispered, brushing his lips over her brow, "are
you sober?"

"Of course I'm sober," she replied.

"I was hoping," he pulled her closer, and she moaned softly.

"Why is that?"

"I knew there had to be a reason why it was so much better than
last time."

Maggie lifted her head to look at him. "You weren't lying to me,
were you, Han, about what happened . . . before?"

"It was all true," he whispered.

Maggie wasn't sure how to feel or react concerning any of this, so she simply chose not to think about it. With no thought of tomorrow, she drifted to sleep in Han's arms.

Chapter Ten

THE DUKE'S BARGAIN

Maggie felt as if she'd only slept a matter of moments before Han roused her in the darkness and whispered, "You've got to get up—quickly. Your cousin has caught up with us."

Fear immediately quickened Maggie's breath and made her heart pound as Han lifted her onto the horse. She vaguely heard the sound of voices nearby, and Nik's stood out strongly. But Han had the horse at a full gallop before it came out of the ruins where they'd slept, and all other sounds quickly dissipated.

"What about our things?" she asked.

"We'll get more," he said. "If we don't get out of here, I'm going to be dead, and you're going to be his."

Maggie said nothing more. She only prayed that would never happen and held on tight. Hearing Han put it that way made her think about this entire escapade from a completely different perspective. Had that been his thinking all along? The very idea made her shudder, and she forced it away, focusing instead on her gratitude that she was in his care. They rode far into daylight, mostly through thick forest, until Han finally stopped, and they dismounted to stretch their legs.

Maggie felt Han watching her, and she wondered how much of all that he'd said and done the past several weeks had been sincere.

"Maggie," he said with serious eyes.

"What?"

"Thank you for letting me kidnap you."

"I didn't let you," she said strongly, but Han caught a hint of humor in her eyes that made him believe the worst was finally over.

"You might as well have," he laughed, and she gave him a vague smile.

They each had a few minutes of privacy in the trees before they mounted the horse again and rode on. It was nearing dark when they came to a town that wasn't as small as the one they'd gone to before, near the cottage where they'd stayed. Han stopped at an inn where he got a room for them under the names of Mr. and Mrs. Bruxen. They ate a hearty supper in the common room, and Maggie swore she'd never been so hungry in her life.

Han watched her closely as she ate. While she seemed comfortable with him, he still sensed a sadness about her, and he wondered if she would fully open up to him.

It was late when they went to their room and freshened up, and then Maggie got into bed and slept immediately from the exhaustion of the past two days. Han fell asleep almost as quickly in his makeshift bed on the floor.

Han awoke in the darkness and realized Maggie wasn't in the bed where she was supposed to be. He became momentarily panicked until he saw Maggie's outline standing near the window.

"Is something wrong?" he asked.

"I thought you were asleep," she said without turning.

"I'm not now."

"Han," she said with humility in her tone, turning to face him in the darkness, "what will we do now?"

"What do you think we should do, Maggie?" he asked.

"I want to go home, but . . ."

"But?" he pressed when she faltered.

"Well . . . can I go back this way . . . after leaving like that, and . . . I mean, what do you suppose people will think? And what about my family, and . . ."

"Maggie," he said gently, "my guess is that Horstberg believes you ran away and eloped."

"With Nik."

"Perhaps, but if you didn't show up to meet him, he probably didn't go looking for you until he made certain you were gone. *I'm* the one who disappeared the same night you did, Maggie."

Maggie absorbed what that meant and allowed it to mix into her already turbulent thoughts. While she was still thinking, Han said,

"I'm not certain you should go back to Horstberg just yet, Maggie. There is no way of knowing what Nik Koenig is really up to, and like it or not, you are a part of it."

The thought sent a shudder through Maggie. How could she have been such a fool? Had she really put her country in jeopardy? She had. She really had. The very idea made her so sick that she had to force it out of her head. Concentrating on more immediate matters, she said, "So, the only way I can return to Horstberg with my honor is to return married."

Han felt both hopeful and afraid by what she was saying. Or perhaps it was the way she'd said it. Even though this was what he'd wanted, what needed to happen, he knew her heart was broken, and he wasn't certain he could ever fix it. Sticking to more practical matters, he took a deep breath and said, "You could put it that way."

Following an unbearable silence she asked, "Do you still want to marry me, Han?"

He felt like crying when he knew he should have been happy. He kept his emotions to himself and simply stated the truth. "Of course I do. Do you think I'd have gone to all this trouble if I didn't?"

"Are you certain?"

"Maggie, what are you getting at?"

"We should . . ." she paused and drew a heavy sigh, "get married."

"I'll not argue with you," he said, "but I'd like to know why you think we should get married now, when you have so adamantly insisted in the past that you would never marry me."

"It's the only right thing to do," she said with just a hint of arrogance. "You kidnapped me, Han. We have been living together—so to speak—for weeks now."

"Is there any other reason?" he felt he had to ask.

"There is no one else for me now," she said sadly, and Han wondered if he was really so bad. "If I was willing once to be given in marriage for the sake of my country, to whatever his name was, then—"

"Rudolf," he provided. "And you'd best remember it. He's probably your brother-in-law by now."

"Yes," she said sadly, "I suppose he is."

"As you were saying," he urged, not wanting her to think about how she'd missed her sister's wedding.

"Yes, well . . . I am trying to tell you that I will marry you, Han, if that's what you want."

"Don't you think I would want to be married to a princess?" he asked, attempting to throw some lightheartedness into the conversation; otherwise, he was afraid he really might start to cry. "I'm certain there are great advantages."

"Like what?"

"Money for one thing. Your father is a very wealthy man."

"Is that why you want to marry me?"

"No. But we must consider power. That's why Nik wants to marry you."

"Yes," she said even more sadly, "we must consider that."

"But I don't want power either."

"What *do* you want, Han?"

"You," he said and wondered if she could hear the sincerity in his voice. "I've always wanted you."

"You have?" she asked, sounding truly surprised, and he wondered why she couldn't believe him.

"Of course I have," he assured her, hoping to be able to tell her things he'd wanted to say for years. "After you told me you would never marry beneath yourself, I tried to hate you because I knew I could never have you. When you called off the betrothal for somebody you thought was nobody, I was upset."

"Are you lying to me, Han?" She turned more toward him.

"I've told you before, my love, I've never lied to you."

"And that is why you kidnapped me? You simply *wanted* me?"

"That's the biggest reason."

"What are the others?"

His heart quickened, certain that if she knew the whole story, she would be angry. She had to know eventually about the bargain he'd made with the duke, but his instincts told him this was not the right time. She already had far too much to think about. "Any other reason is too trivial to mention right now."

"You still haven't answered me directly," she said, and he caught a hint of vulnerability in her voice. "Are you willing to marry me?" she asked.

"Yes, Maggie, we'll get married. I believe it's the only feasible option . . . under the circumstances. But . . ." he added in a light tone, "I want you to promise me something."

"What?" she asked skeptically.

"I want my wife to have fun. Do you think you could learn how to have fun?" He knew he couldn't ask her to learn to love him again, but perhaps if they could have some fun, she would be able to remember more of what they'd once shared.

"Perhaps," she said as if it would be a chore.

"Well, then," he stood up and came beside her, "let's make it official." He went down on one knee and took her hand in his. "Will you marry me, MagdaLena Amelia LeeAnna du Woernig?"

"Yes," she said, and he thought she smiled, but the room was dark and he couldn't be certain, "I will."

"Now that we have that settled," he said, "why don't you come back to bed?"

Through a long moment of silence, he knew she expected him to stand up. But he didn't; he wanted to savor the moment. She kept her hand in his and knelt beside him, resting her head against his shoulder with a sigh. He put his arms around her, and she whispered, "Thank you, Han . . . for kidnapping me."

"You're quite welcome," he chuckled.

"Otherwise," she said, "Horstberg would be lost."

"Yes," he added flatly, trying not to take this too personally, "this is quite a sacrifice we're making for our country."

Maggie awoke alone in the room, but she barely had time to wonder where Han might be when he came in with some breakfast for her.

"Hurry and eat," he said. "I have a feeling your cousin isn't far behind us."

Maggie did as he said, and they were soon on their way again.

"Where are we going?" she asked as they rode. "I mean . . . what exactly are your plans?"

"Well," he said, "I'm not certain exactly. But I was thinking of getting married in Switzerland."

"Switzerland? I wish we could go home to get married."

"As you said yourself, that's not possible if you want to go home with your reputation. When we go back, it has to appear that we eloped right away, or you will be talked about for the rest of your life."

"I see," she sounded dismayed. "How long before we get to Switzerland?"

"That's a good question." He laughed then added, "It depends on how lost we are."

"Han!"

"Don't panic, my love. I was joking. I know exactly where we are. I just hope that Nik Koenig doesn't."

They rode for three days, staying at inns along the way and using a different name in each town. Maggie became continually more weary of all of this running and hiding, and ironically longed to be back at the cottage, safely tucked away there with Han. But it was no longer safe there, and until she and Han were married, she couldn't go home. The entire situation was such a horrible mess. And she was exhausted. Physically, emotionally, and mentally exhausted!

Late one evening as they finally rode into a small town, Maggie counted the minutes until she could have a good meal in her stomach and a comfortable bed beneath her. But Han was certain he saw Nik going into a pub, and they ended up spending the night in a barn, hoping to avoid him.

"Just like old times," he said when they were lying in the straw.

"How can you say that," she asked soberly, "when you haven't got me tied up?"

Han laughed, but Maggie just rolled over and went to sleep. She awoke to a kiss on the brow and looked up to meet Han's gaze. Looking into his eyes, she wondered what it might be like to have him love her. The affection they'd shared as teens tumbled into her mind, and she felt warmed by the memories, although she realized now how innocent their relationship had been. And she'd been extremely naive. She blessed Han for his sense of honor that had kept her from making a very big mistake. For the first time since she'd banished him from her life, she wondered what kind of foolishness had possessed her. He had treated her well, and she couldn't deny the pleasure she'd found from his affection, even as young as she had been. But she was a woman now, and the prospect of spending her future with Han Heinrich no longer seemed so distasteful.

"Good morning," he said softly.

"Good morning."

Lifting his brows, he smiled mischievously. "How would you feel about a bath?"

"Oh," she sat up quickly, "I would die to have a bath."

"Would a pond do?"

"Yes," she said, "it would."

"Come on," Han pulled her to her feet, and they rode through a brief stretch of thick forest before the trees moved away to reveal a crystal blue pond, hidden discreetly by trees on every side.

"Close your eyes," Maggie said when she began undressing. "We're not married yet."

Han chuckled and did as she said. He could only think of how grateful he was for the changes that had transpired between them. They still had to be wary of Nik Koenig. And his relationship with Maggie still had a long way to go, but they'd made remarkable progress, and he could only be grateful for that.

When Maggie was in the water, swimming about carelessly, Han undressed himself and went in too. He kept a deliberate distance from her but watched her closely as she tried to work the tangles out of her hair. He contemplated the changes in her. She had agreed to become his wife now, and she had turned to him for comfort when she'd needed it. But unlike Nik Koenig, Han wanted more than just formalities. They had come far, but he would not be happy until she was his completely. He had no control over whether or not she could ever love him the way she'd once claimed to. But he also wanted her trust, her affection, and perhaps most important, he wanted her respect—not out of fear as she had shown before, but because she saw him for what he was. He would not spend the rest of his life feeling like a man who had been lucky enough to marry a princess. He wanted a complete lack of social barrier between them, not unlike the friendship shared by his father and Maggie's mother. He couldn't make her love him, but he was determined to earn her trust and respect. And that was something he *could* control. If he worked at it long enough, surely he could deserve at least those things from her.

"You look beautiful," he called, "Your Royal All-Wetness."

Her expression didn't change and he said, "Wasn't it even a little bit funny?"

"What?"

"Don't you like it when I make up new and original titles for you?"

"Not really."

"Why not?"

"Because I know you're trying to insult me."

"I am not!" he insisted, glad they could clear *that* up. "I'm teasing you. There is a difference, you know."

"Not much."

"You just don't know how to have fun." He smirked, certain that keeping matters light would be best for the time being.

Maggie only shook her head and swam farther away from him. A few minutes later, Han got out of the water and put on his breeches before sitting down to watch her. She made him close his eyes while she got out and got dressed. By listening carefully, he could tell when she was dressed. Before she even realized he was watching her again, he had one arm around her to keep her from running while he tickled her right at the bottom of her ribs in the spot where he knew from their youth was the most ticklish.

At first Maggie just yelled protests, trying in vain to hit him. When he wouldn't stop, she gradually began to laugh. She finally laughed so hard, she was nearly crying. Only then did Han stop.

"I love it when you laugh," he said triumphantly.

Trying to catch her breath, she said, "Is it really so important to you?"

"It most certainly is. And now that we've cracked that sober face, I intend to keep it smiling."

Maggie studied Han while he gazed at her as if he were doing the same. She wished she could see inside his mind, if only to know the true source of his motives. She wondered what her life might be like with him, but it would certainly be better than having Rudolf as a husband. At least Han intrigued her, and surely what they had shared in their youth meant something. And being married to Han meant that she could live in Horstberg as opposed to having to move to her husband's home country, which is what Sonia had surely done by now. Marrying Han certainly had its advantages.

Maggie was surprised when Han interrupted her thoughts by kissing her softly, but she wished it hadn't been so brief. When he kissed her again, she wondered if he could sense her desires so easily. Or was this the result of his *own* desires? Either way, she enjoyed his lengthy kiss and held tightly to his shoulders when her knees felt a little wobbly. She felt Han beginning to lose his balance only a moment before he fell backward into the water. Maggie laughed again when he came up gasping for breath. She couldn't deny that it felt good to laugh.

"Help me out of here," Han said, wondering if she had any clue that he'd just done that on purpose. Hearing her laugh made it all worth it. He held out his hand toward her, silently implying that she help him. Maggie reached toward him, and he couldn't believe she actually fell for it. She knew he had walked out of here not ten minutes ago, and now she believed he needed help. He laughed as he took her hand and pulled her into the pond with him.

"Ooh," she muttered and spit water, trying to hit him. Then she laughed even harder than she had a minute earlier. Han pulled her into his arms, loving the way she didn't resist his affection. Even more than that, he loved the evidence that she actually wanted him to kiss her, and she enjoyed it at least as much as he did.

Han met her eyes and couldn't help smiling to think of the changes he'd seen in them since they had left Horstberg. But he had to begrudgingly give a lot of the credit to Nik Koenig for being stupid enough to let her figure out what he was really like. Pulling her up into his arms, Han carried Maggie onto the shore. He set her down and bent gallantly, doing his best to wring the water out of her skirt, and finding a great deal of pleasure in the way she kept laughing for no apparent reason.

Maggie was thrilled and relieved when Han found an inn for them to stay in that night, an inn that was far nicer than any they had stayed in so far. The food they served tasted heavenly, and she ate until she was stuffed. Han teased her about getting fat if she didn't slow down, but in his eyes she saw something that made her believe he would keep looking at her with that perfect adoration for the rest of his life, no matter what she looked like.

Maggie relished the comfortable bed where she slept deeply.

And since the room had a nice sofa, Han didn't have to sleep on the floor. She awoke alone in the room the following morning and became impatient when Han didn't return for quite some time. She began to wonder if she should be worried and was pacing with subdued panic when he finally came into the room with an armload of packages. For the first time since all of this had begun, Maggie wondered where he'd gotten all of his money. She reasoned that his father was a very important man and would likely be wealthy from all the years he'd worked for the duke. That had to be it.

"Good morning, my love," he grinned, setting the packages on the bed.

"Where have you been?"

"I've been busy." He smiled then held out his arms elaborately so she'd notice he was wearing new clothes from head to toe. "There now," he said, "I'm dressed to escort a princess."

"So you are." She couldn't help smiling.

"And," he said, "you shall be dressed like a princess." Tearing open one parcel after another, he brought forth new shoes and stockings and a silk chemise—which she scolded him for purchasing because it was scandalous. There were ruffled petticoats and some miscellaneous sundries. And to top it all off, a blue traveling suit and a matching hat and handbag. Maggie squealed with delight, and he laughed from her happiness.

Not completely convinced that there wasn't something suspicious about his abundance of funds, she asked cautiously, "Where did you get the money, Han?"

"That's my secret," he said.

"You didn't steal it, did you?"

"No," he laughed, "I didn't steal it. I just came upon a king's ransom."

He seemed sincere enough, so she just smiled and admired her new dress. "As long as you came by it honestly, I suppose it's your business."

Han smiled in return, certain she would tear his eyes out if she knew where he'd *really* gotten the money. She would have to know eventually, but for now he preferred to keep her distracted. "Try them on," he said with enthusiasm and took great pleasure in watching her excitedly reform herself, covering his eyes when necessary.

"How did you know what size to get?" she asked when the skirt fit perfectly around her waist.

"I took your old clothes with me," he told her and pulled a satin ribbon from his pocket as if it were a magic trick. Her resulting giggle made it *feel* magic. With her hair brushed through and tied back in a blue ribbon, she put the hat in place and turned dramatically for him to see the results.

"You look beautiful," he said with sincerity, "Your Royal Highness." She smiled at him, and he added, "How do you feel?"

"Like a princess," she said, "and it feels good. Thank you, Han."

"You are very welcome," he grinned.

"But Han," she looked distressed, "I can't ride a horse dressed like this."

"Oh, didn't I tell you?" he grinned, knowing he hadn't. "I traded the horse in . . . for these." He pulled tickets out of his other pocket with the same magician affect.

"What?"

"Train tickets. We are going to Switzerland, my love, and after I've made you my wife, we are going to honeymoon our way to Italy and go home through France."

"Oh, Han," she squealed again and clapped her hands together, "it sounds wonderful, but . . ." She looked downhearted again.

"What now?"

"Won't we be gone an awfully long time? Shouldn't we get home?"

"Maggie," he pulled her into his arms, "have you ever left Germany before?"

"No."

"Have you ever really talked to anyone who was not from Horstberg?"

"I talked to that lady downstairs last night," she said.

He smiled. "There is a big, beautiful world out there. I haven't seen much of it, but I've seen more than you have. You and I are going to see it together. Horstberg will not change while we're gone. We'll go back, and everything will be the same, but we will have had the time of our lives. That's what honeymoons are for, my love." She still looked a bit distressed, and he added, "We will be home before Christmas, for certain."

Maggie smiled, satisfied with his promise. And his reasoning certainly made sense. She realized in that moment that she was actually looking forward to marrying Han. Having gotten used to the idea, it was perhaps even exciting. Certainly a great deal more exciting than she'd once felt at the prospect of marrying Rudolf.

Maggie's thoughts stayed with her as they boarded the train. With Han sitting across from her, his long legs stretched out and his arms folded across his chest, she tried to imagine him as her husband. Though she hadn't consciously thought about it for years, Maggie had to admit that Han Heinrich was a handsome man. His pale, fluffy hair was as soft as it looked. She knew that from experience. His green eyes almost glowed when he was happy—which was most of the time. And his smile was remarkable. Despite his slender frame, she knew from experience that he was very strong. And she liked his height. He made her feel secure and protected when she was near him.

Maggie couldn't help remembering how it felt to be in his arms, having him kiss her. To look at him now, it was difficult to believe this was the same man. The thought spurred a rush of excitement that mingled with a fluttering in her stomach. The cruel things he'd done to her in the past didn't seem to matter anymore; or perhaps she was beginning to understand his motives.

As the miles passed mostly in silence, Maggie thought about where all of this had begun. Han Heinrich was a stablehand, for heaven's sake! Even now, dressed finely and smiling often at her, she couldn't help but see the groom. He had always been a servant, and it was difficult to think of him otherwise. His father having prestigious employment and the friendships their parents shared didn't change the fact that he'd grown up a servant, and his parents had done the same. He certainly had brought her down to his level over the past several weeks, but she wondered what it would be like when they returned to Horstberg.

Deciding for now to just do as Han was determined to do—see the world and have fun—Maggie chose to put her speculations away and enjoy herself. She leaned eagerly toward the window to admire the scenery as it passed by.

"It *is* beautiful." Han smiled.

"It is," she agreed. "Are we almost there?"

"I think so. Do you want to get married today?"

Maggie turned to meet his eyes, and they seemed to delve into her with a sense of anticipation. Feeling fluttery again, Maggie turned back to the window. "Today would be fine."

"We'll have to see what we can arrange," he said. "The first thing we must do is find you a wedding gown. What kind do you want?"

"It doesn't matter," she said.

"It *does* matter," he retorted emphatically. "A princess must look like a princess when she marries." She smiled toward him and he added seriously, "Will this make me a prince or you a groomess?"

"Neither," she said too seriously. She thought a lot of his self-made words were ridiculous.

The train arrived at last in Zurich. With the purchase of a new gown and some quick arrangements, Maggie actually became excited. There was a genuine happiness apparent in Han's eyes, and she couldn't help feeling satisfied to see it there. She had to admit that the elaborate gown Han had chosen did well for her, and she felt a fresh exhilaration as the reality began to take hold.

The ceremony was simple, as was the binding kiss they shared. With a finely etched gold band on her third finger, Maggie became Mrs. Han Heinrich. They went together to one of the finest hotels in the city, where an elegant meal was brought to their room. When they'd finished eating, Han took Maggie's hand across the table and kissed it. His eyes met hers strongly, and she read anticipation in them.

"Well," he said lightly as he stood and pulled her to her feet, "should I tickle you or take you to bed?"

Maggie felt embarrassed by his bold reference and looked away, not knowing how to respond. His teasing tone of voice couldn't hide the severity in his eyes, and she knew he didn't take any of this lightly. She simply didn't know what to say. She'd known this moment was coming, but she'd not once considered how to handle it.

Han watched Maggie a long moment, wishing he knew how she really felt about all of this. He sensed her anticipation, but he also sensed confusion. And whether or not she was at all afraid, he simply couldn't tell. He didn't want her to believe this was some kind of obligation now that she was his wife. But oh, how he wanted to stop avoiding the boundaries that had been necessary between them before now! Not at the expense of her feelings, however. Realizing it was futile to try and read her mind, he decided to just come right out and say what needed to be said. "Maggie," he lifted her chin with his finger, "just because we're married doesn't mean you have to—"

"Love me, Han," she whispered, and a lump gathered in his throat. He looked deeply into her eyes, searching for any indication of her true feelings. He knew her biggest reason for being with him had to do with circumstances she'd been forced into, but he clearly read a desire in her that perhaps matched his own.

"MagdaLena, my love," he whispered, pressing his fingers over her face before he kissed her. Everything had changed now, and nothing more needed to be said.

Maggie worked the pins out of her hair while Han unbuttoned the back of her wedding gown. As he carried her to the bed and lay close beside her, she felt herself come alive. She had never dreamed that any experience in this world could be so remarkable. Surely it couldn't be wrong for her to be with Han if they shared something so wondrous. And mingled with the passion they shared, she felt serenity, knowing that she was his. He was hers. They would always be together. A perfect peace and contentment fell over her when their passion was spent, and she eased her head to his shoulder, marveling over what she had just experienced with him.

While they lay in silence together between the cool sheets of the huge bed, Han eased Maggie closer to him. He had never felt so satisfied in all his life. Through all the years that he'd been imagining this moment, he'd never dreamed it could be so perfect. Maggie lay still for a long while, and Han felt certain she was asleep when he whispered close to her face, unable to hold back the words, "I love you, Maggie. I love you with all my heart."

He was startled when she lifted her head quickly to look at him, and he nearly expected her to accuse him of being mad. But she only gazed at him intently until he saw a subtle mist rise into her eyes. She quickly buried her face against his chest to hide the tears, and Han eased her closer. He took her hand into his, fingering her wedding band, praying their future together might be as good as this moment.

In commencing a honeymoon, Han made it clear that it was

important to spend a great deal of money. They stayed for several days in Zurich, during which they managed to fill trunks with new clothes and other odd paraphernalia. And he'd never seen Maggie so happy. She would smile brightly as she tried on new gowns and laugh as they walked and held hands, taking in all of the sights of the city. The days were filled with fun and excitement, and the nights with passion and respite. When Maggie finally proclaimed she could think of nothing else to buy or see in Zurich, they moved on.

Taking the journey slowly in order to enjoy themselves along the way, they traveled south through Switzerland and into Italy—with no sign of Nik Koenig. Han tried to be careful, certain at times that Nik would show up any day. He knew Nik's motives well. But for the most part, he didn't worry about it. He never talked about it. And they had a glorious time.

Maggie was amazed to realize that Han did a fair job of communicating any necessary exchange in English, French, and even Italian. When she commented on it, he reminded her, "I was taught by the same tutors who taught you, Your Highness."

"So you were," she had to admit.

A slight impedance interrupted their fun when Maggie unexpectedly became ill. It didn't seem overly serious, but when it persisted, Han insisted she see a doctor. They stopped at an inn located in a small town not far from Venice. After Han made arrangements for the local doctor to come, they sat in the common room together to eat.

Maggie was vaguely aware of a very overweight woman sitting on the other side of the room, chatting with the innkeeper's wife. She'd never personally known any person so large, but she knew it would be improper for her to pass judgments or be impolite in regard to this woman or anyone else, no matter their differences. Han distracted her with a typical chuckle.

"What's so funny?" she asked with a mouthful of food.

"You," he smiled. "You're always eating. You eat more than I do these days. If you don't stop eating, you're going to look like that lady over there."

"Han!" she scolded and wondered if he'd been reading her mind. She just smiled at him and continued to eat. "She looks like a nice lady. Even if I did get fat, I would still be nice."

"There would be more of you to love," he laughed and relaxed more into the comfortable chair. He marveled at how he never grew tired of just watching Maggie, and the way she enjoyed food so thoroughly was a trait he found endearing. She enjoyed eating even more than she enjoyed buying new clothes—and that was really saying something. Since he'd never actually been shopping with her during their youth, it was something he'd never realized, but he enjoyed making her happy—whatever it took. And he loved to just watch her and take in the happiness of the present, as if it could go on this way forever and Nik Koenig would never have to be faced.

"Maybe *you* will get fat when you get old," she said with her mouth full. He chuckled to think of how the duchess would have scolded her politely for doing such a thing.

"I doubt it," he replied. "It takes too much exercise to keep up with you."

"If I get fat," a smile touched her lips, "will you still kiss me like you did last night?"

"Was the way I kissed you last night different from any other night?"

"No," she said, "I was just wondering . . . about kisses in general, I suppose."

"And other things," he grinned, "that go along with kisses."

Her eyes sparkled. "And other things," she admitted.

"I don't know," he teased. "You'll have to get fat and test me."

"I'd rather not." She laughed.

"I bet that lady gets kissed," he said.

"Oh, I don't know," Maggie said skeptically, grateful that they were managing to talk about this discreetly. "She looks kind of lonely."

"I'll bet she's married."

"No," Maggie argued, just for the sake of it. "She's probably an old maid."

"I bet her husband is handsome and kind and very good to her."

"I bet she's an old maid. I bet she knits and cooks and that's about it."

"I bet that . . ." he paused and grinned when a tall, nice looking, middle-aged man entered the room, "I bet that's her husband."

"Don't be ridiculous."

"Are fat people supposed to be married to fat people?" he asked.

Maggie didn't have a chance to reply before the man walked over to the fat lady and placed a tender kiss on the side of her face while he was helping her to her feet. Maggie watched with astonishment then noticed Han grinning smugly. But his complacency was interrupted when the couple they had been discussing approached their table.

"Ah, Mr. Bruxen," the man said with a thick French accent, "it is nice to see you again."

"It is indeed," the fat lady said, and Maggie glared at Han while he lifted his brows playfully.

"Hello," Han said, "please sit down. You must meet my wife."

"Ah," the man said as he took her hand to kiss it, "this is no doubt the beautiful Maggie you told us about. But your words did her no justice."

Maggie smiled. The gentleman was indeed very handsome. He was near Han's height but bore a larger frame. And he had a youthful attitude about him that contradicted the signs of age in his hair and face. The woman, despite her obesity, was quite attractive and very sweet. The contrast made them an interesting couple.

"Maggie," Han smiled affectionately toward her, "this is Claude and Josette Dormante. I met them earlier when I went in search of a doctor."

"It is a pleasure to meet you," Maggie smiled as they were seated, Claude tenderly helping Josette since her obesity made it difficult for her to do so on her own.

"By the way," Han said toward Mrs. Dormante, "did you get what you needed for your backache?"

"Oh, yes," she said, "Dr. Latini is very good. I feel much better."

"I'm glad to hear it," Han said.

"And what about you, Mrs. Bruxen?" Mr. Dormante said. "Your husband told us you weren't feeling well."

"I dare say she looks a bit pale," Mrs. Dormante inserted.

"Oh, it's nothing serious," she smiled. "It comes and goes. Han thought it would be wise to see the doctor, but I—"

"And he's coming here shortly," Han added, "to make certain it's *not* anything serious."

"That's very wise," Mrs. Dormante added adamantly. "If there is a problem, it can be corrected, and if not, you will have peace of mind."

"Very well put, Mrs. Dormante." Han smiled toward her.

"Please," she said, glancing at both Han and Maggie, "call me Josette. I do so hate formality. You know I was just telling Claude last night that we haven't met nearly as many interesting people on this last excursion we've taken. We usually always come back with new friends, and well . . . it looks as though we might have finally found some. Don't you think so, Claude?"

"It would seem so." Her husband smiled warmly at her.

"Where is it that you've been?" Maggie asked.

"We've just now returned from France," Claude said. "We are originally from Nice, but we now prefer the charming little Italian palazzo where we stay when we're not gallivanting about the world."

"You enjoy traveling, then?" Han asked.

"Oh, yes indeed. Where is it that you come from? Bavaria, didn't you say?"

"Yes," Maggie said nostalgically. "A small country called—"

"It's so small," Han interrupted, not wanting to leave any obvious clues for Nik Koenig, "it's hardly worth mentioning. I'm certain you would have never heard of it."

Maggie glared at him, but he ignored it, and Claude said, "There are many small countries in that area. What is it you people call them, uh . . ."

"Duchies," his wife provided.

"Ah, yes of course. We have traveled that way before. Very beautiful place, Bavaria."

"It is indeed," Maggie said.

"The Germans do well with castles," Josette inserted. "The French have nice castles, but I do think I prefer the German ones. We've seen some very fascinating ones, and . . ."

Han was grateful when Dr. Latini came into the common room, interrupting their conversation. He knew that Maggie could have easily started talking about Castle Horstberg and her being a princess. It could easily compromise their anonymity and leave them wide open for Nik to find them. He made a mental note to let Maggie know later what she should and shouldn't say to others. Since they'd not had any significant conversations with anyone else up to this point in their adventures, it simply hadn't come up.

Han excused himself and Maggie, and they walked up to their room with the doctor. He stayed while the doctor asked a few questions, then he went back to the common room to chat with Claude and Josette while Maggie was examined. The doctor came down a short while later and Han stood to meet him.

"Your wife is fine," he said with a smile, and Han sighed with relief. "I've told her everything, and I must be going, so I'll let her relay the diagnosis to you."

"Thank you, Doctor," Han said and settled with him. He then said good evening to the Dormantes and went quickly upstairs.

Entering the room, he found Maggie standing near the window with her back to him.

"You're all right, then?" he asked, closing the door.

"Yes," she replied, turning toward him.

"What did he say?"

"It's so simple." She smiled. "I don't know why I didn't figure it out before now. I suppose I've been having too much fun to think about it."

"What?" he asked impatiently

"Well," Maggie drawled, feeling the urge to hold off a little and tease him, "first let me ask you something you once asked me."

"All right."

"What do you think we should name it?"

"Name what?" he asked quickly, and she smiled. "Maggie," he drawled and tilted his head. "Are you trying to tell me that . . ."

"Yes," she said, "we're going to have a baby."

Han smiled. Then he laughed. Maggie laughed with him, and he pulled her into his arms.

"How do you feel about that?" he asked, watching her closely.

"What do you think?" She grinned.

"You seem happy enough."

"I am," she stated adamantly. "I think it will be fun."

"Oh, Maggie," he said and kissed her warmly, "you've made me happier than you could ever know."

She laughed softly then told him the doctor's instructions concerning things she should and should not do. They sat together on the bed, planning the remainder of their honeymoon, set at a slower pace for the benefit of Maggie's health.

They were surprised to hear a knock at the door, but Han smiled when he answered it to see the Dormantes standing in the hall.

"Forgive the intrusion," Claude said, "and you needn't tell us if you prefer, but . . . we only wondered if your wife is well."

"Yes," Han smiled, "she's fine. It appears we are going to have a little one."

"Oh," Josette clapped her hands together as Maggie came to stand near her husband, "that's the very best news a doctor can bring! How very exciting!"

"It's late," Claude said, "we're delighted with the news, but we should be getting off to bed. We'll be leaving early so that we can get home."

"You live not far from here, then?" Maggie asked.

"Just a few hours away. We take the traveling at a slow pace. It's more enjoyable that way."

"It was very nice meeting you," Han said.

"And you," Claude replied, handing him a small piece of paper. "I've written down where we live. If you get in the area, stop and see us any time."

"Thank you," Han said, "we might do that."

"We'd love to have you," Josette added gleefully, and they walked slowly together down the hall to their own room, one door down.

"So," Maggie said to Han when they were alone, "what should we name it?"

"We've got plenty of time to figure that out."

"But you were quite adamant about choosing a name right away the last time this came up."

Han looked down abruptly, overcome with a rush of guilt. "I'm sorry about that, Maggie. I was—"

She interrupted him with a kiss, as if none of that mattered anymore and there was no need to talk about it. Han smiled as she turned and began undressing for bed. He couldn't believe this was the same woman he'd kidnapped. He thought of the changes and then of the circumstances that had made him do what he'd done. Sooner or later, she had to know the truth. Now seemed just as good a time as any. He would be very glad to stop dreading the inevitable.

"Maggie," he said carefully, "there is something I must tell you."

"What is it?"

"It's about the reason I kidnapped you."

"You already told me. You wanted me."

"And that's absolutely true, but it's more than that," he said with caution.

Maggie thought back to their wedding night when he had whispered that he loved her. Though he'd not said it since, she wondered if that's what he was getting at. He certainly behaved as if he loved her.

"What is it?" she urged, noticing his apparent distress.

"Maggie," Han paused too long, remembering just how wrathful she could get. Knowing she would not be pleased, he pressed forward cautiously. "What I have to say will likely make you angry, but I want you to stay calm and hear me out. It's something you need to know."

Maggie nodded, feeling wary but certain it couldn't be anything too serious.

"Your father," he began, "suspected that you would try to run away with Nik." Maggie's eyes widened. Already, this was not what she had expected.

"How did you know that?" she insisted.

"He said that your mother had figured it out."

Maggie thought that sounded feasible. Her mother knew her very well. "But when did you talk to my father about it?" she asked, becoming more attentive. It wasn't like her father to talk with Han so openly—especially about something like that.

"You see, Maggie," Han cleared his throat as if his voice was finding it difficult to get through, "he called me into his office, and we talked, and . . ." he drew a deep breath and blurted it out, "your father asked me to kidnap you."

Maggie laughed. Surely this had to be a joke. But Han's expression told her it wasn't, and she had to stop and absorb what he'd said. Her heart began to pound from the severity in his expression.

"Please tell me you're teasing me," she said. He only shook his head, and something close to regret rose in his eyes.

"I can't believe it!" Maggie shouted when she recovered from the shock.

"Shhh! Keep it down. You promised to stay reasonable and hear me out."

"I don't believe you," she chuckled dubiously, but at least in a softened tone.

"I've never lied to you, Maggie."

"But you told me you did it because you wanted me."

"And that was the truth."

"And now? Han! Why on earth would my father want me to be kidnapped?"

"So you wouldn't marry Nik. He knew what was happening. But you were too bullheaded to listen to reason. He had no choice."

Maggie tried to catch her breath. "So," she said curtly, "you did it because the duke asked you to. How very noble!" With her sarcasm, tears burned her eyes, and she fought to hold them back. "How much did he pay you?"

"He gave me the money we've been living on," Han justified quickly. "He told me to show you a good time, to have fun, to buy you presents."

Looking back on the situation, it was easy enough for Maggie to understand her father's motives and to see that he was looking out for her. But it was Han's motives—Han's feelings—that disturbed her now. All this time she had found comfort, and perhaps a degree of pleasure, to think that a man would have gone to such great lengths—just because he wanted her. And she couldn't help but feel hurt, and perhaps feel deflated, to learn the truth. The rejection felt distantly familiar. And while she couldn't quite pinpoint the incident, associated memories rushed in with their accompanying pain. She reminded herself that she was a princess. It all came down to that. Matters of friendship and love all came down to that one fact—and she hated it.

Resigning herself to focus on the problem at hand, Maggie pushed the memories away, wishing her emotions would relent as easily. She looked Han in the eye and asked, "Did my father also want you to marry me?" He hesitated, and she added firmly, "I want the truth, Han. I am your wife. There will be no more secrets between us."

Han looked down sullenly. "My father . . . and your father . . . agreed that—"

"So," she said, fighting to keep her desire to explode under control, "I was put into an arranged marriage after all. Is that it?"

"Yes," he said, "I suppose it is." Maggie squeezed her eyes shut and willed back the knot in her throat. If she started to cry, she'd have no pride left at all.

"And what's in it for you, Han?" Anger always made it easier to avoid other, more sensitive emotions. "It's difficult to imagine your being talked easily into such an ordeal. What's waiting for you when we go back?"

Han took in her fierce gaze and told himself he could have expected no less. He'd known this moment would come. While she glared at him hotly, waiting for answers, he realized she was more perceptive than she often let on. "Answer me, Han!"

Han gazed back at her firmly, trying not to sound apologetic. "I've been guaranteed my father's position, working with Erich as he takes over."

Maggie sucked in a painful breath and had trouble letting it go. She turned her back to him and attempted to gain some composure. She had only hurt this deeply once in her life, and she could *not* allow herself to think about that. Not now. She couldn't believe this! It had been difficult to believe that *any* man would go to so much trouble for a woman—especially when she had been so cruel to him. She'd convinced herself it was because he'd wanted her. And believing that he'd actually loved her all along had made everything Han had done seem more plausible. But she'd been a fool. It all made sense now, and she could see what an absolute and utter fool she had been. She could see now how tempting it must have been to be given such on offer. His desire to work with Erich and have all the advantages of royalty available to him surely would have been too much to resist. She wouldn't be surprised if that had been at least partly his motive for showing an interest in her even when he was seventeen. She could well imagine how difficult it might have been for him, growing up almost a brother to the du Woernig children but denied all the rights of royalty. But she was the key to his having it all. Marrying her was clearly the easiest route to achieve everything he'd ever wanted. It was just so perfectly convenient. Remembering that he was waiting for her to speak, Maggie forced her hurt safely behind the anger. She'd been so perfectly happy not so many minutes ago. And now . . .

"Maggie?" Han said when the heart-pounding silence went on

too long. He'd far rather take her wrath head on than have to wonder what she was thinking. "Talk to me."

When she spoke at last, her tone bit deeply. "How low can a man get?" She turned to look at him, her eyes storming. "You are no better than Nik Koenig. I can see now that I am a woman of great value. You won't get the duchy, but you'll get the next best thing. I've seen what your father does. He has very nearly as much power and recognition as my father. He's the one who does everything important. He has prestige—and respect. People are every bit as much in awe of him as they are any of the royal family.

"Ooh!" she muttered, turning quickly away. "How could you do this to me? After all this time! I really thought you cared about me, and now . . . now I—"

"Maggie," he interrupted and turned her to face him, holding tightly to her upper arms, "you must hear me out."

"What else could you possibly say?" She squirmed away to put distance between them. "Did he offer you the family jewels and—"

"Don't be absurd, Maggie. Listen to me. I am not like Nik Koenig. Any amount of money or power could not have made me do something if I thought it wasn't right. I *did* want you, Maggie. I always have. Before you resign yourself to being a great martyr, I want you to look at me and tell me that I've made you unhappy." She gazed at him dubiously, but at least she was listening. "You and I are happy together, Maggie. It's a good marriage. When your father told me what he wanted me to do, I couldn't believe it. It was like a dream come true. It was everything I'd ever wanted."

"Power?" she retorted. "Wealth? A princess for a wife? Of course! You can't stand there and tell me that the benefits of being my husband are not enticing. If something were to happen to Erich without progeny, it would be your son—*your son, Han*—who would be the duke."

"That doesn't matter to me, Maggie. That's what I'm trying to tell you. If I had to choose between you and that position, I would choose you. I would work in the stables all my life and be happy, as long as I had you. If I were a prince, and you were a servant girl, it would not have been any different."

"I don't believe you," she said, fighting to hold back the tears burning in her head. "It's easy to say that now. Now that we're married, now that I'm going to have your baby. It's all tied up neatly. It's a dream come true, all right," she growled. "Yes, it's evident you've got everything you've ever wanted."

"Stop it, Maggie! You don't have any idea what you're talking about."

"No," her voice became cynical, subtly sarcastic, "I'm nothing but a simpering fool . . . a brainless princess with a cold heart, who—"

"Listen to me, Maggie." He took hold of her firmly. "Do I have to spell it out in black and white?" His tone was desperate.

"Yes!"

"Fine! You tell me, MagdaLena—if I had even suggested to you, at any time in the past five years, that I wanted to marry you, do you think you would have even considered it? No!" he answered for her. "You wouldn't hardly give me the time of day. You would have laughed in my face. If it hadn't happened this way, it would not have happened at all. Don't get angry with me because you were too bullheaded and arrogant to see things the way you should have. You should have known Nik Koenig was a louse, just like you should have known that I have been in love with you for as long as I can remember!"

Han felt the tenseness in Maggie's arms disintegrate, and she hung weakly in his grasp as tears spilled from her eyes.

"Don't accuse me of lying," he said softly, "and please don't tell me I'm mad. I love you, Maggie. I always have. When you turned me away, I tried to get over it. I used to hate myself for feeling that way, but I did my best to accept it. You were a princess. And when you came up with that pathetic betrothal . . . I wanted to die. Then when you called it off for that . . . *bastard,* I was angry, Maggie. I wanted you so badly! It's time you knew. I never stopped loving you! I love you with all my heart."

Maggie was stunned speechless. She wanted so badly to be angry with him, to believe that it wasn't true. But there was no way that she could retort. And in truth, she didn't want to. She wanted him to love her. She wanted to believe him. Still, a part of her just couldn't believe that his entire motive was love. There were simply too many other things tangled into the situation. While something inside her wanted to just crumble in his arms as if everything was all right, something stronger overpowered it with a hurt that oozed from deep inside. She took a step back and Han's expectant expression fell into disappointment.

"You don't believe me," he stated. The obvious hurt in his eyes made her *want* to believe him. She turned her back, fearing once again that she would betray her emotion. She reminded herself that he had been good to her, in spite of her stubbornness. He was looking out for her best interests, and taking good care of her. He was her *husband*. She was going to have his baby. Some things just couldn't be undone.

Swallowing her tears, Maggie spoke straightly, "You're right about one thing, Han. I must admit that it's a good marriage. I can see that you've tried very hard to make me happy, and I'm not such a fool that I can't appreciate your efforts."

Han felt his heart breaking as he began to absorb what she was saying. She sighed as if she were resigning herself to doom, and Han had to fight back the urge to just shake some sense into her.

"I'm certain we can have a good life together, Han. There's no reason we can't be happy. I mean . . . we have been, and . . . we can just go on as if . . ."

When she faltered, he interjected, "As if a black cloud weren't hanging over us, threatening a storm that won't go away? That's not good enough for me, Maggie."

She turned to glare at him. "You've got what you bargained for, Han. My heart was not my father's to give you."

"And what do I have to do to win your heart, Maggie? Name it, and I'll do it!"

She looked down and wrung her hands. "I'm not sure it can be won—not now."

"I don't believe that," he said.

"Believe what you want if it will make things easier for you. I'll be a good wife to you, Han. I'll give you children and do my best to raise them well. But don't expect something from me that I can't give."

Han felt his breath quicken, and his heart pound while he stifled the urge to cry. Once again, she was sentencing him to cope with something that he was supposed to be satisfied with, completely against his will. But what could he do? He couldn't force her to love him. He couldn't control her feelings. He didn't even understand them. He reminded himself that she was his wife. And with her being a part of his everyday life, he would find a way to win her heart. He would!

Gathering courage, he stepped forward and took hold of her shoulders, relieved when she didn't attempt to retract.

"I love you, Maggie," he said, whether she believed him or not. He pushed his arms around her and squeezed his eyes shut. Tears of relief pressed through when she took hold of him, clinging to him almost desperately.

"Oh, Han," she cried softly, pressing the side of her face to his chest. "Love me now, Han," she whispered. "Please love me now."

Han lifted her chin with his finger and looked into her eyes. What was it he saw in them that contradicted everything she had just said? What made her want him as much as he wanted her, in spite of so many unvented emotions—or perhaps because of them? He told himself he should be grateful she wasn't pushing him away—at least not physically. Trying not to think about the rest for fear of falling apart, he pressed his mouth over hers, allowing his love for her to come through, unleashed and desperate. She clung to him with the same desperation, and he thought he'd die from wanting her. Deftly, he carried her to the bed and kissed her hard. But somewhere in the midst of their lovemaking, he felt Maggie sob, and when it was done, she turned her face into the pillow and cried.

"Oh, Maggie," he whispered, his voice quivering, "why can't you believe me?"

She only cried harder. Han held her tightly until she drifted to sleep, and he lay staring at the ceiling, wondering why he'd ever been fool enough to believe that a stableboy could ever become a prince.

Chapter Eleven

THE ACCUSATION

Han slept very little. Somewhere in the night, Maggie got up and put on a nightgown, but she said nothing to him before she got back into bed and went to sleep. He reminded himself to look at the positive aspects of this situation. They had come far, and surely time would soften the blow of what he'd told her. At least it was in the open now, and he could stop dreading the conversation. He certainly couldn't take her back to Horstberg without her knowing the full truth. He only prayed they could both learn to live with it.

Feeling restless, Han finally got up just past dawn and got dressed. He felt an uneasiness that he couldn't explain, although it was difficult to tell if it had to do with Maggie or if his instincts were telling him something more. Perhaps he was fearing that Nik Koenig would yet catch up with them again. He began quietly packing their things, thinking it might be best if they left this town right after breakfast.

Han was pleased to see that Maggie slept soundly despite his being up and about, and he took time every few minutes to admire her, wishing there weren't dark clouds hanging over their future together.

He couldn't explain why his eyes moved to the doorknob when it twitched, and a chill of fear rushed down his spine. He'd barely found his pistol before the door flew open. In a split second the gun was knocked out of his hand, and some foul-smelling lug had both Han's arms pulled painfully behind his back. An equally gruesome character headed straight for the bed, pulling Maggie, dazed and frightened, into his arms. Han fought with everything he had to break free, turning to land a healthy blow against his assailant's jaw. It momentarily stunned the man, and Han turned to get Maggie. But immediately, he was met with a fist in his own jaw, and he reeled backward, right into the grip he'd just escaped from. His head swimming in pain, Han was barely aware of Maggie crying out to him as repeated, painful blows assaulted his face and then his belly while he was held helpless from behind.

Maggie couldn't believe what was happening. She struggled with all her strength and managed to worm her way out of the arms that held her just as Nik Koenig came into the room. He began hitting Han over and over, and she ran to him, trying to pull him away.

"No, Nik—please," she screamed. "Please don't!"

"I'm not letting him get you away from me again, my sweet," he said, relentlessly hitting Han over and over while Han's arms were held behind him by another man. Memories of how she'd once believed that Nik loved her and would rescue her from Han now made her sick.

"No, Nik," Maggie cried, "you don't understand." She kept pulling at him, but he paid no attention. "He's my husband, Nik."

Nik paused briefly and turned to Maggie in angry astonishment. "He's *what?*"

Maggie took a step back. "He's my husband."

Nik drew his arm back, and Maggie was almost afraid he would hit *her*, but he swung around, landing his fist in Han's ribs as an enunciation to his angry words. "Well, you are about to become a widow, my dear."

"No!" she screamed. "Please stop—please. I need him!"

Nik obviously didn't care about that as he continued his assault. "Get her away from here!" he shouted.

The order was immediately followed, and Maggie felt strong arms come around her belly. She kicked and fought, but the grip tightened abruptly, pushing the air painfully out of her lungs, and she slithered to the floor, gasping for breath.

Maggie landed on top of Han's pistol and discreetly took hold of it. Trying to catch her breath, she turned and fired, hitting the leg of the man who had held her. Nik turned in astonishment at the same moment the door flew open and Claude Dormante rushed into the room. With no hesitation, he sent one fist into Nik's belly and the other to his jaw. Maggie marveled at his strength. The man holding Han finally let go in order to fight off this newcomer, and Han slid to the floor with a groan.

Claude struck that man as well, then he hit Nik again, and Nik went to his knees. Before Nik could stand, Josette came into the room and laughed as she sat on him, leaving him pinned face down on the floor while Claude got the other brute under control.

"Han!" Maggie scrambled across the floor toward him, trying to ignore the pain in her belly. She pulled one of her blouses from where it hung over the edge of a trunk and wiped frantically at his face, trying to find it beneath all of the blood.

"Oh, Han—don't die. Please don't die," she sobbed, but he made no response. "Oh, Han. What have they done to you? Oh, please God, don't let him die! Speak to me, Han," she pleaded, and his eyes came feebly open. She mingled a smile with her sigh of relief, wiping blood from his nose and mouth.

Han managed a crooked smile and whispered, "I don't think your boyfriend likes me."

Maggie couldn't hold back a chuckle. Then she pressed her face against his shoulder and cried. Even now, he just had to be funny.

Maggie stayed close to Han, barely aware of other people coming into the room in response to the ruckus. A doctor was sent for, as well as the police. Josette and the innkeeper's wife brought clean, wet towels to help Maggie clean the blood away from Han's face. Nik and his friends were taken away by officers of the law, but still the doctor hadn't come, and Maggie felt frantic. Josette remained nearby and kept a soothing hand on Maggie's shoulder.

"I'm so glad you showed up," Maggie said to her.

"We were just about to leave," Josette explained, "when we heard the racket. I am glad we were here. You poor dears."

Maggie expected her to ask questions about who the thugs were, but she didn't, and Maggie was relieved. She was in no mood to explain.

Dr. Latini arrived a few minutes later. With Claude's help, they got Han to the bed, while Maggie sat close by, still fighting with the pain in her belly as the doctor tended to Han's wounds. Han didn't speak and hardly moved, and she knew he was in a great deal of pain that was surely more crucial than her own discomfort. When a sharp pain took her off guard, she doubled over with a groan, and the doctor's attention turned to her. Han became frantic and tried to sit up, moaning from his own pain.

"What is it?" he demanded. "What's wrong?"

Han wanted to scream like a frightened child when he realized that something was wrong with Maggie. His own pain became irrelevant, and he wanted only to help her, but his body wouldn't respond the way he wanted it to, and he could barely move. He heard Josette offer use of the room that she and Claude had left just a little while earlier. The doctor's gentle hands guided Han's shoulders back to the bed while Han was keenly aware of Claude carefully helping Maggie toward the door. He was only alone a minute before Claude returned to be with him.

"What's wrong with her?" Han asked in panic before he'd even closed the door.

"I don't know," Claude said with a reassuring smile as Han attempted to sit up again and failed. "But the doctor will take good care of her. You need to try and relax. Josette is with them. They will come and talk to us as soon as they have something to tell us."

Han wanted to jump off this bed and rush to her side, but he found it impossible to move even though his mind raced frantically with questions and concerns in regard to Maggie. The innkeeper came to check on Han, bringing with him a different doctor who had been eating downstairs at the time of the incident and had offered to help. He gently checked Han's injuries and assessed them while Han could only think of Maggie. He was grateful for Claude being here to speak with the doctor, who kindly helped Han get cleaned up and saw to the injuries as much as possible. After the doctor had left, Claude helped Han sit up in bed against several pillows. It seemed hours that the two men sat mostly in silence, while the worst scenarios marched through Han's mind. He pushed his hands into his hair, trying to ignore the painful throbbing in his head, the result of one very black eye, a slightly broken nose, swollen lips, and a number of bruises and cuts. The pain in his head was only enhanced by the broad range of bruises covering his torso, and a few broken ribs that, despite being wrapped tightly, pained him with every breath. But all the physical pain did not compare to his worry over Maggie. He had no idea what had happened to her.

He hadn't been aware of anything except the fist pounding his face and ribs.

When he felt certain he'd go mad with waiting, he asked Claude to help him get up, and his friend graciously complied. Realizing he could stand and walk on his own, he was just about to go down the hall and demand to know what was going on when Doctor Latini came into room, looking morose.

"What?" Han demanded, feeling unsteady again.

"She's going to be fine," he said right off, but his expression contradicted the statement, and Han felt afraid.

"What happened?" Han asked, grateful for the way Claude helped him step back and sit on the edge of the bed.

The doctor sat on a chair to face Han, and Claude moved away, silently offering to give them privacy.

"Please stay," Han said, stopping him with a hand on his arm. Instinctively, he didn't want to be alone. He wanted this new friend of his to know what was going on, and he had no desire to repeat whatever it was.

"Mr. Bruxen," the doctor said solemnly, "I'm afraid she has lost the baby."

Han was so stunned he couldn't even think. He couldn't speak. He just waited numbly for the doctor to go on. "Because of the early stage of pregnancy, it was not a serious loss, even though the process was difficult for her. There was no permanent damage. She simply needs to rest and take it easy, and she can get pregnant again as soon as she's feeling up to it."

Han tried to console himself as the doctor finished his report, thinking it could have been so much worse. But the pain was still difficult to take, and he felt like killing Nik Koenig with his bare hands. He suddenly wished they were back in Horstberg, where they had a strong network of family to lean on.

"She really shouldn't be traveling," the doctor said. "At least not yet. But then," he smiled wryly, "you're not exactly in any position to be doing that either. You should stay here for at least a few more days."

"Nonsense!" Claude interjected. "They can't stay here. There's no one in this place to look after them. They will come and stay with us."

Han's eyes widened. This man was an answer to prayers he hadn't even had a chance to utter.

"How far is it to your home, Mr. Dormante?" the doctor asked.

"Not more than three hours, if we take it slowly. They can be comfortable and stay for as long as they like. Josette and I would love to have them, and we'll take good care of them. I can assure you they'll not be up and about before they're ready. Josette is quite a natural at caring for people, and we have an excellent serving staff."

"It sounds like a good idea to me," the doctor said to Han. "You're in no position to take care of your wife right now—or the other way around."

Han managed a sober chuckle and looked toward Claude. "How can we refuse?"

"Very good," Claude said exuberantly. "Josette will be thrilled. We'll stay here one more night and set out in the morning—taking it slowly, of course."

"Very good, then," the doctor said. "Mrs. Dormante is with your wife now, and I've given her some instructions. I'll check back in the morning before you leave."

"Thank you, Doctor," Han said.

"Why don't you go and see her. She's been asking for you."

Han stood carefully with very little help from Claude, who then left to escort the doctor out. Han held his arm against his painful ribs as he made his way slowly to the room Maggie was in. Josette opened the door for him, and he whispered, "I think your husband has something to tell you." She lifted her brows in question, and he added, "It looks as though you'll be having company."

Josette smiled and left the room. Han moved slowly toward the bed, sitting carefully on its edge. He watched Maggie and felt sick inside to see her drawn, pale face against the pillow. She reminded him of when she'd been ill during their stay at the cottage. So much had changed since then, and much of it felt like a dream—or a nightmare.

"Hello, my love," he said, and her eyes came open.

"Han." She reached her arms out for him, and a sob escaped her. He carefully pulled her as close to him as he could manage. Their argument last night seemed irrelevant now.

"What have they done to you?" she asked, touching his face carefully.

· "Nothing I won't recover from." He tried to smile. "But what about you?" he asked.

Maggie's expression faltered. "Our baby," she cried. "Oh, Han, our baby is gone."

Han felt a burning behind his eyes and held her tighter, ignoring the pain in his side.

"How can I bear it?" she asked, pulling away to look at him.

Again Han tried to smile. "You'll be pregnant again in no time." He added with a slight chuckle, "I've figured out how to make that happen."

A wan smile crept into Maggie's countenance before she was overcome with tears. Han carefully lay down close beside her, and she cried until she slept.

Later that evening, two local officers came to the inn to ask some questions about this morning's incident. They'd already spoken to everyone they'd been able to find who had seen or heard anything regarding the incident. Now the officers sat down alone with Han and Maggie in order to complete their official report of the crimes committed. Han did most of the talking while Maggie kept her hand tightly in his. Having opted for the truth, he told the officers exactly what Nik was after and the entire situation, making it sound as though he and Maggie had eloped, rather than trying to justify his kidnapping her.

Han knew Maggie shared his relief when the officers assured them that Mr. Koenig and his companions wouldn't be bothering them any further. By the time these men served their time in jail, Han and Maggie would likely be back in Horstberg. They were both grateful to know they would have time to recover and return home without having to fear that Nik Koenig would catch up to them again.

Abbi came awake with a gasp, held bound to her sheets with the fear that had accompanied her from her dream. In the minute it took her to reassess the images she'd seen in her sleep—and the feelings that had come with them—she reached across the bed for Cameron and took hold of his arm firmly enough to stir him.

"What is it?" he stammered and fumbled for her in the darkness. "What's wrong?"

Too breathless to answer, she was relieved to feel his hand on her face and hear him ask gently, "A dream?"

"Yes," she managed.

"Was it Maggie?" he asked in a fearful tone that reminded her of the tension they had felt as parents since the moment they'd realized their daughter was gone. For all that they had to believe that Han was keeping her safe, the uncertainty was unnerving. And knowing that Nik Koenig and his friends with deplorable reputations had disappeared from Horstberg did not help at all. Abbi knew that Georg and Elsa were also concerned about their son's absence, and the four parents had secretly shared their grief and concerns. For all that they had a great deal of faith in Han, and they knew he would do everything he could to protect Maggie and take good care of her, he was only one man, they were on the run, and Maggie was more likely to be uncooperative than anything else.

"Yes," Abbi said again.

She heard Cameron let out a long sigh of concern before he asked with caution, "Was it . . . one of *those* dreams?"

Abbi knew well what he meant. She'd always had a gift of occasionally seeing something premonitory in dreams. Her gift had brought them together, and it had saved them more than once. It had many times given her insights into situations that were otherwise impossible to discern. But there had also been many times when the dreams had mostly left Abbi feeling helpless and distraught when she couldn't completely understand the meaning of what she'd experienced in her sleep. Still, there was a certain feeling that always accompanied dreams that held significance—a feeling that seemed to alert her to pay attention. And she certainly felt that way now.

"Yes," Abbi said still again.

"Is she all right?" Cameron demanded, as if Abbi might immediately know the answer to that question.

Trying to keep perspective and not overreact, Abbi said quietly, "I think so." She took a deep breath and forced the words out of her mouth that needed to be spoken, holding tightly to Cameron's hand. "I only saw vague images . . . flashes . . . of something happening." Fear and concern threatened to choke her voice. "They were being hurt, both of them. It was Nik. I know I saw Nik. And there were . . . others . . . with him. But . . ." She knew Cameron was holding his breath, and his grip on her hand had become almost painful. "They're all right," Abbi added and felt him relax slightly as he exhaled near her face. "I saw . . . people helping them . . . intervening . . . caring for them. Like angels in human form. They were surrounded by good people. And it feels as if . . . they're all right."

"Oh, I pray you are right," Cameron muttered and pressed his face to her shoulder.

Abbi put a hand into his hair. "Part of the dream was so horrible, Cameron, but . . . it feels as if the overall message of the dream is for us to know that . . . they're all right."

She felt him heave a deep sigh and ease closer to her. He spoke in a calm and measured voice that contradicted his words. "I want to kill Nik Koenig; I want to kill him myself."

Abbi shuddered slightly and had to say, "Well, I know you're capable of killing a man when it's necessary to protect your country."

"Or my family," he added, mildly indignant.

"Yes," she said. "But I also know you would never take a life unless you could do it in good conscience, knowing you could face God with your intentions."

"You're right, I know. But sometimes what I *want* to do is not the same as what I would actually do. And I *want* to kill him with my bare hands. When I think of how he's forced this ridiculous separation from our daughter, and how Erich could have easily died, I just . . ."

His words faded, but Abbi felt his anger heightening. She stroked his hair gently and pressed a kiss to his brow. "There is nothing more we can do right now. They're all right. Somehow, I just . . . know they're all right. We must hold onto that and just . . . pray it remains that way; pray that we all remain safe."

"Yes," he said with resignation and a hint of the peace she knew he could find in his belief that God would keep his loved ones and his country safe.

Nothing more was said between them, even though neither of them went back to sleep. The room was barely lightening with the approach of dawn when a knock at the door startled them both.

"I hate it when that happens," Cameron said, quickly on his

feet and putting on a dressing gown. "They rarely bother me before breakfast unless it's bad news."

Abbi knew he was right as she quickly tried to tally the reasons they'd been disturbed in the night. Through the years there had been many things that had warranted interrupting the duke's sleep, but few of them had been personal. Given the present circumstances, it was doubly unnerving, but she had a great deal of experience maintaining her dignity at such moments, and she stood near her husband, tying a robe around her waist.

Abbi was not at all surprised when Lance Dukerk entered the room; it was almost always either him or Georg that awoke them when circumstances made it necessary. He looked as if he'd been awake for quite some time, and she wondered which officer had been given the unfortunate duty of waking the captain in the wee hours of the night.

"An official communication arrived by special messenger a short while ago . . . from a small city in Italy."

"Italy?" Cameron echoed, and Abbi reached for his hand.

"We can discuss the details later," Lance said, "but Nik Koenig and three men who were with him have now been incarcerated there and will be serving a sentence of some months for breaking into a premises illegally and for assault."

"Assault?" Abbi repeated his last word this time, her heart quickening.

"A young couple going by the names of Mr. and Mrs. Bruxen were—"

"That's Elsa's maiden name," Abbi said, even though she suspected both men already knew.

"Yes," Lance said and went on. "They were both injured in the assault, but they are recovering in the care of some good friends there, and they will return to Horstberg before Christmas."

Abbi almost fainted with relief at the implication. She leaned into Cameron, who wrapped his arms around her, and she couldn't hold back the evidence that she was crying. They all knew that this communication was surely about Han and Maggie, and the authorities in this Italian city would not have known where to send it if the alias Mr. and Mrs. Bruxen hadn't told them. For the first time in months, they actually knew that Han and Maggie were all right—even if they had endured some measure of abuse at Nik Koenig's hands.

"Thank you, Captain," Cameron said, his tone making it evident just how deep his gratitude went. "Is there anything else?"

"That's all for now. I just thought . . . you would want to know right away."

"Of course," Cameron said. "Thank you."

Lance left the room, and Cameron pressed his lips into Abbi's hair before he said, "It would seem your dream was correct. Perhaps it was given to us as an added witness that they are well." He sighed loudly. "I am . . . so relieved."

"As I am," Abbi muttered.

"I still want to kill Koenig with my bare hands. I don't even want to think about what this *assault* actually entailed."

"We *mustn't* think about that," Abbi said. "We must simply . . . look forward to Christmas."

"Yes, we must look forward to Christmas."

"If it's any consolation," Abbi added, "I want to kill him, myself."

Cameron chuckled and held her closer, even though it wasn't at all funny.

The Dormantes' palazzo proved to be an exquisite example of Italian architecture. It was an elegant home, but it also had a coziness that was typical of the Dormantes. Han didn't see much of the house and grounds when they arrived, since they were both in great need of some rest. And Maggie had no interest in anything but being able to go to bed and recuperate. Han hardly left her side the first few days, doing his best to make certain all was well, and grateful for the graciousness of the Dormantes and their kind and helpful staff. On the fourth day, Han was doing better and left Maggie to rest while he went exploring a little. He returned to the elaborate room that had been provided for them and sat next to Maggie on the bed to give her a report.

"You can't believe this place," he said. "You've got to get better so we can have some fun."

"Tell me," she insisted. "I need a distraction."

Han knew that meant her body was weak and sore, and her emotions were still fragile. He kissed her and smiled and gladly complied. "The first thing we're going to do," he said with a smirk, "is go swimming in the fountain." At her questioning gaze, he clarified, "There is an enormous fountain in the garden that's almost as big as the pond by the cottage. It's beautiful! I think we should sneak out there some night and go swimming."

"Han," she gave him a wan smile, "you're so . . ."

"Fun!" he provided dramatically.

"Yes," she said, "I suppose that about sums it up."

"How are you feeling, my love?" he asked.

"Better," she said. "Still weak, but much better."

"Good." He smiled and chose not to specifically bring up the baby. As far as he could tell, she was determined to put the loss behind them and move forward with a positive attitude.

"And you?" she asked. "You still look terrible."

"The ribs hurt far worse than my face," he said. "I will heal with time; it's nothing I can't live with. That is," he teased, "if you can live with a deformed man."

"Deformed?"

"Look at my nose. It's crooked."

"It doesn't look much different to me," she said. "Although it's too swollen and discolored to know for sure."

"Are you trying to tell me it's always been crooked?"

"I'm trying to tell you," she smiled, "that whether or not your nose is crooked, I . . ." She hesitated and glanced away.

"You what?" he asked tenderly.

"I'm still more than happy to be your wife," she replied simply. Han kissed her gingerly and lay next to her to rest. They still had much to overcome, but he knew it could be worse.

Through the following days, Claude and Josette provided every possible comfort for Han and Maggie. Their hosts managed to achieve the proper balance of not letting them get bored, but still allowing them privacy and quiet time. It didn't take long to see that Josette enjoyed social activity. Just as soon as Maggie was up and about, Josette was taking her to all the little social gatherings that women went to. And Claude did the same for Han, doing all the things that gentlemen in Italy did with their spare time.

Han and Maggie both quickly realized that this was a very social area that attracted wealthy people on a regular basis. There was a composite of people from all over Europe who had summer homes here, or who had moved in permanently like Claude and Josette. Rarely was there a day without at least one social event, and staying with these people was never dull. Even at the dinner table it was rare for laughter to be absent. Josette had an unbeatable sense of humor, and she and Han were always trying to outdo each other with witty observations.

As some color came back to Maggie's face, and Han's regained some normality, they began getting more involved in the local social circles. They often went riding horses or playing croquet, among other things. And Han did as he had promised and took his wife for a midnight swim in the fountain.

They stayed at the palazzo far beyond any necessity concerning their recovery. But if it even crossed their minds that they were outstaying their welcome, they were quickly assured by Claude and Josette's gracious hospitality. They had truly become good friends.

The social life increased as people came from cooler climates to settle in for the winter. And the Dormantes took Han and Maggie to several gatherings where they had a wonderful time. Han had told Maggie before they'd left the inn that it was best—despite Nik now being taken care of—that people didn't know their true identity. She'd looked dismayed when he told her that no one should know she was a princess, but she had complied. And now as they became involved with these people, Han realized that it was probably good for Maggie to temporarily lose that identity. He knew her position had stifled her, and here she could see that it made little difference who she was. These people accepted Han and Maggie as equals in social status, and Maggie was able to see that there was a world outside of Horstberg.

When Josette announced she was going to host a garden party of her own, Maggie became excited and caught up in helping Josette with the plans. Han was pleased with the way that Maggie truly enjoyed helping with party arrangements. And with a new gown and the big day at hand, she was full of smiles and anticipation.

"You look beautiful," Han smiled warmly at her as they descended the stairs together, her hand over his arm.

"You look very nice yourself," she replied, and they moved outside, where the party was already getting underway.

Maggie breathed in the fresh air, glad to note that physically she felt back to normal, and any thought of the baby could be placed on the hope of future children. They quickly began to mingle, which she thoroughly enjoyed. She had found that one of her greatest pleasures at these gatherings was simply to mingle and listen to bits and pieces of people's conversations. She had never considered herself secluded, yet she was amazed at what she was able to learn about the world just by watching and listening. She liked studying the variety of beautiful gowns, and in her mind, she was planning things to tell the dressmaker when they returned to Horstberg.

Although it was typical for the men and women to divide, Maggie always kept her eye on Han. And she was pleased each time he caught her with a glance and gave her a warm smile. A little flutter erupted inside her as she noticed the fit of his slender breeches and the tapered brocade waistcoat, buttoned over a cream-colored shirt with full sleeves. The fine coat he'd been wearing had been set aside, as all of the other men had done with the evening being so warm. She couldn't help but think how handsome he was, and at this moment the stable groom was impossible to imagine.

As usual, Josette introduced Maggie around the crowd, and she enjoyed helping her with the hostess duties. Maggie spoke with several gentlemen of varied ages, some who showed more than a polite interest in her. But it was easy to laugh off their attention and defer the conversation, knowing that Han was all she ever needed or wanted. The Comte Marchess—an aging nobleman with more money than scruples—proved to offer enjoyable conversation, but it was difficult to convince him that she was not available or interested in anything more.

"I am married, sir," she laughed to cover her discomfort.

"As is everyone here," he said, overtly seductive. "You should know that makes little difference. I could entertain you well for an evening, Madame Bruxen."

"I must confess that I am quite content with my husband's entertainment," she said and smiled toward Han, who nodded to acknowledge her.

"As is my wife," the Comte observed, indicating the woman

who was engaged in animated conversation with Han. Maggie felt something formless stab at her. She purposely moved away from the Comte, not caring if she appeared rude. As she watched her husband across the crowded lawn, and the way the Comtesse Marchess hovered near him with interest, she found herself seeing him in a whole new light. These people didn't see him as a stable groom. He fit into this life very naturally, and he had a certain dignity about him that was not lessened by his playful personality.

In her mind, Maggie assessed the changes she had gone through since the day he'd kidnapped her, and a light of revelation crept into her. At first Han had managed to bring her down to his level—even below it—by forcing her to do menial chores and to care completely for herself, and even by sleeping in barns. And now that she had experienced such things, he had quite naturally brought himself up to her level. There was no division of social status between them here; they were equals. And she'd been blind not to see it before.

Maggie looked at Han Heinrich now and could hardly comprehend that he'd been a servant. He reminded her of his father, the very dignified and respected Georg Heinrich, who had mingled with the royal family since childhood. In spite of the sore point involved, she couldn't deny that Han would make a good advisor to the duke. He was intelligent and a good man, and she felt confident that Horstberg would be in good hands. She actually looked forward to returning there with him as her husband. His revelation about the position he'd been promised had come as a shock to her, but now that it had settled in, she was surprised to realize it had settled in very comfortably.

Maggie's thoughts were interrupted when she saw the comtesse slip Han a note. She had learned quickly in these worldly social circles that affairs were common and easily accepted—just as the comte had recently reminded her. Claude and Josette were in the minority of those who remained loyal to their spouse, but they had spoken very openly about how many in their social circles did not adhere to the same kind of commitment. Claude had made a point of telling them how he and Josette had married for love, while many marriages among the upper classes were arranged, and people who were unhappy in their marriages often went elsewhere for affection. While the idea had initially been startling to Maggie, she couldn't deny that she'd been naive to believe that all people in the world were as devoted in their marriages as her parents and the other couples she'd been close to through her upbringing.

Maggie now observed the comtesse's expression as she gave Han that piece of paper, and the lewd glance she passed him as she walked away. She knew exactly what the woman was after. At first it made her angry, then a little sick. But as she watched Han reading the note with no expression, she became overwrought with fear.

The party seemed to go on forever. Han said nothing to her about the message he'd received, and she couldn't bring herself to ask about it. Dusk settled in, and Maggie felt exhausted and needed to lie down. She told Claude and Josette she was leaving and thanked them for a lovely evening. When she whispered to Han that she was going up to bed, he met her eyes and asked, "Are you all right?"

"Yes, of course," she said. "Just . . . tired. Stay if you want to. I'll see you later."

He kissed her cheek and said, "I'll look forward to it."

Their eyes met again, and he smiled. Nothing seemed different about him, but she couldn't help feeling suspicious. Oh, if she could only know his thoughts!

Lying on the huge bed, Maggie introspected deeply on the turn her life had taken. While there were aspects of her relationship with Han that disturbed her—most specifically his motivations for marrying her—she couldn't deny that she was happy. Han had been right in saying this was a good marriage. She'd had more fun with Han in the past few months than she'd had in her entire life. And she had every reason to believe he would take good care of her, and their future together would be good.

A nauseous feeling crept into her while she tried to rest, and she became certain that her recent hunch had to be correct. She was pregnant. The reality of having a baby filled her with a new sense of peace, and though she had been keeping it a secret until she was certain, she decided she would tell Han as soon as he came up from the party. She wondered again about the note the comtesse had given to Han and how he felt about it, but she dismissed it as insignificant in light of everything else she shared with Han, and she was finally able to relax.

Maggie fell asleep with the anticipation of Han's return and woke somewhere in the middle of the night. Alone in the bed, she thought she must not have been asleep long. But lighting a lamp to check the clock, she realized it was half past four, and Han was not with her.

Fear gripped Maggie in the pit of her stomach as the only possibility of where he might be engulfed her. Haunting images of the comtesse passing Han that message crowded into her mind. But rather than looking over the past and seeing Han's dedication to her, Maggie could only see how she had taken his affection and attention for granted. She had never stopped to analyze how she really felt about Han. But now in a fearful turmoil, she knew that he was everything to her.

Had she realized it too late? She had not once told Han she cared for him. Her affection toward him had been an automatic response rather than something she had thought about. Panicked beyond all reason, Maggie wondered if perhaps Han had not found the emotional satisfaction from her that he needed, and he'd taken the opportunity to seek affection elsewhere.

Trying to take hold of her senses, Maggie noticed Han's clothes from the party thrown over the back of a chair. He must have come back to change. Remembering how Han had stuffed that dreadful piece of paper into the pocket of his waistcoat, she hurriedly searched and her heart beat madly when she found it. Hot tears surfaced as she read: *There is a terrace on the south side of my palazzo where a pleasant breeze often brings me out near midnight. The peacefulness is very inviting, for my husband sleeps soundly in the far north bedroom and prefers to be left alone.*

Maggie crumpled the paper and threw it to the floor. Then she stood at the window, gazing into the darkness with silent tears flowing down her face. Nightmarish images assaulted her of the man she now knew she loved, holding another woman. She was haunted by the comtesse's tall, shapely frame, glistening dark hair, and penetrating eyes. Her fear gradually became replaced by anger as she wondered how Han could be so quick to turn his back on her without giving her any warning or chance to prove herself. She thought of her family, and for the first time in many weeks, she missed them dreadfully. She wanted to cry on her mother's shoulder and feel her father's comforting arms around her.

Maggie leaned against the window crying until dawn approached. That nauseous feeling crept into her again, adding to her fears with the reminder that she was carrying this man's child. She thought of the ways Han had been deceitful in the past, however subtle, and the knot inside her tightened. Even if Han *did* care for her, the advantages of being her husband were certainly enticing. She didn't doubt that he loved her. But how much? And if he had loved her all these years, did his feelings compare to those she felt now? It was as if her heart's blood was spilled over the floor to be trampled upon. And she realized now that the love she felt—however sweet—had a bitter edge in the fear of not having it returned. Did Han understand those feelings? Had he given her so much of himself with so little in return that he had gone elsewhere? Or were his feelings for her tangled into politics enough to make the luring of another woman's affection just too tempting?

Maggie became so lost in thought that she was startled when the bedroom door came open. Breathlessly she turned to see her husband.

"What's wrong?" Han asked, noting immediately his wife's tear-stained face and distraught expression.

Maggie quickly took in his disheveled appearance. As her nausea combined with the reality of what she was facing, she clapped a hand over her mouth and turned back to the window, trying to suppress a sob.

"Maggie," he said, coming closer, "whatever is the matter?"

"When I woke up," she cried softly, "you were gone and . . ."

"What?" He nearly chuckled. It felt good to see that he was missed.

"I . . ." she began again, but in an effort to hold back her emotion, she said no more.

"Maggie," he said and pulled her close to him, "I'm here now. There's no need to be upset."

"Where have you been?" she asked, praying there was some explanation—though she couldn't imagine what.

"Claude woke me just before midnight. I've been helping deliver a foal for his friend, the baron."

Maggie looked at his eyes, searching for sincerity. But her vision was clouded with nightmarish images of the comtesse and her lewd glances. And if that weren't bad enough, she could hardly bear the harsh reality of all he would gain from returning to Horstberg with her as his wife. While she had managed to put it out of her mind most of time since she'd learned the truth, at the moment it was impossible to ignore.

"I don't believe you," she said, turning away.

"What do you mean, you don't believe me?" Han asked, stunned.

"I wonder now if it hasn't all just been a long string of lies. You are a suave and charming man, Han Heinrich. I dare say you could eventually make me believe anything for the sake of getting what you want."

Han recalled saying similar things about Nik Koenig. Had her experience with Nik made her so skeptical? But then, hadn't she been seething with cynicism long before that? "What on earth are you talking about?"

"That!" She turned and pointed to the crumpled piece of paper on the floor. "How could you, Han?"

There was no need for Han to pick up the note. He knew what it said. And he knew now what he was being accused of. His initial reaction was satisfaction. Maggie cared for him, and it felt good. But his satisfaction became quickly replaced by hurt and anger. She cared, but she didn't trust him. Despite how hard he'd tried to mend the bridges between them, she was immediately willing to think the worst.

"That's it, then," he said petulantly, not wanting to even try and defend himself. She'd already made up her mind that he was guilty. "You don't believe me. Well, fine, Your Royal Highness! Believe what you want. I have been up all night with a laboring horse, and I am in no mood for this. I am going to bed!"

"Then you don't deny it!" she said vehemently.

"I told you where I've been, Maggie. If you don't believe me, that's your problem. It's apparent that no matter what I say, you will believe the worst. I get the impression that in your eyes I am little more than a lying, cheating, power-thirsty *louse*, who will stop at nothing to get what I want. Well, maybe it's all true, Maggie. Maybe I *am* like Nik Koenig, but I'm your husband and you're going to have to live with it!"

Maggie said nothing as Han undressed, pulled the drapes closed, and got into bed. She felt like crying. She felt like begging him to tell her the truth, and she would forgive him, and they could start over.

She wondered if it would make any difference if he knew that she was pregnant. She wanted to tell him. There was so much she wanted to say. But her pride overruled, and she got dressed and went downstairs to find something to eat, hoping to ease her nausea. She went to the kitchen and coerced the cook out of some dry biscuits, which helped ease that sick feeling. But there was an emotional knot in her stomach that would not go away. She wandered aimlessly about the palazzo, waiting for breakfast to be served, wishing she didn't feel as though her life were falling apart.

It seemed forever before anyone but the servants were up and about, and she was relieved to finally be seated at the breakfast table, hoping a good meal would help her feel better. Claude was the last to come in, as he'd obviously already been out somewhere this morning. Claude and Josette chatted easily with the other guests present that had stayed the night following the party. She was glad they weren't alone, since her friends surely would have noticed her sour mood.

They said little to her until Claude commented, "Maggie, my dear, I see your husband isn't with us. No doubt sleeping like a baby after last night's ordeal."

Maggie felt her nerves tighten as she tried to smile toward Claude in response.

"I've been out to see the baron again this morning. He asked me to express again his gratitude to Han. Apparently it was rather serious. He would have surely lost both the mare and the foal if it weren't for your husband's expertise."

Maggie stood abruptly in reaction. It couldn't be a false alibi. Han hadn't had a chance to request any such thing. She felt freshly sick inside—now from regret. How could she have been so blind, so foolish, so quick to judge the worst? Han had been right. He'd been right about everything.

"Is something wrong?" Claude asked.

"No," she managed a smile. "I just . . . well, yes, Han is very good with horses. I'm glad he could help. I . . . was just thinking I would like to . . . well . . . perhaps you could have breakfast sent up to our room, so that he could eat, as well."

"Splendid idea," Josette said. "We'll do that shortly."

"Thank you," Maggie said and whisked herself out of the room and up the stairs. She had to see him, to hold him, to tell him how wrong she had been. She prayed he would forgive her. She prayed he would still love her. She couldn't imagine either with how cruel she had been.

Maggie had expected Han to be asleep and opened the door quietly. But she found him facing the window despite the drapes being closed tightly. He was clad only in breeches, his hands clasped behind his back.

"Han," she said and closed the door, breathless from her quick ascent up the stairs. He turned quickly to face her. Seeing his woeful expression, her regret deepened.

"Han," she repeated and fled across the room toward him. She touched his face and hair, and tears crept from her eyes as she whispered, "I don't know what to say. I'm so sorry. I shouldn't have even thought such a thing. I was wrong. I'm so sorry. Forgive me, Han."

"Maggie," he sighed her name with relief and pushed his arms around her.

"Will you forgive me?" she asked with pleading eyes.

"Yes, of course. Yes!"

"Oh," she laughed softly, "I'm so glad, because I . . . oh, Han, I love you. I do. I would die without you, Han."

Han had to remind himself to breathe when his chest began to burn. Then he laughed—a stunned, ecstatic, laugh. And Maggie laughed with him as he pulled her up into his arms and turned her around.

"Oh, Maggie," he whispered as he set her down and pressed the side of his face to hers. "I love you too, Maggie. I love you more than life."

"Han," she whispered, and he met her eyes, "we must be together—always. You are a part of me, Han. You see," she smiled and drew his hand to her belly, "your baby, my love."

Han's eyes widened. "Are you certain? Already?"

"I have not seen a doctor yet," she said softly, "but I have felt these things before. Yes, I am quite certain."

"Maggie," he laughed her name softly, "life just keeps getting better and better."

"Yes." Needing reassurance, she added, "Tell me you'll never leave me, Han. I need to know."

"I will always be here," he said, his sincerity readily evident. "You are everything a man could ever want. There is no need to look else-where. Do you know," his voice softened, "what went through my mind when I read that note she gave me?"

"What?" Maggie asked, wondering if she wanted to know.

"I looked at her and thought about you—in the cottage, with your hair down, wearing simple clothes. I used to watch you work and marvel at how beautiful you looked. A woman like the comtesse would be nothing if she didn't have her expensive gowns and jewels. If a woman like that were put into such a situation, she would have fallen apart; she would have been nothing. But you, Maggie—you shine! You don't need all of those things to be beautiful. And that is one of the many, many reasons I love you as much as I do. Don't ever forget it, Maggie. You are all I will ever need—or want."

Maggie sighed and pulled herself close to him. "Again, I am sorry."

"Forget about it," he whispered then lifted her chin with his finger and kissed her, softly at first, but then a familiar passion crept in, and Maggie melted against him. A knock came at the door, and they both sighed, hesitantly easing away from each other.

"Come in," Han called.

"Breakfast for you," a maid announced as she entered with a large tray.

"Thank you," Han said as she set it down and left quickly.

"I asked for it to be sent up. I wanted to eat with you."

"Well, then," he said, "let's eat."

They sat on the bed to eat and giggled like children as they fed each other, and Han kept making her close her eyes and tell him about the different textures of the foods as she ate them. Maggie enjoyed the little game and recalled the many times in their travels that Han had taken the time to play it. He was aware of things in ways most people weren't, and he enjoyed having Maggie share such simple experiences. Gradually, she had become more aware of her senses, and she could now understand his motives.

When breakfast was finished, Han moved the tray to the bureau, locked the bedroom doors, and came back to the bed. He pulled off Maggie's slippers and threw them comically onto the floor, then he lay down beside her and moved his fingers gently up and down her arm.

"What do you feel?" he asked intently.

"Your hand on my arm." She laughed. "No, wait." She closed her eyes. "I feel the touch of an angel, my guardian angel. It's like . . . a summer breeze against my face. I feel secure. I know when you touch me that way that you love me. I feel . . ." she drew a deep breath, "anticipation."

Han smiled and moved closer, taking her hand into his, kissing the tip of each finger. "Now what do you feel?" he asked.

"It's like," she smiled, her eyes still closed, "the day you fed me berries in the black forest, and you made me lick the juice from your fingers."

"Why is it like that?" he asked, pressing a gentle kiss to her brow.

"Because," she opened her eyes, "I had the same butterflies in my stomach then that I have now."

Han's eyes widened, remembering how much she'd hated him back then. He kissed her and couldn't keep from laughing. *She loved him*. She'd actually admitted that she loved him, and he had no reason to question her sincerity.

"Remind me," she whispered after he'd kissed her again, "when we get home, to tell my father something."

"What's that?" he asked in a raspy whisper.

"I want to thank him for offering you the job of being my husband."

Han looked at her in surprise. Needing clarification, he said gently, "Maggie, I did it all for you."

She smiled, but there was something in her eyes that made it evident she didn't entirely believe him. Han reminded himself that they'd come one step closer. She'd admitted for the first time since she was fourteen that she loved him. But her trust was not complete. A part of her still doubted his motives.

Han sighed and forced the thought away with a quick prayer that eventually they could be free of this dark cloud—once and for all.

Chapter Twelve

RETURN TO HORSTBERG

Claude and Josette were intensely disappointed when Han told them that he and Maggie would be leaving. But they were pleased to know that Maggie was expecting again. And they understood their desire to return home before Christmas. It was difficult to say good-bye, but promises were made to see each other again. And Josette insisted to her husband that they must make a point to visit Bavaria before too much time had passed.

"It sounds like a good idea," Claude said and winked at his wife, "if you think we could find somebody who would put us up while we were there."

They all laughed, and Han said, "You know you're more than welcome any time." He smiled toward Maggie then added, "You especially, Josette, might find our home rather fascinating."

"Really?" she said. "Why is that?"

"And where exactly do you live?" Claude inserted. "We can't come if we don't know where to find you."

"Well," Han said, "there is this little country—very beautiful, nevertheless—called Horstberg."

"One of those duchies," Claude said.

"Yes, one of those. Well . . ." Han smiled slyly at Maggie, and she wondered how much he would tell them. "I must be honest," he said. "Our name is not Bruxen."

"It's not?" Josette seemed surprised yet amused.

"We used the name to try and stay away from that . . . man who—"

"We know who you mean," Claude said. "What is your name, then?"

"Heinrich," Maggie provided.

"And you were saying . . . about your home," Claude said. "How do we find it?"

"It's easy," Han said. "As soon as you come into the valley, you look east, and there is this ominous, imposing, stunning, elaborate—"

"Get on with it." Maggie nudged him her elbow.

"Castle."

"Oh, I love castles!" Josette clapped her hands together. "Can you see it easily from your home?"

"Actually, no," Han said, and Josette looked disappointed. "But then, I suppose that depends on where you're standing at the time."

"I think what he's trying to tell us," Claude said, "is that they live *in* the castle."

"That's right," Han said proudly. "We live at Castle Horstberg."

Josette seemed intrigued and curious, as if she were trying to imagine Han and Maggie as royalty. They talked for a few minutes about the ways of the Bavarian duchies, then Josette asked, "Whose home was it originally?"

"We both grew up there," Maggie said.

"Really?" Josette lifted one brow.

"It is Maggie," Han said, "who is the duke's daughter."

"And you, Han?" Josette asked.

Han remained silent, almost expecting Maggie to tell them he had been a stablehand; not that it really mattered to him, but he still had no idea exactly where she stood on their division of social status.

"Han's father," Maggie interjected, "is my father's highest advisor. Han will take over his father's position when my brother inherits the duchy. Our fathers arranged the marriage, actually," she smiled, "but I believe they knew what they were doing."

Han returned her smile and cherished the warmth inside of him.

"Obviously," Claude said. "You are both happy together. That is quite apparent."

"And we will certainly look forward," Josette said, "to coming to this country of yours and learning more about it."

They reluctantly proceeded with their good-byes. Han and Maggie were put onto a train by their new friends and were soon heading for Venice. Though they had originally planned to go home by way of France, neither of them were disappointed to have traded that for the time they had shared with the Dormantes, going instead through Austria and back into Germany. They took the journey slowly, allowing time to see the sights and also to keep Maggie from becoming weary from her condition.

The honeymoon had been glorious, and they agreed that the time away from Horstberg had been exciting and fruitful. But both Han and Maggie were glad to be nearly home. Maggie grew impatient with anticipation when she knew the train would soon be arriving in Regensburg, and it was only a matter of hours by carriage from there to Horstberg.

"Han," she said, "do you think they'll be happy about it?"

"Who?"

"My family; your parents."

"Our fathers will be overjoyed," he grinned. "As for the rest . . . well, I don't see why they wouldn't be. We're happy about it," he added, "and that's all that matters."

"Who should we see first?" she asked expectantly.

"Well," he said, glancing at his watch, "if my memory serves me correctly, we should be arriving home just about dinner time, and . . ." he added with a contriving smile, "do you know what today is?"

"What?"

"It's Thursday, and our parents usually dine together on Thursdays because it's often a long day of meetings. If we're clever, we can catch them all in the same room at the same time."

"Oh, Han, you're so much fun."

He laughed and said, "So are you, my love."

She touched his face and met his eyes with a gaze that always warmed him. "It's a pleasure to be your love, Han."

He kissed her and returned her gaze, wishing there were words to tell her how much that meant to him. She had come far since they'd left Horstberg together.

Even though darkness had settled over the valley, both Han and Maggie moved near the carriage window to absorb the familiarity of the scenery. Maggie caught her breath and felt Han squeeze her hand tightly when Castle Horstberg came into view. The moonlight illuminated the high turrets, adorned with splotches of snow. The majesty and grandeur of the structure was breathtaking no matter how many times they saw it or how clearly they remembered it.

Ten minutes into the dinner hour, the carriage pulled up in the courtyard, and Han stepped down. He held out his hand and assisted his wife. The luggage was unloaded while Maggie sensed an excited chatter among the servants. Han squeezed her hand tightly, and she asked, "Are you nervous?"

"Not really." He chuckled. "Maybe a little. It all just feels . . . strange."

"Yes," she agreed as they came through the main entrance into the great hall and she glanced around nostalgically. "But it feels so good to be back."

"It does indeed," he said. "But you can reminisce later. If we don't hurry, the servants will have the secret out before we've had a chance to make our entrance."

Maggie moved quickly down the hallway with Han's hand at the small of her back. She felt an excitement that overcame her own nervousness and hoped that Han felt the same. Coming to the open door of the dining room, they could hear familiar voices inside, and Maggie bit her lip to keep from laughing. Han kissed her quickly and whispered, "Here goes." She held back a moment, letting him enter first. She had liked the little plan he'd come up with for the best impact.

Han took a deep breath and stood just inside the door for several moments, watching the little dinner party, thinking again how good it was to be home. He ignored the fast pace of his heart and said, "Excuse me, Your Grace."

Conversation ceased, and the room became eerily still. All eyes turned toward him with stunned expressions. Cameron du Woernig came to his feet, and Han added, "I hear you're offering a reward for the safe return of your daughter."

"Han!" His mother stood breathlessly and put a hand over her heart. He glanced affectionately toward her, then his eyes met the duke's again as he waited for a reaction.

"Do you know where my daughter is, young man?" Cameron asked sternly, but Han caught the subtle spark of amusement and relief in his eyes.

"I have found a woman who strongly resembles her," he said coolly, "but I'm not certain if she's the same woman who left here seven months ago."

Maggie appeared from behind him. Abbi broke away from the dinner table and nearly ran to take her daughter into her arms. "Maggie! Oh, Maggie!" she said with tears in her eyes.

Elsa followed the duchess across the room and gave her son an exuberant hug, going up on her tiptoes to kiss him. Georg followed and embraced Han, then he shook his hand firmly amid an outpouring of laughter, while Cameron hugged his daughter and looked as if he were on the verge of tears himself. When all other greetings were completed, Han found himself face-to-face with the duke.

"It's good to see you, Han," he said, holding out his hand.

"And you, Your Grace," Han replied and took his hand. He shook it with confidence, hoping to let the duke know that he had succeeded. Their eyes met, and Han knew he had perceived the silent message.

"Maggie," Cameron turned toward his daughter, and she hugged him again. "You look prettier than ever," he said, pulling back to look closely at her.

"Father," she said, "Han and I are married. But then," she smiled, "you already knew that, didn't you."

"I'd hoped," he admitted.

"But Father . . . Mother . . ." She took Abbi's hand and smiled toward Han, who had his arm around his mother. "First I must apologize for not trusting your judgment and for trying to do what you had forbidden. I know now the way things really are. Han has taught me a great deal. And I must thank you, Father . . . for seeing the good in him and knowing he would be good for me." She gazed affectionately toward Han.

"Oh, Maggie," Abbi started to cry again, and Maggie did her best to hug both her parents at the same time.

"And," Han added with a dramatic lilt in his voice, "you are all officially old now. You'll be grandparents by next summer. Maggie's going to have a baby."

They all laughed, hugged again, and the duke ushered Han and Maggie to the table, and the duchess asked Heidi to have dinner brought in for them.

"So," Cameron said when they were all seated again, "I want to hear everything—right from the start."

While they ate, Maggie enjoyed hearing Han recount the happenings of the past seven months. He had everyone roaring with laughter as he dramatically explained how he had managed to kidnap her, and the duke nearly fell out of his chair as Han said, "When I got her into a barn and took the towel from her mouth, she looked at me and said . . ." he raised his voice to mimic Maggie, "'My father is going to kill you!'"

They talked far past the end of the meal, and the conversation stayed light and humorous until their story reached the morning when Nik Koenig had bombarded into their room at the inn, along with his brutal thugs. Everyone became silent until Maggie said quietly, "He nearly killed Han. He just kept hitting him over and over, and I . . . tried to stop him and . . ."

"Maggie was pregnant then, though not very far along," Han said sadly. "She lost the baby that day."

Abbi and Elsa both showed tears in their eyes, and there was another long reign of silence before Han said more cheerfully, "But thanks to our friends the Dormantes, everything turned out fine."

Cameron told them how a message had arrived from Italy concerning the incarceration of Koenig and his associates. It was evident from the expressions and comments of all four parents that these past seven months had been difficult for them. But they were all now equally grateful to be reunited, and Han went on to tell of their experiences from that point, and the story ended on a happy note with their return home.

"And now," the duke said to Han, "I suppose you'll be wanting to collect that reward."

"No, Your Grace," he replied. "I've already got my reward. Besides, I'm the thief who stole your daughter away from her home. It would be hypocritical to actually collect the reward."

"All for a good cause," the duke said, lifting his wine glass toward Han.

"By the way," Han said, "have you seen or heard anything from the distinguished Mr. Koenig?"

"Not a thing," Cameron said. "We had feared when he disappeared that he would be on your trail, and we felt better knowing he was in jail. But we were not informed of how long he would be there."

Han reported, "We haven't seen any sign of him since that dreadful day they arrested him."

"With any luck," Maggie said, "he's still dwindling away in some foreign jail cell."

"Where is everybody else, anyway?" Han asked, looking around.

"Everybody else?" Abbi questioned.

"Erich, Sonia." He chuckled and added, "Of course, Sonia is married by now."

"Yes," Abbi said. "In the summer. She writes regularly, and she's doing very well."

"I'm glad to hear it," Maggie said with some sadness. She wanted to know her sister was happy, but already she missed her.

"It was a beautiful wedding," Elsa said. "We all wished the two of you could have been there."

"We were busy," Han stated and looked intently at Maggie, who gave him a wan smile. He knew she felt some disappointment over what they had missed, but they both knew that under the circumstances it couldn't have been helped.

"And Erich," Abbi continued, "is dining with the family of a certain young lady this evening."

"Ooh," Han smirked. "Anyone worth mentioning?"

"Not so far," Cameron said wryly, as if Erich's courting experiences were giving him personal grief. Han let the subject drop, but he couldn't wait to see his old friend. They had a lot of catching up to do.

"Speaking of weddings," Georg said.

"Were we?" Elsa asked.

"We were," he said. "It's too bad we couldn't have all been there for yours."

"It was nice," Han said. "Simple, but very . . ."

"Beautiful," Maggie provided.

"And where did you say you were married?" Elsa asked.

"Switzerland; Zurich to be exact."

"Well," Cameron said, "we must have a celebration."

"That's a splendid idea," his wife added.

"Celebration?" Maggie asked, lifting her brows.

"Sonia had incredible wedding festivities in her new country," Cameron said. "And you, my dear girl, are going to have them as well."

"We don't need all of that, Father," Maggie said.

"She's right," Han agreed. The duke glared comically toward him, so he added, "Your Grace."

"On the contrary," Cameron continued, "it's important for the people to see publicly that you are married and happy and that we as your families accept the marriage."

Han didn't like the idea of being a public image, and he knew it must have showed in his expression. Cameron grinned at him and said, "Welcome to the diplomatic world, Han. It's all part of the job. You'd better get used to it. Which reminds me, you can have tomorrow to get settled in, but the following day I want you in my office right after breakfast. We've got work to do."

"Yes, Your Grace," he said with a satisfied smile and a quick wink toward Maggie. She smiled in return, and he was glad to know that she understood what this meant to him.

"And, Han," Cameron said, "*sir* would be fine. When we are only with family, *Father* would be preferable. Or you can simply call me by my name."

"I don't know about the rest of you," Maggie said as she stood, "but I'm exhausted."

"It has been a very long day," Han added, standing as well.

"We'll be staying in my room for now," Maggie added as she kissed her parents—all four of them. "And," she took Han's hand and added as they moved together toward the door, "we'll most likely be late for breakfast."

"Some things never change." Cameron smiled toward his wife, and they all said good-night.

"Are you always late for breakfast?" Han asked Maggie as she led him by the hand down long hallways and up two different staircases.

"Usually," she replied.

Feigning exhaustion due to the long walk from the dining room, he said, "No wonder you're always late for breakfast."

Maggie laughed and pushed open the door to her room, sighing wistfully to see that it looked exactly the same—except for the trunks that had been brought up from the courtyard where they'd been unloaded from the carriage.

"There are some larger rooms that will be prepared for us, but this will do for now."

"Larger!" Han said. "Good heavens, Maggie, I could get lost in this one."

"But we will need rooms with a nursery," she smiled.

"So we will," he replied, still looking around, "and this place no doubt has many of those. It has everything else."

"You should know that. You grew up here."

"Not in this glorious royal residence of the castle," he teased and sat on the edge of the bed to pull off his boots. "My room wasn't like this."

"It is now," she said and took his hand, drawing his attention completely to her.

"Welcome home, my love," he whispered, pulling her back onto the bed with him.

"With you here, home is better than it ever was."

Han smiled and kissed her. He wondered how he might have felt eight months ago if he'd been able to foresee this day. The very thought made him believe in miracles. If he could only conquer that one part of Maggie's heart that he still didn't understand, he'd have everything a man could ever want.

The following morning, Han stood at the window for several minutes, adjusting to the view. He recalled well his feelings in the past about the view from the apartment where he'd grown up and lived with his parents, as opposed to those of the royal family. And now, in a relatively short time, the view had changed dramatically, along with every facet of his life.

He left Maggie getting dressed and went to Erich's room before breakfast. But the maid making his bed told Han that he'd left early. Certain he'd gone riding, Han went to the stables, hoping to catch Erich when he returned.

Memories washed over Han as he walked in. He wondered how many hours he'd spent here, caring for the horses of the du Woernig family and their most prestigious associates. He chuckled to himself at the ironies in his life, and then he was greeted by the young man who had been hired to replace him permanently about six months ago. They visited for a short while before Erich came riding in and dismounted.

"Good morning, Your Highness," Han said, and Erich turned on his heel.

"Han?" Erich laughed and stepped toward him. "I don't believe it!" They grasped forearms and laughed together as they shared a hearty embrace.

"I see you've recovered," Han said, tapping his shoulder lightly where he'd been shot the day before Han had left.

"No thanks to you," Erich laughed as they walked out of the stables together. "I can't believe that you, of all people, would run off without so much as a word, while I'm on my death bed."

"Your *death* bed?" Han echoed.

"Well, it *felt* like my death bed," Erich said lightly. He stopped walking and just looked at Han, shaking his head with a hearty chuckle. "I can't believe it. Where in the world have you been for seven months?"

Han sobered. "Surely your father told you."

Erich put his hands on his hips. "Told me *what?*"

Han looked down at the toe of his boot as he shuffled it over the ground. "He must have told you *something.*"

"My father told me nothing. My mother told me they hoped you were keeping Maggie away from that bastard. Is Maggie—"

"Oh, she's here." Han looked up and smiled. "Everything's fine . . . now."

"Now?"

Han chuckled and glanced away briefly. "I can't believe he didn't tell you."

"If he knew something and didn't tell me, then he must have had his reasons. Apparently, he didn't want me to know."

"But . . ." Han felt completely caught off guard. He had never imagined having to explain any of this to Erich. "Your father tells you everything," he insisted, as if that might change the fact of Erich's ignorance.

"Not *everything,*" Erich said, picking up on Han's severity. "Whatever you were doing, it must have been pretty important. You're right; there isn't much he *doesn't* tell me."

"Well," Han shrugged, attempting to keep this light, "I suppose it was a matter of political security. If Maggie had married Nik, we'd all be destined for trouble."

"I won't question that, but . . . you've been gone seven months, Han. You're here now. I think you can tell me what—"

"Erich!" Maggie called, and they turned to see her running across the courtyard. Erich moved toward her and laughed as she catapulted herself into his arms.

"Oh, Erich," she cried as he twirled her around then held her suspended off the ground. "I missed you so much." She took his face in her hands and kissed him with a loud smack.

"*You* missed *me?*" Erich laughed and kissed her again. "Mercy, girl, I thought I'd die without you."

"What about me?" Han asked. "Did you miss me, too?"

"A little," Erich said wryly. He set Maggie down and took both her hands into his. "You look fabulous," Erich said, and she beamed. His eyes intensified, and he added, "You look . . . happy." She laughed, and he said, "You're laughing!"

"It's good to see you."

"Is that all?"

"Well, I *am* happy." She moved into Han's arms, and Erich's eyes widened.

"He doesn't know," Han said to Maggie.

"Know what?" Maggie asked.

"Anything."

Maggie laughed. "Truly?" She laughed again. "Surely there has been gossip about us running away together."

"I don't pay attention to gossip," Erich insisted, sounding indignant.

"Do you want to tell him?" Maggie asked Han. "Or do you want me to tell him?"

"Tell me what?" Erich erupted with an infuriated laugh.

Han forced a severe expression and said, "I hope you won't let this come between us Erich, but I've been sleeping with your sister."

Erich barely had a chance to absorb the implication before Maggie lifted her hand to show him her wedding ring.

"I can't believe it," Erich said breathlessly.

"It's true," Maggie said, hugging Han tightly. "I'm Mrs. Han Heinrich, and we're going to have a baby."

Erich chuckled and shook his head. "I can't believe it."

"A man of many words," Han said with light sarcasm.

"But . . ." Erich looked utterly dumbfounded and was unable to speak.

"Now, Erich," Maggie said lightly. "You can't honestly think that Han and I could be away together for so long without coming back married. Surely it must have occurred to you."

Erich didn't answer, but Han wondered if it either *hadn't* occurred to him, or if he'd chosen to dismiss the possibility because he was against it.

"It's nearly time for breakfast," Maggie announced more to Han. "If I don't eat something soon I'm going to be sick. Are you coming?"

"You go ahead." He kissed her hand quickly. "We'll be there in a few minutes."

Maggie nodded and kissed Erich once more. She kissed Han quickly and hurried away.

"Well," Erich said as if he were in shock. Han laughed, but he knew that Erich knew him well enough to sense the tension in it. "You've been sleeping with my sister."

"Regularly, if you must know."

"So, will you please explain all of this to me?"

"Before breakfast?"

"Just give me the nutshell version."

"All right." Han took a deep breath. "Your mother suspected Maggie might try to run away with Nik. Your father asked me to kidnap Maggie and keep her away from here for at least six months. Of course, I had to marry her for the sake of her reputation and all."

Following a moment of stunned silence, Erich said, "But I thought you *detested* Maggie."

"Think again," Han said, slapping Erich on the shoulder. "Come on, let's eat."

They paused a short distance from the door as Erich said, "My father *asked* you to *kidnap* my sister?"

"Exactly."

"How much did he pay you?"

"Actually," Han said, "he just gave me a new job."

"I hope he didn't give you *mine.*"

"Fortunately, your job takes du Woernig blood. *I* wouldn't want it. But I'm afraid he came close." Erich glanced at him in question, and Han clarified, "I'm not only part of the family, I'm taking my father's position."

Erich frowned. "Is *that* why you did it?" he asked with an imposing demeanor that Han had rarely seen directed at him. Again, he was taken completely off guard. He never would have expected Erich, of all people, to question his motives.

Han replied with the same severity. "If there is a reason you don't want to work with me, Erich, then just—"

"I asked you a question," he interrupted. He was clearly the prince now. "Is *that* why you married my sister, so you could have the most prestigious occupation in the duchy?"

Han took a step toward him and lifted a finger. "There are many reasons I did what I did, the least of which is that job. I most emphatically did not want the esteemed Mr. Koenig marrying into your family and worming his way to the top. And in the same respect, I did not want to see Maggie sentenced to life with the creep just because he was low enough to take advantage of her stubbornness and naiveté. But the bottom line is simple, Erich. With Maggie as my wife, I would work my fingers to the bone to make her happy—at *any* profession—and I'd not begrudge it." His voice lightened. "Instead, I have to work with *you.*"

When Erich made no response, Han looked into his eyes and felt a little sick. He knew that look, that subtly skeptical, distrusting look that Maggie was famous for. Han and Erich both turned when they caught movement and they realized they weren't alone. Maggie was standing in the doorway. She'd obviously come back to see what was taking so long. And she'd obviously overheard. *She* had that look in her eyes, too.

"For the love of heaven," Han snapped. "Does incertitude run in the family, or do the two of you just have it in for me?"

Neither of them answered. They both looked a little stunned.

"Come along, my dear," Han said, taking Maggie's arm abruptly. "You'd best eat before you get sick." She said nothing, and Erich followed close behind, exuding the same implicating silence.

There was no conscious reason why Han felt uneasy at the break-fast table. The conversation was pleasant, and it was evident that the duke and duchess were delighted to have their daughter back. But Han felt undeniable tension. Erich talked and laughed as if everything were perfect. But that look was in his eyes. And Maggie—in spite of her smiles—became especially tense when the duke started discussing the advantages of having Han work with Erich.

After breakfast, Han found a moment alone with Erich. He came right out and asked, "Is something bothering you?"

Erich looked a little alarmed, but he chuckled nonchalantly as he said, "It could take some time getting used to having you in the family."

Han reminded himself that it would take time for all of them to adjust to the change in circumstances. He decided to take that at face value and not make something out of nothing. Attempting to keep things light he said, "Speaking of family, have you found the next Duchess of Horstberg yet?"

Erich snorted and seemed more like himself. "I don't think she exists. While you've been out having the adventure of a lifetime, I've been enduring stodgy dinner parties with garish and deplorable women throwing themselves at my feet."

Han laughed. "Not to worry. Your day will come."

Han and Erich went riding together for a while, as if nothing had ever changed. But *everything* had changed, and Han wasn't certain if he could live with it. Erich did fairly well at behaving as if nothing was any different between them, but Han had known Erich all his life. And something was definitely different.

When Erich went to the office to get some work done, Han went up to his room where Maggie was rearranging the clothes in her closet and putting away the new things she'd acquired on their journey. She smiled and kissed him in greeting. Everything seemed fine as he put his own things away and acquainted himself with his new living quarters, but he could feel that something was wrong with Maggie just as surely as he'd felt it with Erich. Although the feeling was so abstract and vague that he doubted he could confront either of them without having them deny it. And that made it worse.

Lunch wasn't quite as uncomfortable as breakfast had been, and Han tried to comprehend that this was where he would be eating his meals for the rest of his life. It was still difficult to believe that he'd become a part of the royal family of Horstberg. But when he glanced briefly at Erich and Maggie, it was blatantly evident that he wasn't a part of them at all. He still felt like a dinner guest, as if it should be some great honor for him to be sitting here, and his reasons for being invited were dubious.

Near the end of the meal, Cameron said, "Han, your father

wants to see you for a few minutes. He said he'd be in the office. Erich and I will be away on business this afternoon."

Han nodded to acknowledge him. He made a gracious exit and hurried to the office, where his father was seated in the duke's chair, busily writing something. Han found some comfort in the simple picture before him.

"Ah, come in," Georg said, motioning him toward the chair at his side. Han closed the door and sat down. "We missed you, Han," his father said. "It's good to have you back."

"It's good to *be* back," Han admitted.

"Are you settling in all right?"

"I think so," Han said, trying to sound enthusiastic. He briefly contemplated asking his father's advice, but the very thought of even voicing his concerns was less than appealing at the moment. *Perhaps another time*, he thought.

"There's something I need to talk to you about, son," Georg said in a severe voice that made Han uneasy. "We'll be spending a great deal of time together in our work from here on out, but it's rare that you and I will have the opportunity to be alone, especially in this room. You have a wife now, and things will be very different."

Han nodded and motioned for him to go on, not certain he liked that idea, given certain aspects of the present situation. Georg leaned back in his chair and turned more toward Han. "You know son, His Grace has always paid me well. The salary for this position is ridiculous, in my opinion. You'll work up to that salary eventually, but I would assume that, in the meantime, your resources are limited."

Han thought of the money the duke had given him. He actually had quite a bit left, but it was difficult to think of it as his. Beyond that, he'd been pretty much broke when he'd left here. Working as a stablehand hadn't come with much of a salary. "I guess you could say that," Han stated.

"Your mother also made good money in the years she worked for the duchess. The thing is . . . there was little to spend it on. We were always provided with a nice place to live, and it didn't cost a whole lot to raise one child."

Han watched his father closely, wondering where this conversation was headed. "I assume you're getting to a point," he said.

Georg smiled. "Yes, I am. We have both put away a percentage of our earnings into different funds through the years. One of those funds is to care for us when we're too old to work. The rest is for you."

Han inhaled deeply. "What are you saying?"

Georg folded his arms across his chest. "You're a married man now, Han. You have a baby on the way. I have no question about your ability to make an adequate living. I'm certain that once your salary starts coming in—which will be soon—you can provide for Maggie's personal needs without any difficulty. You—just as myself—are blessed to have a roof over your head as an added benefit. But I've thought a great deal about the situation between you and Maggie. And I just want you to know that you are not financially dependent upon the du Woernig family—at all."

Han didn't know what to say. He could never express to his father how much his insight was appreciated, but he had to try. "You're a very wise man, Father. Just knowing you understand something like that means more to me than I can ever say."

"Maybe I don't understand fully," his father said. "I married into my own social class. I have never had any difficulty with such distinctions with the du Woernigs, but I know that Maggie has struggled with her identity as a princess."

Han was in awe of his father's perception. Perhaps he was getting advice without having to ask for it.

"You see," Georg went on, "I believe it's important for you to know that not only could you make it on your own, Han, you are a wealthy man—in your own right."

Han sucked in his breath and held it. "Are you trying to tell me that . . ." He couldn't finish.

Georg slid a piece of paper across the desk without taking his eyes off Han. "This is your inheritance, Han. No need for you to wait for me to die to receive it. Be discreet, and use it wisely."

Han hesitated shifting his eyes down to the paper. Heart pounding, he finally forced himself to look at it. He recognized it as a bank statement. It had all the information he needed to access what his father had just given him. His eyes moved down the financial figures penned in neat columns.

"Merciful heaven!" he gasped to see an amount more than twenty times what the duke had given him last spring, which had been more money than he would have made working five years as a stablehand.

"You can't just *give* this to me," he protested.

"Why not?" Georg asked.

"I didn't *earn* it."

"Han," Georg leaned forward and looked him in the eye, "I am not even remotely concerned about your using this money wisely. If I were, I *wouldn't* give it to you. I can assure you that Erich has accounts far exceeding this one at his disposal. And for what? Because he was born the son of a du Woernig. It's as simple as that. Well, you were born the son of a Heinrich. The du Woernigs are independently wealthy, Han. The taxation of the people benefits the people. The monies are not intermixed. My life has been richly blessed as a result of being a part of the country and the family. I am bestowing that blessing on you now. And I pray in my heart that it will aid you in making a good marriage and in raising children worthy of *both* their bloodlines."

Han glanced again at the statement in his hands. "I . . . I don't know what to say."

"Say thank you."

"Thank you," Han chuckled.

"Now, when you get a few minutes, go thank your mother. She worked hard taking care of Abbi for many years and certainly contributed to that."

Han thought of his growing years when his mother usually left early and came home late, always close to Abbi du Woernig, meeting her needs. He'd been well cared for, usually in the castle along with the du Woernig children and the children of others who worked there. The irony was difficult to comprehend. He looked up at his father, not ashamed of the tears in his eyes.

"And while you were both working hard, what was I doing?" Han asked.

"You don't remember?" Georg chuckled. "I'll tell you what you were doing, Han. You were diligent to your studies, never giving the tutors any trouble, always bringing in high marks in your education. You cooked and cleaned when the housekeeper was ill or too busy, and you kept me and your mother company when one or the other of us had to work extra hours. Once you had your own job, you did it well and made us proud. And you still cooked and cleaned. You never caused us any trouble, Han. You never gave me a moment's dismay at having you raised and tutored with the royal family. That's what you did. And you were there when the Duke of Horstberg had a very delicate and severe problem on his hands. He trusted you, and he knew he could count on you. And you didn't let him down. You're a man of integrity, Han, the finest son a man could ask for."

Han choked back his emotion and said, "I had the finest example a boy could ever hope for." He slid to the edge of his chair and reached over to embrace his father. "Thank you. I won't let you down."

"I know," Georg said as they settled back into their chairs. "I'm looking forward to working with you, Han. Nothing could make me happier."

"I'm looking forward to it, too," he said.

"And your mother," Georg chuckled warmly, "is so proud of you. Your marrying Maggie has made her so happy. She was there to help bring Maggie into the world, you know. And a woman has never been more excited to become a grandmother."

"I'm glad," Han said, wishing he could ignore the sadness that rose in him.

"What's bothering you, Han?" Georg asked gently.

Han felt a little unnerved at being read so easily. He considered brushing it off, but perhaps he *did* need his father's advice. "Well," Han decided to get right to the point, "it seems that Erich and Maggie are both a little . . . skeptical about my reasons for marrying Maggie. They both seem to believe that my taking this position was a stronger motivation than my love for Maggie."

Georg blew out a long breath. He was thoughtfully silent, and Han allowed him the time to think. Georg Heinrich was well known for thinking before he spoke. When he had apparently come to a conclusion, he simply said, "Then you'll have to find a way to make it clear to them what your motivations were. Think it through. You'll know what to do."

Han wanted to ask if he had any more specific ideas, but he felt certain his father would tell him he needed to solve his own problems. They embraced again before Han left the office. In spite of the issue before him with his wife and his best friend, he had to bask in the warmth of all that his parents had given him. The money meant a great deal—more than he could ever say—but knowing his father and mother were proud of him meant even more.

Through the remainder of the day, Han followed his father's advice and pondered carefully how he might solve the problem at hand. He hid the bank statement where he knew Maggie wouldn't come across it. Until things were a little more settled between them, he preferred that she didn't know about the money. While Maggie was visiting with her mother late in the afternoon, Han wandered idly through the castle, getting temporarily lost more than once. He came across the castle chapel quite unexpectedly but found it calming to sit there and ponder his dilemma for over an hour. He'd attended Sunday services here throughout his life, along with the royal family, some high-ranking military officers, and the higher level servants and their families. He remembered watching Maggie through many of those services, fantasizing about a future with her more than paying any attention to the sermon. Now with the struggle he was facing, he wished he'd paid more attention. He could use some divine inspiration right now. How could he work with Erich if they didn't have complete trust? And how could he share his life with Maggie and raise a family with that same horrible dark cloud that kept reappearing in her eyes? The more he thought about it, the more angry he became. What had he ever done to discredit their trust? He just didn't understand.

Han slept little that night as his mind went through memories of his relationships with his wife and his best friend, attempting to put pieces together. He didn't come to any definite conclusions, but the following day only made it more and more clear to him that the problem was not his imagination. The tension was evident between him and Erich as he settled into his first day on the job. Maggie was kind to him, but she'd developed a cool condescending attitude that nearly sickened him.

"What is it, Maggie?" he asked as they were getting ready for bed following his first day of officially working for the country of Horstberg. He thought that she might ask about his work, how it had gone, how he felt about it. Something!

"What?" she asked with apparent innocence after not having uttered a single word since supper.

He pointed a finger at her, no longer willing to let her deny it. If they didn't face this now, the problem would only get worse. "The way you're treating me, Maggie. I can feel it."

"I don't know what you're talking about," she insisted.

"It all started that day . . . that day when we met in the garden and it was raining. It was the same day you rode out into that storm and nearly got yourself killed."

"That was years ago. What has that got to do with anything?" she asked.

"That was the day you changed toward me, Maggie. I don't understand what happened, but I'm going to. If it takes me the rest of my life, I am going to figure out what happened to you that day. Do you remember that day, Maggie?"

"Oh, I remember it, all right," she said, clearly perturbed.

"And then we came inside and . . ." Han paused as a piece fell into place, and he wondered why he'd never made the connection before. "And the baron's daughters had arrived early and . . ." Han stopped when Maggie's eyes filled with . . . what? Fear? But of what? The memories? "That's it," he said. "Something happened with the baron's daughters."

Maggie turned away abruptly, but he took her arm and forced her to look at him. "What did they say to you, Maggie?"

"You don't know what you're talking about," she snarled, but her demeanor had instantly become the cynical, cold Maggie he'd lived with in the black forest.

"They were horrible, cruel girls, Maggie. They saw you come in out of the rain—with me—and they said something, didn't they."

"Leave me alone, Han," she snapped and hurried from the room as if the devil were right behind her.

Han nearly followed, but he thought it would be better to leave her in peace. Perhaps he'd at least given her something to think about. *He* certainly had something to think about. But he couldn't figure it out if Maggie wouldn't talk to him. She didn't come to bed until after the clock had softly chimed two. She said nothing, but once she had slid between the sheets, he pulled her close to him, pressing a kiss to her brow. No matter what difficulties might be between them, he would never let her wonder over his love or the fact that he would always be there for her. She relaxed when it became evident he wasn't going to press the issue they'd been arguing over. Within minutes she fell asleep. Again, Han slept little, but before dawn he knew what to do. His idea seemed brash, but he couldn't go on with this tension another day. If he didn't do *something*, he'd go insane.

Maggie woke up alone the following morning, but a quick glance at the clock let her know she'd slept late and had long missed breakfast. She found a note from Han that said he wanted to let her sleep, he loved her, and he had something to take care of in town, but he would see her at lunch.

She had some food sent up to her room if only to help ease her nausea. Even though it was nearing time for lunch by the time she was dressed and had her hair put up, she couldn't get by on an empty stomach. Glad to once again have Klara there to help her, she complimented the maid on the beautiful work Klara had done on her hair and thanked her for her help. Klara smiled kindly, and Maggie realized that Han had taught her to appreciate all the little things the servants did to make her life easier, things she'd never thought of before.

After Klara had left her alone, Maggie's mind wandered to the conversation she'd had with Han last night. To say that it had left her uneasy was an enormous understatement. But she hated the memories, and she didn't want to think about them, let alone talk about them—not to anyone. Most of all she didn't understand why Han was apparently upset with her, and why he seemed determined to make an issue out of something that happened such a long time ago.

With careful proficiency, she pushed away her difficult thoughts and went downstairs for lunch with the family.

"Where's Han?" Abbi asked as lunch commenced without him. It was evident from Erich's expression that he hadn't seen him either.

"He told me he had something to take care of in town," Maggie said. "But I thought he'd be back by now." She turned to her father. "Have you seen him?"

"No," he replied in a tone that made it evident he wasn't happy about Han's absence from work that morning with no apparent explanation.

A few minutes later, Han erupted into the dining room. Maggie knew immediately he wasn't in a good mood, but she wasn't prepared for the way he strode toward her father and slapped down a thick envelope on the table.

"What is this?" Cameron asked without picking it up.

"It's the money you gave me before I left Horstberg—in full."

Cameron looked baffled as much as concerned. "Han, that money was to take care of Maggie while—"

"Maggie is my wife," he interrupted. "From the moment we rode out that castle gate, I considered her *my* responsibility. It was a loan. I'm paying it back."

Maggie's heart pounded over the sudden awkwardness in the room. She saw her father glance at her mother in a typical way, as if she might give him some insight on how to handle this. She looked as baffled as he.

Maggie felt her palms sweating while she wondered what Han was trying to say.

"Han," Cameron said gently, "it's really not necessary for you to—"

Han kept his eyes focused on the duke while he took in the surprised silence of everyone in the room and hoped he was doing the right thing. But he'd done it now. He couldn't back down. And in his heart he knew this had to be done.

"It *is* necessary!" he said with a tone of controlled anger, knowing the duke would never tolerate any disrespect from *anyone*. Cameron looked so stunned that Han had to remind himself who he was talking to. He glanced quickly around the room, his eyes resting briefly on Erich, then Maggie, then back to Cameron. In a softer tone he added, "And as long as we're all together, this is a good time to tell you something that needs to be said. The deal is off, Your Grace. You'll have to find somebody else to stand by Erich. I can't take the job under these circumstances."

"What on earth are you talking about?" Erich interjected. "What circumstances?"

At Erich's apparent ignorance, Han felt fresh anger rising and knew this was not the time to get into it any further if he hoped to remain in control. "Perhaps we should talk about that later. I don't think I'm in the right frame of mind to—"

"Han," Cameron said, pushing his chair back slightly, "you're suited to the position. You earned it. There is no reason for you to—"

"I don't *want* it!" Han nearly shouted. He reminded himself to keep his anger in check, but he didn't feel hopeful at the moment that he'd be able to do so. "I'll work my fingers to the bone if I have to in order to support my wife and children. Put me back in the stables. I don't care! But I will *not* take a job that's tangled into friendship and marriage. I won't!"

Maggie watched her husband and felt confused—and afraid. She didn't understand what was happening, but she had to do something. "Han!" Maggie stood abruptly, her heart pounding. He turned to look at her, his eyes on fire with something she didn't understand. "You are entitled to that job. You can't possibly go back to the stables after—"

"Why?" he interrupted, taking a step toward her. "I'm good at what I do, Maggie. It was my father's original trade, and he taught me well. Maybe that's where I belong."

"But look at what you're turning down. It's just not right for you to—"

"Right for *whom?*" he retorted. "What's the matter, Maggie? Does it offend your noble senses to bear the name and children of a lowly stablehand?"

Maggie sat down as if she'd been slapped. Hot tears stung her eyes, and her head pounded as she fought to hold them back. She couldn't believe what he was saying any more than what he was doing.

"For whatever reason you married me, Maggie—whether it was for the sake of your honor, or your country, or if I was just the only man available during the crisis—I will not have my life's work caught up in the ring on your finger. I am who I am. No amount of money, or prestige, or power will ever put royal blood in my veins. But you are my wife, and you're going to have to live with that!"

The tears rolling down Maggie's cheeks startled Han to reality. His impassioned speech echoed through his head as he glanced around at the stunned expressions of Cameron, Abbi, and Erich.

Fearing he would either sit down and cry or erupt again with anger, he turned on his heel and left the room. Once alone in the hall, he leaned against the wall and attempted to catch his breath and calm his anger. He squeezed his eyes shut in self-recrimination for the scene he'd just caused. He'd done what he'd needed to do, but he wished that he'd handled it a little more civilly.

Chapter Thirteen

ABDICATION

Maggie could hardly breathe after Han's exit preceded a minute of complete silence at the dining table. Cameron stood to leave with the money in his hand.

"Cameron," Abbi said, sliding her chair back.

"Believe it or not," he said, "I think I can handle this." He glanced briefly at Erich, then at Maggie, as if he were trying to gauge their reaction to what had just happened. It was one of those rare moments when Maggie knew her father was a sovereign, and she almost felt like a criminal. But she had nothing to say.

Han heard the door open and looked up to see the duke as he stepped into the hallway and the dining room door closed behind him. Han turned to walk away, but he stopped when Cameron said, "Han. I want to see you in my office—right now."

"Is that an order?" he asked, turning back to face him.

"Yes, dammit. It's an order."

Han took a deep breath and followed Cameron into his office. He'd certainly heard the duke curse before, but never had it been directed at him. He doubted this encounter would go well. After the door was closed, Cameron motioned Han to a chair. He tossed the money down on the desk and took his usual seat behind it. Han felt sweat rise over his lip while he waited for the inevitable eruption. He'd just caused an ugly scene, and he'd been less than kind with the duke's daughter. He felt certain he deserved a scolding, and he was determined to take it like a man. He was dealing with a sovereign, the ruler of Horstberg, one of the most powerful men in Bavaria. However, this man was also his father-in-law now. He simply didn't know *which* side of Cameron's persona he might be dealing with at the moment. But when Cameron turned to look at him, apparently searching for the right words, his eyes were concerned, almost sad.

"Han," he said at last with no hint of anger, "did I do the wrong thing?"

Han sighed and looked away, trying to grasp the depth beneath his question.

"Tell me, Han, was it wrong of me to put you in the position you're in now?"

"Forgive me," Han said. "I should not have expressed my anger so . . . inappropriately. What I'm struggling with right now has nothing to do with you."

"It certainly *does* have something to do with me. I'm the man who told you to manipulate my daughter into marrying you, at all costs."

"Well, I did that, didn't I." Han said as if he hated himself for it. Maybe he did.

"Yes, Han, you did it. You did everything I asked you to do. And I was under the impression that Maggie was happy with the way it turned out. But apparently you're not." He glanced toward the money on the desk. "If you're giving me a refund, does that mean you're not pleased with what you've procured?"

"I didn't do it for the money *or* the position."

"I know that."

"Well, your children don't know it!" Han shouted softly.

Cameron leaned back in his chair and sighed. An enlightenment in his expression made it clear the problem had begun to make sense.

"Why did you do it, Han?" he asked gently.

Han admitted readily, "I love Maggie. I've loved her for as long as I can remember. But maybe I was just too big for my breeches. Maybe it was ridiculous for me to ever believe that I could fit into her world."

"Perhaps I'm missing the point, Han, but I was under the impression that you've *always* fit into our world, as you call it. You were raised right alongside my children. I held you in my arms when you were barely a day old. Is this social distinction such an important issue?"

Han looked Cameron in the eye and got to the point, "To Maggie it is."

"We didn't raise her to be that way."

"I know."

"You're suited to the job, Han. The reasons I want you to have it don't have anything to do with your marriage to Maggie."

"I know that, too. But it's not you that I have to work with, Your Grace—not directly. And I cannot be an effective advisor to your son without complete trust and acceptance. If Erich—"

He was interrupted by a knock at the door. "What?" Cameron called, and Erich opened the door.

"Well, speak of the devil," Cameron said. "Come in, by all means. Maybe you can talk some sense into your brother-in-law."

Erich closed the door and leaned against it a moment, seeming apprehensive. Han deliberately avoided looking at him.

"Sit down," Cameron said, and Erich did. "This concerns you more than it does me. Who you have working as your highest advisor should be up to you. Perhaps I was out of line in not consulting with you on this before I offered Han the job. It's up to you." The duke motioned elaborately toward Erich and leaned back in his chair.

"I can't force him to work with me," Erich stated.

"Do you want him to work with you?" Cameron asked as if Han were absent.

"Is that relevant?" Erich asked.

"Oh, come on, Erich," Han said with disgust, unwilling to remain silent. "Why don't you act like a duke? Just cut through the muck and get to the point!"

"And what point is that?" Erich asked tersely.

Han leaned toward him. "You and I have been like this," he crossed his fingers, "since we were babies. There is only one thing that's ever come between us, and that's your sister. When we were teens, I was well aware that you didn't approve of my interest in Maggie. You seemed to think that just because I didn't pour my heart out to you with confessions of my love for her that I surely had dishonorable motives. It was as if seventeen years of friendship wasn't enough for you to give me the benefit of the doubt that I would want what was best for Maggie. Once Maggie slapped me back into place and told me she wanted nothing to do with me, you could be chummy again. And now it's evident that little has changed. As I see it, you can trust me, lean on me, turn to me—except when

Maggie is in the middle. But she's my wife now, and she will always be in the middle. After all we have been through together, what makes you think that I am the kind of man who would marry a woman just so I could get the highest paying job in the country?"

Erich turned away. He said nothing, wouldn't even look at him.

"Well," Han added, "if you can't trust, lean on, and turn to your highest advisor, then how the hell are you going to run a country? Get somebody else, Your Highness. You can find me in the stables." Fearing he would erupt again, Han stood and left the room.

Erich winced when the door closed, even though Han hadn't slammed it. He felt utterly humiliated and wished his father hadn't just witnessed that conversation.

Following a miserable silence, Cameron said to Erich, "Is he right?"

"I don't know." Erich shook his head. "But he's certainly given me something to think about."

"You think good and hard about it, boy. Whether he works directly with you or not, he's family now, and he deserves to know that our acceptance is unconditional. From where I sit, Han has never behaved in a way that would not warrant my greatest trust and respect. If there's something you know that I don't, maybe you'd better let me in on it."

Erich said nothing. What could he possibly say? He pressed a hand over his face as if it could make him think clearly, and he was relieved when his father dismissed him, saying simply, "Make certain you're at that meeting in an hour."

Han went upstairs to change his clothes. He was hoping to avoid Maggie until he cooled down, but she was sitting in the middle of the bed, crying.

"Where have you been?" she asked when he said nothing.

"I had a little meeting with your father." He pulled his most comfortable clothes out of the closet and began to change.

"What did he say?"

"He was wondering if he'd done the right thing . . . concerning you and me."

"And did he?" she asked with a sniffle.

"I don't know, Maggie. You tell me."

She said nothing until he was pulling on his old boots. "Where are you going?" she asked.

"Someplace I can feel completely at home. Should you decide to go riding, my dear, I will be waiting to do your bidding."

"That's not fair, Han," she snapped.

"No," he said with his hand on the doorknob, "it's not fair. There is nothing even remotely fair about conditions of the heart being measured by my occupation."

"I love you, Han," she said firmly.

Han took a deep breath and turned to face her. "Yes, I know you love me, Maggie. But it feels to me like a condescending kind of love. I feel as if I'm being granted some great favor to have earned the love of one so noble. I get the impression that deep inside you're still believing that my love for you was always something *convenient.* You seem to think that right from that first kiss when I was seventeen, I've been somehow using you to worm my way into a world I wasn't allowed to be a part of without having du Woernig blood. So, I'm going to prove the truth to you, Maggie. After you have seen me working in the stables for fifty years and never taking anything from your father that I didn't earn, then—maybe then—you will believe me when I say that I did it all for love. I did it all for you."

Emotion pressed close to the surface, and Han hurried from the room before she could see the tears leak from his eyes. He quickly wiped them away and hurried outside and across the courtyard. The young man on duty in the family stables seemed surprised by Han's offer to help, but he made no protest. While Han was scrubbing down one of the duke's stallions, he began to relax. The familiarity of the work was calming, and he felt better. In spite of the dramatics, there was relief in knowing he'd said what he needed to say. Maggie and her family knew exactly where he stood. He'd vented the feelings that had plagued him. Now he could only hope that the results would be favorable.

Maggie sat on the bed, stunned and afraid, for more than an hour after

Han left. While the life she had shared with Han—right from their childhood—was complicated and full of many different emotions, one fact stood out strongly. She *did* love Han. And she knew he loved her. When it came right down to it, hadn't his speech in the dining room been a declaration of just that? He was refusing the job and the money to make it clear that he loved *her*. Suddenly needing to see him, Maggie jumped from the bed and opened her closet. Pulling out an old skirt and blouse, not unlike those she'd worn in the Black Forest, she hurried to change and brushed out her hair.

Maggie entered the stables to find Han dumping a bucket of water over the back of one of her father's stallions. For a moment, it felt as if they'd gone back in time. How clearly she could remember walking in here as a young woman, wanting only to have him close. The same excitement surged through her. He looked as young and firm as he had at seventeen, though his shoulders had broadened and his maturity was evident. Quietly, she moved toward him while he bent to wash the horse's belly, unaware of her presence. Standing directly behind him, she pressed her hands down over his hips.

Han gasped and straightened himself abruptly. He closed his eyes briefly to absorb the feel of Maggie's hands moving with purpose down his legs and up again.

"What *are* you doing, Your Highness?" he asked.

Maggie leaned her chest against his back and pushed her arms around his waist. "Something I've always wanted to do but never dared."

"Always?" he questioned, wishing he could see her face.

"Even when I hated you, I often walked in here and had an irresistible urge to just touch you in a way no respectable woman ever would."

"So, the truth comes out," he said lightly. "It was merely lust that made you marry me."

"That too," she said, but there was no humor in her voice. "Are you alone here?"

"Anton went to take care of something."

Han turned to look at Maggie and caught his breath. Her appearance took him aback. She had come out here a common woman. He looked into her eyes, questioning her purpose. Tears pooled there immediately, spilling over her face as she said, "I love you, Han." She glanced away briefly and bit her lip. "It's apparent that I have made things difficult for you."

Han looked down and cleared his throat unintentionally loud. "It would seem there is much we both need to adjust to," he said, hoping to avoid any further contention.

"Can we talk . . . later?" she asked.

Han met her eyes and felt warmed by her concern. "Yes," he said, "I would like that."

Maggie eased into his arms, heedless to the water on his clothes. She sighed with relief to feel his embrace tighten around her. As long as he held her this way, she believed everything would be all right. Looking up into his eyes, her relief deepened when he bent to kiss her. He kissed her long and hard, holding her so close she almost felt like a part of him. Then somewhere in the distance she heard an elaborate "Ahem." They both turned to see Erich watching them, his arms folded over his chest, his expression a combination of amusement and disgust.

"What is this?" he asked. "A little serious necking?"

"Oh, no," Han chuckled, turning to look at Maggie. "I have every intention of making mad, passionate love to your sister . . . whether you like it or not."

"Well, for heaven's sake, go someplace besides the stables. Those of us who are not fortunate enough to find a tolerable woman to share life with have no desire to be affronted by those of you who have."

Han chuckled, but Maggie heard a tenseness in it and realized that their bantering was not as light as it seemed. Noting the severity in Erich's expression, she thought it best to give them some time alone. She eased away from Han and said graciously, "I'll talk to you later, my love."

Han nodded and reluctantly let her go. He watched her until she had disappeared, then he turned his attention to Erich. "Did you need something, Your Highness?" he asked. Erich said nothing, and he added, "A horse saddled, perhaps?"

"Don't be ridiculous."

Han turned back to rinsing down the stallion at his side. "It's not ridiculous. It hasn't been so long since I was doing just that. Do you think that marrying your sister should magically change everything?"

"It does make you part of the family. But . . . there's more to it than that . . . obviously."

Han met Erich's eyes briefly. "What's obvious? You tell me. Because apparently I'm missing something."

"What do you mean by that?"

"You've known me all my life, Erich. With what you know about me, do you honestly believe my interest in your sister was for the sake of my personal gain?"

"I admit," Erich said, pushing his hands behind his back, "if I look at everything I know about you, my assumptions concerning Maggie don't fit."

Han took a deep breath and reminded himself to stay calm. His best friend had as much as admitted that he'd always assumed the worst.

"But," Erich went on, "what you said a while ago certainly shut me up. I've been thinking, and . . . and I'm not too proud to admit that I may have been wrong. I don't know, maybe I was jealous somehow . . . that you and Maggie shared something I couldn't be a part of."

"And what did you and Maggie share that *I* couldn't be a part of? Do you think I never felt excluded?"

"I'm certain you did," Erich said. "But you always handled it so graciously that I never even considered that it might have bothered you."

"It *didn't* bother me," Han said, concentrating more on his grooming of the horse, "until Maggie told me she would never marry someone beneath her. And I never felt that social distinction between you and me . . . until it became evident that you disapproved of my romantic interest in your sister. As I see it, there were only two possibilities for that. Either you didn't trust me, or you figured I was beneath her social station. I never had any other indication that you considered my lack of royal blood a problem. So my conclusion is obvious."

Erich looked down and sighed loudly. When he said nothing, Han added, "If I'm wrong, Erich, feel free to straighten me out."

Erich sighed again and said, "I don't know, Han. I honestly can't go back in time and tell you why I behaved the way I did when I was seventeen. But I can tell you how I feel now."

"By all means . . ." Han motioned elaborately with his arm.

"I must admit that I've had my doubts. I couldn't blame you for wanting your father's position, or for wanting to get out of the stables. We both knew all along you had the brains to do it. It's just that . . . I got the impression through the last few years that you didn't like Maggie at all."

"And how was I supposed to behave when she'd turned me out like an old pair of shoes?"

Erich looked away, apparently thoughtful. Han continued his work with the horse, attempting to ignore the tension. He knew they needed to work this through. He only hoped they could come to a favorable resolve.

"Han," Erich finally said, "I want to ask you something. And I want you to look me in the eye when you answer."

Han turned with purpose toward Erich, completely confident. He had nothing to hide.

"Tell me, Han, why you married my sister."

"I married Maggie because I love her. I've always loved her. But I wasn't fool enough to wear my feelings on my sleeve where even *you* could throw pity my way if she'd married some prince or baron. Your father's offer was an answer to my every prayer, and I won't apologize for taking full advantage of it. But if I hadn't believed in my heart that I could make her happy, I would have done my best to keep her from marrying Koenig, and I would have kept her safe, but I would not have even attempted to get her to marry me—under any circumstances. But I knew I could make her happy. My methods were a bit brash at times, I admit, but she wasn't exactly in the frame of mind for civil negotiation."

Erich almost chuckled and glanced down briefly. He looked Han in the eye again and said, "There's something else I need to know. Perhaps it's none of my business, but I must admit it's bothered me."

"All right. Let's get it all in the open and get it over with. If I'm going to be saddling your horse every day, we certainly don't want misunderstandings between us."

Erich ignored the gibe and persisted with his purpose. "When Maggie was fourteen . . . I know you were . . . involved. But did you . . ." He couldn't bring himself to say it.

"Are you trying to ask me if I took your sister to bed?"

"I suppose I am."

"And if I did? Is it forgivable?"

"Just answer the question."

"I assume you want me to be honest."

"Get on with it, Han," he said with the imposing quality of ducal authority he'd learned from his father.

"All right. We did a lot of kissing, Erich. And I certainly enjoyed being close to her. But I never once—let me repeat that—not once, did I ever do anything with her that was inappropriate."

"And that's it," Erich said to reassure himself.

Han put his hands on his hips. "Let me put this plainly, since it's obviously concerned you a great deal. I could have had her, Erich. She practically begged me to make love to her. She was a passionate young woman, acting purely on instinct. But she was fourteen years old. She was the duke's daughter, and my best friend's sister. And I loved her enough to know that crossing that line would only bring pain into her life. I knew it wouldn't be right. It was as simple as that. I was alone with Maggie for many weeks after we left here last spring, but I swear to you Erich, our relationship was not consummated until she was my wife."

"You didn't have to tell me that, you know. You could have told me it was none of my business."

"Yes, I could have."

"But I appreciate knowing."

"I'll tell you anything you want to know, Erich, if it will strengthen the trust between us. I have nothing to hide. Maybe I should have made a point of telling you years ago. In truth, I would be disappointed if you didn't care about Maggie enough to let her virtue and happiness come between us. If I *had* wronged her, I would expect you to beat the hell out of me. Maybe you should have anyway."

Erich chuckled and shook his head. Then his eyes filled with severity. "You must forgive me, Han, for my poor judgment. I pray that I can learn enough from this to become a better man—and a better ruler." He cleared his throat and took a deep breath. "And I'm asking you to work with me . . . as a friend, as my brother, and because you have what it takes to do the job well."

Han absorbed Erich's declaration for a lengthy moment. "Don't patronize me, Erich," he said, not wanting even a tiny degree of doubt in taking this step. "We're talking about running a country. You know more than anyone the seriousness of what that means."

Erich lifted his chin slightly, and his innate regal quality came through. "That's why I want *you*. I was wrong, Han. I admit it. Do you want me to beg?"

"Maybe," Han chuckled and reached a hand out toward Erich. Erich hesitated only a moment before he took it firmly. "It would be an honor to work with you, Your Highness," he said with genuine respect. "I pray that I will have the courage and intellect to serve you well."

"Your willingness and integrity are all I will ever need," Erich said.

Long after Erich walked away, Han just stood there. It would seem he'd done the right thing, but he'd not expected results so quickly. Looking forward to talking with Maggie, he hurried to finish the chore he'd started. Young Anton returned and thanked Han for his help. Han was leading the now-clean stallion to its stall when he heard the boy say, "Good day, Your Grace. Would you be wanting a mount?"

"No thank you, Anton," Abbi du Woernig said kindly.

Han turned to look at her as he closed the stall and latched it. Their eyes met, and it was evident she'd come to see him.

"Hello, Han," she said.

"Your Grace." He nodded and walked toward her. "What might I do for you?"

"If you're finished here, I was hoping you might join me for coffee."

"I'm a bit wet," he admitted, glancing down at his shirt.

"A little water never hurt anything," she said, putting her hand over his arm.

They walked slowly across the courtyard and to one of many drawing rooms in the castle, as if she had all the time in the world. She talked of the weather and reminisced about her children when they were young. They sat across from each other while she briefly recounted the story of her meeting Cameron du Woernig and becoming his wife. A maid brought a tray in and Han watched as the duchess poured out the coffee and passed him a cup. Her natural grace, her movements and mannerisms, reminded him so much of

Maggie. And yet Maggie was so different from her mother. They finished their coffee and set the cups aside before the duchess stated her purpose for this visit.

"I just wanted to thank you, Han."

"For what?"

She smiled serenely. "Once Cameron told me that he'd put Maggie in your care, I knew everything would be all right. I missed her, and I admit that I worried about the both of you, knowing Mr. Koenig was on the loose. It was difficult. But I knew that you would do everything in your power to see that she was safe. I knew she was in good hands. With you at her side, her life is in good hands. That's all I wanted to tell you."

When she said nothing more, Han knew he had to ask, "You didn't want to talk about my little outburst earlier?"

"No," she said. "Did you?"

Han chuckled. "You are an amazing woman, Your Grace. Your son-in-law burst into the dining room, caused a scene, yelled at your daughter and made her cry, and you have nothing to say?"

She smiled again. "Apparently you'd like me to say something."

"I just assumed that's why you wanted to talk to me."

"I've been wanting to talk to you since you returned. I felt now might be a good time. Under the circumstances, it seemed that you could use some friendly company." Han smiled at her perception, and she went on. "As for what happened earlier, I admire your courage, Han."

Han sat up a little straighter. This was certainly not what he'd expected.

"It takes courage to confront misunderstanding and hard feel-ings, especially with people you care for and respect. There are some things that Maggie needs to face up to, but I suspect those things are painful for her. In my experience, most people don't face up to their pain unless someone cares enough to force them to. Maggie's very lucky to have a man who loves her enough to have the courage to confront her behavior when it becomes difficult. And as for Erich." She chuckled softly. "Well, he's got a little of that du Woernig arro-gance. As long as it's honed properly, it makes for a good ruler. That's part of the highest advisor's job, you know, to keep that arrogance and power from getting out of hand."

"Is it?" He grinned.

"You would be good at it, should you change your mind."

"Oh, Erich's already begged me to come back. He apologized, and he wasn't even arrogant."

Abbi smiled. "Well, good for him. He came around faster than I thought he would. Your friendship means a great deal to him."

"Do you think so?"

"Oh, yes. He nearly went mad while you were gone. A day didn't pass when he didn't talk about you, and Maggie, too, of course. I believe he's nearly as glad as I am that she'll not have to move away as Sonia did."

"Well," Han chuckled, albeit tensely, "I'm glad about that myself." Han felt suddenly sad that Sonia wasn't around as she always had been.

"You love Maggie very much," the duchess said.

"Yes," Han looked her in the eye, amazed at her perception, "I do. I always have, I believe."

"It must have been very difficult for you when she severed your relationship. You were, what . . . seventeen at the time?"

"We were both . . . far too young. I believe now it would have been better to keep my feelings to myself until she'd had a fair chance to grow up a little more."

"Perhaps, but . . . I never worried about how you would treat her. And that's not what we were talking about."

Han felt a little uneasy at her insight. But he simply responded to her previous comment. "Yes, it was difficult."

"And yet you continued to look out for Maggie." Abbi smiled serenely. "Even as children, I recall your being drawn to her, always protective of her."

Han shifted slightly in his seat, wondering what she was getting at. But her next statement took him completely off guard. "It was you who informed me that the nanny was drinking on the sly . . . and that she didn't treat Maggie very well."

"I'd forgotten about that," Han said.

"So had I." Abbi's confident demeanor faltered slightly. She glanced down at her hands and smoothed the wrinkles from her skirt. "Sonia brought it up around the time all of this drama was getting stirred up with Maggie in the spring. She said that Helga had treated Maggie differently, perhaps because she was more of a stubborn, strong-willed child. And she wondered if the way Helga had treated Maggie might have had some influence on Maggie's personal struggles."

Han leaned forward, setting his forearms on his thighs as he began to perceive what she was getting at. The memories became more clear as he thought it through, but he hardly knew what to say. He was relieved when Abbi continued.

"Although the changes in Maggie occurred when she was older, I can't help wondering if there isn't a connection. Still, I have difficulty understanding exactly what changed her. She was never the same after that illness."

Han met her eyes, marveling at her wisdom and perception. He wished that he could somehow combine it with everything he knew about Maggie. Then he wondered if that was her purpose. "I have an idea," he admitted, and she seemed relieved.

"I was hoping you might. My concern is for Maggie's happiness, Han—and yours as well. If there is something painful bottled up inside of her, I believe it will impede her life as long as it remains. Perhaps if we understand it, we could help her to be free of it."

"I'm just guessing," Han said, "that it had something to do with those awful girls . . . What were their names? Ah yes, Anastasia and Esmerelda."

Abbi's eyes widened. "The baron's daughters?"

Han nodded. "They were here when Maggie rode out into that storm. Earlier that day, Maggie and I had been walking in the garden in the rain. When we came in, they had just arrived—earlier than expected—and Maggie looked as if her world had ended. When she had recovered from her illness, she told me straight out that—" Han stopped himself as a painful knot erupted into his throat. He stood and walked to the window.

"Are you all right?" Abbi asked.

Han sighed. "It would seem Maggie's not the only one with painful things bottled up inside." While Han wanted to be free of these feelings, he didn't know where to begin.

"What did she say, Han?" Abbi asked gently.

Han cleared his throat and leaned against the window pane. Drawing a deep breath, he said, "She told me that she would never marry beneath her."

Abbi's stomach tightened. She gasped before she pressed a hand over her mouth to hold back the emotion spurred by this revelation. While it was difficult to acknowledge that her own daughter would harbor such a hurtful attitude, she couldn't deny that it helped many other things make sense. She cared for Han like her own son; she always had. To know that Maggie had hurt him this way was difficult. The past couldn't be changed, but it could usually help the present be understood more fully.

"I can't comprehend how that must have hurt you," Abbi said with compassion.

Han chuckled as if he could force the pain to go away, but his voice was shaky when he admitted, "I always wondered why she couldn't just treat me with the same respect you gave my parents—whether she wanted to marry me or not."

"Have you ever told Maggie how you feel about this?" she asked.

He chuckled again while the tension inside him increased. He told himself it shouldn't have surprised him that Abbi du Woernig would be so easy to talk to, but he had difficulty comprehending that she was his mother-in-law; though in a way, she had always been like a second mother to him. "I don't know what I've told her, to be quite honest. The last several months feel like a tornado when I try to piece everything together in my mind. I know I should be grateful for the progress we've made. We're married. She's admitted that she loves me, and I believe she means it. But there's something so condescending about it that—"

Han stopped when the doorknob turned and the door came open. His heart quickened when Maggie peered inside, her eyes going to her mother.

"Oh, there you are," she said, closing the door behind her. "I was wondering if we could talk."

By the way she moved toward her mother, Han knew she was unaware of his presence in the room.

"You would be welcome to join us," Abbi said, motioning toward Han.

Maggie stopped and turned to look at him, startled. "Oh, I'm sorry," she said, a little unsettled to imagine what they might have been talking about, especially considering everything else that had happened today. "I thought you were alone. If I'm interrupting, then—"

"You're not interrupting," Han insisted.

Abbi spoke cheerily. "We were just talking about that horrible nanny we had when you children were younger; I believe her name was Helga."

Han saw a visible tension overtake Maggie's countenance. She sat down near her mother and said nothing while Han and Abbi talked about Helga for several minutes. Han was amazed at the casual way Abbi influenced the conversation to a point where Maggie began to express her hatred for Helga. As Maggie gained momentum, it seemed easier for her to talk about her difficult memories of the woman. Han had no doubt that Abbi was as astonished as he was by the expression on Maggie's face when she tearfully admitted to Helga's attempts at manipulating her behavior in order to give the nanny peace and quiet. Helga had repeatedly told Maggie that if she were really a princess, she wouldn't be so fidgety and prone to physical activities; she would instead prefer to sit still and mind her manners. She'd been told that any child with royal blood would never be so high-strung and willful.

"What on earth was she implying?" Han asked angrily.

Maggie realized all she'd just admitted to and glanced warily toward her mother before she chose to concentrate on the pattern in the carpet. "She said more than once that Erich and Sonia looked so much like my father, but that I . . ." She couldn't finish the sentence due to a large inexplicable knot blocking her voice.

"Was she implying that you were not Cameron du Woernig's child?" Abbi demanded, and Maggie nodded.

Abbie was so quickly overtaken by fury that she had to clench her fists *and* her teeth to keep from exploding. Taking a long moment to put all of this into perspective and take in deep, calming breaths, Abbi at least felt relief that the nanny had long ago left Horstberg, or she'd be tempted to hunt the woman down and punish her for this. She couldn't even comprehend the emotional impact this had had on Maggie, and yet so many things that had been confusing to Abbi over her daughter's behavior made so much more sense given this new revelation.

"Maggie," Abbi said, her voice trembling with anger, "I can assure you that I was never unfaithful to—"

"I know that!" Maggie insisted. "I *never* wondered about that! It's just that . . . I always wondered what was wrong with *me*. I wondered why I couldn't . . ." She became lost in tears again, and Abbi put a comforting arm around her.

Han blinked back his own tears and pushed a hand through his hair, grateful beyond words for Abbi du Woernig's presence. When Maggie calmed down again, her mother gracefully led the conversation to the incident with the baron's daughters. He was grateful that Maggie seemed to forget he was there as she spilled her heart concerning the way their tormenting had pressed sore points created by Helga. Something had shut down inside her at that time as she'd tried to convince herself that it was necessary to prove that she was a princess at all costs.

"I know I hurt Han very badly," she admitted. "But I didn't know how to fit my feelings for him in with everything else. I only knew I was hurting, and I couldn't fix it."

Again, she fell apart in tears, and Han discreetly left the room, fearing he would do the same. Abbi obviously had everything under control, and it was a mother's love and understanding that Maggie needed now. He went up to the room he now shared with Maggie, needing to be alone. Knowing his wife would look for him there if she needed him, he tried without much success not to think about how the conversation downstairs might be going. It was well over an hour before she arrived, and he turned from the window when she came in and closed the door. Her eyes were red and swollen; she'd obviously done a lot more crying after he'd left.

When she didn't seem prone to speak, he asked lightly, "Did I miss anything?"

Maggie twisted the handkerchief in her hands. "My mother told me that I should always trust my instincts and listen to what my feelings are telling me, in spite of what others might say or do." Han completely agreed but made no response, wanting her to go on. "I can see now that rather than trusting my feelings, I was ignoring them. That's why I couldn't see what Nik Koenig was really after, and . . . that's why I was such a fool to not . . ." She faltered with emotion, but Han held out a hand toward her, and she rushed into his arms.

"Oh, Han," she cried, "you must forgive me for being so cruel to you. I was so insensitive . . . so shallow. I know you loved me right from the start. And I think that deep in my heart I always loved you. I just . . ."

"It's all right," he whispered. "I understand, Maggie. I really do. It's all in the past now. Oh," he held her tighter, "I love you, Maggie."

Maggie drew back to look at him as a thousand questions from the last several months came together, needing one firm, final answer. The sincerity in his eyes was evident. But she could see now that it had always been there. She just hadn't known what she was looking at. Her strongest and deepest instincts bathed her with peace as he bent to kiss her. She was indescribably grateful for his love, for his patience on her behalf, and for his courage in not allowing her to become caught in Nik Koenig's trap. As his kiss gained fervor, she wondered if any woman had ever been so happy as she was in that moment.

When their kiss ended, Han erupted with laughter and lifted her off the floor, turning with her in his arms. Maggie laughed and leaned against him to gain her balance when he set her feet back down.

"I have something for you," he said, digging into his pocket. He held a closed fist in front of her. "When I was seventeen, I saw something just like this in town, and I wanted more than anything to buy it for you, but I couldn't afford it. I know it doesn't compare to all the jewels that a princess owns, but . . . it comes from the heart."

Fresh tears welled up in Maggie's eyes as he took her right hand into his and she felt a ring slip onto her finger.

"What's behind us doesn't matter anymore, Maggie."

She glanced down and blinked the mist from her eyes, attempting to focus enough to see what he'd given her. The jade stone in the center was flanked by two small diamonds that sparkled in the gold band.

"Oh, Han," she said, "it's the most beautiful thing I've ever owned." She pushed her arms around him. "I'll treasure it always." She kissed him and added, "I love you, Han Heinrich."

Han laughed again then reluctantly reminded her that it was time they went downstairs for supper. They walked hand in hand to the dining room and paused outside the door, where Han kissed her, believing they were alone. When he drew back from the kiss, Cameron and Abbi were standing nearby, and he resisted the urge to tell them they shouldn't be so sneaky. Han chuckled when he saw Maggie blush with embarrassment.

"Everything's all right, I assume," Cameron said, opening the door to the dining room.

"Everything is perfect," Maggie said, going in first. Cameron lifted an eyebrow toward Han. He smiled and shrugged. Abbi winked at him as she passed by, and the men followed her into the room. Erich was already seated, looking at a newspaper.

"It's about time," he said, setting it aside.

"What?" Cameron asked. "You're not eating out tonight?"

"I turned down three invitations," Erich said. "I've had enough of romance . . . if that's what you call it."

"You could take a lesson from Han," Maggie said, showing him her new ring as she was seated with Han's assistance. "Look what he gave me."

"Ooh," Erich looked at it closely then smirked toward Han, "jade and diamonds. Expensive, eh?"

Han just shrugged again, grateful to feel no tension between them, whatsoever.

"When did you get paid?" Erich asked. "You still owe me a couple of drinks from last February, I believe."

"I didn't pay him anything yet," Cameron stated, and it occurred to Maggie that Han had produced evidence of an immense amount of money just today. He'd paid her father back in full, and he'd given her an expensive gift. She sensed a certain purpose in her father's demeanor just before he added, "Han doesn't need *my* money."

Han saw the duke look him straight in the eye, as if seeking his approval before he said anything more. Han just smiled and nodded subtly. Now that he knew where he stood with Erich and Maggie, he had no problem with having the secret out.

Maggie looked pointedly at Han, silently demanding to know what secret he might be sharing with her father. Again, he only shrugged. "You're not saying much," she said directly to Han.

"I said more than enough earlier." He smiled and took a long swallow of his wine.

Maggie turned to her father, as if to get an answer.

Cameron smiled playfully. "I hear a rumor that Han received an inheritance. He's rather well off, actually."

"You are?" Maggie asked her husband.

"I guess the secret's out," Han said with exaggerated dismay. He smiled and added sweetly, "I didn't want you to marry me for my money."

Chapter Fourteen

THE VALET

Once the dust of the initial drama had settled, Han found it easy for his life to fall into place with Maggie at Castle Horstberg. He liked his position already, and he enjoyed the time he spent with Erich—who usually worked closely with Cameron and Georg—learning the tricks of the trade. Ruling a duchy was a complicated business, but Cameron du Woernig was a good duke. Han respected the way he worked side by side with Erich, rather than expecting him to just take over when Cameron could no longer hold the position.

Maggie spent a great deal of time with her mother, who was ecstatic to have her daughter back. Abbi declared often how she'd nearly gone crazy with both Maggie and Sonia gone, and she was grateful to have at least one of her daughters remaining at the castle forever. Maggie also spent a lot of time with Han's mother, and the more she got to know Elsa, the more she loved her. Abbi and Elsa had always been close, and Maggie enjoyed being with the two of them as they speculated on the grandchildren they would share.

Maggie quickly loved her new life in the home she'd always known. Everything that had always been good became better, and many things that had felt challenging in the past took on a new perspective. She even came to enjoy the time she spent doing needlework, chatting with her mother and the other ladies that joined them. She grew to admire Nadine Dukerk in ways she'd never paid attention to before. And Dulsie, for all that she was very quiet and much different from Maggie, had admirable character traits Maggie had never bothered to take notice of. While Maggie spent very little time actually putting any stitches into the piece she'd been slowly working on, she did enjoy the conversations that took place and found she looked forward to them, as opposed to finding them dreadfully boring.

Han and Maggie were up late one night, discussing these very things, when she impulsively said, "Let's go riding, Han."

"But it's past midnight."

"That's exactly why I want to go."

"Ah, yes, I'd almost forgotten how much you like that. Well then, let's go."

The night was cold and their ride brief but nonetheless exhilarating. They returned full of laughter, like a couple of children, and fell asleep tangled together with an assurance that life was good, and they were grateful for the circumstances that had brought them to this day.

Han awoke late and nearly panicked. Not only had he missed breakfast, but he knew he should have been in the duke's office long before now.

"Ah, Han." The duke grinned when Han entered the room. "Did you have a long night?"

"You might say that," Han replied. "Where is everybody?" he asked, noting they were alone.

"Your father and Erich have gone to see my solicitors about a trivial matter."

"I'm sorry I was late. I—"

"It's no problem, Han. Your job has certain flexibility. I would have sent for you if there had been something urgent. Actually, I've been wanting to talk to you alone for quite some time."

"Anything in particular?"

"Nothing terribly important; more a formality, really." He opened a desk drawer and took out a ring of very old-looking keys. He closed the drawer and dangled the key ring on his finger. The keys of different sizes clanked together as they settled, and Cameron appeared briefly fascinated with them. "Abbi thinks they're *rather pretty;* that's what she said. The craftsmanship of each key is unique, and there is a certain artistic quality to them, I suppose. They were made to *look* special, as well as to open doors—which of course is what keys are for." He moved the keys into the palm of his hands and added, "There are a very limited number of this exact set of keys; only certain people would be allowed to have them in their possession. They are safeguarded carefully, and are due a certain . . . respect."

Han sensed where this might be headed, and his heart quickened slightly, but he just listened as the duke went on, not wanting to jump to any conclusions. "The keys fit certain locks here within Castle Horstberg, but not one of the doors these keys will open is ever locked. There are officers of the Guard posted at each of these doors every minute of every day . . . therefore, no key is necessary to keep what's behind those doors safe."

"Trusted men do that job instead," Han commented.

"Precisely. Therefore, the keys are more of a formality. It's an honor to have this particular set of keys in your possession, and no one but the Duke of Horstberg—which is currently me," he added with a smile, as if Han might not know, "has the right to determine *who* will have possession of them." He held the keys out toward Han. "This set is for you. Keep them safe, even though they are only a matter of formality."

"Me?" Han said, a bit breathless. "Truly?" He chuckled in disbelief and took the keys when the duke pushed them further toward Han. "I'm the stableboy, Your Grace."

"*You,*" Cameron said, "are a member of the royal family, and you are working to help run this country. You will be both for as long as you live, and neither is any small thing, not in Horstberg, and not to me."

Han took a deep breath and fingered the different size keys that each had their own unique design. "What doors *do* they open? Just curious."

"The main front door of the castle adjacent to the courtyard, which we go in and out of all the time."

"Which is always guarded and never locked."

"Correct. Also, there is a key to the armory and a key to this office."

"And the other? There are four; you only mentioned three."

Cameron chuckled. "I have no idea. Your father has a set of those keys; so does Erich. None of us have ever figured out what it goes to—not that it really matters, and not that any of us has put much effort into figuring it out. I don't know if my father told me and I forgot, or if he didn't know, either."

"Strange," Han said with a chuckle. "And may I ask who previously owned this set?"

"You may, but don't take it personally."

"What?" Han countered, not liking the way that sounded.

"The previous owner of the keys has nothing personally to do with *you*. It's simply a matter of . . . well . . . this set became available when he died."

Han didn't even have to ask. "Your brother."

"That's right. And in my opinion, you deserve them more than he ever did. Put them in a safe place."

"I will," Han said. "Thank you." For now he tucked them into a deep inner pocket of his jacket where he knew they would be safe until he could put them away in his room later.

"Since it's just the two of us," Cameron said, "I would like to tell you again how grateful I am for what you have done for Maggie. She's like a different person—and I can see that she is very happy."

"It was actually my pleasure." He chuckled. "Well . . . now that it's all behind us, *most* of it was a pleasure. I love Maggie very much."

"I can see that. I'm sorry for the trouble you had to go through, but I am glad things worked out well."

"So am I. It was well worth it."

"You know," the duke chuckled nostalgically, "when you were telling us about your time in the cottage, I couldn't help being reminded of the time when Abbi and I were . . ." he paused and smiled.

"What?"

"Oh, it's not important; just reminiscing a bit. I'm sure you wouldn't be interested."

"On the contrary," he urged.

"It's just that, well . . . I fell in love with Maggie's mother while we were in a situation very much like that."

Han was hoping to hear more, but a manservant entered the office.

"What is it, Franz?" Cameron asked.

"A letter for you, Your Grace, from Italy."

"Italy?"

Cameron met Han's eyes before he took the paper and Franz

left the room. "I don't know anybody in Italy," Cameron said, "but I know you do."

Cameron broke the seal and put on his glasses while Han waited what seemed a terribly long time for the duke to read. Impatiently, Han asked, "Does it concern what I think it does?"

"Most likely." He cleared his throat then began to read aloud. The letter was from the same officer of the law who had questioned Han and Maggie after Nik had been arrested; he had also written the previous letter that had stated the circumstances in detail. This letter reported that Nik Koenig had been imprisoned there since that time, and it ended saying that Mr. Koenig and his companions had served their time and had now been released. The officer wanted to let the authorities of Horstberg know the situation so they could do what they felt was best.

"What will we do?" Han asked when Cameron threw the letter angrily onto his desktop.

"There's not really anything we *can* do. He hasn't done anything to justify having him arrested here in Horstberg. The consequences for his crimes in Italy have been met. All we can do is remain alert and hope he doesn't stir up any trouble." Cameron sighed then added tersely, "But I know he will. I know just as well as I know I'm sitting here. It's only a matter of time."

"We can handle him," Han said easily, even though his memories of what Nik Koenig had done to him and Maggie in Italy were difficult. But being here in this great fortress, surrounded by loved ones, with a military force on their side, he felt much more secure. "If you and my father outdid his father, surely the four of us can handle *him*."

Cameron smiled. "I hope you're right. At least you and Maggie are here with us now. I am glad for that."

"So am I . . . Father."

"Come along, Han," Cameron said as he stood. "We're supposed to meet Erich and your father at the Red Lion for a drink, and on the way, we'll discuss one of our best mutual interests."

"What's that?"

"That woman we both love." The duke smiled, and they walked out to the stables.

As Han rode by Cameron's side, descending the hill that supported the castle, he couldn't help feeling a sense of pride. He knew his father often rode with the duke when he left the castle, but Han had never personally been present. It came as a surprise when they approached the center of town and became surrounded by people. There was a certain awe and respect for the duke, and the people all seemed to want to get near him. Cameron was apparently quite accustomed to it. He shook hands and spoke lightly with people as he rode slowly through the streets, and it was obvious he had a comfortable rapport among the citizens of Horstberg.

The people treated Han with a respectful deference, and he did his best to follow the duke's example, nodding and smiling and offering kind greetings. He was vaguely aware of whispers and speculations, as if they weren't certain who he might be. But it seemed that if he was with the duke, he deserved respect.

When they arrived at the Red Lion and went inside, it was immediately evident that the duke came here regularly.

"Good day, Your Grace." A portly man wearing an apron addressed him as they were escorted to a table in the corner. "And how are you today?"

"Very good, Max," Cameron replied. "And you?"

"Fine as ever. Can I get the usual for you?"

"Yes, please," the duke said, and it was evident that Max owned the place but didn't interact a great deal with customers. Cameron du Woernig coming through the door had brought him out from behind the bar.

"And who is this fine young man, Your Grace?" Max turned toward Han as he was seated.

"Ah," Cameron smiled, "this is my son-in-law; Georg's son, Han."

"Ah. It's no wonder he looks so familiar. Then this must be the one who eloped with the fair princess."

Han felt embarrassed, but Cameron chuckled. "This is the one."

"Well, it's good to have you, my boy. What can I get for you?"

"Whatever His Grace is having," Han replied.

"Very good choice." Max bustled off and quickly returned with two tankards of his own special beer.

"Do you have the time, Han?" Cameron asked.

"Yes," he pulled the watch from his pocket, "it's nearly noon."

"We're a bit early. I'm sure they'll be here soon."

"I've missed this place," Han said. "I used to come here quite a lot."

"Really?"

"In the evenings, mostly. Sometimes earlier."

"Your father and I have been coming here ever since we were . . . well, probably younger than you are now."

Han thought of how he rarely came here without Erich.

"Hello, Your Grace," a mellow voice said lightly. In the split second before they both looked up, a deep annoyance came into the duke's eyes. "How fortunate to run into you like this," Nik Koenig said with his hands placidly on his hips.

"Fortunate for whom?" Cameron replied dryly.

"Oh, come now," Nik said, "surely you've been expecting me."

"I did get word you were coming. I'd hoped it would be longer, but apparently the post is traveling more slowly than you these days."

Nik nodded at Cameron before he turned and acknowledged Han with a self-satisfied smirk. "Mr. Heinrich. You're looking a bit better than the last time we met."

"I feel much better too, thank you," Han replied lightly. "But I do recall that you met your match that day."

"Indeed." Nik seemed perturbed.

"Oh, don't feel too badly about it," Han said. "After all, such a burly aggressor could hardly be too humiliating."

Nik's dismay increased, and Cameron glanced at Han in question. "Her name was Josette," Han provided, and Cameron smirked.

"Well," Nik persisted, "the important thing is that I'm here now. And I'm certain I was missed." He smiled devilishly toward Cameron.

"Quite."

"I was sorry to hear about your daughter's marriage." Nik glared at Han. "But then, such is life. The fair princess will never know the broken heart she has left behind."

Han sighed and rolled his eyes. "Yes, I can just see your heart breaking right now."

"What really breaks my heart," Nik said, "is to think of all that room . . . that huge castle. And your favorite nephew is—"

"You've not met my sister's son," Cameron said coolly.

"Nevertheless," Nik smiled, "here am I, living in such a lowly manner, and—"

"If you're trying to get pity, it won't work. And if you're trying to get an invitation to move in, you won't get it. That's something that won't happen as long as I'm alive."

"I'll bear that in mind," Nik muttered.

"I'm certain you didn't come here to discuss domestic arrangements."

"Actually, no. I am in need of my allowance, as you call it . . . Uncle Cameron," he finished with a smirk.

"It is *Your Grace* to you, boy. And I will have your allowance sent by courier as soon as I get back. You may leave now."

"So His Royal Highness has dismissed me."

"Very perceptive," Cameron said. "And if you want that allowance to keep coming, you'll find a way to keep yourself scarce."

Nik laughed, bowing elaborately. "It was a pleasure." He then left the pub.

Cameron cursed under his breath, and Han said, "Do you really think he is capable of any harm, or has he just got a big mouth?"

"I don't know, Han," he said soberly. "I used to think my brother just had a big mouth. But he managed to kill my wife, frame me for the crime, and take over my duchy—all in one day. I don't know what Nik Koenig is capable of, but we have evidence enough that he's cruel and manipulative. I'm taking him on his father's merits, and we will not get too comfortable as long as he's around."

Han appreciated the duke's common sense and felt good about his precautions.

"You must tell me more about this Josette," Cameron said, and Han grinned.

Georg and Erich came into the pub then, ordered the usual, and sat down at their table. "So," the duke said to Georg, "what's the report?"

"Everything looks fine."

"And what about you, Erich? Do you understand it?"

"I'm getting there."

"Well," Cameron went on, "you were both fortunate enough to miss a quaint little meeting with Mr. Koenig."

"Oh, terrific," Erich said sarcastically. "So the beast is back, eh?"

"And as amiable as ever," Han added.

"A toast," Cameron said, lifting his tankard high, and the others did the same, "to Mr. Nik Koenig. May he never cross our paths again."

"Hear, hear," Han said, and they all drank.

The men returned to the office to see to their business, but they'd barely begun when a knock came at the door.

"Come in," Cameron called. Heidi entered and curtsied.

"Excuse me, Your Grace," she said, "but the duchess requested that I summon young Mr. Heinrich upstairs, and that I inform you the princess is ill."

"What's the matter?" Han asked, bolting from his seat.

"The doctor's with her now, sir," Heidi said toward him. "I could tell you no more, sir." She turned her attention back to the duke, who was making no effort to hide his concern. "Her Grace said that she will call for you when the doctor has left."

Cameron nodded, and Han followed the maid into the hall.

"Where is she?" he demanded.

"In your chambers, sir," she said, and he ran past her.

Han was stopped in the doorway of his room by Abbi as she ushered him back into the hall. "The doctor's with her. You can see her in a few minutes."

"What happened?" he insisted. "Is the baby—"

"I don't know about the baby, Han," she said straightly, and he could see worry in her eyes, "but Maggie will be fine."

"What happened?" Han repeated.

Abbi bowed her head and swallowed hard. She looked up to meet his gaze. "She started having some pains late this morning and some minimal spotting of blood. I don't know what—"

She was interrupted as the door opened and doctor came into the hallway, closing the door behind him.

"Is she all right?" Han asked.

"It appears that everything is fine," he stated. "The bleeding has stopped completely, and I believe if she stays flat in bed a few days, the problem will solve itself. Beyond that, as long as she has no further symptoms like those experienced today, she should be able to continue normally, and the baby should be fine. You should plan on having extra help for her until the baby comes. She must not lift anything or do any riding at all."

"But you say the baby will be all right?" Han asked.

"As far as I can see now, yes. I will keep a close eye on her, and we'll do everything possible to make certain that it is."

"Can I see her now?" Han asked.

"Yes, go on in. Oh," he added, and Han paused, "there is one more thing. It's not necessarily always the case, but I want to be honest with you right off. In some cases, when a woman loses more than one child, it diminishes her chances for having more. She must be very careful."

Han nodded barely enough to indicate he'd understood, then he went into the bedroom to see Maggie. He found her sitting up in bed looking far more perky than he'd expected. She smiled when she saw him, and he sat on the edge of the bed to embrace her.

"You talked with the doctor?" she said, and he nodded. "I suppose this means no more midnight rides," she said lightly.

"How are you feeling?" he asked, brushing a loose curl off her forehead.

"Fine," she said, but he gave her a dubious stare. "Really," she smiled. "It hurt for a while, but now I feel fine. A little worried perhaps," she admitted.

"You do what the doctor tells you, now," Han admonished.

"I will," she promised, and a grin filled her face, "and we'll have four children."

"How about three?" he said, wondering how many times they could suffer through this.

"How about five?" she added, and they both laughed.

"One at a time," Han said. "Let's get married first."

"We are."

"I mean this other wedding we're supposed to have. Do you think you're up to it?"

"The doctor said that as long as I have no more problems before then, I should be fine."

"Good." Han managed a smile before he put his face on Maggie's shoulder. "I love you, Maggie," he whispered and squeezed her hand tightly. "I was really scared; I can't deny it."

"I love you too, Han," she answered, "and everything will be fine."

Within a few days, Maggie was up and around as if nothing had happened. She continued to be careful, as the doctor had admonished, but Han couldn't help feeling concerned. If nothing else, he was grateful to have both their mothers looking out for her while he was kept busy with his work. And in spite of his worries, a day didn't pass without evidence that his every dream had come true.

Erich walked in for breakfast late, obviously not in a good mood.

"Is something wrong?" his mother asked as he was seated.

"My valet quit," he muttered. "Left town, just like that!" He snapped his fingers and began to eat. "It's the third one in six months. I'm beginning to think something's wrong with me." He took another bite, then looked at Han. "Am I so difficult to work with?"

Han shrugged. "I like you, but then . . . we're related."

Maggie smiled toward Han and said to Erich, "Perhaps you should consider the frequency of your bathing. Or maybe you should use mouthwash more often, or—"

"You're a shrew!" Erich laughed and threw his napkin across the table at her. "How do you put up with that?" he asked Han.

Han grinned and lifted his brows comically. "Being Maggie's husband does have its . . . benefits."

"I don't want to hear about it," Erich said with exaggerated disgust.

Cameron and Abbi exchanged a discreet smile as they observed their children.

"I'd like to know what I'm supposed to do without a valet," Erich grumbled. "Tomorrow's one of those court-then meetings-then-banquet-then meetings-then social days."

"Perhaps we could find some pretty little maid to fill in for him and—"

"Cameron!" Abbi scolded, but she couldn't hold back a smile.

"I have one suggestion," Han said.

"And what's that?"

"Pray," he stated severely, and Erich scowled.

Later that morning, Han accompanied Erich to the tailor's for a fitting, since the prince would be traveling with his father on a diplomatic visit the following week while Han and Georg stayed behind.

"I don't understand why I need new clothes for these dreadful things," Erich said as they walked from where their horses were tethered.

"Face it," Han said, "you love this. You're a fashion connoisseur, just like your sister."

"And you should be grateful I am," Erich quipped. "If I didn't tell *you* how to dress, you'd end up awfully embarrassed at those dreadful socials."

"So I would," Han admitted.

"It's not the new clothes I mind. It's these dreadful fittings."

"Stop grumbling and smile like a prince," Han said quietly as they entered the shop and the tailor, Mr. Keimer, approached.

"Good day, Your Highness . . . Mr. Heinrich." Mr. Keimer nodded graciously. "I'll be ready for you in just a moment."

Erich sighed and decided he truly hated this kind of thing, even more than he'd let on. He didn't mind the prospect of running the country when his father needed him to take over. It was all this flash and fancy he could do without. It was all so tedious!

The fitting commenced as usual. Erich stood motionless as fabric was tucked and pinned over his shoulders and torso, while Han leaned back in a chair and made bad jokes. They had the tailor laughing more than once, along with a young man who had come in and was waiting to be helped, sitting unobtrusively across the room from Han.

They were nearly finished with the last piece, a tapestried waistcoat, when a commotion could be heard from behind the shop, where Mr. Keimer lived with his family. Mr. Keimer looked nervous and agitated but seemed hesitant to leave.

"If you need to see to that . . ." Erich said, "by all means—"

"Thank you, sir. I'll be back shortly."

Erich attempted to relax, but he had pins tucked all over his chest and down his sides. "I feel like some kind of pin cushion," he said.

Han chuckled. "You *look* like a pin cushion, if you ask me."

When Mr. Keimer didn't return after a few minutes, Erich said, "Help me out of this thing, Han."

"What do you want *me* to do with it?" Han retorted. "I can't—"

"Here," the young man who had been patiently waiting crossed the room, saying graciously, "let me help you with that, sir." He deftly helped him out of the waistcoat without disturbing any of the pins, then took Erich's jacket from a hook and helped him into it.

"You look terribly familiar," the man said to Erich. It was something Erich heard often, and he actually enjoyed it when people didn't know who he was, even though his anonymity never lasted long. "I don't suppose we've met somewhere before, or—"

"I suppose it's possible," Erich replied nonchalantly. He figured they were near the same age, though this man was slightly balding and built more stoutly. But he was obviously a common man, and their social circles wouldn't have likely crossed.

"Thank you," Erich said when the man brushed off the shoulders of Erich's jacket. Erich glanced discreetly toward Han, whose expression was a comical exaggeration of being impressed at this man's abilities. Not wanting to leave the shop until they finished up with Mr. Keimer, and also wanting to be gracious, Erich spoke again to the man who had helped him. "Are you waiting to—"

"Oh, I was just going to talk with Mr. Keimer about a job."

Erich lifted a brow. Han's expression was barely concealed amusement.

"Do you have . . . experience with—"

"No, not really. I mean . . . I know absolutely nothing about tailoring, except that I'm not so bad at mending things. My wife always insists I do that sort of thing better than she does. She suggested I try here. She says I have a knack for fashion and I enjoy fussing over details."

"Really," Erich nodded, trying not to grin. "And . . . are you currently . . . unemployed, then?"

"At the moment, yes," the young man said with obvious chagrin. "Actually, my father is a wood craftsman. He's very good, and he's always wanted me to take over the trade, and I've been trying. But it's just not in me. My wife and I are living with him right now, but we have a baby on the way, and I've got to figure out something I can do so we can get a place of our own."

"What do you think, Han?" Erich asked, leaving the young man baffled.

"It's worth a trial, I think."

"What's your name?" Erich asked.

"Theodor Lokberg," he stated. "And you are—"

"I wonder if we might be able to help each other," Erich interrupted, not wanting to complete the introductions just yet. He wanted to bask just a little longer in having his identity unknown. "I am in need of a valet, and I must have him tomorrow . . . early. It will be a very busy day, and I need help. If you could help me out, I'd make it well worth your while, and if tomorrow goes well, maybe I could use you permanently. What do you say?"

Mr. Lokberg chuckled. "I . . . I don't know what to say."

"Well, if you're not interested, just—"

"Oh, no. I am. Thank you. What time do you need me?"

"About six-thirty, I think . . . until evening sometime."

"All right." Mr. Lokberg grinned and shook his hand, behaving as if the Red Sea had just parted before his eyes. "Where do I go?"

"Castle Horstberg," Erich stated and was not disappointed by Mr. Lokberg's obvious surprise. "Just come to the main door and tell them you're my temporary valet. They'll get you to the right place."

"And you are?" Mr. Lokberg leaned forward expectantly, that awed expression on his face growing more obvious

"Erich du Woernig," he stated, and he motioned toward Han while Mr. Lokberg went a little pale. "And this is my brother-in-law, Han Heinrich, who doesn't need a valet because he has a fussy little wife, and he only has to go to half as many dreadful socials as I do."

Before Mr. Lokberg could speak, Erich slapped him lightly on the shoulder. "See you in the morning, my good man." He glanced toward the curtain where the shopkeeper had disappeared and decided there was nothing he really needed to say. "Would you mind telling Mr. Keimer for me that everything looks fine?"

"I'd be happy to," Mr. Lokberg said before Erich hurried out of the shop with Han at his side.

"I think you made his day," Han said as they mounted their waiting horses.

"Well, I hope he makes mine tomorrow. If he's actually worth hiring, I could consider what just happened a miracle."

"Amen," Han said. "I hear the pub calling," he added.

"My thoughts exactly," Erich chuckled, and they hurried down the cobbled street and around the corner to the Red Lion.

Kathe Lokberg rose to her feet and brushed the dirt from her skirt. She turned to absorb the beauty of the garden and sighed contentedly. At the age of twelve, she was a better gardener than Mrs. Burger next door, and she couldn't deny that she took pride in it.

She was washing her hands at the outside water pump when her sister-in-law, Leisl, came outside. Kathe noticed that she was beginning to look pregnant, and she wondered what it would be like when the baby came. Kathe liked Leisl. In the year since her brother had married this woman, they'd become friends in a way. Truthfully, she far preferred Leisl's company over her brother's. She and Theodor simply had little in common, and she didn't understand why he was determined to avoid taking on their father's craft. It was a continual source of tension in their home, and since their mother's death just prior to Theodor's wedding, it had only steadily worsened.

"Has Theodor come back yet?" Leisl asked. "I've got lunch nearly on."

"I haven't seen him," Kathe reported.

"Oh, I do hope he's found some kind of work. I fear if we don't move out of this house, he and your father will *never* get along."

"I suppose you're right," Kathe said, walking back into the house by Leisl's side. "But I don't want you to live anywhere else. I could live without Theodor, but . . ."

The two giggled as they entered the kitchen, and Leisl said, "Just don't let him hear you say that. You'll hurt his feelings." They laughed again.

"What's funny?" Karl Lokberg asked, sauntering into the room from the hallway.

"Oh, nothing," Leisl said, pressing a quick kiss to her father-in-law's face. "Are you hungry?"

"Famished. It smells wonderful, as always."

They'd barely started eating when Theodor erupted into the kitchen. "Oh, Leisl. Leisl. You won't believe it." He was so excited he was nearly dancing, while Kathe and the others looked on in disbelief. "I went to the tailor's, just like you suggested, and Mr. Keimer had to go in the other room right in the middle of fitting a waistcoat for a fine gentleman. When Mr. Keimer didn't come back, I helped this gentleman out of his waistcoat, you see, and we started talking, and he said he needed a valet, and he'd try me out tomorrow, and if it worked out, he'd hire me permanently."

"That's wonderful!" Leisl said, standing to put her arms around him. Kathe noticed her father scowling slightly. "If he needs a valet, then he must be well off or—"

"That's the incredible part." Theodor drew back and took his wife's shoulders into his hands. "Once I'd agreed to it, he told me to report . . . Are you ready for this?" Leisl nodded. "I'm to work at Castle Horstberg."

Leisl's eyes and mouth rounded simultaneously. "That's incredible."

"And the man I'll be working for is none other than the prince himself—Prince Erich."

Leisl gasped and put a hand over her heart.

Kathe snorted. "That's just what you need," she said to her brother. "As if you aren't stodgy and arrogant enough, you've got to go and work for a prince. In no time you'll have such a big head, we won't be able to tolerate you at all." She finished with a smile; they'd always been comfortable with such teasing between them.

"Where did such a young lady get such a sassy mouth?" Theodor retorted, albeit lightly. She knew he had learned to take his little sister's antics in stride.

"But then," Kathe ignored his question, "they're all probably the most stodgy and arrogant people in Horstberg. You should fit right in."

Theodor frowned at Kathe and turned back to Leisl, who appeared to be in shock. "I don't believe it," she said.

"Neither do I."

"Do you think you can do it?" she asked, seeming concerned. "I mean . . . you've never been a valet. Is it—"

"Oh, I'll manage, I'm sure. I can learn fast. I'll *make* it work!"

Theodor left before dawn the following morning and didn't return until well past dark. He walked into the parlor where his father was reading the weekly newspaper, Kathe was mending some stockings, and Leisl was knitting something for the baby. He slouched into a chair and all eyes fell on him.

"You look exhausted," Leisl said.

"I am. I never imagined that any one person could change clothes so many times a day. First court, then meetings, then a banquet with visiting dignitaries, then more meetings, then a social."

"Surely he can't be finished with an evening social at this hour," Leisl observed.

Theodor smiled. "He assured me that he was quite accustomed to dressing for bed on his own and sent me home."

Nothing more was said when no one wanted to pose the obvious question. Karl finally spoke up. "So, how did it go, son? Does he want you back or not?"

Theodor's grin broadened. "Actually, he does. He wants me to meet with his secretary in the morning to discuss wages and living accommodations."

Leisl gasped and erupted with a little laugh. "Living accommodations?" she echoed.

"The job comes with an apartment at the castle," Theodor reported, beaming. "Some days he'll have me quite busy, like I was today. And on rare occasions I would travel with him. But most days I would only be needed for short periods through the day, and I would be able to be with you, my dear."

Leisl mirrored his excited demeanor. Theodor turned to his father, waiting for a reaction. Following an uncomfortable silence, Karl said, "If it's what you want to do, son, I wish you the best."

"Thank you, Father," he said, taking Leisl's hand. "And who knows? Maybe we'll have a son who'll be better suited to being a craftsman."

"Maybe," Karl said and went back to the newspaper. Theodor kissed his wife, and they laughed together.

Kathe returned to her task, feeling rather glum. She was happy Theodor had found work, and knew their moving out might lessen the tension between her father and brother, but she wasn't sure she wanted to them move all the way to the other side of the valley.

Chapter Fifteen
CELEBRATION

Maggie eased carefully into her mother's wedding gown and heard gasps of approval from the other women in the room as she turned to adjust the dress over her shoulders.

"Oh, it's splendid!" Sonia said eagerly. "I do wish it would have fit me."

"You're built too much like Father," Maggie sniggered.

"At least Sonia has more shape than a mouse," Abbi said, and Maggie smiled warmly at her. Abbi had always taught her children that the body they were born with, however much it might differ from the shape and form of others, was beautiful and unique and that being content with what they'd been given was a far better attitude than indulging in any kind of envy. For all that Maggie and Sonia were shaped very differently, they had always readily admitted to their different types of beauty.

"Oh, it *is* beautiful," Elsa said as Maggie surveyed her reflection in the long mirror.

"I thought Han wanted you to wear the wedding gown he bought for you in Switzerland," Sonia said.

"He did," Maggie replied. "But it's a little too tight around the middle now. And he agreed this would be appropriate under the circumstances."

"I must admit this is exciting for me," Abbi said as she finished fastening it and stood back to admire her daughter. "It's every bit as beautiful as when I wore it. Perhaps more so," she added with a smile.

"It certainly does well in hiding my condition," Maggie said. "Not that it matters. Everyone knows we're long married, nevertheless . . ."

"I ordered the dress with that in mind," Abbi confessed. "Of course, we had been married privately long before the cathedral wedding. Your father was finally able to admit publicly that we were already married and I was with child, so it ended up making little difference."

Maggie sighed and waited for Abbi to put the veil in place.

"That should do it," Abbi said. "You look beautiful."

"I feel . . . like a princess," Maggie beamed. "Han said that a princess should look like a princess when she marries."

"I dare say Han is right."

"He *is* a good kisser," Sonia said, and Maggie's eyes widened.

"And how would you know?" Maggie asked as Sonia gathered up the train and they all followed the bride into the hallway.

"I took some of that love potion," she whispered dramatically, "and then I set my eyes on Han, and . . . ooh!"

"Oh, I see," Maggie smiled. "Well, I'm glad you got Rudolf."

"So am I," Sonia sighed with a dreamy smile.

"So am I," Abbi repeated.

"And I'm glad you were able to come for the wedding," Maggie added, squeezing her sister's hand.

"I only wish you could have been there for mine," Sonia replied warmly.

"Let's stop chattering and hurry along," Elsa inserted. "The coaches are waiting."

The day was beautiful for this time of year, and the warm sun eased the cold nip in the air. Maggie stepped into the courtyard and was escorted by two officers of the Guard to an open coach, draped with wedding streamers and bells, harnessed to four white horses. Maggie was seated with her back to the driver, with Abbi and Elsa facing her. Georg mounted his horse to ride behind them with a company of uniformed horsemen and the other high officials of the duchy who took up the rear of the procession. As soon as Sonia joined Rudolf and Abbi's father, Gerhard, in the ducal coach, the duke called out an order that was repeated by Captain Dukerk. Trumpets sounded and a drum cadence began. The hooves of a hundred horses moved forward, circling toward the castle gate to begin their descent into the valley.

At the head of the procession was a troop of caparisoned horses whose riders carried ducal flags. Behind them, the duke rode his stallion with the Captain of the Guard at his side and a battalion of foot soldiers behind him, marching in perfect synchronization. Han and Erich rode at the head of the cavalry, followed immediately by the ducal coach. And behind them were a dozen uniformed officers of the Guard to lead the bridal coach.

People lined the streets of Horstberg to watch the elaborate procession. It wasn't often that such an event as a royal wedding occurred. Maggie felt all eyes on her, but she had grown up with such things and was quite accustomed to it. Enveloped in billowing white, she knew she made a striking contrast to the rest of the procession, adorned completely in black, red, and gold. All of the men, including Han, wore uniforms deemed of their position, and the coaches too were adorned with the official ducal colors.

Han felt as if he might be living in some kind of dream. The uniform he wore still felt strange, especially since he had no military experience. He'd grown up seeing his father wearing a uniform to many events; it was more of an honorary thing, since he served so closely with the duke. But he wondered if Georg had ever felt so strangely overwhelmed when he'd initially been becoming accustomed to all of this.

The procession slithered along unhurried in time with the unwavering drum cadence, the horses moving at a slow canter. Occasionally, Han glanced over his shoulder and got a brief glimpse of Maggie through the garrison placed between them like some great barrier that would be absent on the return journey. He would have expected this to affect him very little. They were already married and this glorious event would hardly change anything. But he had to admit that he was nervous. It was as if he were really just now getting married. Or perhaps having the marriage made public forced him to face more fully the implications of his now being an official member of the royal family.

It certainly made the reality of his position sink in. For many years, he had longed for a position that would challenge him and offer him fulfillment in his life, but he had never believed that he would actually end up following in his father's footsteps. Something a little further down the chain of authority would have suited him fine. While he was deeply grateful to have this position, and he knew he was capable of doing it well, he had never imagined that his work would be tied into his marriage. He had always envisioned being married to Maggie as being able to sleep in the same bed with her and share her life in every respect. He had never thought much about this public aspect of being Maggie's husband. Even in realizing now that he would take over his father's position, he had rarely witnessed the grandeur that went along with it, and he hadn't thought about it all in regard to himself. He'd more imagined that he would spend most of his life holed up in the duke's office with a lot of paperwork.

But Han realized now that this side of the situation was very real. He was only just embarking on a life where he would frequently be in the public eye. He felt certain it was this aspect that appealed to Nik Koenig, but Han far preferred the quiet retreat of the castle and hoped he wouldn't have to do this sort of thing terribly often.

"You look scared to death," Erich said, interrupting Han's thoughts.

"I am," Han said.

"You've been married to her for months. What is there to be scared about?"

"Do we have to parade around like this often?" Han asked.

"Only on national holidays and special occasions."

"That's a relief," Han chortled.

"Actually, once this part is over, it's not so bad," Erich said. "Of course, we'll have festivities after the wedding."

"Terrific," Han said, only slightly sarcastic.

"You really shouldn't say it like that," Erich said. "I envy you, actually."

Han turned toward Erich in disbelief, grateful for a distraction that made the crowds around them easier to ignore. "Me? Why on earth would you envy me?"

Erich looked straight ahead and said earnestly, "You're married to a woman you love, and you're settled into life. My position can be stifling at times when—"

"I thought you enjoyed your position," Han said in surprise.

"It's not that," Erich replied. "I mean, I feel no qualm about being the duke. The more Father turns over to me, the more I feel confident that I can handle it. Let's just say it's a precarious position to be in when you're my age and . . . well, let me put it this way. It seems that every young lady in the valley is a contender for a prize. And I am the prize."

"Oh, I see," Han chuckled. "You feel like they might as well display you on market day with the rest of the wares."

"Precisely," Erich scowled.

"Forgive me if this is presumptuous, but . . . what about Dulsie?" he asked, referring to Captain Dukerk's oldest daughter.

"What *about* Dulsie?" Erich countered.

"She's so quiet that I hardly know her personally, but I know the two of you have a certain . . . closeness. You always have."

"She's a dear friend," Erich said. "I don't feel that way about her, nor does she feel that way about me."

Han took note of the way he'd said that. "The two of you have discussed it . . . your feelings?"

"We have," Erich said. "And I can assure you that she does *not* want to be the next Duchess of Horstberg . . . for several reasons."

Han let that sink in. "Fair enough. But don't you think that—" he was interrupted when trumpets sounded and the procession came to a halt.

"Oh, terrific," Han said as his heart quickened with nerves.

Within minutes, he and Erich were standing together at the head of the cathedral while Maggie walked the long aisle toward him, on her father's arm.

To Maggie this was like a dream come true. All her life she had dreamed of such a wedding. And while she had tried to convince herself that she would never marry Han Heinrich, she knew beyond any doubt he was the best thing that had ever happened to her. She was deeply grateful now for the difficulties that had brought her and Han together. And the experiences were such that she knew she could never take him for granted. He was a wonderful man, and she loved him with all her being. She was truly happy.

A rush of butterflies seized her as Han came into view at the head of the cathedral. He looked so handsome and dignified. In truth, he looked every bit as regal as Erich, who stood at his side. Maggie glanced up through the veil to meet her father's eyes. He smiled warmly and squeezed her hand. How grateful she was to be part of such a family!

As they reached the foot of the huge stone steps, Cameron kissed his daughter's hand and placed it gently into Han's. Together, she and Han ascended the steps and knelt before the Bishop of Horstberg to repeat their vows. Han's eyes glowed with love as he lifted the veil to kiss her. And with full acceptance of the royal family and the people of Horstberg, they left the cathedral riding together now in the bridal coach.

Han felt less nervous now as the procession moved into the square in the center of town, where they participated in Horstberg's age-old folkdance, according to tradition. The first set was exclusively for the bridal couple, but Han had no awareness of anyone or anything except Maggie. And doing this dance with her was one more facet of a dream come true. He'd learned the dance at a very young age and had participated in it each year on Reclamation Day when Horstberg celebrated a traditional fair, just as it had done for centuries. The duke and duchess joined them on the next set, then crowds began filling the square to join in the celebration. The clapping and stomping became louder each time they went through the dance, added by whoops and hollers of enjoyment. He knew that Maggie was being careful not to overdo it in regard to her delicate condition, but she still looked as if she'd never had so much fun.

When the celebration in the square was finished at last, the procession moved on to Castle Horstberg where a reception and dinner were held to honor the wedded couple. Following that was more dancing in the grand ballroom. Han was concerned that Maggie would become weary, but she insisted that she'd never felt better, and she hardly had a moment off the dance floor.

Maggie enjoyed every moment of her wedding day until she was asked to dance by the Baron Von Bindorf, who ruled the neighboring country of Kohenswald and who was also earnestly trying to match up one of his daughters with Erich. His foul breath alone was enough to make her nauseous, and she knew from the things her father had said that he was a man of no morals and little integrity. But she smiled and endured his company, reminding herself that one of Horstberg's highest priorities was keeping peace with the baron's country. She caught Erich's eye as he moved past her, dancing with Dulsie Dukerk. At least she knew her brother was aware of her predicament and would rescue her if the need arose. She was relieved when the song ended, until the baron possessively guided her to the side of the room, where his daughters were standing close together whispering.

"You remember Anastasia and Esmerelda," he said to Maggie.

"Of course." Maggie managed a smile. How could she ever forget the hateful humiliation she'd endured from these girls?

"I'll leave you young ladies to catch up," the baron said and slithered off to find another unwary dance partner.

"So," Esmerelda said, "you went and married the stablehand after all."

"After all," Maggie repeated, glancing toward Han, wishing he would rescue her.

"I must confess," Anastasia's eyes followed the direction of Maggie's gaze, taking Han in as if he were a piece of jewelry, "he does clean up rather well." She looked back at Maggie and added, "But then, so do you."

They both giggled as if they hadn't matured a bit in all the years Maggie had known them. She was grateful to see Han and Erich approaching cautiously, as if they'd sensed her discomfort.

"And Erich's looking fine too, I see," Esmerelda said. "I wonder sometimes if he even likes women. He doesn't seem to pay much attention to them."

"Do you think he'll *ever* get married?" Anastasia asked.

"I can assure you," Maggie said, "when Erich finds a woman worth paying attention to, he'll pay attention." She forced a smile and added, "If you will excuse me. I think my husband is waiting."

Maggie hurried toward Han, forcing back her anger and hatred. She was determined to not let anything mar this day—not even those nasty little princesses from Kohenswald. Her plan went awry when she bumped into someone and looked up at the face of Nikolaus Koenig. She gasped aloud as a mixture of memories came rushing over her. Before she could think how to react, Han and Erich were standing at her sides.

"It is a pleasure to see you again, Mrs. Heinrich," Nik said and gallantly took her hand to kiss it.

"What are you doing here?" Erich insisted quietly to avoid any attention from the other guests.

"It would appear," Nik smiled toward Erich, still holding Maggie's hand, "that someone overlooked inviting me to my cousin's wedding. Nevertheless, I won't hold that against anyone. I did, however, wish to congratulate the bride personally, and—"

"You're not welcome here," Erich stated firmly while Han put a protective arm around Maggie, appearing calm.

"I only wish to share a dance with my dear cousin," Nik said, perfectly respectful. "I would ask nothing more, nor intrude any further on your celebration."

Nik nodded toward Maggie with a patronizing smile, and she could see no way out of it without causing a scene.

"I don't think that—" Han began to say, but Maggie nodded carefully toward him, thinking perhaps it would cause less trouble if she patronized Nik a bit. Surely he could do no harm here in front of all these people.

"It's all right," she said and placed her hand on Nik's arm, moving gracefully onto the dance floor.

"What do you suppose he wants?" Erich asked Han scornfully.

"I don't know, but I don't trust him."

As Nik eased Maggie into a waltz, holding her closer than necessary, she was vaguely aware of Han and Erich tensely observing them, like two lions ready to pounce at the slightest indication of trouble. She couldn't deny that their presence made her feel more safe.

"You look lovely in white," Nik said casually.

"Thank you."

After a brief silence, Nik added, "It should have been me, Maggie. This should have been *my* wedding."

"I love Han," she stated, trying to avoid the political aspects of the situation.

"And I love you," Nik retorted, seeming genuinely hurt.

"I don't believe you," Maggie stated.

"Why not?"

"There is no reason to discuss it now."

"I have a right to know. You went to sleep in the carriage full of gratitude for my rescuing you from Mr. Heinrich, and the next time I saw you, you were married to him. Don't you think that warrants an explanation?"

Maggie wondered what to say. She glanced toward Han, and his watchful eyes gave her the courage to tell Nik the truth.

"I overheard you talking about your plans. Knowing your true intent, I couldn't possibly marry you. Han is very good to me, and I have no doubt that I have done the right thing—for myself as well as for my country."

Nik seemed briefly taken aback but recovered quickly and appeared to be his normal self, poised and nonchalant. She expected him to deny the charges, but he said coolly, "If you ever change your mind, I'm certain that you and I could—"

"How dare you even imply such a thing!" Maggie said, fighting to remain calm.

"It will be difficult for me to live without you, Maggie," he said, as if he actually meant it.

"Me or the duchy?"

"Maggie," he said, seeming appalled at her implication, "in spite of everything, surely you must know how I care for you."

"That is difficult for me to accept after you were responsible for me losing my baby and—"

"How is that?" he asked in astonishment.

"One of your thugs was far from gentle when he—"

"I was attempting to rescue you, Maggie. At the time, I had every reason to believe you wanted to be rescued." He smiled. "You can't hold me responsible for—"

"I most certainly can. And because of it, I've already had difficulties with this pregnancy and must be very careful. I am paying daily for what you did to us in Italy, and if I lose this child, it's likely I'll have no more. See if you can measure that in your conscience, Mr. Koenig." Maggie took a deep breath, wishing the music would end.

"You know, Maggie," Nik whispered, "you du Woernigs are all alike. One day your arrogance will see all of you put into your proper place."

"And where is that?" she asked with defiance, feeling suddenly weak.

"I will have what should have been mine," he stated with a subtle smirk. "And when that happens, you will wish you had married me when you had the chance."

Maggie attempted to move away as her anger got the better of her and she feared showing her temper in front of all these people. But Nik held her tightly, and any further attempt to break free would have brought undue attention.

She was aware of Han moving cautiously toward them with Erich close behind. Nik glanced toward them and gave a devilish smile that made her wonder how she could have ever been blind enough to believe that what her parents had said about him wasn't true.

"Perhaps," he said slyly, "you'll have another chance yet."

The music ended on a timely note, and Maggie scooped up the train of her dress and brushed past him toward the stairs. A vivid memory assaulted her of how it had felt to watch Nik hitting Han repeatedly while he declared that she would be a widow. A quick glance over her shoulder let her know that Han was following her up the stairs, while Erich followed after Nik, likely to make certain he left the castle without any more opportunities to prolong his visit.

When she was away from the ballroom, Maggie let the train of her dress fall, and she leaned against the wall to catch her breath.

"Are you all right?" Han asked, placing a gentle hand on her shoulder.

"Just tired," she said with a sharp tone.

"What did he say?" Han asked carefully.

"Nothing worth repeating," she said, turning to look up at him with a winsome smile. "And nothing worth ruining my wedding day."

Han smiled and kissed her. "Perhaps it's time we retired, my dear," he said dramatically.

"That would suit me fine," she said. "I doubt anyone will miss us too badly."

"You're still feeling all right, I presume," he said as they walked slowly toward their rooms.

"Yes, fine," she said, and then added tensely, "I'm sorry about tonight."

"What about it?" he asked in surprise.

"Oh, you know," she said timidly, "doctor's orders. It won't be much of a wedding night."

"Ah," Han chortled, "we had a wonderful honeymoon. And we've got the rest of our lives for that." He smiled toward her. "We'll make up for it."

"I dare say we will," she said and soaked in the unbridled love for her that sparkled in his eyes.

"I'm glad I don't have to be the Duke of Horstberg," Han said as Maggie finished fastening his coat for him and straightened it meticulously. "This uniform is bad enough. Can you imagine how your father must feel with all those medals and things he has to wear every time we attend one of these dreadful things?"

"I can't imagine." She sniggered. "But you don't have to worry, my dear. Father and Erich will take care of the medals."

"Lucky Erich!" Han laughed. "I don't envy him."

"There's no reason to. I know you're quite happy with your position. You can complain all you like, but you won't fool me."

"You're right," he admitted. "I love every minute of it—now that I'm getting used to it. But then, I think I always wanted it. Just like I always wanted you." He pulled her into his arms and gave her a torrid kiss. "Now I've got everything a man could ever want."

"You'd do well to hurry along," she said breathlessly after he kissed her again. "The others will be waiting."

"The others will be waiting for Erich," Han said as he moved toward the door. "By the time Theodor can drag him out of the dungeon to help him dress, it's usually already time to be there."

"He does like it down there," Maggie said.

"What he needs is a woman," Han muttered. "But even a woman probably couldn't keep him out of his laboratory."

"Probably not," Maggie said.

Han kissed her once more and headed down the hall, arriving at Erich's room to find a scene that was becoming typical. Because Erich was always the last one ready, Cameron, Georg, and Han often ended up in Erich's room, all comically harassing him.

"I've got more assistance than I know what to do with," Theodor said as he helped Erich into his coat.

"What you need is someone to bodily drag him from that dungeon an hour earlier," Cameron said.

"What he needs," Han said as he sat down and stretched out his legs, "is a woman."

Cameron laughed, but Erich gave Han a sidelong glare.

"That ought to do it," Georg said. "A pretty woman could lure him out of there once in a while."

"It would probably just give him a different excuse to be late," Cameron added.

"As much as I like the chemistry," Erich said, "I'd trade it any day to be free of this dreaded search for the next Duchess of Horstberg."

"No need to concern yourself," Cameron said with confidence. "If you live the way you're supposed to, the right woman will come along."

"I hope she does," Erich said. "The prospects of falling in love at this point don't seem promising."

"It happens when you least expect it," Georg said.

"I know the perfect woman for you," Theodor added.

"I've heard that before," Erich said. "Everyone in Horstberg has a perfect woman in mind for me."

"Who is this woman?" Han asked.

"My sister." Theodor paused to grin at Han before he made certain the medals fastened to Erich's coat were all straight.

"Just how old is this sister?" Erich asked, as if he might seriously consider meeting her.

"Twelve," Theodor stated, and everyone except Erich laughed.

"Oh, that's very funny," Erich said with sarcasm. "I'll be nearly dead by the time she comes of age."

"Not quite," Cameron said. "I was thirty-one when I married your mother. She was . . . what?" he turned to Georg.

"Nineteen," he provided, and Cameron smiled nostalgically.

"Well, let's see," Theodor said to Erich, "you're only eleven years older than my sister. That's not bad."

"But she has to grow up, obviously," Erich said. "What do I do with myself in the meantime?"

"Stick to the laboratory," Han said.

"No," Erich said. "I appreciate your offer, Theodor, but I think I'll have to find somebody sooner than that."

"I don't know," Cameron laughed. "I'd listen to him if I were you."

"And why is that?" Erich asked as Theodor stood back to survey his appearance with an indication that he was ready.

"Remind me to tell you sometime how my valet told me that I should marry his daughter."

Theodor watched Erich leave with the others, gratified once again with the results of his efforts. More and more he was finding fulfillment in helping the prince look presentable for every public event. All of the men moved toward the door, except for His Grace, who held back, putting a hand on Theodor's arm. He felt briefly alarmed until the duke said kindly, "I was sorry to hear about your wife losing her baby. Erich mentioned it. Please give her my regards."

"Thank you, Your Grace," Theodor said, managing a smile. He was left a little stunned by such personal kindness from the duke himself, but the others exited the room, and he had to fight back how His Grace's comment had touched a sore spot for him. He forced himself to clean up Erich's room and get on with his work.

Erich slowed down and turned back, waiting for his father. He suspected the reasons Cameron had taken a moment to speak with Theodor privately and respected him for doing so. They exchanged a wan smile as if to privately share what they both knew about the personal tragedy in Theodor's life, but they wouldn't talk about it any further at the moment.

Instead, Erich turned the conversation elsewhere and asked his father, "Who was your valet?"

Cameron didn't answer, but Georg grinned, and Erich persisted, "Well?"

"Gerhard Albrecht," Georg provided.

"Grandfather?" Erich asked in astonishment. Then he chuckled. He had surely heard that story, but it suddenly seemed a lot funnier than it had been before.

When the four men were all comfortable in the carriage on their way to Kohenswald, with Georg and Cameron taking the opportunity for a little nap, Han asked Erich quietly, "Still down about women, eh?"

"Quite," Erich replied. "Do you know I have had a dinner invitation nearly every other night for four months from people who want me to marry their daughter? I'd like to start eating at home more often. Not to mention that the way these girls behave is pathetic. I didn't think there could be so many simpering women in one country. I wonder where they get this misconstrued idea that I'm looking for someone with pomp and flash."

"What *are* you looking for?" Han asked, amused.

"Oh, that's easy," Erich said. "I want a woman like my mother."

Han lifted his brows, and Erich continued. "Just look at her. She's got dignity and grace, and she's got an intelligent mind. She's kind and warm, and she doesn't let this duchy business go to her head. We all know that the position our family holds is actually a humble place to be. Bearing the responsibility for a country is a great burden. My mother knows that, and she takes it seriously. But a lot of these women seem to think that we live in some fairy-tale world where everything is magic."

"That's how my first wife was," Cameron said with no other indication that he wasn't sound asleep. "A woman like that could destroy a country."

Erich sighed as the evidence of his father's experience strengthened his resolve and also added to his burden. He looked toward Han as if he might offer some great, mystical solution.

"Don't ask me," he said. "Maggie didn't marry me for my money—or my power. Well," he added thoughtfully, "maybe it was my power. I am pretty strong." He flexed his arm comically, and Erich chuckled.

"And you didn't marry Maggie for her power or money either," Erich said.

"Your father's bribe could be misconstrued if some knew the truth. But I know why I did it."

"And why is that?" Erich asked.

"As if you didn't know. We went through all of this quite miserably not so long ago, if you'll recall."

"I want to hear you say it."

"I love the woman," Han said proudly.

"You have for years."

"You know the first time I realized I loved Maggie?"

"When?"

"Well, I think I was always drawn to her, but I remember this day when I was barely sixteen. They moved me from the cavalry stables to work with the family's horses, and Maggie walked in like some haughty little queen and said . . ." Han raised his voice to mimic her, "'Heinrich! Get that horse saddled for me right now. I'm in a hurry.'"

Erich laughed, and Cameron opened one eye to glare at him for the disturbance. Georg continued to snore.

"That's a good reason to fall in love," Erich whispered.

"I don't know why I loved her." Han shook his head. "I could never understand it. I'd lay awake at night wondering why I should care so much for a snippy little thing. But I did." Han turned to Erich and said intently, "And she's the best thing that ever happened to me. She is really amazingly brave and strong underneath all of that silliness we often see on the surface."

Erich sighed with understanding but said nothing about the hovering emptiness in his heart. He only turned toward the carriage window and said distantly, "I long to feel that way about a woman."

"You will," Han said, slapping him on the knee. "I've no doubt about it."

"And how do you know?" Erich asked.

"Look at your parents. They've been married all these years and they still melt every time they look at each other."

Cameron smiled but didn't move.

"Go to sleep!" Han said, and Cameron opened his eyes to glare at him again. "Your Grace," Han added in mock respect, and Cameron grinned before he resettled himself.

"But then look at my parents," Han said. "They act like newlyweds most of the time. Except when my mother yells."

"None of that is a guarantee that I'll find the same," Erich said.

"Nonsense," Han chortled. "Your parents have fire in their blood. It'll happen. My advice as one with great wisdom and experience," he said, only slightly sarcastic, "is that you just enjoy life and don't worry about it. If you don't like going out to dinner, then don't go. You'll find someone. I'd bet on it. She's out there somewhere right now, probably as lonely and worried as you are, wondering if she'll ever find the right man and fall in love."

"You know," Erich said, "hearing you say that reminds me of a dream I've had more than once."

Cameron opened his eyes and leaned forward curiously.

"What?" Erich asked him, wishing he hadn't brought it up.

"If they're anything like your mother's dreams, I'd take notice."

"Why is that?" Han asked.

"Hard to explain," Cameron said.

"Oh, go back to sleep," Erich insisted, hoping the subject would be dropped. "You're more of a busybody than the maids."

Cameron frowned then settled himself again, but Erich knew he was still listening.

"So, tell me about this dream," Han said in a tone to imitate a fortune teller he'd watched once at the fair. Erich sighed, knowing he would never be able to get out of it. Han would never drop the subject now that Erich had brought it up, but perhaps it was best that he said something; maybe doing so would stop the memory of the dream from rolling around his head several times a day.

"It's not much, really. I can see a young woman with red hair. She reminds me a lot of Mother. She's just wandering in a mist. It's like she's alone and lost, searching, perhaps."

"Oh, that's easy," Han said, still sounding like a fortune teller. "She represents the woman out there looking for you. She reminds you of your mother because you want someone like her."

"Sounds logical," Cameron said, his eyes still closed.

"No," Erich said carefully, "that's not the way it seems. I can't explain it, but that's not quite right."

"Maybe it doesn't mean anything," Cameron said, finally sitting up straight as if he'd resigned himself to do without a nap. "Your mother has had a particular dream several times since I met her, where I'm lying on the floor, and she can't wake me up. She's says it's like I'm dead. Either it doesn't mean anything, or I've got something to look forward to."

"Do you believe that dreams can be portentous?" Erich asked.

"Yes, I do," Cameron said emphatically. "At least for some people. Your mother has a gift that way. Her dreams had a great deal to do with how we came together. She's had many dreams that were somehow a presage. Ask her about it some time."

Erich looked thoughtfully toward the window again, considering how his dreams had made him feel. He'd heard tidbits through his life about his mother having strange dreams, but he'd never paid much attention before. Now it seemed important.

As if Cameron knew where his thoughts were, he said, "Don't worry about it, boy. Han's right. You'll find someone to love. Just let fate take its course and don't be so preoccupied with it."

"I suppose you're right," Erich said.

Han changed the subject by telling them a joke he'd heard in the pub the day before, which started a round of old jokes that they loved to repeat. The jokes got so bad that they were all glad to arrive in Kohenswald, only because it got them that much closer to having this diplomatic conference over with so they could go home.

Many long hours later, the carriage thundered up the castle hill, nigh to three o'clock in the morning.

"Ah, home," Cameron said.

"Home to the women we love," Georg grinned.

"Yes," Erich said with sarcasm, "it's always nice to see my mother."

"Don't worry about it," Han insisted. "You'll find the new Mrs. du Woernig when the time is right."

Erich believed that in his heart, but as he thought of the relationship he knew Han shared with Maggie, he had to admit he was truly envious. He knew he was young yet, and there was certainly no hurry. But a part of him felt impatient to have that kind of love in his life and be settled. Surely there had to be a woman out there who could love him for who he was—not because he was the next Duke of Horstberg. The trick was finding her before he was too old to enjoy it.

Maggie came awake in the middle of the night long enough to give Han a kiss when he came to bed, then she rolled over and went back to sleep. When she woke to sunlight, she left quietly, not wanting to disturb him. Since the men all slept late, Maggie had breakfast with her mother before they went together to the conservatory to paint. Elsa came in to visit, and she and Abbi started telling stories about Han and Erich when they were children. Maggie enjoyed listening to their comfortable chatter, even though she'd heard all the stories before. Now, hearing about Han's childhood antics had taken on a whole new meaning.

When lunch was announced, they all went to the dining room to find the men already seated, laughing again over Han's new joke.

"Ah, what a sight," Cameron said as the women entered and the men all stood to greet their wives with a kiss. Except for Erich, who waited until his parents had exchanged an appropriate greeting so that he could kiss his mother on the cheek.

"Good morning, Mother," he said warmly when she went up on her tiptoes to return the kiss.

They were all seated, and Abbi asked how the meetings in Kohenswald had gone. After the women were filled in on the details, Cameron asked, "So did anything exciting happen while we were away?"

"Nik Koenig came by," Abbi stated, and a tenseness descended over the room. Maggie reached beneath the table and took hold of Han's hand. He squeezed it as if he she had no need to explain why just hearing his name made her uneasy.

"The son of a . . ." Cameron began and stopped himself. "It's just like him to wait to come around until everyone's gone. What did he want?"

"His allowance," Abbi stated. "I gave it to him and sent him on his way. But I don't like the way he looks this place over when he's here."

"Neither do I," Cameron said.

"What can he possibly do?" Han asked, hating the vague sense of vulnerability they all felt over the situation but unable to imagine what power Nik could have against them.

"I don't know," Georg said. "But I have a feeling he'll do something. I don't know why; I just do."

"I have the same feeling, and I hate it," Cameron said.

"Do you suppose it's just habit . . . because of his father, I mean?" Erich asked.

"Perhaps," Cameron said, "but I'm not getting too comfortable."

"Very wise," Han said with mock wisdom, and Cameron passed him a comical glare of disgust.

"You must be nice to Han," Maggie said to her father. "After all, you offered him the job of being my husband."

"So I did," Cameron laughed.

"By the way, dear," Abbi said to her husband, "I wanted to tell you something earlier, but you were asleep."

"What's that?"

"I had the strangest dream last night."

Quick glances of expectancy were exchanged between the men, and Maggie wondered why.

"What's the matter?" Abbi asked.

"Nothing," Cameron said. "I was just telling Han and Erich yesterday about the dreams you have on occasion."

"It's certainly never been any big secret," Abbi said. "Although they happen seldom, and it's usually something trivial, or it's private."

"Was this one different?" Cameron asked.

"The mood was much the same, but it . . ." She stopped deliberately then said, "Perhaps I shouldn't have brought this up here. I—"

"It's all right," Han said. "We'd like to hear about it . . . only if you wish to tell us, of course."

"Well," Abbi said, "it seemed to go on and on. I walked through the halls of the castle. It's as if I paced every section of hallway, every staircase."

"That's at least a hundred miles," Han said.

"But it wasn't really me," Abbi said. "Actually, the castle was completely empty. There was no one. It seemed that even I wasn't there. I was just viewing the situation from a distance. Does that make sense?"

"I think so," Cameron said, and a familiar look of love and understanding passed between them. "Was that all?"

"More or less," she said. "As in my other dreams, it wasn't so much what happened as the way it made me feel."

"And how is that?" Cameron asked.

"As I watched the castle halls pass before me," she said quietly, and everyone stopped eating as they hung expectantly on her words and the almost eerie tone in which she spoke them, "I seemed to realize that the castle had lost its soul."

Maggie felt a sudden, unexplainable chill and noted that her father caught his breath audibly and leaned back in his chair. Abbi glanced around the table to see silent, dazed expressions, as if a mutual sense of foreboding had overcome them.

"What do you think it means?" Abbi asked her husband, and he forced a smile.

"I hope nothing," he stated. "But if I were to guess, those of us seated at this table are what comprises this castle's soul."

"I don't know about you," Han said lightly with his ability to ease the formless tension, "but I'm not leaving."

"Well, that's a relief," Cameron laughed. "At least the castle will always have spirit."

"Or a bad joke," Erich said.

Chapter Sixteen

TRAPS

$\mathcal{M}$aggie brought her hands down on the keys of the piano, and a clear note rang through the room. With intensity, she worked through the piece she'd been practicing and felt gratified by her efforts in trying to make it sound as the composer had intended.

For the first time in her life, Maggie found that she was enjoying the music training her father had given her personally. With the restrictions of her condition, she found playing the piano a welcome pastime. And when she wasn't at the piano, she was often in the conservatory with her mother, taking art more seriously than she ever had in her life.

Maggie felt the music move through her, and the piece took on the passion she derived from life. Her emotions rode high with it, and inwardly she felt grateful for her father's gift of music, her mother's gift of art, and the awareness of her senses that Han had given her through his love.

She finished with a final run and a resounding high chord. Hesitantly, she pulled her hands away from the keys, wiped the trace of sweat from her brow, and drew a deep breath. She heard hands clapping from behind and turned, startled. For a moment, she clearly recalled a similar incident when she was fourteen.

"Han," she said breathlessly and rose to greet him. "I thought I was alone."

"I'm glad you weren't." He kissed her in greeting. "The song was beautiful. It would be a shame to have it go unappreciated."

"Thank you," she smiled, "but *I* appreciated it."

"Your father sent me to tell you that we have company."

"Really?" she said, moving with him into the hall. "Who?"

"He told me not to tell you," Han added wryly, and Maggie gave him a sidelong glance.

They approached the drawing room, and Maggie could hear her father laughing from inside. Han pushed open the door, and Maggie stepped into the room.

"Aunt Magda!" she exclaimed. "Oh, I don't believe it!" She laughed as her father's sister rose and they embraced.

"Maggie, my darling," Magda said, pulling back to scrutinize her. "You've become such a lady." She turned to Cameron. "Why, she was barely beyond a child when I saw her last."

"You should come more often." Cameron grinned proudly.

"Have you met Han?" Maggie asked.

"Just barely." She smiled toward him. "Although I do remember him as a child." Magda then whispered loudly, pretending she didn't want to be overheard, "I must say he's a handsome one, my dear. He looks very much like his father." She winked at Maggie. "You did well."

Han looked down sheepishly, and Cameron chuckled. Magda moved to the sofa and urged Maggie to sit beside her. "Your father wrote and told me that you'd married Georg's son. I was so delighted to hear, but he was just filling me in on the details." She giggled. "What an adventure the two of you must have had."

"It certainly was," Maggie declared.

"And I hear you pawned your first betrothed off on your sister," Magda said, and Han chuckled.

"It wasn't exactly like that," Cameron interjected. "Sonia and Rudolf are very happy."

"Oh, I know that," Magda scolded her brother. "I just think it's funny how it all worked out. When did you say Sonia was coming? I do so long to see her—and to meet this Rudolf."

"She'll be here in a few days," Cameron said. "It seems we're all going to be together for Christmas . . . for the first time in years."

"Do you mean Lena is coming, as well?" Maggie asked with excitement. She so dearly loved her aunts and hadn't seen them both together in more years than she could remember.

"She'll be here tomorrow," Cameron provided, and Magda giggled again.

"Can you believe it?" Magda said. "It was your father's idea to try and get us all together," she said to Maggie. "He wrote to both of us and implored us to come. We decided that one Christmas out of ten we could leave our husbands and children behind to be home again."

"You could have brought them along," Cameron said.

"Oh, I know, but they are so busy these days. Perhaps next time. I'll celebrate again with them when I go back."

Abbi bustled into the room, greeted her husband with a kiss, and turned her attention to Magda. "Come along, dear," she said. "It's time we ladies had some time together." She swept her sister-in-law toward the door and motioned for Maggie to join them. "I'm certain the men can find something to occupy themselves with." Abbi tossed a warm glance toward Cameron before they hurried out of the room.

Cameron and Han sat silently for a long moment before Cameron said, "Do you know, my boy, what makes a room feel really empty?"

"What?" Han asked, genuinely interested.

"The absence of skirts rustling," Cameron said quite seriously. "The last thing you always hear when a lady leaves the room are their rustling skirts. Have you noticed?"

Han chuckled. "I must admit that I have. And," he went on as if this were an important business matter, "a room feels really empty without that red hair. What would our lives be like without it?"

"Utterly miserable," Cameron retorted.

Sonia and Rudolf arrived the day after Lena and only hours before the snow started to fall. It fell until Christmas day, burying Castle Horstberg and the valley below in billowing white. It was a delightful time to be inside near the fire, and the spirit of Christmas combined with the reuniting of the family made the days priceless.

Maggie had always loved Christmas, and since she'd been born on Christmas Eve, there was always a birthday celebration mingled into their festivities. But never had it been as good as this! She enjoyed more than ever their traditional celebrations that included a number of different festivities, along with some charitable projects to assist those in need. Some of their festivities were more public and involved many people, and some were more private. One of the most enjoyable gatherings was the sharing of a fine feast with the Dukerk family. Maggie knew that in earlier years, when the children had all been young, the families had spent more time together socially. But as all of the children had grown up and the families had changed, traditions had shifted slightly, which Abbi had declared was the natural evolution of traditions. Still, Maggie felt entirely comfortable with Captain Dukerk and his sweet wife Nadine. The captain was thrilled to have Magda and Lena there for Christmas, since he had grown up with them and knew them well.

Maggie loved observing the older generation together, reminiscing and laughing about times gone by. Although she and Han gravitated more toward their own generation since they had grown up alongside the Dukerk children. She knew their oldest two—Dulsie and Jacob—the best, since they were nearer her own age. Although their three younger children were also like part of the family. Erich also had a closer relationship with Dulsie and Jacob; it was typical for him to be found with one or both of them during such gatherings, and Maggie knew he socialized with them at other times as well. All in all, the combining of these families left Maggie feeling completely at home and content. She loved the way that her marriage to Han had connected their two families officially, even though they had always been connected in every other way throughout their entire lives.

With the feasts and parties all behind them, Maggie enjoyed most of all what she considered to be the height of the celebration on Christmas day, when the family gathered in the central music room to carry out a long-standing tradition.

"I can't even imagine life without music," Maggie said as Cameron seated himself at the piano and Erich picked up the guitar.

"Music has filled this castle for as long as I can remember," Cameron said, looking through a pile of sheet music in search of a desired piece.

"There wasn't much of it when Nikolaus was the duke," Magda inserted.

"Those were dreadful years," Lena added.

"They were less dreadful than they were . . ."

"Oppressive," Lena provided for her sister.

"I know that when we were children, hardly a day passed without music," Cameron said. "It meant everything to Mother."

"Yes," Lena agreed, "and I don't know about you, but I am forever grateful for her efforts to leave it with us."

"Most definitely," Magda added, and Cameron smiled toward them.

"Have you found it yet?" Erich asked, toying idly with the strings.

"It might help if you had your glasses on," Georg said, handing them to Cameron, who looked briefly disgusted but put them on.

"Aha!" Cameron exclaimed. He set the piece before him on the piano and began to play. Erich came in on the guitar, and the whole family joined in singing "O Taunenbaum."

On the next song, Maggie took the piano and Cameron took the guitar, and through the course of the evening, anyone who had even the slightest idea how to play took a turn. Even Abbi, who considered her ability mostly worthless, was coerced by her husband into picking out at least one song on the piano. Since Rudolf had also grown up with some music training, he and Sonia joined in as well.

"Are there any more?" Abbi asked Georg, who was sorting through the sheet music.

"I think we've about covered it," he replied.

"Let's start over," Erich offered.

"It is getting late," Cameron said.

"But it's Christmas," Han declared. "After we go to bed, it won't be Christmas anymore."

"We must consider Maggie's condition," Lena inserted.

"I feel fine," Maggie replied exuberantly.

"What about *my* condition?" Sonia said, and all eyes turned to her abruptly. She was grinning broadly, and Rudolf laughed.

"She's been waiting for the appropriate moment," he said. "I think she hit on it."

Everyone jumped up and hugged Sonia and Rudolf. "Two grandchildren coming?" Cameron asked, and Sonia nodded, her face serene.

"You're getting old," Elsa said to the duke. "I'm glad I'm not old enough to have two grandchildren on the way."

"That's right," Georg agreed. "We've only got one on the way. That makes us not as old as you."

"If I'm that old," Cameron chuckled, "I'd better go to bed."

"Not yet, brother," Magda insisted. "It's Christmas, and we need to take . . ."

"Advantage," Lena provided.

"Of our time together," Magda finished.

"How do the two of you complete a sentence when you're not together?" Cameron asked his sisters. They looked at each other as if they didn't know what he was talking about, then Erich started to play a song, and they were soon singing again.

Maggie moved close to Han and slipped her hand into his. Their families had been celebrating together this way for as long as she could remember. But now it was different. Han's love and the life they shared made everything better.

With the arrival of the new year, all of the Christmas visitors departed from Horstberg leaving extremely cold temperatures behind. Han found himself becoming more acquainted with his work and, as a result, enjoying it all the more. Each day, he got to know the duke better, and he came to know his father and Erich in a different light, coming to appreciate their intelligence and the mutual respect that continually deepened between them. Not only was his position satisfying, but it could be fun sometimes, as well. There were days when they stuck to working intently, and then there were days when it seemed more important to have a good laugh intermittently, and they ventured to the Red Lion almost daily for a drink, or occasionally, a meal.

At first, Han thought the short journey into town was just an indulgence, but he came to realize that it was accomplishing something very important. Here at the pub, and on the way in and out of town, the duke and his team—as he called them—had the opportunity to see and talk with the people, establish a rapport with them, and be aware of life from the people's perspective as a result. It gave the people a sense of security to see their ruler come and go daily.

The busy hours spent in the duke's office were occasionally interrupted by Maggie, who would peek in just to say hello, and Han always excused himself to give his wife a kiss. The duke especially would tease him about it, but Han always admitted in good humor that he was young and in love and he had a right to act that way.

It came as a surprise—though Han figured it shouldn't have—to see how the duke reacted when his wife appeared unexpectedly one afternoon. The men were in the principal library, along with Captain Dukerk and a few officers of the Guard, with maps spread over a long table, studying them. With the door open, there was a minor distraction when the duchess was heard in the hallway giving instructions to a servant: something to do with redecorating.

The voices were ignored at first. Then, without a word, the duke stepped into the doorway and leaned there while his men watched silently. He stood there a long moment, just watching his wife while she wasn't aware.

"Good afternoon, Your Grace," he said at last, smiling as she turned.

"Good afternoon." She smiled back. "I'm sorry if I disturbed you."

"Oh, no," he said, "I was in need of a disturbance."

Abbi smiled at him again before leaving the hallway, and Cameron watched her until she disappeared. He turned back into the library and continued the meeting as if nothing were out of the ordinary. But the incident left an impression on Han.

"If you're not careful," Georg said to Cameron later when they were all back in the office, "you're going to get gossip started."

"Really?" Cameron looked confused.

"People are going to say that the duke is in love."

Cameron laughed it off, but again, Han couldn't help but take notice. He wondered if he would love Maggie that much after more than twenty years of marriage. He knew without a doubt that he would.

Maggie loved seeing signs of spring as it spread over Horstberg. With the melting snow and the color of blossoms and the flower gardens appearing, she became nostalgic in thinking over the happenings of the past year. It had been in the spring that she had met Nik, and not long after that, Han had abducted her, and nothing would ever be the same. It had certainly been an eventful year.

As weeks passed and she had no further problems with her pregnancy, she was able to go about normal living with the exception of riding and lifting. There was a peaceful contentment present in her that could not be compared, but perhaps it coincided with the state of the country. Maggie had heard her father declare that, politically and economically, things were going well. With the alliance they had made through Sonia's marriage, and the progress they were making in establishing unity with Kohenswald, Horstberg was doing better than it perhaps ever had.

As the weather warmed, there was a natural urge to be outdoors. The ladies spent more time in the gardens, and Han and Erich quickly got into the habit of riding each morning before breakfast.

Han opted to stay in bed with his wife one morning, knowing Erich would only wait a few minutes before he went out on his own.

"Ooh," he whispered and pulled Maggie closer, pressing his hand over her belly, "you are getting fat, my love. If you're not careful, you're going to be as fat as Josette."

Maggie giggled. "I wouldn't say much about it if I were you."

"Why not?"

"Because it is all your fault!"

He laughed, and she sat on top of him, attempting to tickle him without success.

"Just wait until I get really fat," she said. "I'll sit on you and squash you flat."

"What a way to go." He grinned.

He rolled her onto her side and kissed her hungrily. "Oh, Han," she whispered.

"Now, now," he said in a scolding tone. "We'll be late for breakfast."

"So?"

"Every time we're late for breakfast, your father smirks at me. I know he knows what we've been doing."

"Well," she smiled, "I happen to know that he's every bit as guilty."

"And how do you know that?"

"I'm living proof." She grinned.

Han kissed her again, and they were late for breakfast. They were met with the typical greetings, accompanied by a smirk from the duke. Han gave Maggie a knowing smile and was beginning to eat when Abbi asked, "Where is Erich?"

"He must still be out riding," Han said. "I didn't go this morning."

"I see," she replied.

A short while later, the duke broke the silence. "I don't recall Erich ever being late for breakfast."

"I was just thinking the same thing," Abbi said tensely.

Cameron pushed his chair back and stood to go and find his son. He'd only taken two steps toward the door when Erich strode into the dining room and threw his jacket abruptly into a chair.

"I was just coming to find you," Cameron said.

"That's slightly reassuring," Erich said curtly.

"What's the matter?" Abbi asked as the duke sat back down.

"I was just shot at," Erich stated, and the duke stood up.

"You *what?*" Cameron demanded.

"Just like last time," Erich said, visibly shaken. "I thank heaven they missed. I might not have been so lucky as to just get it in the shoulder again."

"Were you riding in the same place?" Cameron asked.

"Yes."

"Did you see anything . . . anyone?"

"It was difficult to pay much attention," Erich said angrily, "with repeated gunfire heading my way."

"Repeated?" Cameron shouted as Erich sat down weakly in his chair, looking a bit ashen.

"How many shots?" Han asked.

"Three . . . four maybe."

"And you're certain the shots were aimed at you?" Abbi asked softly as if she desperately hoped there was some explanation beyond her son's life being threatened.

"When a bullet hits a tree not a hand's width from my head, I'd say I could be pretty certain. And seeing the fact that I've been going there every morning at the same time, and this is the first time in weeks I've been there alone, well . . ."

Cameron sat down hard with an angry sigh. "Han," he said, "I want you to go with your father and Captain Dukerk to that meadow just as soon as you're finished here and see if you can find anything."

. "Yes, sir," Han complied.

Georg and Han followed the duke's orders, taking with them Captain Dukerk and a couple officers of the Guard. They searched carefully and found evidence of shooting materials in a spot that was ideal to remain hidden and aim where Erich had been on both occasions. But it looked more like someone had had a picnic rather than a quick shot.

Han and Georg returned to the office with Captain Dukerk to give their report to the duke. The captain suggested that he and Georg, along with a trusted officer, go to the place in question the following morning and carefully conceal themselves, while Han and Erich rode as usual. The captain hoped to gather some information and try to prevent this from happening again.

That night before bed, Han told Maggie about their plan. She hated it as much as he'd guessed she would, but he assured her that all would be well. Captain Dukerk was an experienced and wise man, as were his highest lieutenants, and they surely knew what they were doing.

The following morning, Maggie once again expressed her fear as she kissed Han goodbye and repeatedly admonished him to be careful.

"Don't tell *me*," he said with a smirk, attempting to keep the matter light. "I'm not the duke-to-be."

"Well, then," she said, "tell Erich to be careful."

"I'll take very good care of him." Han kissed her again then left as usual.

Their ride in the meadow passed without event, and they returned to the castle for breakfast. Georg came into the dining room before the meal was finished. "Excuse me for interrupting your meal, but I believe we have found the guilty party."

Cameron, Erich, and Han all stood at once and left the room. Captain Dukerk was waiting in the hall, and he quickly explained as they all walked out of the castle and across the courtyard to the keep. They had found the culprits arriving early at the very spot, bringing with them rifles that they had claimed were only meant to be used for sport, saying they had simply been intending to do some target practice. Han felt as skeptical as the other men appeared until they all filed into an interrogation room to see three very frightened boys, no more than twelve or thirteen.

"All right, boys," the officer who was standing guard at the door said, "you'd best straighten up. The duke's here to see you."

The boys all stood close together with wide, fearful eyes as they came face-to-face with the tall, imposing man who ruled their country. The Captain of the Guard, who stood at his side, was equally stern and imposing. Han stood back a little with Erich and Georg to observe the drama. He did not envy being one of these boys.

"So," the duke said sharply, "you've been doing a little shooting, have you?" No reply came, and he shouted, "I expect an answer!"

"Yes, sir," one boy spoke up.

"It's Your Grace, boy," the captain corrected.

"Yes, Your Grace."

"And are you aware that you were trespassing on my grounds?" Again, there was silence, and he added sharply, "Were you?"

"No, Your Grace. We didn't know that."

"Did someone tell you to come to this particular place?" Cameron asked.

The boys exchanged glances of confusion with each other until one said, "We heard some boys talkin' about it."

"What boys?" Cameron demanded.

"We don't know," another boy said. "Just boys. We don't know 'em. We just heard 'em talkin'."

"And were you also aware that you nearly shot my son yesterday morning?" Cameron asked.

"We didn't see him, Your Grace. We was just shootin'. We didn't know anybody was there."

"Well, I don't like the coincidence." Cameron placed his hands firmly on his hips. "How would you boys feel about facing an attempted murder charge?"

The three gasped in unison.

"Well?"

"But we didn't . . ."

"And you can add treason on top of that."

"But we didn't mean to do it. We was just havin' some fun."

"Your Grace," the captain insisted.

"Your Grace," the boy added.

"Well," the duke said with a cruel expression, "I'll have to think about what to do with the three of you. In the meantime, you think about the seriousness of what you've done. And you learn how to use firearms properly. You don't shoot if you can't see what you're shooting at!"

"Yes, sir . . . Your Grace."

"I assume you have a cell ready for these young men," Cameron said to the captain.

"Indeed we do, Your Grace," Captain Dukerk said.

"Then take care of it," he said and exchanged a knowing glance with the captain before he left the room abruptly with his son and advisors close behind.

"What will you do?" Erich asked when they were back in the courtyard.

"Oh," Cameron said, "I'll have their parents sent for and release them about suppertime. That much wondering ought to give them enough of a scare to humble them."

"So, you think it was innocent?" Han asked.

"I don't know," Cameron said. "It appears that way, but I still don't like the apparent coincidence of the whole thing. It's possible that whoever's behind it just took advantage of the boys. Either way, Erich, you won't ride alone anymore."

"Yes, sir," he complied without question.

"I'll protect him," Han said with mock gallantry as they came back into the castle to finish their breakfast.

Maggie became caught up with excitement when the redecorating in the rooms for her and Han was completed and all of their things were moved. The new bedroom in and of itself was huge, with a massive, curtained bed and a view of the main garden. To the left of the bedroom was a nursery that Han declared was perfect except that it didn't have enough toys. On the other side of the nursery were rooms for the nanny. And to the right of their bedroom was an elaborate sitting room, which Han declared must be called a sitting room because there were a lot of places to sit.

Having the nursery nearby and ready, Maggie became more preoccupied with the forthcoming birth, and Han shared her enthusiasm completely. They talked often of the birth, and Maggie insisted that she wanted Han to be there. Although it was not customary, her parents encouraged it since the duke had stayed with Abbi when their children were born, and he had relished the experience of being present through the duration of labor rather than leaving the mother without a husband's support. He'd also declared that being there when the baby took its first breath was a moment beyond compare. Since Georg had been with Elsa for Han's birth, Han heartily agreed.

"I know what to name the baby," Maggie said to Han one evening as they walked down the stairs to go to dinner.

"Really? Do tell. Which lucky relative will our child be named after?"

"None, actually. I was considering giving her a completely original name—like yours. You're the only Han around here."

"Her?" he questioned.

"Well, I've only come up with a girl's name. If we have a son, you'll have to name him."

"And what is this girl's name?"

"From the Bible; it means grace. She was the mother of Samuel, who—"

"What is the name?" Han insisted with a grin.

"Hannah."

Han stopped walking and was silent a moment while Maggie bit her lip expectantly. He smiled. "I like it."

"I thought you might," she added, and they walked on together to the dining room.

"I was just beginning to think we were going to eat alone, Abbi," the duke said when Han and Maggie entered.

"Sorry," Han said, "we're here. No peace and quiet tonight."

"Where is Erich?" Maggie asked.

"Last I heard," Han said, "he was going to his dungeon. Would you like me to go and get him?"

"Would you, please?" Abbi said. "I get nervous when he's late for meals."

Han smiled his understanding and set out quickly. He hadn't thought to bring a lamp along, but he'd come down here in the dark before, so he held to the rope bannister to guide him and moved easily down the winding stairs. About halfway down, a horrible stench hit his senses, and he laughed to himself, wondering what the prince was up to this time.

Just as Han realized the steps were slippery for some reason, he felt the rope in his hand break loose and it was nothing short of luck that enabled him to grab one of the upright posts that supported the rope, preventing him from falling to what surely would have been death.

After the initial shock subsided, Han became aware of only two things. His heart was beating so loud he could hear it, and the post that had saved him was beginning to feel slippery from the sweat in his palms.

"Erich!" he shouted as loud as he could, but no response came. He tried to push his feet against the wall and move upward, but the stone was slick and smooth and there was nothing to grip onto with his shoes. Dangling helplessly, he shouted again and again while his mind kept wondering if he would ever live to see the name Hannah given to his daughter.

"Erich!" he shouted again, hating this castle for being so blasted big with such thick walls. Pressing his face against the cold stone, he took a deep breath and prayed, feeling sweat rising on his lip as his hands became wetter and the post more slippery.

Miraculously, Han heard the familiar squeak of that iron door coming from somewhere below, and he shouted again, "Erich!"

"Han?" came the distant reply. "Where are you?"

"I'm hanging on for dear life . . . about half way up this stupid staircase . . . and if you don't get here fast, you're going to be gathering flowers for my grave."

Han took a deep breath and tightened his grip, knowing help was on the way. A light gradually filtered up the stairs as he heard Erich's footsteps ascending.

"Be careful," Han said, "the stairs are slippery."

"Hold on," he heard Erich say as the lamp was set down, and then he felt Erich's grip come over his wrist.

Erich lay on his belly on the steps, pulling Han upward by his wrists with a deep groan. Han could do nothing to help, and he prayed Erich had enough strength to save him, given the odd angle of the stairs. Seconds seemed like hours before Erich was finally able to lift Han up high enough to crawl onto the stairs, where he collapsed. They both leaned against the wall, laughing with relief and trying to catch their breath.

"I'm sure glad you heard me," Han said.

"Heard you what?"

"I called your name at least a dozen times."

"I didn't hear you. I got hungry."

Han laughed. "Well, I'm glad you didn't have an afternoon snack. I'm certain that hell is literally waiting where I almost fell."

"It probably is."

"But the real hell was thinking that the last thing I'd be aware of before I died was that terrible stench in the air. What have you been cooking down there?"

Erich laughed. "You wouldn't want to know. What were you doing down here, anyway?"

"I came to get you . . . to tell you that you're hungry."

"I guess that means we're late for dinner."

"That's what it means."

As they stood up, still leaning against the wall, Erich picked up the lamp and held it high to illuminate the broken rope. "That rope must be three thousand years old."

"At least."

"It's a wonder it hasn't broken before now."

"And it's even more of a wonder," Han said, "that the floor is slippery here."

Their eyes met as Erich's thoughts were obviously the same as his own. Han bent down and ran his fingers over the floor and smelled them.

"Lard," he said, glancing soberly at Erich. "Someone has greased the steps with lard."

"Good heavens!" Erich gasped.

"Amen," Han repeated in the same tone.

"But who?"

"Who would know you come down here every day?"

"Anybody," Erich said. "Everybody in the whole blasted castle knows that. It could have been any one of the servants."

"Terrific," Han said sarcastically. "That's just terrific."

"I suppose we'd better tell Father."

"I'll let you tell him." Han managed a smile as they started up the stairs, holding carefully to the center wall. "He always yells when he talks about things like this."

"That's one of the privileges of being the duke," Erich chuckled. "I can't wait until I'm the duke, so I can yell. Being a prince, I can only use an average shout."

Han laughed as they came through the door at the top of the stairs, but he realized he was still a little shaky. He knew they were both using humor to cover their shock over what had just happened—and how much worse it could have been. "I should remember that," Han said. "It is no doubt the most important thing I've heard yet concerning the ruling of this duchy."

"No doubt."

They hurried to wash their hands, then Erich walked into the dining room just ahead of Han. Cameron was just coming to his feet, apparently to go and find them.

"What took so long?" the duke demanded.

"Well," Erich tried to smile, "Han had a little accident."

"Accident?" Maggie stood quickly.

"Don't panic," Erich said. "He's fine."

"Barely," Han added. Now that the drama was over, he realized his hands were actually shaking. He couldn't decide if that was from fear or the actual strain they had endured. Probably both.

"What happened?" Abbi asked fearfully.

Between Han and Erich, the circumstances were explained, and Maggie started to cry somewhere in the middle of the second course of their meal. Surprisingly enough, the duke remained silent, but a blatant intensity appeared in his eyes. And Han suspected it would not easily be erased.

That night Han held Maggie close to him, thinking she was asleep until she moved her head against his shoulder and whispered, "Oh, Han, I can't stop thinking about it. I've never felt so afraid in my life as when I realized how close you'd come to dying."

"Well, don't think about it," he said. "I'll admit it was unnerving, but I—"

"Unnerving! Surely it was more than that. You must have—"

"Yes, I'll admit it," he said, "to you, anyway. It scared me to death. But it's over, and I'm fine."

"I love you so much, Han," she whispered. "I would die without you."

"And I love you," he whispered. "Do you know," he said, "what I kept thinking while I was hanging there?"

"What?"

"I could see you so clearly, holding a baby girl and calling her Hannah. I was praying that I would live to see that day."

Tears filled Maggie's eyes, but Han kissed them away and pulled her against him.

"You know," he said, "you get more beautiful every day."

"I get fatter every day."

"But you look beautiful fat. And I love you more because, as you said, it's my fault that you're fat."

"Stop talking and kiss me."

"Yes, of course," he complied, "Your Royal Fatness."

Cameron had the entire castle staff called in and questioned thoroughly by officers of the Guard regarding the accident that had nearly killed Han—and had obviously been intended for Erich. A thorough investigation was carried out, including an exhaustive search of all the residences and living quarters of every single servant—even though they weren't quite certain what they were looking for. Anything at all that seemed even mildly suspicious is what the captain had ordered. Some servants lived elsewhere and came to the castle to fill their shifts, but many lived in apartments or dormitories that were a part of the castle structure, which meant they could come and go from performing their duties without any notice. The very idea was deeply unsettling to everyone involved, but Cameron insisted that more than a hundred loyal and faithful servants could not be punished because one person might be up to something unsavory.

Since the military force of Horstberg included men with special training to do covert work, there was also extensive effort put into trying to connect any of the servants to Nik Koenig or any of his known associates. Every military officer—even those with high-ranking positions—was also questioned and investigated, even though both the captain and the duke felt certain they were loyal. But nothing turned up—at all. There was no way of knowing who had done it, but Cameron had a good idea who was most likely behind it. Still, there was no proof or evidence, so Cameron could only insist that Erich be extremely careful, and if he was ever to be alone, it would not be for long. As an added precaution, the captain assigned officers to regularly patrol certain areas of the castle, and one man would stand guard continually at the door that went to the stairs leading down to the dungeon so that no one could set any more traps that might bring harm to Erich or anyone else.

Even with every feasible precaution being taken, Han felt an uneasiness that he knew was shared by everyone else involved. It was as if they all knew there was an enemy in their midst, but they could do nothing to combat it when they had no idea who it might be.

Han was sitting with his father and Cameron in the ducal office, chatting more than getting anything done, when the duke glanced at the clock and said, "Erich is late. He should have been here by now."

Han reported, "He went down to his dungeon about, well . . ." he glanced at the clock as well, "not more than twenty minutes ago. He said he wouldn't be long."

"Would you go and see if he's all right?" Cameron asked.

"Yes, of course." Han stood immediately.

"And Han," the duke added, "don't hold the rope . . . please."

"Yes, sir," he smiled.

Han took a lamp with him, not willing to face the stairs in the dark again. But the moment he came around the corner of the hallway, he knew something was terribly wrong. Instead of seeing an officer posted at the door, there was a uniformed man on the floor, clearly injured. Han ran to his side, panic strangling his heart. The panic bolted through his every vein when he got close enough to realize the officer was dead. It only took a second to observe the knife in his back, the pool of blood on the floor, and the way the man's eyes were unnaturally still and wide open.

"Heaven help us," Han muttered, knowing what this had to mean in regard to Erich. He also knew he needed help. He ran back around the corner where he yelled loudly enough to get the attention of the officers standing guard at the door to the duke's office. "Get me some help. Now! Something is wrong."

Knowing the officer had heard him, Han ran back to the door that led to the dungeon and went as quickly as he could manage down the seventy-eight steps, terrified of what he might find when he got to the bottom. His fear heightened when he saw smoke pouring out from beneath the iron door.

Putting the lamp down, he pulled at the door and found it locked from the outside. The key always hung nearby on the wall, but it wasn't in its usual spot. Han stepped back, looking for anything he might use to break the lock. He stepped on something and looked down to see the key.

In a frenzy, he unlocked the door, aware that the smoke was not from fire. It had a chemical smell. He choked and coughed. Covering his mouth and nose with his hand, he fought his way through the smoke and found Erich unconscious on the floor. Recalling with horror the dead officer he'd just found, he prayed that Erich was still alive. Holding his breath, Han took Erich beneath the shoulders and dragged him out of the room, slamming the door to confine the smoke. Heart pounding, he wondered again if Erich might actually be dead.

"Erich!" he shouted, slapping his face and jerking his shoulders. "Erich—wake up!" Han felt more fear now than when he'd believed he was dying himself. Again he shook Erich, looking for any kind of response . . . anything to let him know that Erich was alive.

Trying to think rationally, he pressed his ear to Erich's chest and sighed to hear a heartbeat, and he could feel him breathing. Knowing he couldn't carry Erich all the way up those stairs by himself, he was grateful to hear multiple footsteps coming down. He looked up to see two officers and hurried to report what he knew.

"We'll carry him up," one of the officers said. "Find His Grace and send for the doctor."

Han was grateful for their help as well as their level-headed thinking. Hurrying up the stairs, he tried to comprehend that these men were well-trained enough to remain calm and in control even while they knew one of their own had just been murdered while doing his duty to protect the prince.

Trying to be careful and still hurry, Han fled up the stairs and ran past the body of the dead officer, around the corner into the long corridor that led to the duke's office. He immediately saw a couple of servants and shouted, "Stop! Do *not* come this way. Get His Grace."

They both looked stunned and afraid but turned back toward the duke's office. They only took a step before Cameron and Georg came running out the door, with an officer right behind them.

Han immediately turned back and ran around the corner just in time to see the other officers carry Erich through the dungeon door. They laid him on the floor, and Han fell to his knees at Erich's side, trying once more to wake him without success.

Cameron wondered if he had ever felt so sick in his life as when he saw the scene before him and took in what it meant. An officer dead. Erich unconscious with Han and two officers kneeling beside him.

"I think he's still alive," Han said in response to the question in Cameron's eyes. "But I can't get him to wake up."

"What happened?" the duke asked, more fearful than stern.

"I found the officer dead. I called for help and . . . went down. The other door was locked . . . from the outside . . . and the room . . . was full of . . . smoke . . . and I . . ." Han bit his lip, unable to go on.

Cameron knelt beside his son and fought to hold back an urge to cry or scream.

"Someone has gone for the doctor, Your Grace," an officer reported, making him aware that he was surrounded by a number of officers. And Georg was ever faithful at his side.

Cameron nodded and glanced toward the dead officer on the floor nearby. He'd lost officers in the line of duty, but never within the walls of Castle Horstberg. The very idea made him literally nauseated, and looking again at Erich made it difficult to keep his composure.

The doctor arrived within minutes, out of breath as he knelt at Erich's side, and Cameron went to his feet, pacing breathlessly while he waited for a report. The captain was now at his side, and the dead officer had been covered with a sheet, but Cameron's focus was completely on his son. The doctor checked several things, and then he sighed and looked up at the duke. "His breathing and heartbeat are steady, but he appears to be in a coma. It could last hours, weeks, or . . . he could never come out of it."

Han squeezed his eyes shut, and a harsh lump gathered in his throat. He was barely aware of the duke as he turned and slammed his fist into the stone wall. Only a moment later, Maggie and Abbi came around the corner, having been summoned by one of the servants. The doctor repeated his report to the duchess as he stepped back.

"Oh, please God—no!" the duchess cried as she went to her knees beside her son and Maggie came into her husband's arms.

Han stumbled through the following days as if he were living a nightmare. And everyone around him had the same numb, somber countenance that he knew mirrored his own. Beyond the fear and pain that everyone who knew Erich felt over what had happened to him, they had to face the reality of the circumstances. Erich lay unmoving and lifeless in his bed while a hired nurse attended to him, and the duke or duchess—or often both at the same time—were almost constantly by his bedside.

The horrifying death of the officer who had been killed made the danger of the situation all the more real and undeniable. A funeral was held with full military honors, and most of the royal family attended. The young man was fairly new to serving with the Guard and had lived at home with his parents, who were understandably devastated.

Another thorough investigation was carried out, overseen by Captain Dukerk and criminal analysts who were constantly employed on the duke's committee of national security. But they could find no leads or information that offered anything helpful whatsoever. They had no idea who had done this to Erich and had murdered the officer, even if they all suspected who was likely behind it. Regardless of any suspicions, they could prove nothing.

It was despairing to see the way Erich's parents became almost as lifeless as Erich. The thought of losing him was clearly more devastating to them than to anyone. The duke especially grew completely silent, and a grave expression on his face became permanent.

The day after the officer's funeral, Han went to Erich's room and found the duke alone by his son's bedside. They had spent many hours in here together without a word exchanged, and the silence was something he'd come to expect. Han was doubly worried today since he'd just come from his own room where Maggie lay resting, feeling unusually ill. He had decided to send for the doctor, but recalling that he came here daily to check on Erich, Han would just have him check Maggie at the same time. He didn't bother mentioning the problem to Maggie's parents. They had enough to worry about.

Han was surprised to have his thoughts interrupted. "Han," the duke said softly. "If . . . Erich doesn't make it through this, I—"

"He will," Han stated.

"Even if he does, his mind may not."

"He'll make it."

"If he doesn't, I . . . well, you should know, if you don't already, it will be your son who will inherit this wretched duchy. And if I'm not around, well . . . you've got to raise him right, Han. You can't leave the fate of the country and the people up to chance. You have to raise him to be a duke . . . to know what's expected of him. He must be a good man."

There was a long reign of silence as Cameron watched his son and tears came into his eyes. Han knew that Cameron had succeeded in raising and training his son well to be the duke. And it was heartbreaking to see this situation. But Han replied with impeccable confidence, "Erich will make an excellent duke."

Chapter Seventeen

STARTING OVER

Han began to feel an inward anxiousness when Maggie worsened with each passing day, until she declared that she didn't have the strength to get out of bed. Doctor Furhelm examined her as he had several times since this problem had begun, and he took Han aside to talk with him.

"What is it?" Han asked fearfully.

"I think," the doctor said, "we should perhaps seek out your father-in-law. I believe he will want to hear this, as well."

Apprehension churned inside Han as he led the doctor to the duke's office. They sat down together, and the doctor began asking questions rather than stating a verdict.

"Has Maggie ever shown any signs of lethargy at any other time in her life?"

"No," Cameron answered easily. "She's always been very healthy beyond an occasional illness . . . which you would have been aware of."

"And did any sign of this occur before I was summoned concerning it recently?"

"No," Han answered. "She was a little tired at the beginning of the pregnancy. But you said that was normal, and it went away."

"That *was* normal," he stated. "This isn't."

Panic struck Han. He wondered what was wrong with the baby—or worse, Maggie.

"There is something very unnatural in the symptoms," the doctor said thoughtfully. "Something I've never seen before. And considering the timing of certain other events around here . . . Well, let me ask you . . . who sees to Maggie's meals?"

"The servants," Cameron said.

"But *who* in particular?"

"Uh . . . I don't know," the duke continued, tossing Han a glance of barely concealed terror. "There are probably at least a dozen hands it goes through before . . ." He stopped talking as if he couldn't even put a voice to the possibility being implied.

"And when the meals are served," the doctor asked, "is everyone served out of the same dish, or is each person served separately?"

"Both," Cameron answered dryly, "but usually separate."

"She's mostly been eating in her room for several days now," Han reported.

"It's just a guess," the doctor said, "but I would bet that if you start feeding Maggie something that's . . . well, let me offer a specific suggestion. Say for instance, we have Han's mother prepare Maggie's food, and it doesn't even come near the servants. That wouldn't be too difficult to arrange."

"You are saying, then," Han said, "what I think you're saying."

"If you mean that I believe Maggie is being drugged, yes."

Han and Cameron exchanged a harsh glance before Cameron asked what Han didn't want to. "Drugged or poisoned?" Cameron erupted to his feet and slammed a fist on his desk. "Is this a temporary problem that can be solved . . . or is someone trying to kill my daughter, too?"

The doctor showed nothing but compassion in his expression. He knew Cameron well enough to know the anger was not directed at him. "I can't be completely certain, Your Grace," the doctor said gently, "but I would guess it's more something temporary, that it *can* be remedied. Even given my limited knowledge, I would tend to think that symptoms of slow poisoning would make a person ill, with some serious problems. Given that she seems to be completely healthy but simply lethargic in an unnatural way, well . . . that sounds more like the effect of a pain medication, or something similar."

Cameron sat back down and blew out a harsh sigh as he took in the information. Following a long moment of silence, Han asked another question that he didn't want to say aloud, but they had to know. "What kind of effect will it have on the baby, even if it's stopped now?"

"That's impossible to know," the doctor said. "I don't know for certain what they're using. But I must be honest; I've never been anything less, and I know you expect me to be straightforward." He looked at Cameron, who nodded, then back toward Han. "Hopefully, Maggie will be able to carry this baby to the end, and not miscarry again as we have feared. And I have no way of knowing how the drugs would have already affected the baby. The drugging didn't start until the child was well developed. It could be fine. It could be born with problems. It could not make it here alive."

Again, Han met Cameron's eyes, seeing his own torment reflected in them. But there was little to be said.

"All right," Han said, trying to look at this objectively. They had to do their best to take this on in the most positive way or they would all go mad. "I like your suggestion, Doctor. My mother procures and cooks her own food, and she sees Maggie often, anyway. We'll make certain Maggie doesn't eat or drink anything that isn't brought directly to her from my mother, either personally or by one of us."

"I might be wrong," the doctor added, "but I firmly believe that will remedy the problem. And when she *does* get feeling better, she should take it easy." Han liked his optimism and listened with growing hope. "She is getting rather far along. Keep her out of even potentially dangerous situations. Don't overlook anything. Don't even let her walk down the stairs without holding her arm. I know I don't have to say this, but I'm going to anyway." He focused directly on the duke. "There is obviously a crisis underfoot right now." He glanced toward Han then back to the duke. "You are both very aware of what happened to Erich. And forgive me if I step beyond my bounds as a physician, but I can see the threat here. It appears to me that whoever is trying to get rid of Erich is trying to get rid of the alternate heir: Maggie's child. And if Maggie has a serious miscarriage, after already losing one child, it could be difficult for her to have children at all."

A dark pall of silence followed the doctor's words until Han sighed and mustered up a confidence he didn't entirely feel, but he hoped to ease his father-in-law's concerns. "We'll take very good care of her," he said. "I'm not going to let her out of my sight unless she is resting in bed or with another member of the family." He shrugged and forced a smile. To even consider the possibility of what the doctor had told them was simply too horrible to think about.

"Well," the doctor stood, "I think that covers it. You be careful now," he added. "All of you. And I'll check in with you daily."

"Thank you, Doctor," Han said.

"Yes, thank you," the duke added. "By the way, how is your father?"

"Doing very well. I care for him just as I do my other patients."

"Tell him hello for me," Cameron added, and Doctor Furhelm left.

"You know," Han said when they were alone, "if we ever find a way to prove that Nik Koenig is behind all of this, I'll kill him with my bare hands."

"Not if I have my way," Cameron said sternly, and Han saw something in his eyes that he'd never seen before. Someone was trying to do away with his children. The very idea was unimaginable, but Han felt certain the duke meant it when he said, "If anybody is going to kill him, it's going to be me."

Though Erich's condition remained the same, it was a great relief to see that the doctor's advice for Maggie worked well. Within a few days she was feeling much more like herself. Cameron and Georg seemed to manage the work well enough on their own. Of course, they'd been working that way for years, with the assistance of Captain Dukerk and several committees. But there was a harsh solemnity surrounding every matter of business that took place in the ducal office; every person who knew and had grown accustomed to having Erich by his father's side the last few years could hardly not be keenly aware of his absence. Han had joined the team more recently, but for him it was difficult to do any work at all without Erich by his side. They'd been meant to work together just as their fathers did. Now everything simply felt all wrong. Given the pall hanging over the office, Han was grateful that both Cameron and his father insisted that he spend most of his time with Maggie and make certain she remained safe and healthy.

Han enjoyed the opportunity to be around his wife more, as long as they avoided talking about their concern over whether or not the baby would be all right, which went right along with their concern over whether or not Erich would come out of his coma, or if he was lost to them forever. Han did his best to show a positive attitude around others when they were in need of encouragement. They were all struggling, and he fought hard to use his gift of humor and optimism to try and help the people he cared for get through this. But inside he didn't feel nearly as hopeful as he pretended to be. He could only pray that God might see them through this and that miracles would happen.

With a great deal of time on their hands, Han offered to tell Maggie some stories. She let out a little laugh, which was the first hint of laughter he'd heard since Erich had been found nearly dead. He told her every story he knew, and when she insisted he relay them all again, he couldn't help but be reminded of their time in the Black Forest. When he mentioned his memories to her on a particularly cold afternoon, Maggie said, "I miss it, Han. I wish that you and I were back in the cottage without a care in the world."

"When this is over," he said gently, "we'll go back."

"Will it ever be over?" she asked, treading into that territory they usually tried to avoid.

Maggie watched her husband put a careful grin into place. She knew the expression well. He was trying to keep the mood light and his attitude positive, but she could see through him and knew he was as worried as everyone else. Still, she couldn't fault him for his efforts, and in fact, she was very grateful for them.

"Of course," Han assured her with confidence in his voice. "Everything will be fine."

Maggie didn't press the matter. She knew that Han couldn't possibly know that everything would be fine, but they all had to hold onto the hope that it would be. She hardly dared acknowledge the fear she felt to even consider the possibility that Erich might never recover. And added to that, she could only pray that this child would make it into the world healthy and strong. She tried to comprehend—as her father suspected—that Nik Koenig was behind all of this. Thoughts of her brief relationship with him made her sick. She thanked God every day for the events that had prevented her from marrying him. She couldn't even think about what that would have done to her life, her family. And the country. Thinking about it was simply unbearable, so she tried her best to follow Han's optimistic example and hope that everything would be all right.

As Maggie's health continued to improve, she felt in need of fresh air. The doctor said it would be all right for Han to take her for an occasional walk in the gardens. Maggie hadn't been beyond her room since Elsa had started bringing her meals, and the prospect of going out was very inviting.

"Are you nearly ready, my dear?" Han asked while Klara put up her hair.

"Almost," she said exuberantly.

"It's just a little walk in the garden," Han said.

"And the first time I've been out of this room in years—or so it seems. To me it's an occasion, so hush. Besides, Klara is enjoying herself. Isn't that right, Klara?" Maggie said.

"I am," the maid smiled. "It's been a long time."

"You do well," Han said to Klara. "Maggie's hair always looks beautiful."

"It's beautiful hair," Klara replied. "It is a pleasure to dress it. There." She stood back triumphantly. "All finished." She put a hand over her heart and actually got a glisten of tears in her eyes when she added, "It is so wonderful to see you up and about! I admit that I was worried."

"Amen to that," Han said, and Klara hurried away as if she might want to have a good cry in private.

Han gallantly offered his arm, and Maggie took it. Coming to the top of the stairs, Han held her arm firmly, remembering the doctor's advice. How grateful he was for that advice when three steps down, Maggie slipped. By the way she completely lost her balance, it was only his holding her that prevented her from falling clear to the bottom.

"Good heavens!" Han said, taking her quickly back to the top step, where he sat her down and she took a deep breath. "Are you all right?"

"Yes," she said, "I'm fine. It just scared me."

"Well, it scared me, too," Han said. He went carefully back to the third step, ran his fingers over the marble surface, and wasn't at all surprised.

"Lard," he stated. "Exactly like we found it on the stairs going down to the dungeon. Someone just about succeeded in making certain your baby was never born. Or worse."

Maggie gasped and felt as if her pounding heart might kill her, in and of itself. And the anger and fear in Han's eyes was something she didn't know how to respond to.

"Come on," he said, picking her up in his arms. "I'm taking you back to bed."

Maggie didn't argue. She felt too terrified to even speak.

"What happened?" Klara exclaimed as Han brought Maggie back into the bedroom, where she was barely starting to clean up.

"She just fell on the stairs," he explained.

"Good heavens!" Klara exclaimed. "Are you all right, my lady?"

"I'm fine," Maggie insisted, wanting to believe it wasn't as bad as Han had said. "Surely anyone could have fallen there," she muttered breathlessly as he placed her on the bed.

"On the contrary," he said soberly, "we are the only ones living in this wing. And *you* are the only one who doesn't use the back staircase."

"That's right, my lady," Klara agreed, and Han glanced toward her in question. "Is it true that someone is really trying to do you harm?"

The horror in her expression affirmed her complete innocence and ignorance. Maggie had never had any cause to question Klara's integrity. She'd been working with her for years, and Klara was a fine young woman. But Maggie suddenly wondered if she could trust *anyone* outside of her family. Instinctively she knew she could trust Klara, and there was some relief in that. But it was all so horrible!

Han soberly answered Klara's question. "It appears that way." He nodded toward her with silent appreciation for her concern and added, "You can clean up here later. Thank you."

"Ring if you need anything at all," she said, looking again as if she might start to cry before she rushed out of the room.

"Oh, Han," Maggie cried, and he pulled her into his arms. "I'm so afraid. I don't dare touch anything . . . or go anywhere . . . or eat or drink anything that hasn't come from the right place. Han, will we always have to live this way?"

"I hope not," he said and forced a wan smile that she knew was an attempt to reassure her. But their eyes met, and she knew he felt every bit as terrified as she did.

Han didn't want to tell anyone about Maggie's accident. With Erich still in a coma, the family hardly needed something else to worry about. But only hours after Maggie's fall, she began having pains and spotting blood. Han immediately sent Klara to summon the doctor, and once Klara had returned to sit with Maggie, he went quietly to Erich's room, where he was sure to find one or both of Maggie's parents.

"Is something wrong?" Abbi asked as soon as he entered, but Cameron remained expressionless as he watched his son drifting on in unconsciousness.

"Maggie's in trouble," Han stated, and Cameron turned his head abruptly.

"What happened?" he insisted.

Han explained briefly, making every effort to assure them that it was surely nothing serious. But Cameron and Abbi left Erich in the care of the nurse that had been hired to be on hand, and they went with Han to check on Maggie. Han prayed each step of the way that they would find her doing better and there would be no cause for alarm, but they entered the room to find Maggie writhing with pain, holding tightly to Klara's hand. The maid's expression showed alarm and helplessness before Han thanked her and she hurried out of the room.

"Maggie," Han whispered and sat next to her. She clung to him desperately, oblivious to her parents who were standing nearby. Han glanced once over his shoulder to see them holding to each other, looking horrified and frightened. He felt certain they had to be wondering what they'd ever done to deserve having their family destroyed this way.

The doctor arrived quickly and ushered all of them out of the room. Cameron and Abbi sat quietly in the hallway holding hands while Han paced back and forth, feeling more afraid than he ever had in his life.

Though Cameron appeared calm, Han knew it was otherwise when he stood abruptly and said, "I'm going to find your father."

Han nodded, and Cameron left in haste. Abbi said quietly, "He depends on your father a great deal when things get difficult."

"So do I," Han said and continued pacing.

Moments later, the doctor opened the door and appeared with his sleeves rolled up, looking concerned.

"Your Grace," he addressed Abbi, and she stood, "could you please summon someone to assist me. It appears we're going to have a baby."

Han leaned against the wall for support and bit his lip.

"But it's too soon," Abbi protested. "Will the child survive?"

"At this point," Doctor Furhelm said, "it may either be Maggie or the baby. It's too late to stop labor now."

Han watched Abbi suppress her fear and put forward her most courageous self. He doubted he had the strength that she did, but he felt indescribably grateful when she said to the doctor, "I'll help you."

The doctor didn't hesitate to usher her into the bedroom, leaving Han alone in the hall, wondering if he'd ever see Maggie alive again. He thought of how they'd planned for him to be present when the baby was born, but apparently he wasn't welcome now that it had become a medical emergency. He couldn't decide if that was better or not. Perhaps he should have been grateful to be banished from the room, but he felt as if he would lose his mind. At least he derived some comfort knowing Maggie had her mother with her.

Han paced back and forth, first slowly, and then gaining momentum as if that might make this nightmare end more quickly. He heard Maggie cry out in anguish, and it took every ounce of strength he had to keep from bursting into the room. When she cried out again, he knew he couldn't bear it any longer and moved away where he couldn't hear her. Aimlessly, he wandered the halls, finding himself at the door to Erich's room. He entered quietly to find only the nurse there.

Han nodded toward her in greeting, then sat close to Erich's bed. The painful knot in his stomach tightened as he beheld the sallow look about his friend that only intensified daily. There was little evidence that Erich was still living, and the reality made Han want to die inside. His wife and dearest friend were both on the verge of death, and here he sat, completely helpless to do anything about it.

"Excuse me, sir," the nurse said softly, interrupting his thoughts. "If you're going to be here a few minutes, I'll take care of a matter and leave the two of you alone."

Han nodded and attempted a smile, grateful to have some time with Erich. Impulsively, he took his friend's hand and squeezed it, wishing in vain for some kind of response.

"I don't know if you can hear me," Han said quietly, "but I need to talk anyway. If there is anything inside of you that has the will or power to live, I beg you to find it. Hearts are breaking here, Erich. You must live!" he insisted and closed his eyes, choking back his emotion.

"Maggie's in trouble," he said quietly. "The doctor says that we could lose either her or the baby. I don't care if I ever have any children, Erich," Han went on, his tears refusing to be held back. "If I lose Maggie, I don't know if I can make it. I need her! And I need you!"

Han went to his knees and leaned his head against the bed, holding Erich's hand in his as he prayed with all his might that this family might survive and they could be free of this atrocious oppression. When his prayer was done, Han remained with his head against the bed, even when he heard the door open and close, and he assumed the nurse had returned.

"Han, my boy," Georg said gently, and he felt his father's hand on his shoulder. Han mopped his eyes with his sleeve and came to his feet to be greeted by a firm embrace.

"Cameron told me what happened," Georg said quietly. "Are you going to be all right?"

"I will be if she is," Han stated.

The nurse came quietly back into the room, and Han and Georg went out, walking slowly through the halls.

"I recall well when you were born," Georg said, and Han looked toward him in surprise. "You came into the world backward and grabbed something on the way out. For a while there, I wondered if your mother would ever recover."

Georg smiled at his son. "But she did, and I've never doubted it was a miracle. We were told she would likely never conceive again, and of course, you've figured out by now that you are an only child."

Han had to smile.

"She actually recovered very quickly," Georg went on nostalgically. "Once she got her health back, we forgot about the difficulties and thoroughly enjoyed just having you in our lives." He looked toward Han with affection. "You have been a great joy to us."

Georg moved his eyes straight ahead. "Miracles do happen. And I could be wrong, but I have a feeling Maggie's going to come through this just fine."

Han felt warmth from his father's words, and a degree of peace settled into him.

"And," Georg added, "I would dare say that sooner or later, you will have a beautiful family."

They exchanged a smile and walked in silence for several minutes until Georg said quietly, "Your mother's going to have a baby, Han."

Han stopped walking and turned to face his father, immediately seeing that he was serious.

"Can you believe that?" Georg smiled. "After all these years."

Han chuckled and shook his head in disbelief. "I thought you were too old for that sort of thing."

"Never," Georg grinned, and they started to walk again. "When you live with a woman as beautiful as your mother, it's . . . well, what can I say?"

"I understand," Han said.

"I believe you do," Georg replied.

"A baby?" Han nearly laughed. "Really?"

"Really," Georg assured him. "I'll admit that twenty-four years is a bit far between children, but . . ." he trailed off with a chuckle.

Their conversation brought them to the hallway by Maggie's room, where Cameron sat quietly with his arms folded, glancing up with a sober expression when he saw them.

"Anything?" Han asked as the reality sank back into him like a knife through his heart.

Cameron shook his head, and Georg sat beside him, but Han proceeded to pace the floor. When he finally grew tired of that, he sat beside his father, continuing to pray in silence that all of this would end the way he so desperately wanted it to.

When the door to the bedroom finally opened, the three men stood at the same time. Han's heart was gripped with a fear that he knew the others shared when they saw Abbi standing before them, looking weary and distraught. Meeting their expressions, she covered her mouth with her hand and began to cry.

"Oh, no," Cameron said, and his voice trembled. Han sat back down and felt his father take his hand. "What?" Cameron demanded of his wife.

"It's all right," Abbi finally managed to say. "Forgive me. I'm just so grateful." She looked directly at Han. "Maggie's going to be fine."

Han laughed aloud as he stood up and embraced his father, and Abbi moved into Cameron's arms. Once the embraces of relief were complete, Han turned expectantly toward Abbi, and she led him through the door. His heartbeat quickened to see signs of Maggie's ordeal in the room, which smelled of blood and sweat. But joy swept over him to see Maggie, however pale and weary, turn her face toward him and reach out her hand.

"Han," she said faintly, and he put one knee on the bed to carefully lean over and embrace her, so grateful to know she was alive. "I love you, Han," she said as tears filled her eyes, and he was reminded of the time she'd lost their first baby.

"It'll be all right," he said carefully, brushing his hand over her face. "All I need is you. As long as I have you, nothing else matters."

Maggie smiled weakly, and he embraced her again.

"Han," Abbi said from behind him.

"Yes, Mother," he said, not taking his eyes from Maggie.

"I have something to show you."

Han heard Georg and Cameron chuckle as he rose and turned around. Abbi said nothing as she placed the infant in his arms, and Han sat weakly on the edge of the bed, afraid he'd drop the baby as he suddenly lost his breath.

"She's very small," Abbi said.

"I can see that," Han chuckled breathlessly.

"But she appears to be perfect and handling this world just fine so far."

"I don't believe it," Han said, turning toward Maggie, who was consumed with a proud smile. "She's beautiful."

"Brings back memories, eh?" Cameron said, nudging Georg in the ribs.

"Sure does," Georg replied with a smirk, "Grandpapa du Woernig."

Cameron laughed and slapped Georg on the back. "Sure does make me feel old—Grandpapa Heinrich."

They both laughed while Han continued to admire his daughter, in awe of her tiny fingers against his hand.

"Her name is Hannah," Maggie said.

"Yes, I know," Han smiled.

"Princess Hannah," Georg added.

"Hannah MagdaLena Heinrich," Abbi declared, and Han bent to kiss his wife, knowing that as his father had said, miracles really did happen.

"I never would have believed," Georg said quietly, "that my grandchildren would have royal blood."

"I would have believed it," Cameron said. "Imagine that. Heinrich has become a royal name."

Han smiled up at these two great men he admired and loved so deeply. They'd been friends since childhood, and now they had both become grandfathers at the same time. He chuckled and said, "I bet the two of you didn't drink to *this* when you used to meet in the pub as young bachelors."

"No, I don't think we ever could have imagined *this*," Georg said.

"It's perfect," Abbi said, leaning against Cameron, who put his arm around her. She took Georg's hand, and they all moved a little closer to get a better look at the baby. Han only wished that Erich could be there with them in that moment, but he felt certain that everyone else had the same thought, even if no one wanted to say it.

Han developed a continual swell of gratitude in his heart as he remained close to his wife and baby. Although Maggie was weak through the days following the baby's birth, Doctor Furhelm declared her recovery miraculous. And little Hannah proved to be strong and healthy, apparently unaffected by the trauma placed upon her mother throughout the pregnancy. The only thing deterring their happiness was Erich's condition, which still showed no sign of change.

"I hope Maggie can have more children," Cameron said to Han

one afternoon when the two men were sitting together in the nursery, admiring the baby while Maggie slept in the next room.

"So do I," Han said lightly, but Cameron's response was severe.

"If Erich dies without progeny, his sister must have a son. And Sonia's son will inherit his father's title."

Han was a little taken aback by the very idea. He didn't know which was more difficult to imagine: *his* son being the Duke of Horstberg, or accepting that Erich would not survive to hold the position. Unable to think too deeply about either possibility, he stated with confidence, "Erich will make it through this."

"I want to believe that," Cameron stated and tried to smile. "Either way, I hope that Maggie has a son. Otherwise, too much is left up to chance."

Han said nothing. He knew how important it was to train the next leader of Horstberg correctly and not let the country fall into a ruler's hands by marriage, or leave it vulnerable to people like Nikolaus Koenig who could move in by way of a dubious bloodline. Han too wanted a son, but in his heart, he wanted most of all for Erich to recover.

"As I have said before," Han added, "Erich will make a fine duke."

Cameron smiled toward him then turned his attention to his granddaughter, making all sorts of foolish noises in an attempt to get her attention.

"Too bad the guys at the pub can't see you now," Han said.

"Some things are better kept in the family," Cameron said sternly, but Han caught a glimmer of humor in his eyes.

Maggie had barely drifted back to sleep after feeding the baby when a loud banging at the bedroom door made her sit up in bed.

"I'll get it," Han said, hurrying to put on a robe. Maggie did the same and was at her husband's side when he pulled open the door to see her father standing in the hallway. Cameron's face was expressionless, and Maggie nearly expected him to say that Erich was dead. She reached for Han's hand and squeezed it tightly, knowing by the way he squeezed back that he shared her fear.

"You're a prophet, Han," Cameron said, and gradually, a smile crept over his face. "Erich is asking for you. You'd best come along. You don't keep the future Duke of Horstberg waiting."

Han laughed and embraced the duke. Maggie embraced them both before they went together to Erich's room, knowing the nanny would be able to hear the baby if she woke up while they were gone. Maggie held her breath as she entered the room, well aware of how tightly Han was still squeezing her hand.

"It's about time you got here," a familiar voice said, and Maggie put her hand to her mouth to hold back an unexpected rush of tears that came in response to seeing her brother leaning against the head-board. He looked pale and sallow, but it was immediately apparent there was nothing wrong with his mind. The doctor had warned them that there could be loss of memory, slurred speech, confusion, or any number of other results. It was a great relief to see that Erich was not only going to live, but his mind was whole.

"How many years did you say I'd been asleep?" he asked, turning toward his mother, who sat nearby, beaming to see her son alive again.

"Too many," Cameron answered for her.

"Only a few weeks," the doctor assured him.

"I had a dream about that woman again," Erich said to Han. "You know . . . the one with red hair." Han nodded. "I was hoping she'd be here when I woke up. No such luck, eh?"

Han and Maggie moved closer to the bed and laughed as they each took their turn to embrace Erich and feel the life in him as he responded, however feebly.

"Guess what?" Maggie said as she sat near her brother and held his hand.

"What?" he asked with a weak grin.

"Han and I have a daughter now." As Maggie made the announcement, Erich's grin broadened. "She's beautiful. I'll bring her to meet you tomorrow."

"I'd like that," he said then turned toward Han and added face-tiously, "Papa!"

Han was so grateful to see Erich alive and well that he wanted to curl up and cry like a baby. For now, he just took in the reality and silently thanked God for yet another miracle.

"I cannot deny," Han said, "that becoming a father is about the best thing that's ever happened to me." Erich smiled again. "Your day will come," Han chortled, but Erich's expression of joy immediately faltered. A sudden tension descended over the room, and Han wondered why. Trying to keep the mood light, he said to Erich, "So, you'll be up and about in no time . . . once you get your strength back."

Erich glanced toward his father, who was standing near the doctor. Han caught the glance of dismay they exchanged, and he knew that Maggie did too by the way she grabbed onto his arm as if to brace herself for bad news.

"I don't know," Erich said stoically, lifting his chin in a regal manner; it was that same look of drawing courage that Han had seen in both of Erich's parents. "I can't feel my legs."

Han felt Maggie squeeze his hand almost painfully, but he tried not to let his expression falter at the news.

"It may very well be temporary," the doctor said quickly, "but we shall see."

"At least you're alive," Cameron said. "We are all very grateful for that. And you can still rule a country. You're not going to get out of it."

"Yes, I *can* do that." Erich managed a chuckle.

"And I'll get a few pretty maids to take care of you." The duke grinned.

"It won't be so bad," Erich said, but Han read a deep sadness in his eyes.

"And how are you feeling, Maggie?" the doctor asked.

"Quite well, thank you, all things considered."

Abbi watched Han and Maggie leave the room and silently thanked God *again* for the miracles that had taken place in regard to her children. The turmoil she had been through as a mother during these recent weeks was the worst in her life. And she knew that Cameron had struggled as well. They had shed many tears together, and countless prayers had been uttered with the hope that the love they had for their children might evoke compassion from a merciful God and grant them the miracles they had been seeking. Now Maggie was doing well and so was the new baby. And Erich had finally come back to life. Knowing there were challenges yet to face, she would keep praying for her children's well-being and safety—just as she always had. But given how bad things had been, she could feel nothing now but gratitude. And whatever Erich had yet to overcome with the adjustments in his life, they would be there beside him. She was just so grateful to have him back! To know that he would live!

Abbi turned her attention to her son, still marveling at the evidence of his being awake and aware. They exchanged a smile before the doctor chuckled and said, "Well, if you don't mind, my wife declares I'm spending far too much time here."

"I dare say she's right," Cameron said.

"I think I'll go home and get some sleep. I'll check back first thing in the morning."

"Thank you," Cameron said.

Doctor Furhelm left, and Cameron declared that he was going to bed. "Perhaps now that I know you're going to be all right," he said to Erich, pressing a fatherly kiss into his son's hair, "I might actually be able to get some sleep and not start snoring in one of those stupid meetings." Erich smiled up at his father, reminding Abbi of when he was a child.

Cameron kissed her and asked if she was coming, but she opted to stay with her son for a while longer. "I'll see you in the morning, then," he said and kissed her once more before he left Abbi alone with Erich.

"How are you feeling?" she asked gently, sitting on the edge of the bed where she could easily reach to push his red curls back off his brow.

"Awful," he laughed, "but I have to assume that I'm feeling better than I have in weeks."

"We missed you." Abbi couldn't hold back tears.

"There's no need to cry, Mother." Erich put an arm weakly around her as she leaned against the headboard to sit closer to him.

"I'm just so happy to have you back," she said. "You are so dear to me, Erich. A mother could not want for a better son."

"No," he chuckled, "it's the other way around." Abbi smiled, and he touched her hair where it hung over her shoulder. "If I ever get married," he said, "I want a woman just like you."

"And why is that?" she asked.

"That's easy," he said. "You, Abbi du Woernig, are practically a legend."

"A legend?" She laughed, pretending innocence. She was well aware of how people talked about her, but in her mind, it was mostly exaggerated nonsense.

"People admire you," he said, "and the way you saved this country with your love for Father. The people of Horstberg are in awe of you." He met her eyes, and she could see that he felt the need to say what was on his mind, but his weakness was evident. "I am in awe of you, too. You are too kind and good to be true, I think. And I want a woman just like you."

Abbi could do nothing but smile warmly. Being paid the highest compliments she could ever recall hearing from her son, she was left speechless and even more grateful for his second chance at life.

"You look very tired," she said quietly, brushing her fingers over his pale forehead. "Why don't you rest, and we'll talk more tomorrow."

"Please stay," he said, slipping his hand into hers.

Carefully, Abbi leaned against an extra set of pillows and lifted her feet onto the bed as she put her arm around Erich and he pressed his face to her shoulder. He didn't know that she had held him this way many times while he'd been in a comatose state. But now she could feel life in him, and she had to fight back the threat of more tears.

"Sing it to me," he whispered as he closed his eyes, and she knew what he meant. "I know I'm at least fifty years too old for such things, but I want to hear it anyway."

Abbi brushed her lips across her son's brow and ran her fingers idly through his red curls as she softly sang the song that Cameron had written for him, long before he was born.

I know a place where snow falls white
That's where I long to be
Where castle turrets strike moonlight
And shine where I can see
I've known my love on mountains high
Where meadows bloom in blue
I know my love is there for me
I know that love is true
There is a place where snow falls deep
And warmth is near the hearth

Deep in my sweetheart's dreams I sleep
There's comfort in this warmth
The world is cold and brash outside
I fear what it imparts
But I know my love is here with me
A fire burns in my heart.

The day after Erich had come back from the dead, Han was with the duke in his office when a knock came to the door. The two of them were alone in the room since Georg had gone with Captain Dukerk to take care of a matter of business in the keep.

"What is it?" Cameron called.

Heidi entered and curtsied. "Mr. Koenig is here to see you, Your Grace."

"Send him in. I've been expecting him."

The maid left, and Han looked toward Cameron in surprise. "You've been expecting him?"

"Quite." Cameron scowled. "Though it surprised even me, I had an urge to talk with Mr. Koenig. But rather than go hunting him down, I simply didn't send out his allowance." Cameron smiled. "I knew he'd show up sooner or later."

"I see," Han said dubiously, wondering why on earth Cameron would want to see Nik.

Heidi entered the office again, curtsied, and announced, "Mr. Koenig, Your Grace."

"Thank you, Heidi." Cameron rose from his chair as the maid closed the door behind her. Nik Koenig strode in with his chin lifted high, and Han felt every muscle in his body become tense. It took great self-restraint not to bodily attack the man and strangle him.

"Hello, Uncle," Nik said lightly. "It seems you've overlooked something."

"Quite purposely," Cameron stated. Nik lifted his brows, seeming amused. "I wanted to see you."

"Really?" Nik asked. "Have you reconsidered . . . letting me move in, I mean?"

"Not in a million years." Cameron placed his palms flat on the desktop and leaned forward. A silent expectancy descended as their eyes met, and Han wondered what Cameron would say. He knew the emotional struggles Cameron had gone through in the past weeks because of Nik Koenig. The pain that had been inflicted on the family was still fresh and raw. And they all *knew* Koenig was behind it, even if there wasn't any proof.

"I'm waiting," Nik insisted.

"There have been some odd coincidences around here," Cameron said softly, yet with a cruel intensity in his eyes, "and I have a word to say concerning them. Ever since you came back from that quaint little jail in Italy, bizarre things have been happening to the people I love. At this point, you're lucky they're still alive."

"Are you accusing me of something?" Nik asked, appearing calm. But Han could *see* the glimmer of guilt in his eyes. Or perhaps it was more accurately some tiny sparkle of self-satisfaction.

"I am implying something that you'd best listen closely to, or you might find yourself wishing you'd never set foot in this room."

"Are you threatening me?" Nik asked, his eyes narrowed but still mildly triumphant.

"Call it what you will," Cameron stated. "Sooner or later, justice will be met."

"You *are* insinuating, then, that I had something to do with it." He chuckled carelessly. "Surely you don't think that—"

"I don't have to think it." Cameron's voice went even lower. "I know with every fiber of my being that you are not without guilt in this."

"You'll never prove it," Nik said dryly. Han saw a muscle in Cameron's neck tighten, and his own nerves wrenched. Nik had just all but admitted it was true.

"Most likely not," Cameron said, "but it's not proof I'm after." Cameron straightened his back and sauntered around the desk. "What I want, Mr. Koenig, is peace." He sat on the corner of the desk and folded his arms. "That is the major obligation of my position. It is my responsibility to keep peace—with my family and with my country. And I will do anything . . . *anything*," Cameron leaned forward, and Nik took a step back, "to insure peace."

Again silence hung for several moments as Cameron's words were absorbed.

"Now bear this in mind, Mr. Koenig," the duke continued. "If anything—anything at all—happens to anyone I care for—your fault or nobody's fault—I will have you tracked to the ends of the earth, and I will have you hung and quartered at the very least. As I see it, you'd do well to concentrate your efforts on praying that this castle remains a very safe place to live. Am I making myself clear?"

"So you *are* threatening me," Nik said, seeming only slightly ruffled. "I would have thought such a thing went beyond your moral judgment. I was under the impression that you were strictly governed by the restrictions of the law. No proof, no guilt."

"Perhaps you didn't hear me correctly," Cameron said. "Let me clarify myself. I want peace. And for the sake of peace, I will be a tyrant if I must." Cameron rolled his hand into a fist and held it near Nik's face. "I'm certain you are aware of the power I hold. If you weren't, you wouldn't be coveting it so badly. But remember this, my boy—as long as I have this power, you will leave my family and my country in peace. If you want the money to keep coming, then you'd best mind your business and your manners. If trouble starts, the first thing you're going to lose is the money, the next is your freedom. The list goes on and on."

"Are you finished?" Nik asked cynically.

Han waited only a moment before he said, "He might be finished, but I'm not." He stepped abruptly toward Nik and felt some satisfaction over the way Nik took a couple of quick steps backward, looking alarmed. Han figured it just put the cretin closer to the wall, which would make it impossible to escape Han's sudden uncontrollable urge to have his *own* conversation with Nik Koenig. Without giving himself time to think about what he was doing or talk himself out of it, Han took hold of Nik's collar and slammed him into the wall. Nik was taken off guard enough that he made no attempt to protest, and obviously, he knew that Han wasn't the only man in the room who likely wanted to do him harm.

"Now, you listen to *me*," Han said, speaking gruffly, his face only an inch away from Koenig's. "You have no comprehension of the self-discipline it's taking to not beat you to a pulp, the same way you and your thugs beat me. But far worse than that is the mental list I have of all the things you have done to hurt Maggie—and it is *very* long. I could beat the hell out of you for that alone. We may not have any proof connecting you to more recent events, but Maggie and I have both seen and heard you do and say things that have put you very close to the edge of a cliff. Your father was very good at exaggerating the truth and creating trumped-up charges in order to put men in front of a firing squad for less than you have done. This is *not* a democracy, Mr. Koenig. So bear in mind that the man standing behind me has the power to wipe your existence off the face of the earth. You can be grateful that he's actually a *fair* man—unlike your father—and he will honor the law. But you would do well to be careful—very, *very* careful. Because if anything goes wrong— anything at all—I will personally use every resource Horstberg has to hunt you down and see you utterly undone. With or without the duke's permission, I will *destroy* you. Are we clear on that?"

Nik's countenance showed anger, but Han could see the fear in his eyes, and he relished it. When Nik didn't answer right away, Han slammed him against the wall again and shouted, "Are we clear?"

"Quite clear," Nik said, and Han reluctantly let go, took a steadying breath, and stepped back.

Only then did it occur to Han that Cameron might not be happy with him for the way he'd just behaved, but overall, he really didn't care. Nik hurriedly straightened his collar and turned his fearful eyes toward the duke, who said nothing as he picked up an envelope off the desk and slapped it into Nik's hand. Nik turned abruptly and opened the door, then paused and looked over his shoulder. Tension rose sharply as his eyes met Cameron's. Nik said nothing, but Han knew there was deep significance for Cameron in that moment, which distracted him from his own outburst toward Nik.

After Nik had left and closed the door, Han just came right out and asked, "What was that about? That . . . look?"

Cameron didn't appear puzzled or taken by surprise. He clearly knew what Han meant. He went back to his chair and sat down with a weary sigh. "I see my brother in his eyes," he said. "Nikolaus du Woernig had an incessant drive for power and a complete lack of scruples." Cameron shook his head and closed his eyes. "I still live with the damage he did in the four years he ruled this country, and when I look at Nik Koenig, I . . ." He hesitated and took a deep breath as if he were trying to control his temper as well as his thoughts. "It's as if the years that have passed since my brother's death are nonexistent, as if it never happened, and he's still here, still trying to undo me simply because he believed he had the right to do so." He shook his head again. "And I will never understand it. Never."

Han thought about that for a minute and said, "Well, I'm glad you said what you did. And I'm glad to know that you meant it."

"I *did* mean it," Cameron said. He gave Han a steady gaze, and he could feel it coming; some kind of reprimand was surely warranted for being so brash with Nik Koenig. But he said firmly, "And I'm glad you said what *you* did."

"You are?"

"Absolutely," Cameron said and looked toward the window as if the answers to his problems might be out there somewhere. "And I'm glad you *did* what you did. I wish I could have done it, but being the duke calls for a certain amount of . . . decorum, I suppose." Cameron chuckled with no humor whatsoever and looked at the floor. "I only wish you'd given him a fat lip, as well."

"Perhaps next time," Han said.

"I pray to God there won't be a next time," Cameron said and sighed deeply, looking out the window again. "Still . . . there is only so much I can do, ironically, because I refuse to be like my brother; I refuse to lower myself to taking tyrannical measures to solve a problem—even one as ugly as this." He sighed. "Let's just hope Koenig will take heed to our threats."

"I think they should at least hold him off," Han said, attempting to lighten the mood.

But Cameron turned to look at him, and the severity in his eyes only deepened. "What just happened might hold him off," Cameron stated, "but it isn't over." He looked toward the door where Nik had just left. "The bastard is too much like his father. Somehow I just know that it isn't over."

Chapter Eighteen

PREMONITION

"It's a good thing I didn't fall in love before now," Erich said lightly to Han, who was sitting cross-legged at the foot of the bed on the other side of a chessboard.

"Why's that?" Han asked and moved his knight.

"What kind of woman would want a man in my condition?" he asked, only slightly cynical.

"One who loves you," Han said easily.

Erich looked dubious, but he turned his concentration to the chessboard to make his next move.

"Have you seen Dulsie lately?" Han asked. He'd hardly seen her at all, but that wasn't unusual. Still, he knew that Dulsie and Erich were good friends, and surely she would have been aware of all that Erich was going through.

"Every day," Erich replied without breaking his concentration. By the way he made no further comment, Han had to conclude that Erich still felt the same way about her—that they were friends and friends alone.

A minute later Erich said, "It's a good thing I had already decided to take your advice."

"What advice is that?" Han asked absently while he studied the chessboard, dismayed by Erich's move that had put him at a disadvantage.

"To not worry about getting married and just enjoy life. I'd already stopped worrying about it. Now I don't have to adjust."

Realizing the severity of what Erich was saying, Han drew his attention completely away from the game in front of him and looked directly at Erich. "But you want to get married, don't you? I mean . . . you should, don't you think?"

"Why?" Erich leaned back against the headboard and folded his arms.

"Well, because you don't want to be alone," Han insisted.

"I can't have children," Erich argued.

"What makes you so sure?"

"Han! I can't feel anything from the waist down. Now how do you suppose I can . . ." Erich didn't finish, and Han had no idea what he could ever say in response. A long moment later, Erich said, "So, what's the point? I am *not* going to sentence any woman to life with half a man. I won't do it!"

"There is more to marriage than that," Han said gently. "Maggie's problems with her pregnancy prevented any kind of relations for months. It didn't stop us from holding each other, enjoying each other's company, or even sharing intimacy. Believe it or not, there are good women out there. And to repeat some wisdom I heard your father say once, if you live right, you'll find someone."

"I can't go out like this." Erich sighed and leaned his head back abruptly. "I have to face the fact that I may be this way for the rest of my life." He looked down, and his voice softened. "I still have nightmares about it. I'd only been in the room a few minutes when I knew something wasn't right. I heard something behind me and turned around just as the door slammed shut. Then the room started to fill with smoke. The next thing I knew, I was in this bed feeling twenty years older."

Erich's eyes became distant as he went on. "Once in a while I do remember little things, though. There must have been times when I was aware of what was going on around me, because I remember people talking about me—and to me." He looked up at Han. "You talked to me."

Han gave him a dubious glance.

"You told me if there was anything inside of me that had the power or will to live, I should find it."

"I *did* say that," Han said and looked into his eyes for a long moment, absorbing the irony. "I don't know about you," he added, "but I'm sure grateful that you're alive."

"I am grateful." Erich smiled. "I must admit."

"But still . . . it's difficult."

"Yes," Erich admitted, "it's difficult." He gave a dry chuckle. "It's your turn, Han." They continued their game in silence. Han wanted to be able to say something that might help give Erich perspective or hope, but he honestly couldn't come up with a single word. Pretending to be entirely focused on the game, he was grateful when Abbi came into the room.

"Hello, Mother," Erich said warmly.

"May I watch?" she asked, taking a chair near the bed.

"If you want to watch me win," Han said.

"We'll just see," Erich retorted.

Abbi enjoyed watching the remainder of the game as Erich put up a hard fight and won. He leaned back triumphantly while Han moved the chessboard from the bed to a nearby table, and Abbi indulged in memories of these boys playing together as children.

"See if I ever play with you again," Han said, imitating a hurt child.

Erich chuckled as Han left the room. "He always says that."

Abbi smiled and took his hand. "How are you feeling?"

"As well as could be expected, I suppose," he answered.

"I have something for you," she said softly, placing a finely etched gold bracelet into his hand.

"What is this?" Erich asked.

"You know what it is."

"Yes, but why are you giving me your mother's bracelet?"

"My father gave it to her when he asked her to marry him. And you know it holds special significance with your father and me. When you find that special girl, Erich, I want you to give it to *her*. And someday she can give it to one of your children."

Erich looked up at her dubiously. "Mother, I don't think that—"

"And make certain she knows what a special talisman it is in this family. That bracelet was the key to saving Horstberg once." Abbi smiled wistfully. "Be sure to tell her the story behind that as well."

Abbi knew her son well enough to know that he wanted to protest. She knew that at this moment he likely felt certain the giving of this bracelet would stop here. But she needed to give him hope that he would continue to improve, so she simply smiled and kissed his brow before she left the room.

Han was glad to see both Maggie and Erich showing improvement each day, and even more glad when Cameron personally asked him to focus the majority of his time for now on keeping track of both of them. The duke was especially concerned about keeping Erich's spirits up as he fought to regain his physical strength, and possibly have to accept that he might never walk again. There was always a nurse close by to help see to Erich's needs, and the nurses had been carefully chosen as kind, efficient, and discreet. But Han felt touched to have Erich's father say that no one but Erich's best friend could help him through this.

"As parents we can give him love and support," Cameron had said, "but there is no one like a true friend to get you through a crisis." Han knew he'd been speaking from experience, and he was referring to the deep lifelong friendship he shared with Georg. But the duke was also very close with Captain Dukerk, and the three men had been through much together. Now Han had been given the unmatchable assignment of helping the next Duke of Horstberg get through what would likely be the greatest crisis of his life; the adjustment ahead could be enormous if his inability to feel his legs—or use them—didn't heal with time.

Han often tried to keep his time with Erich light while they played chess and card games and reminisced over their antics as youth. Maggie came to visit often, as did Erich's parents and other friends and family members. And Erich loved to see the baby and even hold her. He seemed in good spirits and often said that he was grateful to be alive. But there were times when Han was alone with Erich that he could see through Erich's attempts to be brave and dignified, and he knew that his friend was afraid and hurting.

More than once Han forced Erich to talk about his feelings. He even provoked him to get angry over it a couple of times, knowing that he surely had to be angry, and such anger was better expressed than held inside. Following one lengthy bout of anger where Erich had cursed and shouted and expressed exactly how he felt about all of this, he actually shed tears of grief as he admitted that he had to accept that his life would not be what he'd expected, and he would do well to get used to it. Han kept holding onto the hope that Erich would improve over time, and the doctor said that he had read of cases where such a thing was certainly possible. But Erich was less optimistic. And all things considered, Han couldn't blame him.

As Erich seemed to resign himself to his circumstances, and Maggie became stronger after her childbirth, peace fell over the family once again. The strong ties among them deepened as they united to give Erich the sustaining love he needed to face this change in his life. And during this time, Sonia also gave birth to a daughter. They received detailed reports of the event in lengthy letters from both Sonia and Rudolf, and Cameron and Abbi clearly regretted that their daughter lived so far away that it simply wasn't feasible to leave their responsibilities and see their other new granddaughter at this time. Although Han suspected that their biggest reason for not going was more about Erich than it was about running the country. Han knew that the committees who were firmly in place, and the military force as well, could all manage through the duke's absence for a time. He talked with his father about it, and they both decided to encourage Cameron and Abbi to take some time off and go see their other child and her new daughter. Georg agreed that he would do his best when the time was right.

"Still no heir," Erich claimed with mock disgust when he heard the news about Sonia's baby. He seemed to take it lightly, but Han knew how much it bothered him. And even if Erich's parents never admitted it, he knew it bothered them, too. He felt certain they all had to wonder if the du Woernig name would end with Erich.

With a great deal of prodding from Georg and every member of the family, Cameron and Abbi finally left to go and stay with Sonia for a couple of weeks to get acquainted with Hannah's little cousin. The duchy was left in Georg's hands, and he started bringing piles of paperwork to Erich's bedroom and told him to make himself useful. Erich complained, but Han knew he appreciated Georg's insight. Han appreciated it too. He was able to sit with Erich and discuss political matters, and they both felt as if they were becoming more prepared to take on the enormous responsibility of running a country.

During Cameron and Abbi's absence, Elsa's pregnancy began to affect her adversely. Georg became overwrought with concern, and Han was worried about them both. Maggie and Hannah practically moved in with Elsa so they could offer company and help care for her, since the doctor had ordered Elsa to remain confined to bed. Maggie told Han that she was coming to love Han's mother more than ever as they spent endless hours together, and through Elsa's stories, Maggie had learned more of the days before her father's reclamation when life was very different for the du Woernigs and the Heinrichs.

While Maggie spent her time caring for Elsa, Han continued doing the same for Erich.

"If you don't stop grumbling at those nurses," Han scolded—not for the first time—pulling open the drapes, "they'll all quit and you'll be stuck with me to do everything—because I'll be the only one to put up with you. Even Theodor hardly dares step into the room."

"What do I need him for?" Erich snarled.

"Whether you're going out or not, those of us who are coming in would prefer that you stay clean and groomed. Those nurses especially wouldn't come anywhere near you if Theodor didn't put up with you enough to assist in your personal hygiene."

"That would suit me fine," Erich muttered. "They're fussy . . . all of them. They fuss over every stupid little thing, and I'm tired of it. I'm quite accustomed to taking care of myself."

"Face it," Han said, spreading the chessboard out on the bed, "you can't take care of yourself for the time being. So stop grumbling and accept the help you need."

Erich said far too seriously, "I'm not sure what the point is to even go on living if I can't get out of this bed and take care of myself."

"We're working on ways for you to get out of this bed and be able to get around," Han reminded him. "Once you get more of your strength back, you will adjust, and," he shrugged, "maybe we'll get a miracle yet."

Erich just glared at Han and turned his focus to the chess game, but his mood didn't improve. In fact, it became steadily more sour over the next few days. Han could see the spirit fading from Erich even while he was beginning to look more like himself and get some color back to his face. Han felt awful every time he stopped to think about the possibility that Erich's condition could be permanent, but he didn't know what to do about it. He wished there was something—anything—he could do to bring the life back to Erich's eyes. But all anyone could do was pray that Erich could find a way to be at peace and find happiness with the changes that had occurred in his life.

"It's just sad," Maggie said to Han late one evening while she sat next to him in bed, nursing Hannah. "To see a man so young, so full of life, condemned to live that way. It's sad."

Han could only agree. But he didn't want to talk about it. There was nothing he could say that hadn't already been said many times already.

The following morning, Han went early to Erich's room. In the hall he met the maid carrying Erich's breakfast tray and confiscated it from her in order to deliver it personally. He was surprised to find the bedcovers thrown back and Erich staring at his legs that were sticking out from beneath his nightshirt.

"What are you doing?" Han asked, setting the tray on the bureau.

"Shut up and sit down," Erich said, patting the bed beside him.

Han did as he was told. Erich slowly grinned and pointed to his toe. "Watch," he said, and Han realized it was moving.

"You can feel it?" he gasped, making no attempt to hide his excitement.

"Just a little," Erich said, "but . . ." He laughed. "Well, it's enough to make me think there may be life beyond this."

Han immediately sent for Doctor Furhelm and observed with delight as Erich reported the good news to him. The doctor expressed a great deal of confidence that this was a very good sign and that Erich would continue to heal. According to the doctor's instructions, Han began a routine of regularly massaging and exercising Erich's legs, doing all he could to help put movement back into them. Theodor was eager to help when he realized what they were up to. Within just a few days, Erich had a remarkable turnaround. As feeling and movement returned to Erich's body, his spirit came back to life in the process. Reverting to the idea of how much they'd loved to play harmless pranks on others in their youth, they decided to keep the progress a secret from everyone but the doctor, and Theodor was sworn to secrecy. When Han finally got Erich on his feet and helped him take a few steps, they both laughed so hard they nearly cried.

"All right," Erich said to Han the following day, "I'm getting out of this room. Help me get some breeches on. I've had enough of this."

Erich shaved, and Theodor helped him dress, and then, with a firm hand on Han's arm, Erich moved carefully toward the door. They were barely into the hallway when Maggie appeared, looking as if she'd seen a ghost. Han and Erich laughed while she recovered from the shock. She cried with uncontrollable relief and threw her arms around her brother's neck.

A couple of days later, Cameron and Abbi returned from Schmautzberg, arriving just in time to have dinner with the family. They entered the dining room while Abbi was saying to her husband, "As soon as we've eaten, we'll go up and see Erich. I hope he's—" She stopped mid-sentence as they both realized Erich was seated at the table in his usual place. Han took Maggie's hand while they observed expectantly, barely able to keep from laughing.

Following a long moment of silence, Erich nodded casually. "Hello, Mother . . . Father."

Han wondered if they simply believed someone had helped move Erich downstairs. Astonishment, relief, and joy all erupted from both of Erich's parents when he rose from his chair and walked toward them with very little difficulty.

"Oh, thank God," Abbi cried as Erich embraced her. She touched his face and looked down at his legs as if she couldn't believe the evidence. It was difficult to tell if she was laughing or sobbing as she pressed her face to his shoulder. Tears brimmed in Cameron's eyes as he put his arms around both of them, and he ruffled Erich's hair as if he were still a boy.

"We're truly blessed," Cameron said quietly.

"Amen," Erich added. Han shared a knowing smile with Maggie, and then impulsively kissed her, knowing she shared his gratitude for such rich miracles in their lives.

Abbi loved the onset of autumn and often declared it to be her favorite season. This particular autumn was unusually warm. Long after it should have snowed, temperatures were still pleasant, and crisp leaves covered the ground.

"It's a beautiful day," Abbi said to her husband as they approached the center of town on horseback with Georg riding beside them.

"Hannah seems to be enjoying it," Cameron said, glancing at the baby on his lap, his arm securely around her. Adorned in a pale green bonnet and sweater, six-month-old Hannah took in her surroundings with bright-eyed curiosity.

A number of children clambered near the duke as he dismounted near the market square, and even the adults who stood nearby watched with more interest than usual. As Georg helped the duchess dismount, all of the grandparents were full of proud smiles.

Everyone knew who the child was, but this was the first time anyone outside of the castle had seen her. Cameron had impulsively decided that today was ideal for Hannah's debut into public. The duke showed no hint of apprehension as the children gathered close to get a good look at the young princess. He bent down with Hannah in his arms so that she could be seen.

"This is Princess Hannah," he declared, properly introducing her.

"She is beautiful, Your Grace," a young girl replied.

"Yes, she is," he agreed. "And she has her mother's red hair. You can see that, of course, from those curls sticking out from beneath her bonnet."

"Does she have a dolly?" another child asked, and the duke chuckled while Abbi observed, warmed with delight by memories of when she and Cameron had first brought their own children into town.

"She certainly does," Cameron declared. "And she won't sleep a wink without her."

The children giggled, and Abbi allowed her husband another minute to show off his granddaughter before she took his arm, insisting that they had important shopping to attend to. They began to casually browse in a way that was familiar and comfortable, with Georg hovering near them. Abbi knew he wished Elsa could be with them, and they were all looking forward to this ordeal being over for her.

"Cameron, look!" Abbi said to her husband. "Aren't these just the perfect doilies to go in the winter parlor? I've been looking for some like this."

"Imported from France, Your Grace," the proprietor offered, and Abbi smiled toward him.

"If you say they're perfect," Cameron said, "then they're perfect."

"Well, I think they're hideous," Georg interjected. "That winter parlor is gaudy enough without sentencing it to those things."

"I'm buying them anyway." Abbi shot an amused, indignant glare toward Georg. "If you don't like them you'll just have to stay out of there."

"Yes, of course, Your Grace," Georg replied. He took Hannah from Cameron so that he could pay for the doilies.

They wandered on until Georg stopped to look over some scarves. "What do you think, Your Grace?" he asked Abbi, always careful to uphold the title in public. "Would Elsa like this?"

"I believe she would," Abbi said. "You have good taste."

Georg turned Hannah back over to Cameron and paid for the purchase, then Abbi handed her package to Georg for safe keeping while she examined the scarves further. He smiled as he took the wrapped doilies from her, and she threatened him against trying to discard them.

"Try that one," Cameron said, pointing to a particular scarf.

"This?" Abbi asked.

"Yes, that's just the one you need to liven up that dreadful dress you brought home last week."

She smiled at his comment, and he held it against her with his free arm.

"You've got the color wrong," Georg said after scrutinizing her closely. "That red clashes with her hair."

"It's not red," Cameron protested lightly, "it's burgundy."

"It still clashes," Georg insisted. "Try the green one," he added, exchanging it with the one Cameron held. "It matches her eyes . . . and would go better with the dress. Which, by the way, is not dreadful."

"Green it is," Cameron conceded and gave his friend a mock frown. "And it is dreadful." The duchess laughed and moved on while Cameron paid for the scarf. She wondered if these people thought that the worst thing the duke had to deal with was the choice of scarf colors and his aversion to the latest fashion. She watched as he and Georg took turns coddling over Hannah on her first adventure, and she knew that the people had to realize how hard these men worked. Otherwise, life would not be as good for them as it was.

Abbi's thoughts were interrupted when she felt a hand lightly touch her arm and a woman's voice with a thick accent said, "Maggie, is that you?"

Abbi turned to see a pleasant-looking obese woman, whose expression immediately faltered when she realized she had the wrong person.

"Oh, excuse me," she stammered. "I'm so sorry. I thought you were—"

"You're looking for Maggie?" Abbi asked easily.

"Yes," the woman relaxed at her kindness, and a handsome, middle-aged man appeared beside her.

"You mustn't be embarrassed," Abbi said. "People say that she and I look a great deal alike. It is a compliment to me."

"You know her, then?" the man asked.

"Quite." Abbi smiled. "I am her mother."

"Oh, Claude!" the woman clapped her hands together. "Can you believe the coincidence? This woman is Maggie's mother."

"Allow us to introduce ourselves," this man called Claude said in an equally thick French accent. "I am Claude Dormante, and this is my wife, Josette. We've been wandering around Germany over the past few months and decided to pay a visit to Han and Maggie."

"How delightful!" Abbi said. She turned to her husband as he approached. "Look, Cameron, these are the Dormantes. The people Han and Maggie told us about, who helped them in Italy."

"It is a pleasure," Cameron said, offering his hand to Claude.

"What a beautiful baby!" Josette exclaimed, and Cameron grinned proudly.

"This is Han and Maggie's daughter," Abbi said, and Josette let out a gleeful giggle. "You must come to the castle," Abbi added. "I'm certain they'll be delighted to see you."

"We're on our way back now," Cameron said. "Your carriage can follow us."

Josette grinned toward her husband, who glanced toward the

castle suspended high above the valley. "I think we can find the way," he said, and Cameron chuckled.

"Heidi," Abbi said, coming through the door, "are Han and Maggie still in the music room?"

"Yes, Your Grace," she replied.

"Go up and tell them they have guests, and have someone make certain that Mr. and Mrs. Dormante are comfortable in the east drawing room."

"Yes, Your Grace." The maid curtsied and scurried away.

"I'll show you the way," Cameron offered.

"And I will see you in a few minutes," Abbi said to Claude and Josette, who both thanked her profusely and insisted that they not make any fuss.

While Georg went to give Elsa what he'd bought for her and Cameron went with their guests to the drawing room, Abbi took Hannah up to the nursery.

"Look, Hannah," Abbi said, pulling off the little bonnet, "here is Ruthild to put you down for a nap."

"Ah," the plump little woman took Hannah and grinned, "Ruthild missed you, little darling. Did she enjoy herself, Your Grace?"

"I believe she did," Abbi smiled. "She hardly made a peep. We have company who would like to see her, so bring her downstairs as soon as she wakes up."

"I'll do that," Ruthild smiled at Hannah, and Abbi left to join their guests, sitting close beside her husband, who was already engaged in delightful conversation. Georg showed up a few minutes later since Elsa had declared the need for a nap. By the time Han and Maggie came to the drawing room, Claude and Josette were being regaled with stories by Cameron and Georg.

"Oh, my," Maggie said, coming through the door. "I don't believe it."

Han laughed as Claude and Josette rose to greet them.

"You said summer," Han scolded. "We'd about given up on you."

"We wrote to you," Maggie said, "but you didn't answer."

"We haven't been home," Josette replied. "How can you expect us to get your letter if we're not home?"

"We should have known." Han smiled toward Maggie.

"How long can you stay?" Maggie asked.

"At least until after Christmas, I hope," Cameron insisted.

"I must confess," Claude said to Maggie. "Your father has already talked us into staying until January, at least."

"How delightful." Maggie linked her arm with Josette's and moved toward the sofa. "There is nothing like Christmas at Castle Horstberg."

"I can hardly wait." Claude said and smiled toward his wife.

"As long as we're all together," Maggie said, hoping Han wouldn't be angry that he wasn't the first to know, "you might as well have the news." She paused and gazed toward her husband. "I'm going to have another baby."

Maggie was aware of the excited chatter of congratulations going on around her, but her attention was centered on Han. Without a word he rose from his seat and left the room. A hushed silence fell in his sudden absence, and Maggie excused herself to go after him.

"Whatever is wrong?" she asked when she found him in the hall. "I thought you would be pleased." He looked at her but made no response. "Han, surely you—"

"It's so soon," he said quietly. "I didn't think it would happen again so soon."

"They'll be very close to each other as they grow up," Maggie said. "It will be perfect."

"If you survive it," Han said.

Maggie grasped the problem. "You're worried."

"Yes," he retorted, "I am. Do you have any idea what I went through while you were in labor? Which is nothing compared to what *you* went through. And look at what my mother is going through now. I'm truly afraid for her, Maggie. She is growing more and more weak, and it scares me. And I'm afraid for you, as well—especially after what happened last time."

Maggie took this in and realized he'd been holding back his true fears while he'd kept up his typical positive outlook on the surface. She pressed her hands over his shoulders and said softly, "Forgive me if I've been insensitive. I too am concerned about how this will turn out for your mother. Still, I cannot deny that . . . I'm happy about having another child." He said nothing, and she asked, "Are you implying that you don't want any more children?"

"I *do* want more children," he said, pushing his hand through his hair. "You know how I love Hannah. It's just that . . ." He trailed off with a sigh.

Maggie pushed her arms around Han's waist and looked up at him. "Han," she whispered, "I felt nothing but happiness when I realized I was going to have another baby. I suppose there are always risks with bringing a child into the world, but . . . how can we not take those risks when nothing in life brings more joy than a child? I'm sorry I didn't tell you earlier. The moment just seemed right."

"It was a good moment," he admitted. "I'm sorry I spoiled it. I just . . ."

"You didn't spoil it," she said and touched his face. "I simply want you to be happy about this. Think of the joy Hannah has brought to us already. Surely nothing could be more wonderful than to have another. Perhaps this child will be a son. I will take care of myself and do everything the doctor tells me. Everything will be fine."

Han didn't want to bring it up, but the words burst out of him. "If we can make certain Nik Koenig and his accomplices—whoever they may be—get nowhere near you, then we can believe that everything will be fine."

"Father took care of that," Maggie said, and Han resisted the urge to tell her what exactly her father had said to Han about his certainty that they had not seen the last of Nik Koenig. But they could not live in fear, and for the moment they had much to be happy about.

"Yes," Han said and forced a smiled. Still, he felt the need to add, "We are still going to keep a very close eye on you and be certain you're safe and healthy."

"Of course," Maggie said and reached up to kiss him.

Han couldn't keep from smiling. "A son would be nice," he conceded.

"Come along," she said. "Let's go tell your mother. She never naps for long. She should hear the news before anyone else."

Maggie took Han's hand, and they walked across the courtyard to the apartment where Georg and Elsa lived.

"Hello, Mother," Han said, coming into the doorway of her bedroom.

"Han." She smiled and held out her hand. "It's always so good to see you."

"And how are you feeling today?" Maggie asked, straightening things in the room by habit.

"I feel fine," she said, but Han's ongoing worry felt validated by her obvious pallor and weakness, which only added to his concern over having Maggie go through this again. "I just wish I could get out of this bed." Holding up a brightly colored scarf, she added, "See what you're father brought me."

"Very nice," Han smiled. He took it from her and tied it about her throat. "You look beautiful, as always."

"Georg has good taste," Maggie commented. "It goes well on you."

"He is so good to me," Elsa said warmly. "I don't know what I would do without him."

"We have some news, Mother," Han said.

"Oh, good!" she exclaimed. "I could use some news. Is it gossip?"

Han chuckled. "It probably will be before the week is out." He smiled toward Maggie, but he knew she could still see the worry in his eyes. "We're going to have another baby."

"Oh, that's wonderful," Elsa said immediately and held out her arms for Maggie, who came to her side and embraced her. "Nothing could make me happier. Perhaps our babies are together now in heaven, counting down the days until they will arrive in this world."

"I'm certain they'll be the best of friends," Han said and squeezed his mother's hand.

"Perhaps I should get back and see to our company," Maggie said. Elsa looked puzzled, and she clarified, "Our friends, the Dormantes, arrived today from Italy. We'll bring them by to meet you later."

"That would be nice." Elsa smiled.

"You go along, Maggie," Han said. "I think I'll stay a while." Elsa smiled toward her son. Maggie kissed them each and left.

"Tell me a story," Elsa said to Han when they were alone.

"But it was always *you* who told me stories," he replied.

"I taught you to tell stories so you could entertain me when I got old."

"You're not old, Mother," Han chuckled.

"I know," she laughed. "But I feel old . . . so tell me a story."

"All right. Which one do you want to hear?"

"Your favorite," she said and leaned back against the pillows to listen.

Han thoroughly enjoyed having the Dormantes at Castle Horstberg, and Maggie held nothing back about her own pleasure concerning their visit. Claude and Josette quickly merged into life in Horstberg, just as easily as Han and Maggie had done in Italy. Before long it seemed they were almost a part of the family. Han declared that the timing of their visit couldn't have been better, since all things related to family *and* country seemed to be going well in most respects.

Maggie's pregnancy was moving along smoothly, and Nik Koenig finally seemed content with his allowance. Cameron always had the monthly allotment sent out promptly, and Nik never showed himself at all. The royal family of Horstberg was at peace, and the valley they ruled seemed the same. For these reasons and many more, their holiday celebrations were especially enjoyable, in spite of Elsa remaining confined to bed.

Josette and Elsa became good friends, and Elsa declared often how grateful she was for what Josette had brought into her life at this time with her frequent visits to Elsa's bedside and her delightful conversation. Since Elsa was on doctor's orders to stay down completely, Josette's company and charming personality helped fill her hours of boredom. Elsa's condition got neither better nor worse, but the time dragged by for her, and any encouraging distraction was welcome.

Erich too visited Elsa regularly, and he also enjoyed the company of the Dormantes. He had completely regained his strength, and it was as if the nightmarish episode that had nearly taken his life had not even happened.

Han was glad to note how well Theodor had come to work with Erich in a relatively short time. But perhaps their level of comfort had been deepened by the way Theodor had remained so perfectly supportive throughout Erich's ordeal. And now it was as if nothing had happened. Since Han was often ready early for events that required his attendance, it had become typical for him to be waiting for Erich to finish dressing with Theodor there to help him. Cameron and Georg were often around as well, and Theodor had proved to be able to fit in comfortably with these very important men who preferred to be treated as ordinary as possible.

Han liked Theodor and enjoyed listening to the banter between him and Erich while Theodor made certain the prince looked perfect for every event. Occasionally, Han made himself a part of the conversation, but mostly he just pretended to read a newspaper while he listened. He was thrilled to hear Theodor tell Erich that his wife, Leisl, was expecting a baby. And since she'd lost the last one, they all hoped that everything would go well. She was further along in her pregnancy than Maggie, since they had held back on making the announcement. Erich congratulated Theodor as if the baby had already arrived. He laughed and declared that with Maggie and Elsa both expecting as well, they would have babies all over the place.

"And when are you going to settle down and start having babies?" Theodor asked Erich in good humor.

"At this rate, when I'm fifty," Erich replied. "And don't tell me about your sister. She's just a little girl."

"She won't be when you're fifty," Theodor laughed, and Erich shook his head in disgust.

Han just smiled and went back to his newspaper, silently thanking God once again that Erich had completely recovered from the traumatic threat to his life and that he was walking around on two good legs as if it had all been a bad dream. As for all the pending pregnancies, he could only hope and pray—as he knew everyone else who cared for these women were doing—that everything would turn out all right.

Theodor's wife also began visiting Elsa regularly, and they too became good friends. Since Leisl was often left on her own when Theodor was busy with his work, Erich came up with the idea of introducing her to Elsa, and the two women quickly took to each other's company, both sharing the hope that their babies would make it full term and be born healthy and strong. Han was grateful for the women who helped care for his mother and keep her spirits up, especially considering how busy he and his father were much of the time.

He loved the way Maggie had come to treat his mother like her own, and her compassion and genuine caring toward Elsa proved what he'd always known about Maggie; she was an amazing and remarkable woman, and he felt such deep gratitude to be her husband.

The Dormantes stayed as promised until after the holidays. They had come to fit in so comfortably that everyone was dismayed to see them leave, but they promised to return again, perhaps in the summer next time when they could see Horstberg without its continual blanket of snow.

Han felt some letdown—as he knew Maggie did—when the Dormantes left Horstberg, but a few days later, Elsa's condition suddenly worsened in her eighth month. Both families gathered in the parlor of Georg and Elsa's home while the doctor was with Elsa. Han held tightly to Maggie's hand, so grateful to have her there, while it seemed that the doctor was taking far too long. Georg paced the room, looking more upset than Han had ever seen him. He'd always known his father to be calm and methodical over every challenge that had come up, whether personal or political. But now he couldn't keep still, and he was wringing his hands while he walked the same length of carpet over and over, his pace increasing as minutes ticked by. Cameron tried to get Georg to sit down, but instead, Cameron began to walk with him, keeping a hand on his shoulder. Han could barely hear what they were saying to each other on the far side of the room, but he did hear his father say that it was insane for a woman of forty-six to be having a baby.

"She didn't conceive for more than twenty years," Georg muttered, "then all of a sudden . . ." He trailed off and said nothing more.

Han exchanged a concerned glance with Maggie, praying inwardly that his mother would be all right, and he added a prayer that Maggie would be all right as well through the course of this pregnancy and bringing their baby into the world.

The doctor finally came down the stairs with the grim news that Elsa was fully in labor, and he could do nothing to stop it. He also told them that it was likely too early in the pregnancy for the baby to survive, and with Elsa's weakened condition, he was extremely concerned about her ability to get through the ordeal. He asked that Georg and Han each take a few minutes with her before her labor worsened and she was unable to communicate. Han took in the implication and feared he might actually lose consciousness from the sudden spinning in his head. He leaned his head against Maggie's shoulder and felt her arms come around him. Otherwise, he felt sure the floor might swallow him. He was only vaguely aware of the doctor telling Abbi that Elsa had asked that she assist the doctor and remain at Elsa's side, although if she didn't want to be there, Elsa would understand. Han took that in as one more piece of evidence that his mother believed she was going to die, and it wasn't going to be an easy passing. He turned his head to see Abbi pull back her shoulders and say, "Of course I will be with her; I'll do whatever she asks of me." He admired the duchess's courage more than he ever had; personally, he knew he could never have remained near his mother through whatever might take place without making everything worse.

His knowledge of his own inability to face this deepened as he went hesitantly into his mother's room, Maggie's hand still tightly in his. The evidence of Elsa's suffering with labor was far too blatant to ignore, even though Elsa forced a smile and spoke words to him and Maggie of her love and gratitude and her certainty that they would live great lives and be very happy. Han hardly digested the words; he only held his mother close for as long as he could manage before pain overtook her with another contraction and she became lost in it. He watched through a fog as the pain relented briefly and she embraced Maggie. They said something to each other that he didn't hear, even though he was standing right there. The doctor then urged them quickly from the room, and Han only knew that Cameron was waiting just outside the bedroom door to be there for Georg as soon as the doctor expelled him from the room, and Abbi was already busy taking orders from the doctor. She had helped deliver babies before, but he doubted she had ever faced anything like this. They all knew that Maggie's labor during Hannah's birth had been difficult and frightening, but he realized that he'd had much more hope of Maggie surviving then than he did now for his mother making it through. All of the evidence seemed stacked against her, and deep in his gut he knew this was the end for Elsa.

For nearly two hours Han sat in the parlor, shocked and horrified. Maggie remained close by his side, crying silent tears. Erich sat in a chair across the room, never muttering a sound. Cameron said little but was keenly aware of Georg and practically shadowed his every move. Sometimes Han's father would frantically pace, and at others he would just sit and stare at the wall. Han wished that he could offer the kind of comfort and encouragement Georg had given him when Maggie had been in labor. But Han could think of nothing to say. Georg had told Han at the time that he instinctively believed Maggie would make it. Georg had no such feelings now, and Han knew it.

Han both wanted this to never end—if only to feel like his mother was still alive in another room—and at the same time he desperately wanted it to be over. The suspense and anxiety felt as if it would kill all of them.

More than two hours after the doctor had banished them all from the room, Abbi came slowly down the stairs, looking weary and distraught as she had the night Hannah had been born. But there was a foreboding in her demeanor that he couldn't define, even though a part of him knew exactly what it meant.

Georg rose to his feet as she stood before him. Han tried as he often had to imagine Abbi and his father as childhood friends. He knew well that they had always been there for each other, and they understood each other completely. It seemed somehow appropriate that they should share this moment. Han saw Georg bite his lip and swallow hard, and he wondered if his father sensed what Abbi needed to say. Han felt his heart beating quickly and knew the news was the worst possible. He felt the pain already sinking in, but he was more concerned at the moment about how his father was going to take it.

Abbi took both Georg's hands into hers. Her lip quivered, but she pulled back her petite shoulders stoically. "She's gone, Georg," Abbi whispered.

Georg sat down unsteadily. His grip on Abbi's hands tightened. Han leaned into Maggie's embrace and squeezed his eyes shut to fight the sting of hot tears as he realized his mother was dead.

"The baby?" Georg asked with no inflection in his voice.

"She only lived a few minutes," Abbi said, and Han felt the lump in his throat intensify to realize he'd had a sister, if only briefly.

Han wanted to offer comfort to his father, but he knew that

Georg was in good hands, and his own grief was threatening to suffocate him. He hurried outside into the darkness with Maggie's hand in his, where he could pull fresh air into his lungs as if it might save him. He went to his knees on the little patch of grass near the front stoop, and Maggie knelt beside him, wrapping him in her arms, whispering tearful words of comfort. He finally managed to get to his feet and walk within Maggie's embrace back to their room, where he collapsed on the bed and cried in a way that he never had before. Never had he experienced such a deep loss; never had he known such pain. He could only hope and pray that there was some kind of light on the other side of this darkness, and he prayed that everyone else who cared for his mother would be comforted—most especially his father.

The days preceding Elsa's funeral went by in a hazy blur for Han. He knew his loved ones were suffering as well, but he felt helpless to do anything but try to accept his mother's untimely death. Maggie was almost continually at his side, and he knew that Cameron and Abbi were keeping close track of Georg. They insisted that he stay in a room in the castle so he wouldn't be at home alone, and Georg readily admitted that he was glad for such an option.

Captain Dukerk also proved himself a good and trusted friend by the way he offered ongoing support to Georg. And his wife, Nadine, was equally supportive in her compassion and empathy. Abbi had been close to Elsa since they'd been young women, and Nadine had become a friend to both of them not so many years later. They'd shared many years and much history together, and now they were bound in their common grief. Han was grateful for them in ways he could never express, and he was also grateful for Erich's friendship and unquestioning compassion. But most of all, Han was grateful for his wife. Maggie's capacity for perfect understanding and compassion just seemed to grow and grow. He didn't know what he would have ever done without her. He only tried once to imagine how all of this might have been if he'd not been married to Maggie by now, and the very thought was completely terrifying.

Han dreaded seeing his mother in the casket prior to her burial, but in a way it actually made him feel better. While seeing her body certainly made it impossible to believe that this wasn't real, she looked perfectly at peace, as if she were ready to move on. The baby had been placed carefully at her side, and it looked as if mother and daughter had just fallen asleep together.

Having the funeral behind them did not by any means diminish their grief, but it seemed they were all becoming accustomed to this altered state of life as they did their best to press forward and take care of each other as well as continue their work in overseeing the well-being of the country. The entire family rallied together in order to cope. But that unreal, dreamlike sensation hovered over them, as if a deep hole had been carved into the structure of the family, and there was no reason to believe that any of them would ever be the same again.

Georg declared that he preferred to never return to the home he'd shared with Elsa for nearly twenty-five years, and the apartment was cleared out, with Georg's personal things being permanently moved to a suite of rooms in the castle. Georg rarely showed anything but his usual dignified manner concerning all he attended to. But those who loved him knew his heart was broken. There was a distant sadness in his eyes, and they could only pray that time would ease the loss, for Georg as well as for all who had loved Elsa.

For Han, observing his father's pain was almost as difficult as dealing with the loss of his mother. As deeply as he felt her absence, he could not comprehend how Georg must feel, having the woman he loved torn cruelly from his life. A part of him hoped that Maggie would outlive him. He never wanted to experience what his father was going through now.

Not many days following Elsa's funeral, Abbi came awake with a familiar sensation. As the memory of her dream rushed back to her, the horror of what she'd seen made her sit up, heart pounding, struggling to breathe. As much as she wanted Cameron's reassurance, she was glad she'd not awakened him. She needed time, and she forced herself to try and get comfortable and relax, taking deep breaths in and out. But it was more than an hour before she finally drifted to sleep again, only to have the same dream, repeated in exact detail. This time she woke up gasping for breath and knew as soon as she sat up that she'd awakened her husband.

"Is something wrong?" she heard Cameron ask.

She gave the simplest possible answer. "I had . . . a dream."

"A nightmare, apparently," he said, sitting beside her. There was comfort in his embrace, and she held to him tightly while she mentally recounted what she'd seen and attempted to digest it. She moaned unconsciously and then heard him say, "Was it so bad?"

"Yes," she said, "it was horrid. It's the most horrible dream I've ever had."

For a long moment, she sensed Cameron trying to take in what she'd just said. Finally, he moved away to light a lamp before he sat on the edge of the bed and took her hands into his, scowling when he noticed they were trembling.

"Abbi," he said, looking into her eyes. "You know the deep respect I have for your dreams."

"Yes," she answered, her voice trembling as well.

He took a deep breath and tightened his hold on her hands. "Did you dream that something bad is going to happen?" he asked, and she nodded. He took a ragged breath and heaved, "Please don't tell me that someone else we love is going to die."

"It wasn't like that," she said, pressing the side of her face to his chest, where she could hear the quickened beating of his heart.

"Just . . . tell me and get it over with," he insisted with the voice of the duke, while he put a husband's arms around her and pressed a kiss into her hair.

"Oh, Cameron," she murmured and held tightly to him, "it's so horrible I don't know how to even say it aloud."

"Just say it," he said.

"I pray that it's a warning, that it can be prevented. If not, what would be the purpose? We couldn't possibly just . . . stand back . . . and allow it to—"

"Just tell me," he interrupted with gentle impatience.

"It was war. Horstberg was at war." She felt his breathing sharpen and heard his heart quicken further. "There was battle in the courtyard. Parts of the castle were destroyed. There were fires through the valley, smoke rising in many places. There was screaming and wailing. The square was littered with bodies: men, women, and children. Blood ran in the streets."

"No, Abbi!" he muttered, taking her shoulders into his hands, looking hard into her eyes. But she saw no skepticism or doubt in his face. Only fear. "It *must* be prevented. It *must!* War has not come into the borders of Horstberg for more than a century. She is Bavaria's strongest nation. How could this happen?" He looked searchingly into her eyes. "Was there more? There must be more!" She nodded and sensed his relief. In spite of all the times her dreams had proven to be correct, she still marveled that he would display such perfect trust in her and in her dreams. "Tell me," he implored. "Tell me you dreamt the root of such horror, and we will find a way to stop it. We must!"

Abbi sensed his surprise when she answered so quickly. "You received a letter. It was brought to your office in the middle of a meeting. The letter was sealed with dark blue wax, and the sign of a dragon." She heard him take a sharp breath and met his eyes. "What?" He didn't answer, and she said, "You know that mark."

"I do. But do you?" He shifted his gaze while she sensed his mind racing frantically. "You have been at my side in ruling this country for many years, and you've spent much time in the office. But have you ever actually seen me open correspondence with that seal? It doesn't happen very often."

"No," she said.

"Do you know who sent it?"

She answered firmly. "The Baron of Kohenswald."

Again he took a sharp breath then said, "Go on."

"The letter asked you to come and meet with him on a matter of great urgency. You sent a reply that you would come the following morning and stated a time. You took a large military escort." She looked at him hard. "I don't understand that. You *don't* generally take a large military escort, do you?" She sensed him hesitating in his answer, or perhaps his thoughts were too overwhelming. To fill the silence, she nervously added, "I don't spend nearly as much time in remaining abreast of these things as I used to. Tell me what you're thinking."

"We normally *don't* take more than a few officers, but Captain Dukerk recommended recently that we start traveling with a larger escort. There is some . . . idea among the committees that it would be prudent . . . considering recent events."

Abbi gasped. "What do recent events have to do with increasing your military escort?"

He said as if she should already know, "Our children's lives have been threatened." His voice rose in anger, even though she knew it was not directed at her. "And Nikolaus Koenig is still out there. I don't trust him, and I don't believe that any threat he was given by me or anyone else is going to stop him in his quest to avenge his father's death and get what he believes he is entitled to. *That* is what recent events have to do with deciding to increase our precautions."

Abbi took this in and felt her breathing become more shallow. "Are you saying that . . . you believe Nik would dare do something so . . . bold . . . so . . . ." She couldn't find a word she dared put a voice to.

"You tell me, Abbi. Does this dream have anything to do with him?"

"I . . . don't know."

"Tell me what you do know. You need to tell me everything."

Abbi closed her eyes and drew in a sustaining breath, taking her mind back to the dream, trying to recall the details; she knew that even something small and seemingly insignificant could be valuable.

"As I said . . . you went to Kohenswald in response to the letter . . . and you took a large military escort. It felt as if . . ."

"As if what?" Cameron urged impatiently. She knew he was well aware that her feelings associated with the dreams were as important as what she'd actually dreamed. Dreams had brought them together and kept them together, and dreams had been instrumental in protecting the people they cared for many times.

"It was as if he knew that. The baron knew; he knew more than he should have known. I can't explain it more than that."

"Which means that . . . well, it only means one thing, doesn't it? We have a spy. There is someone giving the baron information he wouldn't otherwise have." Cameron squeezed his eyes closed and shook his head, as if it were too much to take in.

"Except that . . . wouldn't any of the people in this country be able to see that when you come and go from the borders of Horstberg, you have more officers with you than you have generally used in the past?"

"Yes, I suppose that's true."

"Then it could be anyone," she said.

"Yes, it *could* be anyone. Which means it could also be an officer of the Guard . . . or someone who serves on one of my committees."

"Or a servant here in the castle," she pointed out, recalling all that had happened under their own roof. Feeling that this was drawing them away from the important points of the dream, she said, "I don't think we should concern ourselves too much with exactly who and how. I believe we need to focus on *what* might happen."

"And what is that?" he asked.

"I saw the thick wooded area between Horstberg and Kohenswald . . . that must be passed through to get there. Is that not where the border between the two countries meet?"

"Yes," he said.

"And there is no other route because of the river," she said, and he nodded. Abbi drew a deep breath, trying to focus on the information of what she'd seen, rather than her emotional response to it. "You were ambushed there," she said and couldn't hold back tears. "Many men died." She omitted the fact that she'd seen the faces of men she knew as they'd perished. She sighed and continued. "The next thing I saw was the baron accusing you of the opposite. He would not see reason. I saw . . . pieces of many arguments. He kept twisting the truth and . . . that's where it started. The men involved in the ambush all swore to a different story than what had actually happened. And that's where it started."

When she said nothing more, he asked, "Is that all?"

"Yes. I had the same dream twice; exactly the same."

She sensed that he was more calm now, that his mind was working. His eyes shifted toward her, taking her in as if he'd never seen her before, then he pressed his mouth over hers with a kiss that expressed overt adoration.

"I must go," he said and got out of bed.

Once he left the room, Abbi cried and prayed that he would somehow be unable to undo what she had seen. Her thoughts drifted naturally to a desire to share what had happened with Elsa, and her tears increased to recall that her dearest and truest friend was gone. If Horstberg was truly facing the possibility of a crisis like unto what she had seen in her dreams, the timing of such a thing occurring so soon after Elsa's death simply seemed too much to bear. All the people who loved Elsa most were the same people responsible for keeping this country safe. But there would be no allowance for grieving when a country was at stake.

Cameron paused his brisk walk across the courtyard and looked up at the eastern horizon where a hint of light was just beginning to show. He inhaled that light and uttered his fifth prayer since he'd left the bedroom. Or was it his sixth? It didn't matter. He couldn't pray enough in regard to the situation before him now. He hurried on toward the long row of fine apartments adjacent to the courtyard and knocked loudly at a familiar door. He waited, knowing it would take a few minutes. But he also knew that Captain Dukerk was well attuned to hearing such a knock, and it would wake him from the deepest sleep.

When the door came open, Lance looked stunned. "What are *you* doing here?" he demanded.

"Is that such a surprise?" Cameron countered.

"Being summoned in the night is not uncommon. You coming personally is not what I expect." Lance opened the door wider, and Cameron stepped inside. "What's wrong?" Lance insisted, closing the door behind him.

"We need to talk," Cameron said.

"I did come to that conclusion," Lance replied with mild sarcasm.

Cameron glared at him, and they went together into a parlor where the doors were closed so they wouldn't be overheard if a member of the family should come anywhere near.

As soon as they were seated, Cameron said, "I came myself because I didn't want to alert anyone else to the possibility of a problem. I don't know who I can trust anymore. And I certainly can't go to Georg right now. I can't even think about Georg without wanting to cry like a baby. If I lost Abbi, I . . ."

"I know well what you mean," Lance said. "I'm having the same difficulty. I pray that both Abbi and Nadine live to be very old. What would we ever do without them?"

"I can't imagine," Cameron said, not wanting to broach the subject most prominent on his mind.

"I understand why you can't disturb Georg right now," Lance said, "but what is this about a possible problem? About not knowing who to trust?"

Cameron looked at him severely. "If I give one of my officers an order, do I know he will remain completely loyal to me in seeing to that order?"

Lance leaned forward and tightened his gaze on Cameron. "You remember that night . . . that night which is one of the most horrible we have ever endured."

"Of course I remember."

"I wasn't asking," Lance said. "But do you remember how it felt when you realized that one of the officers with you had betrayed you? I remember how it felt because I realized it too, and I knew the moment you'd figured it out."

"I remember," Cameron said.

"Do you remember how long it took you to know which man it was?"

Cameron sighed, beginning to grasp his point. "Minutes."

"That's right—minutes. And not many minutes later you put him in his place, and he never acted against you again. Do you remember how you knew?"

"Yes," Cameron said. "He wouldn't look me in the eye."

"That's right. Now, you and I have a great many years of experience behind us since then. We both know that some people can look you in the eye and tell a lie, but we both have good instincts when that happens. With that much said, let me say to you with confidence, Cameron, that this military force is made up of good and honest men who serve you with integrity and honor. If I had any doubts at all, it would certainly not be over the higher ranking officers who have any access to personal information that could endanger anyone in our families or the citizens of this country. Do you hear what I'm saying?" Cameron nodded, and Lance went on. "I'm well aware of how difficult all of this has been, but we are all the more alert and aware because of what happened. We know we can't trust Nik Koenig, but we don't have to."

Cameron nodded again and allowed a minute of silence to let that sink in. Lance finally said, "Is that why you woke me in the middle of the night? To assure yourself that you can trust the men who work for you? We both know the men who serve on the committees even more than we know those who serve in the military. What is this about, Cameron?"

"Abbi had a dream," Cameron said, grateful that Lance was well aware of Abbi's gift. Her dreams had influenced his life a great deal and had in fact saved Nadine's life at one time.

Lance leaned back and drew in a ragged breath. "I see. Something that makes you wonder who you can trust?"

"There is a great deal of detail, but . . . my mind is stuck on two things. The first is that . . . she felt like the baron knew things he shouldn't have known."

"I see," Lance said again, his voice growing deeper. "And the other?"

Cameron could hardly bring himself to say it, and he had to close his eyes when he did, as if that might make it less of a possibility of becoming real. "It was war," he repeated Abbi's words exactly. "Horstberg was at war." He heard Lance gasp, but he didn't open his eyes; he just finished repeating what Abbi had said. "There was battle in the courtyard. Parts of the castle were destroyed. There were fires through the valley, smoke rising in many places. There was screaming and wailing. The square was littered with bodies: men, women, and children. Blood ran in the streets."

"Good heavens!" Lance muttered. "How can that be possible?"

"That's what I need to figure out," Cameron said, now able to look at him. "Abbi said that it surely must be a warning; there surely must be a way to prevent this. But the information I have is . . . cryptic at best. I need your help, Captain. And until we can move forward with confidence in knowing what to do next, we will not discuss it with anyone. Not anyone."

"I understand," Lance said. "What information *do* we have?"

Cameron tried to relax and recall everything Abbi had told him. He repeated the details of the dream as well as he could remember, but he felt certain that both he and Lance would need to hear her tell them the entirety of the dream again. He just had to believe that it was as she'd said, that this horror could be stopped. If not, the world for him and those he cared for was about to come to an end.

Chapter Nineteen

LIKE MAGIC

$\mathcal{C}$ameron's mind wandered through the duration of the standard meeting of the advisory council. Georg's absence was keenly felt, but his time off duty was necessary. Han was also absent for the same reason. While they all agreed that it was most difficult to lose a loving spouse, the grief for Han was still difficult. He and his father were keeping each other company, and Maggie was keeping an eye on both of them. Abbi had been doing much of the same, but Cameron knew that today she had pleaded ill and was remaining close to her bed. Upsetting dreams had a way of doing that to her, and this dream had put her in a state of nearly constant, uncontrollable weeping. Of course, Elsa's recent death surely contributed to her tears, but only he knew the full enormity of what was going on. Captain Dukerk was aware of the situation and was compassionate, even if they couldn't speak of it openly, but he still had no comprehension of how deeply this affected Abbi. Cameron was her husband, and he was more responsible than anyone for the welfare of this country. To say that he was haunted by Abbi's most recent dream was a gross understatement.

Cameron discreetly met the captain's eyes from where he sat at the other end of the enormous table in the ducal office. He saw evidence of his own concerns mirrored there, but he quickly glanced away before anyone else could read any meaning into their mutual severity. He tuned into the topic being discussed long enough to be reassured that nothing new was being said, and again his mind wandered.

The gift of dreams. Abbi surely hadn't come to this world with any comprehension of the gift that had come with her, nor of its impact on her life as well as the lives of many others—most especially his own. He recalled the first time he'd laid eyes on her, and how terrified and in awe he'd been when she'd told him that a dream had guided her to him. She had saved his life—quite literally—and she had saved his spirit. And she had certainly saved Horstberg. He recalled how some time later she had dreamed of a child, a boy with his face and her red curly hair. At the time it had frightened him, but it had also forced him to face up to the challenges that had needed to be conquered in order to reclaim his country and his life. And now they were here. They had a grown son who strongly resembled him, and he had his mother's hair. He was supposed to inherit this country, and Cameron had always imagined that the transition would be peaceful and prosperous—at least for the most part. But insidious threats had nearly taken Erich's life—twice.

And now Abbi had dreamed of war. She had seen Horstberg in a state of utter destruction; it was the worst possible nightmare for a man in his position. And he wasn't certain what to do about it. He couldn't just face down the baron when there was nothing to say to him that would make any sense, and he couldn't declare to his committees and his military force that they needed to be on extra alert because the duchess had seen something horrible in a dream. All he could do for now was wait and wonder and try not to give in to the suffocating fear that hovered over him continually.

Cameron was startled from his thoughts when the door came open and a young officer said, "Forgive the interruption, Your Grace. But this just came. I was told to tell you it's urgent."

Cameron stared at the letter in the officer's outstretched hand for a long moment before he forced himself to say evenly, "Thank you." He took the letter, barely aware of the officer leaving the room and the committee all waiting in silence. He exchanged another brief, barely noticeable glance with the captain and resisted the urge to send everyone but Lance out of the room, which would only draw further attention to the matter. Until he actually read the letter, there was no legitimate cause for alarm. He swallowed hard and willed a nonchalant attitude as he broke the dark blue seal, pressed with the image of a dragon, and unfolded the page. He stared at the words in front of him, trying to think of any logical explanation of how his wife might have known this was coming. But there wasn't one. He had no need to be convinced that Abbi's gift was real, but the evidence in his hand was chilling. And he realized he hadn't expected this to happen so quickly. Some of Abbi's most significant dreams had taken a long time to come to pass. There was one in particular that still hadn't happened, and perhaps never would. But now, this very day, he was holding the predicted letter in his hand.

"What is it?" the committee chief asked with concern, startling Cameron from a slight daze. He hoped these men would credit his somber, distracted mood to Elsa's recent death.

Cameron took a deep breath and quickly examined his instincts. If he combined all that Abbi had told him with everything Lance had said, and his own knowledge of a lifetime of dealing with the Baron of Kohenswald, he could boldly take hold of the problem, knowing he had to act, and act quickly.

"The meeting is adjourned," he said. "I want you to stay." He nodded at the man who had spoken. "And I need to see the head of the security council. Captain," he looked directly at Lance, who was already on his feet, "send for your top six lieutenants. And I want my espionage team. Immediately. Erich, I need you to stay, of course."

"Yes, Your Grace," he heard multiple voices say, and Cameron kept staring at the letter while the men all left the room. He kept it in his hand while his thoughts churned.

"Father?" he heard Erich say and looked up, surprised that he wasn't alone. "What is it? What's wrong?"

Cameron leaned closer to him so that he could whisper, even though no one else was in the room. "Your mother had a dream. She knew this letter would come." He glanced at the letter in his hand, then back at Erich's face as his eyes widened. He told Erich nothing more and was glad that he didn't press him for more details. Erich knew something of his mother's gift, but far from everything. Perhaps when this was all behind them, they would tell the children more. Right now he just wanted all of this to be over.

Twenty minutes after the letter's arrival, Cameron was seated with the men he'd requested to see. He simply told them of the letter he'd received and that he had reason to believe it was not what it appeared. When he was asked over the reasons, he evaded the question and told them what he wanted done, and how. After they'd left with their assignments, he hurried upstairs, but he had to take a deep breath before he entered the bedroom.

He found Abbi in bed but not sleeping. She often feared sleep when dreams were haunting her. By the way she opened her eyes, he knew that was likely true today. He sat on the edge of the bed, and they shared an inquisitive gaze before he said, "I wonder what I did to deserve you. Surely the good people of Horstberg who pray for the welfare of their homes and families are blessed through you, and I am only privileged to have you as my own because I was lucky enough to be born with royal blood." He touched her face, noting the puzzlement in her eyes. "I wonder what the people would think to know that their duchess is also a prophetess." Her eyes widened just before he held up the letter. She sat up abruptly and took it with a trembling hand. He'd refolded it so that the seal came together, even though it was cracked open. She put her other hand over her mouth for a long moment, then she seemed to draw courage enough to open it. "Just as you saw it?" he asked.

She nodded. "What will you do?"

"I've sent word to the baron to expect us tomorrow, but we won't be going—at least not at the time I told him we would. I've already arranged for my very best espionage and military personnel to treat it with high-level suspicion. They've been given the assignment to find proof of malicious intent. Once I have proof, the matter will be over."

"Can it be that easy?"

"We'll see. It depends on many factors, obviously." He touched her face. "But I feel confident that it will go well. I have evidence that God is with us in our endeavors."

He put an arm around her and drew her close, silently thanking God for such a precious gift as this woman among women. After Abbi fell asleep in his arms, he eased carefully away, leaving her to rest. He found Lance, and they talked privately for a long while, helping Cameron find the confidence he needed to go forward into what they would do tomorrow. He prayed that it would go well, and that something unforeseen would not occur to catapult them into the battles that Abbi had seen in her dreams.

That evening the mood at the supper table was especially somber. Georg maintained a dignified and courageous countenance, especially when he was around the rest of the family, but his grief was evident. At least he felt comfortable here among their united family. Cameron was glad Georg had made the decision to live here at the castle. It was surely beneficial for all of them.

After supper, Cameron spent some time alone with Georg, giving him the opportunity to talk openly about his continuing shock that Elsa was really gone. Cameron mostly listened and reassured his friend that he would always be a part of their family. He left Georg in Han's care and found that Abbi had already gone to bed, and thankfully, she was sleeping. He prayed that she slept well and that tomorrow at this time they would all be sighing with relief.

Cameron had trouble falling asleep. He knew that the captain had already sent out a small team of spies who were well trained in clandestine operations. He wondered where they were and if all was well. And he wondered if everything would truly go as smoothly as they all hoped. He finally drifted to sleep, and then it seemed only minutes before he was startled abruptly into consciousness by Abbi gasping for breath.

"What is it?" he asked gently, trying to conceal his own fear with the hope of calming her down. He wrapped her in his arms and held her tightly, whispering reassurances until she took hold of him and sobbed.

"Same dream?" he asked with dread.

"No," she murmured and sniffled. "Actually . . . it was . . . all right. Everything was all right, but . . ."

"But what, Abbi?" he insisted, trying to remain patient. He wanted to hear that she had dreamed of endless prosperity and peace for Horstberg.

"Cameron," she asked, and he could practically hear her mind swirling with thoughts, "what will you do . . . if you get this proof you are hoping to find?"

"I will confront the baron and—"

"No!" she said and tightened her hold on him. "No! No, no, no, no, no!" She sprang to her feet, and he reached for a lamp to light it. He found her pacing as soon as he could see her.

"Why, Abbi? What's wrong? You must tell me."

"It must be Han."

"What?" he asked, completely baffled.

"It must be Han who confronts the baron."

"Abbi," he drawled. "I hate to point out the obvious, but—"

"You don't have to point out the obvious. I know it *should* be you, and I know there are many reasons why it should not be Han. But it must be. I saw it. I felt it. Do you trust my dreams or not?"

Cameron felt almost as if he'd been kicked in the stomach. What she was asking seemed simple enough, except that it went against so many measures of protocol that he couldn't count them. And it was vitally important for the baron to see him as a figure of power. His every instinct in being the Duke of Horstberg felt on the line, even if the matter seemed insignificant. But Abbi knew all of that. She'd been the duchess for more than two decades. She had stood at his side while facing the baron countless times. He didn't have to explain it to her. But she'd asked him a question, and she deserved an honest answer. It only took him a long moment to recount their history and all he'd seen spring forth from this woman's dreams. He lifted his chin and said firmly, "Yes, Abbi, I trust your dreams. If you say it must be Han, then it will be Han."

"Thank you," she said on the wave of a long breath.

"Do you know why?"

"No. And perhaps we will never know. It just feels as if . . . the baron needs to know Han holds such a position of respect from you, and that you stand behind him. Or perhaps it's because Han is more of a personal enemy to Nikolaus Koenig."

Cameron took a sharp breath. "Is that *your* idea? Or is that how you felt in the dream?" She didn't answer, and he added, "Abbi, if you have a sense that Koenig is behind this, then—"

"I don't know," she said. "But . . . I think it needs to remain . . . a possibility . . . if only in the way you think of how to manage the situation. That's all I can say for certain."

Cameron sighed deeply. "Fair enough," he said and took her in his arms again, longing for this to be over and dreading the conversation he needed to have with Han.

The following morning as Cameron stood up from the breakfast table, he said firmly, "Han and Erich, I need to speak with both of you right away. You ladies will have to look out for Georg today; I need Han."

"We would be delighted," Maggie said.

Georg countered, "I'm not some little old man who needs a nanny. I'm just fine."

"Maybe you're fine," Abbi said, "but I'm not certain that I am, so I would prefer your company."

"Me, as well," Maggie said. "Besides, Hannah seems to like you better than anyone these days. She'll be less fussy if you play with her."

"I can't dispute any of that," Georg said, but he met Cameron's eyes with a clear indication that he knew something difficult was taking place, and he knew he'd been kept out of the matter because of Elsa's passing. Cameron wondered if Georg would protest or insist on being involved—or at least told of the situation—but he said nothing, and Cameron hurried out of the room. He hated facing something like this without Georg at his side, but Abbi had only seen him and Erich and Han in her dream. He had to believe this was the way it needed to be.

Cameron entered the office with Han and Erich right behind him. He closed the door and motioned for them to sit down. He usually sat with the desk in front of him, but he moved a chair close to them, and they adjusted the chairs they were sitting on in order to face him.

"Erich," he began, "you're aware of what we are endeavoring to accomplish today."

"Yes," Erich said, but his expression made it evident he knew he was being kept in the dark about certain details.

"Allow me to say something, son, that should go without saying each and every day, but sometimes things just need to be said." He leaned forward and put a hand on Erich's shoulder, looking him in the eye. "You are everything I had ever hoped for in a son, and I am confident you will make an excellent ruler of this country when the time comes. I'm grateful for your integrity, your convictions, and your commitment to this heritage. I just want you to know that."

Cameron saw a subtle glimmer of moisture in Erich's eyes as he nodded and said, "Thank you, Father. But . . . that sounds a little bit like something a man might say if he knew that something bad was going to happen."

"I believe everything will go smoothly today," Cameron said with confidence. "I just need you to know that."

Erich nodded again, and again said, "Thank you. I think you're an amazing man, and I consider it a privilege to be your son, and I don't know if I can ever truly fill your role as well as you do."

"Perhaps better," Cameron said with a smile. He then turned his gaze toward Han and said, "I have purposely kept you and your father ignorant of what's been going on because you are both officially on a leave of absence. But today I need your help."

"Of course," Han said eagerly. "Anything."

By the way he said it, Cameron could well imagine him being willing to step in front of cannon fire in order to save the country or the life of anyone he cared about. Cameron then explained what they would be doing today and why, omitting any reference to Abbi's dreams. He simply told him the plan as it had been laid out in detail the same way the committees had heard it in meetings where Han had been absent.

"What is it you want me to do?" Han asked.

"I need you at my side, along with Erich."

Han glanced dubiously toward Erich, then back to Cameron. "I realize you know this, but . . . I have no military experience, whatsoever. I will do whatever you want me to do, but . . ."

"Good," Cameron said. "I need you at my side, and when it comes time to confront the baron—assuming that is how all of this plays out—I need you to be the one to do it."

Both Han and Erich looked understandably astonished. They were well aware of the matters of echelon and protocol established between the two countries. And they also knew Cameron's convictions in being a strong and visible figurehead for Horstberg.

"What?" Han sputtered. "Why . . . sir?"

"Han," Cameron leaned toward him, putting a hand on his shoulder as he'd done with Erich earlier, "are you aware of the duchess's gift of dreams?"

Again Cameron saw Han and Erich exchange a glance of confusion, then Han looked back at Cameron. "Vaguely, sir. I've heard some stories, but . . . I don't know details."

"Suffice to say for the moment that I trust her dreams completely. She predicted the arrival of the baron's letter, and she knew the intentions behind it." He didn't offer any details of those intentions, including her vision of seeing the horrifying images of war within the borders of their country. "It is because of her dreams that I know what to do today, and I am confident this will be resolved quickly. And she told me very strongly . . . she insisted . . . that it must be *you* who confronts the baron. She saw it. We don't know why, Han. But given the number of times that Abbi's dreams have saved this country, we must trust her and do as she says, even if we *never* understand why."

Han took in a ragged breath and briefly rubbed his hand over his face as if that might help him grasp this more easily. "All right, I . . . understand, but . . . I know nothing, Your Grace. I . . . I . . . am still so new at this, and I . . ."

"Han," Cameron said firmly, "you know everything you need to know. I have seen you put Nik Koenig in his place." Cameron tipped his head slightly. "Just pretend that the baron is actually Koenig, and you'll do fine." He stood up and the others did the same. "Get into uniform, both of you, and we will discuss some details on the way."

Cameron hurried out of the room, trying to ignore how utterly terrified Han looked. Erich just looked baffled. Cameron understood well how they both felt. He just had to think about his trust in Abbi's dreams and nothing else. If he tried to weigh this with any other measure of logic, he would lose his mind before the day was done.

Han straightened the coat of his uniform while he gazed at himself in a long mirror and fought to quell the horrible nerves rumbling inside of him. Hearing the details of what the duke had planned for this day, he'd been glad to think of remaining behind, even if it had made him feel somewhat cowardly. Having been given the assignment of facing down the baron, he wanted to just disappear until this was over.

He was startled when Maggie came into the room and closed the door. "Father just told me that you're going with them, but he wouldn't tell me exactly what's going on." She took hold of his shoulders. "Han, I'm frightened. This is serious, isn't it."

"Yes, I believe it is, but if your father doesn't want you to know details, then it's not my place to tell you. I'm not certain I understand it, myself. I just have to do whatever your father asks of me."

"Which is what, exactly?" she demanded.

"I think we should talk about this when I get back," he said and pressed a kiss to her brow. "I love you, Mrs. Heinrich."

"I love you too, Han—more than life." She kissed his lips and touched his face. "Come back safely."

"I will do my very best," he said and pressed a hand over her pregnant belly. "Everything will be all right."

Maggie nodded, but her eyes told him she was doubtful. He forced a smile and kissed her again before he hurried out of the room, knowing it was nearly time to leave. Thinking of the extensive training endured by officers of the Guard, he wished that he had even a portion of confidence in using the sword and pistol he wore at his sides. He'd had some minimal training, and had done enough target practice with Erich through the years that he knew he could use the pistol with some accuracy. But the thought of needing to made his insides churn. Would it come to that? He knew Erich had endured such training, and so had the duke. But Han's father hadn't. His wearing a uniform had always been more of an honorary thing, and being at the duke's side had always been due to his position, which was to help advise and counsel with him. Not once had Han ever considered that something like this would ever be a part of his job. But he had to do everything in his power to do what was asked of him, and to do as the duke had suggested and trust the duchess's dreams. He couldn't even comprehend what was taking place, but still, he had to do his best.

Once Cameron was dressed in his uniform, he stepped into the bedroom and found Abbi looking out the window toward the courtyard where he knew the military force was gathering. She turned to look at him when she heard the door.

"Seeing you in uniform still takes my breath away," she said, "but I've never felt like I was sending you off to war." She turned back toward the window. "And I've never seen them gathered in such numbers."

"There won't be any war, Abbi. We're taking every precaution. I feel confident it will be over soon."

"Do you really?" she asked, looking at him again.

"I do," he said and meant it. The very fact that this was happening because of her dreams gave him more confidence than anything else could.

"There's one more thing," Abbi said. "Something from my most recent dreams that I forgot to tell you. Only repeat it to Han for now, and he should tell the baron only as a last resort . . . or if he feels inclined to do so."

"Very well," Cameron said. "What is it?"

Abbi went on her tiptoes to whisper a phrase in his ear, as if the walls might overhear. He looked at her in astonishment and said, "Truly?"

"That's what I heard in my dream."

"Perhaps Koenig is involved with this, after all."

"But perhaps not in the way that we might think," she said. "It's impossible to know, and we must be careful not to tread where we cannot tread with confidence."

"Very wise, my dear," he said and touched her face. He took her into his arms and added, "Do you remember that dream you had about me? Before we were married? The one where I was on the floor in the hall downstairs and you couldn't wake me up?"

"I remember," she said. "All too clearly." She sighed and added, "It was almost exactly in the place where the officers laid Erich . . . and there was a dead officer lying nearby."

Cameron felt astonished. "Do you think that's significant?"

"I have no idea," she said.

Cameron returned to his original idea. "Do you remember how you said that Georg was there, but after you'd had the dream a number of times, you said it wasn't Georg, but it looked like Georg? And I suggested it might be Georg's son."

Abbi drew back abruptly and looked up at him. "I'd forgotten that part."

"Obviously, whatever implication is in that dream has nothing to do with this, because whatever it is, and whenever it will happen, it will be here. And today *nothing* will happen *here*. But Han does look very much like Georg did when he was younger. We can't possibly understand the implications, Abbi, but something in me knows it's significant. That's all I can say."

Abbi just nodded as if she understood. He embraced her tightly then hurried to kiss her and leave the room. He knew the troops in the courtyard were waiting for him, but he didn't want to think too deeply about the possibility that, as Abbi had said, it felt as if he were going off to war. He prayed that his confidence would be proven right and this would all be solved very quickly.

Cameron kept his focus on the moment at hand and on his trust and belief that the safety of this country was held more securely in the heart of Abbi du Woernig than anywhere else. According to their carefully laid-out plan, a large number of officers, led by Captain Dukerk, left the castle, heading toward Kohenswald. But long before they reached the border, they would split into multiple groups and tread carefully into the woods that separated the two countries. This they would do only after they had carefully met up with the men who had gone into the woods the previous night.

Cameron followed with a large number of officers in front of him and even more riding behind. Han and Erich rode at his sides to a specified location where they waited. They all remained mounted in order to move quickly when the signal came, but Cameron urged Han and Erich to move with him out of hearing range from anyone else while he spoke mostly to Han about certain protocols for conversing with the baron and his personal suggestions on how to handle him. Han listened and took everything in, and Cameron did his best to reassure him that he would manage this assignment just fine. He concluded by saying, "You're a good man with a good head on your shoulders, Han. But even more importantly, you have good instincts—like your father. And you also have a good heart. You will use all of those qualities today, and all will be well."

"Thank you, sir," Han said. "I'm trying very hard to share in your confidence."

"Perhaps your confidence will be doing better when this is over and you see that I'm right."

"Perhaps," Han said, but he didn't seem convinced.

"Just pretend that you're me," Cameron said then chuckled. "But don't let it go to your head."

"Pretend that I am you," Han said dubiously. "And pretend that the baron is Nik Koenig."

"Exactly," Cameron said. "And as a last resort, Abbi told me there's something you could say to the baron—as privately as possible."

"A last resort?"

"If you . . . feel so inclined," Cameron clarified.

"Yes?" Han asked, and again he glanced at Erich. It was as if the two of them were perfectly in tune with each other. So much like his own relationship with Georg, Cameron thought.

Cameron moved his horse a couple of steps and whispered in Han's ear the same words that Abbi had whispered in his.

"Truly?" Han asked, sounding astonished.

"That's what I said to Abbi," Cameron chuckled. Erich looked baffled and frustrated. Cameron just said to him, "I'll tell you later."

They heard riders approaching and turned to see three of their own officers slowing down to search for their leader. They saw Cameron and moved quickly closer.

"Your Grace," a lieutenant said. "Everything went according to plan." He let out a brief laugh. "It all fell into place so perfectly, it was almost . . . like magic."

Cameron smiled. "I'm very glad to hear it," he said.

Another lieutenant said, "We have sixty-seven soldiers from Kohenswald in our custody, Your Grace; their weapons have been confiscated. The captain is waiting for you to rendezvous with him before we go on."

"Very good," Cameron said. "Thank you, gentlemen. Let's move out."

The lieutenants took over giving orders to the dozens of men on horseback who had been waiting with the duke. Cameron looked at Han and Erich, and he couldn't hold back another smile. "It seems we can go now." He laughed. "I think I am going to enjoy this very much."

They arrived in Kohenswald hours later than the baron had requested that the Duke of Horstberg come and meet with him. Captain Dukerk, flanked by four lieutenants, led his troops slowly down the main road through the country before going up the castle hill, purposely displaying the soldiers of Kohenswald who were in their custody. Cameron rode in the midst of his own military force, with Han and Erich at his sides, most prominently thinking of the vision Abbi had seen of Horstberg at war. Fire. Blood running in the streets. The dead and the dying. He knew now that it truly could have happened. But it hadn't. And his gratitude was deeper than he could even comprehend.

In the courtyard of Castle Kohenswald, Cameron demanded that the baron come out to meet him. By the time he showed his face, the sixty-seven men the baron had sent to start a war were on their knees, their weapons in a heap.

"What is the meaning of this?" the baron demanded, approaching Cameron as he dismounted, Han and Erich doing the same.

Han couldn't begin to imagine why it was important for him to take the lead on this, but when he saw Cameron nod toward him, silently indicating that it was time for him to step forward, he felt a surprising burst of confidence as the words he needed to say came clearly to his mind. His confidence briefly waned as he realized how well everything had gone so far, and he wondered if this might be the moment when it would all fall apart. But he couldn't back down. He just had to do what he'd been asked to do, and do it with all the integrity and conviction he could muster. He saw the duke motion toward him with his hand as he took a step back and met the baron's eyes, silently indicating that Han would speak for him. Han stepped forward and drew back his shoulders the way he had seen Cameron do countless times.

"That is exactly what we have been wondering," Han said to the baron. "His Grace had a suspicious hunch about your message yesterday. Imagine our surprise when we sent military personnel to secure our passage. We have several men who will testify to the things they overheard, and I have in my possession maps and battle plans that prove beyond any question your conspiracy against Horstberg."

The baron's guilt and fear showed clearly through his effort to maintain his dignity. "We are returning your men to you in peace, Baron," Han said and lifted a finger. "They will tell you that their lives were generously spared today. But we consider our country offended. If you so much as breathe in our direction, we will ravage this country and squander her spoils and hang you out to rot. Do I make myself clear?"

The baron looked horrified and cornered. He turned to Cameron and said snidely, "You let this man speak for you?"

"I do," Cameron said. "He asked you a question."

"Do I make myself clear?" Han repeated, and Cameron felt proud of him.

"Quite clear," the baron said with contempt. But the fear in his eyes was undeniable. And that was all Cameron needed to see.

Han glanced at Cameron, then back to the baron, checking his instincts to see if he felt inclined—as the duke had said—to act on what Abbi had called a last resort. It seemed the baron was exactly where they wanted him, but Han felt strongly that he needed to offer this additional piece of information. He quickly took two steps toward the baron and whispered close to his ear before he had a chance to retreat. The baron's expression of horror deepened. He looked at Han, then at the duke, then at Han again.

"Take every last man and get out of here!" the baron demanded.

"As you wish," Han said, taking a few steps back without taking his eyes off the baron. "And remember what I said. We will *not* be seeing you, your family, or any member of your military force anywhere near our borders for a very, *very* long time."

"Fine," the baron snarled. "Just go!"

Han smiled at the baron, feeling just a little bit like Moses might have felt when Pharaoh had finally conceded to let the Israelites leave Egypt with their freedom. He turned and mounted his waiting horse, and they all headed back to Horstberg, once again going slowly through the middle of town. As soon as they were beyond the border of Kohenswald, Erich asked Han, "What on earth did you whisper in his ear?"

Since the duke was riding between them, he couldn't help but hear the question, but he only smiled slightly, which let Han know that he approved of Erich now knowing what had been said.

"I just repeated what your father told me," Han explained.

"And I just repeated what your mother told *me*," Cameron said.

"Which is what, exactly?" Erich asked, impatient.

Han cleared his throat dramatically and said, "I told the baron that a reliable source had told me that Nikolaus Koenig was sharing a bed with his wife."

"What?" Erich asked, looking at Han, then his father, then Han again. "Is that really true?"

"We don't know whether or not it's true, obviously," Cameron said. "Very few of us know the source that guided us through all of this today, and we know she is extremely reliable. Whether or not it's true is not the point."

"What *is* the point?" Erich asked in a tone that was somewhere between frustration and wanting to understand such strangeness.

"The point is in the way the baron responded to what Han said. He knew the name immediately. If he hadn't, he would have said something to indicate that he had no idea who Han was referring to. If the baron hadn't believed that such a thing could be possible, he would have jumped to defend his wife's honor. He did neither. He simply got angry and demanded that we leave."

"If Koenig was actually trying to worm his way into the baron's family," Erich said, "I would have thought he'd be more prone to seek out the attention of one of his despicable daughters."

"Ah, yes," Han said, recalling the damage those wretched girls had inflicted upon Maggie. "The deplorable little beasts."

"I would have thought the same," Cameron said. "Of course, we know practically nothing. And we may not be able to prove that Koenig had anything to do with this, but for those of us who are in charge of keeping this country safe, we all have sufficient evidence to *know* that he is—at the very least—associating with the baron in one way or another."

"After what happened today," Erich asked, "would that not make him guilty of treason?"

"Oh, it certainly would," Cameron said with resignation. "But again, we have no proof. And without proof, we cannot put anyone in front of a firing squad. We can only hope and pray that he gives us proof long before he causes any further challenges. The good news is that we have new evidence that God is with us. He has given Horstberg a most extraordinary gift, and I love her with all my heart and soul."

Han took special notice of the peaceful serenity in the duke's countenance as he spoke of his trust in God and his love for his wife. Something stirred in his spirit as if to alert him to the evidence before him that these two things were intertwined, and more than anything else, they were the keys to keeping this country safe and strong.

Cameron was so deeply overcome with gratitude that he had trouble holding back tears as they rode peacefully into the beautiful valley that comprised his own lovely little dominion. Horstberg was only a tiny dot on any map of the world, but it was his, it was home, and it was safe. He told an officer to tell Captain Dukerk that he was riding ahead, along with Han and Erich. Now that they had returned safely, he had no need for a military escort, and he longed to see Abbi. He knew she would be waiting and wondering, likely pacing the floor, heavy with anxiety. No one else who had remained behind knew what she knew, and he wanted to ease her concerns as much he wanted to just hold her in his arms.

Cameron dismounted in the castle courtyard and ran through the main entrance and down the hall. He knew Han and Erich had followed him, and they all stopped when they saw Abbi and Maggie coming down the staircase at the other end of the hall. They'd obviously been waiting where they could see the courtyard, and they would have seen the men arrive.

"You're all right," Abbi said, rushing toward him.

"I am," he said. "We are. We all are. Everything is fine."

Abbi gasped and sobbed and threw herself into his arms. Cameron held her closely for a long moment, whispering to her of his love and devotion, then he fell to his knees and looked up at her. Holding her hands in his, he said with all the conviction he felt, "You have saved me and my country again, my love. There are no words . . ." His voice cracked and faded. He pressed his face into the folds of her dress and felt her hand in his hair. He was home. It was over.

Han's initial motivation in following the duke when he ran from the courtyard was to see Maggie and hold her in his arms and let her know that all was well. When he saw her, their eyes met with silent understanding conveyed back and forth, and then everything froze as he and Maggie and Erich all focused on the exchange taking place between the duke and duchess. Han could hardly breathe and knew the others felt the same. He had no evidence; he just knew. Cameron's emotional declaration that there were no words seemed a gross understatement, and Han knew—as he suspected Erich and Maggie did—that there was far more to what had happened today than any of them had been told. He watched the ruler of their country fall to his knees with perfect adoration and devotion, and unspoken truths rushed into his own mind and heart, as if this day above any other would be the source of everything he needed to know at any given point in the future as he did his part to serve Horstberg with honor. His eyes went to Maggie just as hers moved to him. He crossed the short distance between them and took her into his arms.

"I love you," he whispered.

"And I love you," she replied.

After a long minute of silence, Erich cleared his throat and groaned with a tone of comical disgust. "Has no one any compassion for the lonely bachelor who has no one to greet him when he returns from war?"

"War?" Maggie echoed in panic.

"He's exaggerating," Cameron said, but Han didn't miss the brief glance he exchanged with Abbi that seemed to imply that there was no exaggeration.

Maggie left Han's side to hug her brother tightly, and Abbi hugged both of her children at the same time. "That's more like it," Erich chuckled.

While they were enjoying their laughter and embraces, Han heard the duke say quietly near his ear, "You did good today, Han."

"Thank you, sir. I just did my best to . . . take your advice."

"And you did it well," Cameron said. "We may never know why it had to be you, but I know more than ever that I can always count on you, and I hope that you know you are capable of doing whatever might be required of you."

Han could only nod in response. He couldn't deny an increase in his own confidence, but he wasn't certain what might be entailed with *whatever might be required*. He could only go forward and continue to do his best.

Maggie held her husband close to her in the bed they shared and stared up into the darkness, overcome with a strange sensation that something truly horrible had brushed past their lives and had moved on, leaving them miraculously safe. It was as if a band of evil thieves had been peering in their windows, making plans to take everything and do them harm. And then something unexplainable had frightened them away, and all was well.

Knowing that Han was still awake, she attempted to explain what she was feeling, even though it was difficult to put into words. "I feel like I could have lost you today, but I didn't. What happened out there?"

Han leaned up on one elbow and looked down at her, touching her face. "I want your father to be the one to tell you, partly because I actually know very little, and partly because I'm not certain of what is all right to discuss openly with you and what is not. You're his daughter; he should be the one to tell you what he feels you should know." Han lay back down on his pillow with a loud sigh. "And maybe he'll even fill me in on the details, because . . ." He chuckled. "I honestly have no idea."

Little more was said before they both succumbed to the exhaustion of a strange and tiring day. The following morning at breakfast, Maggie was surprised but pleased when her father announced that he wanted everyone present to meet in his office as soon as they were finished eating. A short while later, Han and Maggie were sitting at the huge table where the committees met regularly, with her parents and Erich sitting across from them, and Georg sitting on the other side of Han. They seemed to be waiting for something, and then Captain Dukerk entered the room with some large rolls of paper beneath one arm. He closed the door and set them on the table before he sat down.

Cameron sighed loudly and said, "Those of us in this room are the only ones who will ever know the whole story of what happened yesterday. But it is important for all of you to know everything. There are two reasons for that. The first is that those of us in this room are and will be the most involved in caring for this country for many years to come. If there are any future repercussions related to this, you all need to be aware of all the pieces of the puzzle. The other reason is that we—who are quite literally family in one form or another—need to recognize and never forget what a miracle we have experienced." Maggie felt Han take her hand underneath the table as her father continued. "Now that it's over, I'm willing to share with you the horror that Abbi and I have been privately contending with. I shared some of the details with the captain, because I needed him to know the severity of what we could possibly be facing. Now I need all of you to know. My intent is not to give you information that you might struggle with because, quite frankly, it's disturbing. My intent is to give you reason to live in gratitude for every day of freedom this country enjoys."

Maggie felt Han's grip tighten around her fingers, and her own heart quickened with dread. Whatever her father had to say, she was glad she hadn't known about it yesterday when Han had left here with Horstberg's military force and special orders from the duke.

Maggie listened in stunned silence as Cameron explained some details of their plans and the reasons for doing what they'd done. Then he asked Abbi to tell them about the dreams she'd had that related to this situation. Maggie couldn't hold back tears to hear her mother's descriptions of what could have been, and she was well aware of the shock and horror felt by every person in the room. But there was something else they all felt. And that was awe. Her father had been right. They needed to live in gratitude each and every day. The people in this room were special witnesses to a miracle of enormous proportions. When Abbi had finished all she had to say, Captain Dukerk unrolled the papers he'd brought with him, which he explained had been confiscated from the officers of Kohenswald who had been preparing to attack the entourage from Horstberg when it had arrived. They all stood up to be able to clearly see the things that the captain pointed out, black and white, irrefutable evidence that were it not for Abbi's dreams—and Cameron's deter-mination to trust them and follow through accordingly—this day would have been extremely different, and none of their lives would have ever been the same. In fact, it was doubtful, considering the positions they each held, that any of them would have still been alive.

When all of the information had been offered, no one said anything. A heavy, severe silence blanketed the room as the full perspective settled in. Georg broke the silence by saying, "We are truly blessed . . . in more ways than we could ever count."

Maggie looked at her father-in-law, taking in the sincerity in his countenance that echoed his words. He had lost the love of his life, and his grief had been deep and incomparable. And yet he could declare with such boldness that they were all truly blessed. And he was right. She squeezed Han's hand and met his eyes, knowing she could never take for granted whatever good might be ahead for them in the life they would share together. She'd never been so glad to be a princess.

When the meeting was finally adjourned, Maggie happened to be near her father as he opened the door of the office where two men in uniform were always standing just outside in the hall. Cameron reached out a hand to shake that of one of the men, saying with a smile, "Lieutenant, you did well yesterday."

"It's always an honor to serve, Your Grace," he replied with conviction. Then the comfortable nature of their relationship became evident when he added, "Forgive me if I overstep my bounds, but I can't help wondering where exactly you found such valuable information to let you know the baron's true intent."

Cameron just smiled and said, "Let's just say I have a source that's . . . confidential."

"Well, God bless your source, whoever it is. I shudder to think what might have happened. Those plans we found were horrific."

"I know," Cameron said. "God is truly looking out for us."

"Indeed," the lieutenant said, adding with a smile, "which is *why* it is always a pleasure to serve."

Maggie caught the underlying meaning. This lieutenant likely represented an attitude held by the majority of those who served Horstberg in their employment. They could serve more fully and with greater conviction because they knew their ruler's heart was in the right place, and his intentions were good. Maggie's gratitude increased as it occurred to her how horrible it would be to reside in a country where someone like the baron was its ruler. Or worse, one's father. She thought of his daughters, who had always been so unkind to her, and she truly felt sorry for them. But more than that, she just felt grateful. Humble and happy and grateful. Her greatest wish would be to spend the remainder of her life with such feelings in her heart.

Han had trouble sleeping that night as all of the events of the past several months swirled around his mind and with the exclamation point of this brush with war screaming in his head. Out of nowhere a strange thought occurred to him. When the thought wouldn't leave, he got out of bed, lit a lamp, and quietly searched in the back of a drawer without disturbing Maggie. Holding the ring with four keys that Cameron had given him, he wondered if his hunch had any substantiation to it, or if he was just losing a portion of his mind due to recent trauma and grief.

Deciding he would never know if he didn't try it, Han put on a robe, picked up the lamp, and quietly left the room. It took minutes of descending staircases and traversing halls and corridors to arrive at the door in question—the door leading to those seventy-eight fateful steps downward to Erich's chemistry room. He felt suddenly terrified without being able to define the reasons. Was it premonition or regret that brushed over his shoulders and made him shudder and take a sharp breath? Or both?

Drawing a courage that seemed logically unnecessary, Han took hold of the fourth key on the ring—the one Cameron had told him was a mystery. Apparently no one living had any idea what lock in the castle matched this particular key. It had to have been important at one time, he thought. And he also thought of the literally hundreds of doors within these castle walls. He took a deep breath, telling himself he was letting his imagination run away with him. He then put the key into the lock and turned it, gasping aloud to hear the way it clicked effortlessly into place. Just to reassure himself, he tried to turn the handle but it wouldn't open.

Han stared at the handle in one hand, and the keys in the other. If this door had been kept locked or guarded all this time, would anyone have ever been able to put lives in danger? Of course, an officer had been killed while he'd been protecting this door. But if they'd known there was a key, would it have made any difference? He pondered the thought for minutes until he realized his feet were cold and his body exhausted. He unlocked the door and went back to his room, glad to find Maggie sleeping, unaware that he'd left.

The following day Han asked if Cameron, Erich, and his father would indulge him for just a minute. He led them to the door they'd all come to hate and hurried to demonstrate how the key fit perfectly there.

"Good heavens," Cameron muttered, and no one else said a word for at least a minute.

They all went to the office and speculated briefly over why this discovery felt more significant than any of them could define. No one had any clear answers, but Han felt some validation in seeing he wasn't the only one who felt unexplainably uneasy over what he'd discovered.

With nothing to say that made any difference now, Cameron declared that the door would now remain locked—if only as a formality. The matter was then put aside and business moved forward as usual, but Han couldn't help looking at these men and considering how much had changed among them, even if the outcome had been favorable in most respects.

With the passing of days, Han realized he was seeing life through different eyes. And sharing conversation with those he cared for most made it evident they were all feeling the same. The citizens of Horstberg would never comprehend what had almost happened; the important thing for them was that it hadn't. For Han, even his mother's absence felt soothed somehow. It was almost as if she hadn't gone so very far away, after all. He could never explain how he felt; he just knew that it felt real.

Less than a week after Han had come face-to-face with the Baron of Kohenswald, he was sitting in the ducal office with Cameron and Erich and the captain—and his father, who had recently returned to work. They all still missed Elsa dreadfully—no one more so than Georg—but they were learning to get by, or more accurately, to help each other get through. A lieutenant came in the room to inform the duke that a woman was demanding to speak to him. They all knew that no citizen of Horstberg could walk in off the streets and demand to speak to the ruler. They would be guided through other channels to get the assistance they needed, or if they were there to cause problems, those problems would be dealt with accordingly. It was natural, therefore, to hear Cameron ask an obvious question. "Why are you bringing the matter to me, lieutenant?"

"The woman is Klarice Koenig, Your Grace: Nik Koenig's mother. Apparently something has . . . happened to him."

"I see," Cameron said and stood. "Well, then . . . perhaps we should speak to her. Is she in the hall?"

"Yes, Your Grace."

Cameron glanced around the room. "Are you gentlemen going to join me? I have a feeling it could be very . . . interesting."

Han stood along with the others, and they all went together down the long hall to the main entry where a woman was waiting. She looked much older than most of the women Han knew in that generation, and her clothes and jewelry were far too garish to be in good taste. She took in the imposing group of men approaching her and snapped, "Are you going to have me thrown out, then? Is that how it goes?"

"Just state your business," Cameron said.

She looked directly at him. "You're his brother," she stated as if she resented his very existence. Han tried to comprehend this woman as the secret wife of Nikolaus du Woernig—and the mother who had raised Nik Koenig.

"State your business," Cameron repeated, firm but unruffled.

"What have you done to my son?" she demanded.

Cameron looked understandably confused. "I can assure you that I have not seen or heard anything of him for quite some time. I honestly have no idea what you're talking about."

The woman looked even more angry. "But everyone knows you had some kind of uproar last week in Kohenswald, and now my son is in prison there. There is no other explanation, given how you've always been out to do us in; you've conspired against him. You have something to do with this. I know you do. You must go to the baron and insist that he have my son released and—"

"I will not go to the baron for any reason," Cameron said. "As for last week's events, you have absolutely no idea what *really* happened. And there *is* another possibility, madam. If your precious son was putting his nose where it didn't belong, then perhaps the baron has good reason to have grievance with him. And if he was somehow behind what happened last week, he's likely better off where he is—as opposed to being arrested for treason here." He took a step toward Klarice Koenig, and she stepped back. "Is there a reason I should believe that your son had something to do with the dispute between me and the baron, because if that's the case, perhaps you need to have a long conversation with my captain and—"

"I have no idea what you're talking about," she said and turned around, hurrying out the door.

Cameron waited until the door had closed before he turned and asked, "Was it something I said?"

A heavy silence followed that didn't match the lightness of his comment. Captain Dukerk finally said, "So, Koenig was involved. And perhaps the baron is blaming him for the failure of their glorious plan."

"Perhaps," Cameron said, "but once again we have no proof. We can only hope that the baron either keeps him in prison a very long time, or maybe we'll get lucky and Kohenswald will execute him—which will save us the trouble of finding a good reason to do it."

Cameron hurried back to his office with the captain and Georg following. Erich stood where he was, and Han remained at his side.

"Are you all right?" Han asked.

"He scares the hell out of me, Han."

"Who? Your father?" Han asked then chuckled, but Erich only stared at him severely, unaffected by his attempt at humor.

"You know very well who I mean."

"Yes, I know," Han said. "And I feel the same. Somehow . . . I think we all know he'll be back."

"There's just no telling when . . . or what insanity he will bring with him when he comes."

Knowing that Nik Koenig was tucked away in the baron's prison, Han could almost tangibly feel the peace that settled over Horstberg, like the calm following a horrible storm, when the sun would come out and warm everything it touched. Of course, they all knew that more storms were imminent, but for now the peacefulness was enjoyed.

Everything progressed well with Maggie's pregnancy, but Han couldn't help feeling a deep worry over the forthcoming birth. He tried to ignore the feeling, knowing there was nothing he could do but hope and pray that all would go well. And it had become an unspoken rule among the family to not even hint at the possibility of anything going wrong. Elsa's death from childbirth was still too open a wound for all of them.

Therefore, Han chose to focus only on that which was good, and everyone else seemed to be doing the same. They all enjoyed little Hannah so thoroughly that the hope of another child was sweet, and Han tried to imagine how it would be to have another baby. It was the end result, not the process, that he and Maggie spoke of together often. For that, and so many other reasons, they had much to hope for that was good and bright.

Erich relished each day with boring committee meetings that were vital to the welfare of the country but had no mention of disaster or tragedy or possible impending doom. He told his father more than once that he would be glad to inherit such a boring job.

Beyond the family's unspoken concern that Maggie's childbirth would go well, and the ongoing adjustment to Elsa's absence, no one had anything to complain about. Erich never let go of the hope that he would find the right future Duchess of Horstberg, but he'd learned that patience was greatly enhanced by gratitude, and he was overflowing with that.

One of many things he felt grateful for was his amazing valet, and the way that he and Theodor had become friends through their comfortable interactions. Theodor proved over time to have some kind of extra sensitivity to Erich's moods, and he always managed to brighten his days a little with his teasing. Erich admitted to him one day that he'd surely been blessed to find him that day when the tailor had been involved with domestic problems.

Theodor was impeccably reliable, and Erich never had to wonder if he would be there when he was needed—which was the very reason his absence one morning put Erich on edge. He paced his room and glanced at the clock repeatedly. Theodor knew that Erich had a banquet to attend. It just wasn't like him to not show up. Wondering if something was wrong, he decided to have an officer go to Theodor's apartment and inquire. But he opened the door to find Theodor about to walk in.

"I am so sorry, sir." He rushed into the room and opened the closet. "It won't happen again, I can assure you."

Erich watched him closely, knowing that something was wrong.

"Theodor, are you all right?" he asked while the valet spread Erich's uniform over the bed.

Theodor didn't answer. He went to the bureau and opened a drawer, then he set both hands down firmly and bowed his head.

"No," he said with a trembling voice, "I'm not all right, but—"

"But nothing," Erich interrupted, taking hold of Theodor's shoulder. "Good heavens, man. You're shaking. What's happened?"

Erich urged Theodor to a chair and felt a nervous prickle at the back of his neck to observe the way he slumped over and pressed his head into his hands. Erich squatted down beside him and put a hand over his arm. "What is it, Theodor?"

"The baby came . . . early and . . ."

When he didn't go on, Erich asked, "Is the baby all right? Did it—"

"Oh, yes. The baby's fine. It's a boy, and . . ."

Erich's heart rate increased when big tears rolled down Theodor's face. He knew something was terribly wrong. "And?" he prodded.

"The doctor said he'll be fine, even though he's small, but . . ." Theodor choked back a sob and blurted it out. "Leisl's gone."

Erich sucked in his breath and pressed a hand over his chest as the shock provoked something close to physical pain. His thoughts went to Elsa's death and the deep loss that hovered in her absence with those he loved most. And he pushed away his sudden fears in regard to Maggie's impending childbirth. He couldn't even begin to comprehend Theodor's pain.

Theodor struggled to explain. "After . . . the baby came . . . she just bled and bled, and . . . the doctor . . . couldn't stop it, and . . ."

Erich didn't know what to say, but he didn't have any trouble urging an arm around Theodor's shoulder as he sobbed like a lost child.

While he quietly allowed Theodor to cry, Erich's appointments for the day fell into perspective. He knew where he needed to be. Theodor had been loyal and served him well, and they had indeed become friends.

Han knocked at the door and peeked his head in. "What's taking so long. Are you . . .?"

Theodor turned away and discreetly wiped at his face while Erich walked toward the door.

"Will you tell my father I won't be able to attend?" Erich asked in a whisper.

Han furrowed his brow. Knowing the depth of Erich's commitment to duty, he knew something was wrong. While he was wondering how to ask, Erich added quietly, "His wife just died . . . in childbirth."

Han squeezed his eyes shut as he was assaulted with horrible memories and unfathomable fears. "Merciful heaven," he muttered. "Is it some kind of plague or something?"

"I think I should stay with him," Erich said. "I'm sure you can manage."

Han nodded his understanding. "I'll tell your parents."

"Thank you," Erich said, and Han left. He turned to find Theodor pulling his uniform off the hanger. "Leave that, Theodor," he insisted.

"Forgive me, sir. I know you're late, and—"

"I'm not going."

"But . . ." Theodor looked astonished and upset.

"I'm taking you home." He took Theodor by the arm and escorted him from the room, not allowing any argument. "I don't know what you're doing here in the first place. You should have just sent word."

"The baby is at my father's home," he reported. "He is watching out for him. There is no need for you to accompany me there, sir. I can—"

"Nonsense," Erich insisted. "I'm coming with you."

Theodor offered no further protest but instead nodded with unspoken gratitude. Erich rode with Theodor to his home and stayed with him until Theodor's father, Karl, arrived, reporting that he'd found a wet nurse who would help care for the baby for the time being.

"And then what?" Erich asked.

Theodor looked baffled and scared. Concerned, and feeling the responsibility of being his employer, Erich gently talked with Theodor and his father about the possibilities. Karl was more than happy to help raise the child so that Theodor could continue his work.

"That's wonderful," Erich said to Karl, "but can you do it alone? I don't know very much about babies, except that my sister's child requires a lot of time and attention."

"I'll have Kathe to help me," Karl Lokberg reported.

Erich looked confused.

"My sister," Theodor reported. "She's very competent, young as she is." He started to cry again and took hold of Karl's hand. "I don't know what I'd do without you, Father."

Karl put his arms around Theodor with a fatherly embrace. Erich heard a baby's cry and looked up to see a gangling girl with dark stringy hair, holding the wiggling bundle. Her red, puffy eyes and weary countenance made it evident this loss was difficult for her, as well.

"I think he's hungry, Papa," Kathe said, looking uncertain and afraid.

Karl left with Kathe and the baby to take them to the home of the woman who would feed the child. Erich stayed with Theodor the remainder of the afternoon, until Karl returned.

Erich attended Leisl Lokberg's funeral, grateful to have his mother with him. An important meeting with some diplomats prevented any of the others from attending, and Maggie was heavily laden with her pregnancy. But Abbi remained at Erich's side, gracious and kind as always, and Erich wondered as he often did if there was any woman in the world so good. He hoped there was one near his age somewhere who could be the next Duchess of Horstberg, although he felt certain that *no* woman could ever compare to Abbi du Woernig.

Abbi also accompanied Erich to the christening of Theodor's son. He was named Karl after his grandfather, and Erich was pleased to see the way Theodor could smile and find pleasure in holding his tiny son and showing him off. He hoped that the future would not be too difficult for them.

The very night after little Karl had been christened, Erich was awakened by his mother and told that Maggie had gone into labor.

"I need you to sit with your father and Georg," Abbi said. "I will be helping Maggie, and Han needs to be with her, as well."

"Is everything all right?" Erich asked.

"So far," Abbi said and hurried out of the room.

Erich did as his mother had asked and sat in the hallway with his father and Georg, but not one of them had a word to say, and he felt certain they would all go mad. He wondered if the others shared his own most prominent thought: if this child was a boy, and Erich never married or had a son, then the world was about to be greeted by the next Duke of Horstberg. He preferred to keep his mind on *that* thought, as opposed to the possibility that anything might go wrong.

Han held tightly to Maggie and tried to remain focused on a positive outcome. It seemed as if her pain and struggling to get the baby out would never end. Abbi kept assuring him that the pain was normal, and the doctor frequently reported that there was no evidence of anything to cause alarm. Han appreciated the frequent reassurances, as he knew Maggie did, but he also knew that no one would be more glad to have this over with than her—and he right along with her.

At the moment he began to wonder if it would ever end, the baby slipped into the world and began to cry with healthy lungs. The doctor laughed and declared that it was a boy, and a moment later the infant was wrapped in a little blanket and given to Maggie. Han held Maggie in his arms and kissed her face while he hardly took his eyes off the dark-haired boy who had just safely joined their family.

When it was all over and the announcement had been made, the family gathered around Maggie's bed and basked in the joy of this glorious moment. A part of Han kept expecting something to now go wrong with Maggie, but the doctor declared her to be doing especially well, and not many days later, she was up and around with little evidence that her body had endured such strain.

The baby was christened Stefan, which was Georg's second name, and Cameron Han du Woernig was added before the Heinrich to make him sound worthy of the position he was second in line for as long as Erich remained without progeny. But they all agreed that they had been extremely blessed, and surely time would take its course with all things, and Horstberg and its ruling family were in God's hands.

Epilogue

Erich absolutely adored little Stefan. He was fond of Hannah too, but something about Stefan just drew Erich to him, and he insisted on holding the baby whenever he could. As Stefan began to crawl, and then walk, it became quickly evident that Erich was one of his favorite people. Erich appreciated the way that assisting in the raising and care of this sweet boy helped him not think quite so much about the absence of marriage or children in his own life.

The year following Stefan's birth, Sonia also successfully gave birth to a son, who was called Rudolf after his father. And two years after Stefan was born, Han and Maggie had another boy, naming him Gerhard after Abbi's father, who had recently passed away. Erich was fond of all the children, but he continued to share a certain closeness with Stefan.

Georg gradually found peace with his wife's death, though it was difficult to tell if he was actually happy. He declared that it was only because Cameron and Abbi were so good to him that he was sane at all. And he admitted almost daily his gratitude to be living under the same roof with Han and Maggie and their three beautiful children, who enriched his life so much.

Theodor gradually seemed to lose the shadow that had hovered over him from Leisl's death. Erich knew Theodor visited his son regularly and the child was doing well. Erich often looked at Maggie's little Stefan, realizing Theodor's son was near the same age, and tried to comprehend the child being raised without a mother. Erich could well imagine Theodor's young sister caring for little Karl, and from what Theodor had told him, she did well with the child.

Theodor talked about his son daily, and it was evident where he spent his time off. Erich arranged for little Karl to spend time in the castle nurseries on occasion, playing with the other children, where Theodor could spend more time with him. Stefan and Karl, being close in age, quickly began to enjoy each other's company, and Abbi commented once that they reminded her of Han and Erich as children.

Horstberg continued to thrive in spite of some difficulties that arose through a harsh year when hunger became prevalent through much of Germany. But Horstberg came through the ordeal better than most of their neighboring countries, and life continued to flourish. And they heard nothing of Nik Koenig and gladly continued delivering his allowance to his mother. Cameron often declared it was a small price to pay to keep them at bay. They all just hoped it remained that way.

As the children grew and Horstberg remained at peace, the passing of time became evident—especially to Erich. He began to wonder if the du Woernig line would die with him. And the thought was simply not pleasant. Still, he reminded himself often that life was good and he had much to be grateful for. And the future was all just around the corner. Any day now, he knew that everything could change.

lizabeth D. Michaels began writing at the age of sixteen, immersing herself ever since in the lives created by her vivid imagination. Beyond her devotion to family and friends, writing has been her passion for nearly three decades. While she has more than fifty published novels under the name Anita Stansfield and is the recipient of many awards, she boldly declares *The Horstberg Saga* as the story she was born to write, with many volumes in the works. She is best known for her keen ability to explore the psychological depths of human nature, bringing her characters to life through the timeless struggles they face in the midst of exquisite dramas. For more information, please visit her author page on WhiteStarPress.com.

Made in the USA
San Bernardino, CA
01 December 2014